WHEN WE'RE
ENTWINED

JODY A. KESSLER

Please visit:
www.JodyAKessler.com

For news, updates, and a free Ebook subscribe to the newsletter.

Paperback ISBN: 978-0-9862406-9-0

E-book ISBN: 978-0-9862406-8-3

Edited by
Melissa A. Robitille

Cover Art & Design by
Sommer Stein
Perfect Pear Creative Covers

Manufactured in the United States of America

First Edition

Dedication

To all my sisters

Other Works Available

An Angel Falls Series

Death Lies Between Us #1

Angel Dreams #2

Haunting Me #3

Book #4 coming soon

Historical Time Travel Series

The Night Medicine

Granite Lake Romance

Unwrapping Treasure

Chasing Treasure - book #2 coming soon

Witches of Lane County

Heart of the Secret

Chapter One

"The first step is a tiny death." — J. Pyrah

Desperation is a wholly conscious nightmare. It grips me like a stone ogre engrossed in ripping my hair out. She sits on my chest throttling me with hairy-clawed mitts while breathing putrid stink breath in my face. This emotional beast isn't going to let me breathe untainted air while I suffer for days over my inadequacies and failings.

I'm leaving home with my backpack on, dragging a duffle bag full of doubt and crooked memories. The knife of guilt stabs my gut for running away. I should feel worse about leaving Evie and Jonah, instead of Ollie, but my dog needs me. I need her—and I can't take her with me. Evie will be all right. She always is. At least, it's what I keep telling myself. Otherwise, I wouldn't be able to abandon my sister. Jonah is too little to understand what it's like to be a nineteen-year-old. Ollie is already living down the street at a neighbor's house.

"Please don't go," Evie says, hanging on my neck.

Her kid arms are so thin. That doesn't mean she's a wimp. Evie is strong. She has way more strength than I do. Evie can hold up the Statue of Liberty in a hurricane. She grips me like she's clinging to the edge of the world. A piece of my humanity shatters when I make her let go.

I'm breaking something that I can't fix. It's trust, but there's probably a long list of sacred sisterhood principles being flushed down the drain as I make my way to the door. I dismiss the feelings like irrelevant background noise. Not that Evie is irrelevant or that she won't ever trust me again, but I can't trust myself not to hurt someone who I love more than anyone else in the world. If I can't trust myself, then I can never forgive myself either.

She tugs my shirt.

"I love you too, Evie," I tell her as I spin around and press her twelve-year-old body against my heart for a final hug.

She's an amazing person. How can one little girl be the epitome of perfection? I'm sure she has a direct connection to goodness. To the source of all life. "You have to stay with Jonah and make sure he does his homework and stops picking his nose." I try to smile, but it's strained. My little brother does much worse things than dig for boogers, but it really grosses Evie out.

"Why is Geoff so mean to you? I'll make him stop. Or Mom will. I know if you just told her, she would make him stop ragging on you all the time."

Tears start to choke her words. I close an emotional floodgate to hold my own back. We've gone over the injustice in our household like reruns on the television. The same episode plays again and again, and we keep watching the channel, expecting something different, but it never changes. Geoff treats me worse than my siblings. There's no known reason for it. At least a rational reason that makes a scrap of sense. I secretly think I figured it out, but Evie doesn't need to know.

At one point, about two years after my mom met Geoff, I thought he hated me because I was older and I could express myself more clearly than my younger sister could. But Geoff resents me because I make him see himself as the jerk he is. I gave up picking apart every detail of why my mother's husband despises me so much. Geoff is a ginormous prick with an obsession for health food, a ridiculous goatee, and an iron fist.

Evie sees the differences in our family dynamics with unique clarity. Mom? Only what she wants to, which isn't much better than walking around wearing a blindfold. I often imagine my mother living in some tainted Wonderland we're not allowed to visit. This place only exists in her head, so it's not actually accessible to anyone else. She rarely leaves this delusion, so it's been up to me to make sure the rest of us reside in reality. I guess what I'm saying is Mom pretends nothing is ever wrong. She's even told me Geoff is helping me become a better performer. That he's pushing me to be my best like her father did to her. How does she not understand that abusing a kid isn't an acceptable way to "train" someone? There's so much *wrong* with that sentence; I can only duck my head to avoid any more bullets and walk out the door. That's what I'm doing now.

Let me backtrack to give you a brief summary of living with Geoff and my mom, Autumn.

I grew up with the Farinelli World Circus. Mom used to train Evie and me when we traveled nine months out of the year in the performing arts business. In other words, we're acrobats, gymnasts, and dancers. Evie and I? We are the upcoming generation in a long line of circus performers. And these days, you have to be multi-talented to impress a live audience. Anyone can simply open the internet and watch amazing people doing extraordinary things, so live acts better be spectacular. It's a lot to live up to. My mother is a graceful and talented artist. Geoff may be good on the trampolines and the pole acts, but I'd never admit it to him. His attitude and general personality cloud my vision, so all I ever see is a controlling, judgmental, jerk-off doing back flips or showing off his muscles.

After my father had left, Mom's life fell apart, and Geoff walked in to pick up her pieces. Only he didn't glue them back together correctly. Mom let Geoff take over everything including our practice sessions. He eventually moved us away from our traveling lifestyle and into the cruddy rundown house that used to belong to his recently deceased father. My mom went along with Geoff's new life plan and the further we were from The Show and her life of continual travel the more she disappeared into herself. It gets worse every year.

You see, Geoff and my mom were reaching an age where their experience in show business made them valuable to the team, but their bodies were becoming a nagging burden. My mom wasn't ready to quit, but the younger performers were rising every season, and my mom kept being used as an alternate. I think Geoff wasn't ready to retire either, but they hooked up, had Jonah, and our trailer was getting cramped. Then Geoff's dad died. Geoff inherited the dumpy house in the midst of a seventies tract home neighborhood in Crapville, USA. His other major gain from the parting of his father was a liquor store that also happens to sell chips, candy, soda, and cigarettes. We left the show circuit and moved to desert hell. Mom and Geoff made us continue practicing our "talents" by converting the backyard and the garage into a training facility for the unbalanced. I'm not mentally disturbed, and neither is Evie, but who in their right mind practices aerial silks and low wire in the desert heat? I made it a part-time job pointing out this absurdity and refused to practice if it was above eighty-five degrees, regardless of the shade canopies they put in place. Geoff was quick to find a solution to my valid complaints and started making us practice at stupid-o'clock in the morning and sometimes in the middle of the night, too.

When I told them I didn't care about ever going back to The Show, Geoff would say things to me like, "If you could keep your damn legs closed and practice more, then you might be good enough to audition for the next season." He completely missed my point.

Other days he would even inform me, with a thoughtful look on his asshole-driven face, "You'll never make it as a professional. You'll be lucky if anyone hires you to scrub the piss off the toilets."

Mom never seemed to hear these comments. Evie, of course, heard everything. Geoff didn't care if his remarks were overheard. He understood Evie didn't have the power to kick him out or make him stop being a controlling bastard.

Evie excelled at everything she tried. If for some reason, she slipped or couldn't master a new technique, she would cry silently, brush away her tears or take a break, and be back at it with no nasty insults or degrading remarks from our stepfather.

Growing up with Autumn and Geoff Holsteen as parents was about as fun as drowning in Jell-O. There were moments of sweet jiggly goodness, but mostly I could never stand on such an unstable foundation.

A vehicle pulls up in front of the house, and I peer over Evie's shoulder out the window. My boyfriend, Keel, is parked at the curb.

"It's too late, Evie. I'm done with school, and I can't stay here any longer. Geoff is always better to you, so you're going to be fine. I'll call you soon. If anything changes and he starts being mean to you or Jonah, you just have to tell me."

"Then I'll say anything you want, just don't leave."

She's really crying now. The choking sobs make it hard to understand what she's saying. I squeeze her tighter for a second that is an eternity too short and slip out of her arms. She covers her face with her hands, and her body shakes as she bawls her eyes out. The sound of tears crashing to the floor and cracking the ground we live on almost tips me over.

What am I doing? I glance out the window and yearn for my freedom. My boyfriend's truck is the escape I've been waiting for. Keel offered to let me join him and his band on their first tour this summer. The backpack suddenly feels like a protective shell on my back. The straps are digging into my shoulders, but the discomfort is inconsequential compared to the guilt dividing me into two battling halves. I want to stay and protect my siblings, but I have to get out of the house before Geoff and Mom return.

"I'll call you soon," I say again, picking up the rest of my life and hauling it out the door.

I am a certifiable schmuck.

Chapter Two

"Promise me you'll never forget me because if I thought you would, I'd never leave." — A.A. Milne

June 21.

Our first show was tonight.

My performance felt odd and out of place. I didn't expect perfection, but the small stage didn't leave much room for me to move around the guys. Keel and the others seemed fine with what I put together, but none of it was stellar. I'm a gymnast more than a backup dancer. Luckily, I've been surrounded by choreographers and performers my whole life, and it wasn't too difficult to make my style flow with the indie beats and tribal nuances of my boyfriend's band, Paradox 21.

This is the first time since leaving Geoff's house that I've had a minute alone. As I write, I'm sitting on mine and Keel's bed in the back of the truck. Neither of us wants to part ways with our cash for a hotel room, so the foam pads and sleeping bags are good enough. I'm sure we'll get a room sometime soon, but for now, we're using the club's bathrooms to wash and shower—if there is a shower— which wasn't the case tonight.

We'll be camping a lot this summer, and I don't mind. Living out of the back of a truck with an oversized cap over the bed isn't all that different than living in a fifth wheel camper trailer—which is all I ever knew until a few years ago. I think mobile living is harder on Keel than it is on me. He's used to the amenities of a regular house. His parents always gave him everything he could ever want. I think they're actually happy he's off exploring and touring with the band and hopefully growing up a little. They aren't funding his trip, but they told him he's welcome back at the end of the tour, and to have a good time. I can't imagine what it would be like to have parents who lived anywhere near the realm of functioning rational adults. So Keel is my liferaft to sanity, but that doesn't mean he is totally sane, or that he's used to roughing it on the road.

Earlier today, I heard him tell one of his band members he wished he'd brought his game system. I shouldn't care that he likes to play video games so much, but the grating background noise makes me want to jam butter knives into my ears. I'd rather listen to him practice his guitar for hours on end or hang out in silence as he messes around on his iPad. You'd think gaming on his tablet and phone would be enough, but whatever. Did he want to bring his forty-eight-inch flat screen T.V. as well? Maybe next year when his parents buy him an RV. In the meantime, I'll make do with living in the pickup truck.

After our set tonight, this guy, William, approached me. He said he could put Paradox 21 in the lineup for a handful of festivals. He couldn't stop raving about how much he liked the band and was digging my dance moves on stage. Keel came over to check out the guy hitting on his girlfriend. William told us he knows a bunch of promoters. He said he has connections to Riot Fest, Way Over Yonder, Dancetopia, Big Foot, and a bunch of other cool fests. I was willing to listen. It didn't take long to realize he wanted to talk to me and not Keel's band.

Keel was all like, "You should listen to what he has to say." My boyfriend disappeared from my side to go drink and play pool with the band and left me listening to this guy blabber on about bullshit that had virtually nothing to do with getting us in front of an audience. It only took a few minutes to get that, you know, creeper feeling about William. So, from here on out, William's new title will be, Wanker William. Anyway, W.W. was a fast-talking loser looking for a date and happened to know the club manager. He couldn't, or wouldn't, give me any contact information for the music festivals. I finished the spiced rum and coke he insisted I drink and ditched him. I slipped out the back door of The West Coast Nest after telling ol' Wanker William I had to use the bathroom. The man was only slightly less sexy than a sweaty pig's ball sack. I'm trying to be nice. Honestly, I don't think pigs sweat, and I don't like rum and coke.

Keel doesn't even know I'm hiding out inside the truck.

Is this how my first summer on my own is going to go? Fending for myself against blowholes like hippie-smelling William? Does Keel realize he ditched me with a colossal twat? All this for an hour on stage and forty bucks in my pocket—if I'm lucky. It'll probably be closer to twenty based on the pitiful turnout tonight. If the band doesn't make a profit, they won't pay me anything. Did I really agree to make pennies this summer? My cash will only last so long and then what? Leave again? Go home? I doubt Geoff will let me come back. If he does, life in the Holsteen household is going to be worse than unimaginable.

I ditched home. I ditched the club. Leaving seems to be the only thing I'm good at.

Earlier today, before the show, we took a walk along the beachfront to kill some time and check out the town and marina. On one of the hundreds of multi-colored flyers posted to every available surface across Southern California said in large bold type print:

"The best way to predict your future is to create it." — Abraham Lincoln.

The address on the bottom of the paper said, "QuotesForLife.org".

I need a future that I want to be a part of. Having something to look forward to is the only way I'm going to make it to this unforeseeable destination called a future. If Mr. Lincoln suggests I should create what I want for my future, then I'm doing that now. I can't be Geoff and Mom's indentured servant any longer. The words on the flyer made me think about what else I need other than my future freedom. To be honest, I don't know yet, but traveling with Keel this summer will give me the opportunity and the time to figure it out.

***

I close my journal and push it down to the bottom of my bag. Keel isn't nosy, but I don't want him reading it. This part of my life is for my eyes only. My Aunt Summer sent the journal for my eighteenth birthday. Her card read, "I have given you a place to jot down your dreams, or rant about the injustices of life. Either way, if you choose to write down your thoughts, you may catch a glimpse of the treasure which is your spirit and soul. Your true self. Your higher being. It's worth looking at, my sweet and beautiful niece. I hope you will seek and find the words to express who you are."

I gave the card and the journal a doubtful look and stashed it in my dresser for nearly a year without touching it. The night I brought my dog to the neighbor's house crying and begging them to adopt her was the night I made my first journal entry. I scratched three words across one page. "I HATE HIM!" Then I fell apart so completely I was unable to write anything else. I ripped the page out before leaving his house and left it on my bed and took the journal with me.

The door latch clicks, and I glance up, seeing the city lights through a small crack in the door. Keel's face appears.

"Hey, what happened to you?" he asks as he climbs into the truck bed with me.

The sweet and sour stench of stale alcohol oozes from his damp breath.

"I needed to get out of there." I yank clean shorts and a shirt out of my bag so I can change out of my stage outfit.

Keel lies down on his back next to me and clasps his hands behind his head. "So did you get the email address of the booking agent William talked about? Or his card or something?"

"No. I don't think that guy is legit." I shimmy out of my skirt and leggings.

Keel cuts me off. "Are you being serious right now? I trusted you to make that connection. William Strauss is the real deal. His cousin owns O.C. Event Promoters."

Keel sits up and runs a hand over his scalp. His russet hair is a disaster, and this only serves to make it even messier, and cuter. The more tousled it is, the more it appeals to my baser instincts.

"Shit. I wonder if he's still inside."

"I'm sorry. I swear he was just spinning bullshit so he could stare at my chest."

"Every straight guy in there was staring at your chest, Tara," Keel says as if I'm playing dumb.

"Fantastic. So you think it's okay for me to act like a slut as long as you benefit from it?" A smoldering fire ignites somewhere inside my chest with his implication. "You left me alone with him on purpose," I accuse, as it finally dawns on me my boyfriend wants me to play this sick game to get hooked up with a potential lead.

"You could have at least tried a little harder. Festivals are good exposure for all of us. There are too many open dates this summer."

"I'm sorry," I say again even though I know I shouldn't be apologizing. Disappointment on his face makes me turn away with shame. "I tried talking to him," I say as I pull my shirt over my head.

"Whatever," Keel says. "I thought you were going to help us on the tour, not hold us back."

"What?" I ask, hardly able to believe what I'm hearing. "I am here to help the band. I'll do anything you need me to."

"Apparently not." Keel's disgust is clear. "I'm going back inside. Hopefully, I can fix this."

"Wait!" I hold up my hand, but Keel leaves without saying anything else.

I grab my pillow and lie down, curling up on my side and feeling terrible about my screw-up. The scene inside the club plays over and over inside my head. Wanker William is a perv. How was I supposed to know I should put up with the ogling and the obnoxious flirting long enough to get an email address or phone number?

It's late, but I can't sleep. I'm terrified Keel will tell the band what I did, and they'll fire me after our very first gig. I don't have enough money to rent my own place, and I don't have my own car. Keel promised we would spend an amazing summer together and then see what happens after. Like maybe we could rent an apartment. He even said not to worry about what I would do after the tour and mentioned I could stay with him and his parents if that's where he ended up. Counting on that offhand remark, said right after we had slept together, suddenly feels like a vast and terrible mistake.

We've been on the road for two whole days and already fighting. *What if he wants to break up?* In seven months we haven't had a real fight. Keel's personality is strong, but he's mostly laid back. I love that about him. He knows what he wants and isn't afraid to tell it like it is, but he's never talked to me like he did tonight. Never. *That's why it hurts so much*, I think as my chest constricts and places unwanted pressure on my heart.

Numbness settles in my bones by the time Keel returns. He doesn't say anything at first, and neither do I. I pretend to be asleep as I listen to him take off his shoes and pants. He slides up next to me and puts his arm around me. Then he gathers me in close to his body.

"Hey," he whispers.

I nuzzle his chest as a response. I'm almost afraid to say something that will cause more arguing. He smells of alcohol mixed with pot smoke.

"I told Will you got really sick and left. I said you're my girlfriend, too, so he'll stop looking at you."

"You did?" I'm mildly shocked and confused.

"Yeah. He was cool. Said he didn't know, and he was sorry."

I swallow and peek up at Keel. His eyes are closed, and his hands are moving up and down my back.

"So did you talk to him about any bookings, or about his cousin?"

"Yeah. He was sort of distracted by this girl, but we have a definite in."

I sigh against Keel's chest and try to relax. His hand slides inside my shirt. I want to be in the mood, but it isn't happening. I'm still insecure about everything and the way we spoke to each other.

"I don't like fighting, Tara. God, it's weird calling you that. Why can't I just use your real name when it's the two of us?"

"I don't like my old name. I want everyone to call me Tara from now on. I'm starting over."

"It is a hot girl's name." He lowers his head to kiss the side of my neck.

"It's so much better than my other stupid name." Tara is the name of a goddess representing peace, compassion, and protection. Or Tara simply means "star". In any case, I just like the name, Tara. The peace and protection aspects feel like a bonus. New beginnings and the fact I don't like my birth name drove me to start fresh with a new identity. It's kind of strange hearing Keel call me something new, but I insist my old name can stay in the past with my previous life.

"Okay then. You've sold me," he mumbles against my throat. "I need you, Tara, the hot girl. Will you make up with me?"

"I guess I will." A tenuous smile tugs at the corners of my lips.

Keel brings his mouth to mine and makes me remember why I love him so much.

Chapter Three

"The second step isn't any easier." — J. Pyrah

Our morning wakeup call is the unpleasant and unwanted interruption of someone banging on the back of the truck.

"Wake up boys and girls. Time to exit the shag wagon."

I roll over and bury my head in the crook of my elbow. The voice belongs to Saul, the lead singer of the band. His morning alarm is completed by two more loud thumps of him slapping the truck cap. Mercifully, I hear him walk away. Keel stretches out next to me and his morning wood presses into the side of my hip. It isn't that I'm repelled by this phenomenon, more like shocked and curious that he can wake up every morning ready to go, especially after the night we had. We won't be fulfilling his caveman needs, however, because the door on the back of the truck swings open and a rush of salty sea air mixed with traffic exhaust sweeps over us.

I pull the blanket up over my half naked body as a female voice I don't recognize says, "Hey. Great setup in here." There's envious morning energy in her voice. "We're having breakfast on the beach. Get up before it's gone, losers."

The door clicks shut.

"You should have locked it," I whisper.

"Forgot," he mumbles as he starts to rise from our bed.

I guess his stomach gets priority over morning sex. Or, he knows me well enough to know I'm not interested while people are randomly opening and closing the door.

"Who was that?"

"I think it was the girl I met last night. Her name is Caspar or some other cartoon name. Maybe it was Dinah. You know, Caspar rhymes with Ja—"

"Don't say it. My name is Tara now, remember?"

He half yawns and half chuckles as he slips on a pair of shorts. Keel's opening the door to leave by the time I sit up. My eyes widen with surprise that he's so quick to join the others. I wasn't drunk or stoned when I fell asleep last night, and I'm moving ten times slower than he is. His eyes are red, and his shirt is wrinkled, but he doesn't seem to notice or care. I swallow and try to think of something to say that will keep him here for another five minutes while I dress and brush my hair.

"Meet you out there." He pauses for half a second and turns back to me.

I sort of shrug and give a half-hearted nod. A braid might be in order since my hair tends to become my enemy after visiting a breezy beach. I turn to my bags in the corner wondering what I should wear. Keel puts his hand on my calf, and I turn back around. He inches back inside the truck and tugs me toward him. Keel places his lips against my bare knee. Keeping his warm palm pressed to my skin, he says, "Don't punk out on me. It's only breakfast with the guys."

"I'm coming." I try to hide my pleased smile. *He loves me. Our fight is officially over.*

He tickles the back of my knee and hops out of the truck, slamming the door closed behind him.

There's no overnight parking on the streets around San Diego, but we had permission from the club owner to sleep on his lot as long as we were gone before they opened again. The West Coast Nest owns a piece of beachfront property and has a postcard view of the Pacific Ocean. Keel and the others are across the parking lot and down a small embankment which leads to the beach. They're eating leftover pizza and drinking cokes by one of the public fire pits.

Eyeballing their breakfast makes me doubly glad I brought the box of donuts, banana, and a jug of apple juice. A girl is attempting to control Zeb's hair with a hairbrush and a rubber band. Her own crimson dreadlocks are secured at the back of her neck with a strip of calico fabric. A couple of yellow and black dreads stripe one side of her head as if she is fire incarnate. She laughs as Zeb pulls away from her nimble fingers.

"Forget it," Zeb, our bass player says, pointing at my head. "I don't want to be Tara's twin."

The salty breeze is mild. I could have gotten away with just pulling my hair back, but I'm not going to undo my braid now. Zeb shakes out his shag of wavy toasted pecan brown hair and stuffs his hat on over the mess. He grabs a slice of pizza from the box on the picnic table and inserts it into his mouth as if he's planning to swallow it whole.

Keel sees me and tips his head toward the table. "Leftovers from last night. Grab some before Demian eats it all."

I hold up my bag of groceries. He wiggles his brows and flashes his sexy grin as an acknowledgment of my offering, then goes back to talking to Saul and Demian, the drummer for the band. I set my stuff down on the table and uncap my bottle of juice.

The morning is lukewarm, and I barely need the light sweatshirt I'm wearing. Someone started a fire in the pit, and it warms my back enough that I pull my hoodie over my head and set it on the bench. Saul's talking about the next venue up in Oceanside and how he wants to play the second set list to mix things up from last night's show. I tune him out after a few minutes. The sound of the waves crashing against the shore is hypnotic and lulls me into something that resembles the dream-state I had reluctantly left with my bedroll. My eyes catch the sweep and play of the gulls flying over our heads. One lands on the sand just outside of our circle. I grab a donut and watch the assertive gray and white bird stare at my breakfast like he's considering how he can wrap his beak around it without me noticing. As I take my first bite, the seagull charges a smaller gull for looking at me the same way he just was. The littler bird takes flight, lifts eight feet into the air, and lands a few yards away.

That's when I notice the homeless man sleeping against the concrete retaining wall separating the beach from the sidewalk. He's stuffed inside a dirty red sleeping bag on his bed of California beach sand. His face is unshaven and a mane of scruffy dishwater blond hair sits on top his head. His mouth is hanging partially open. I wonder if anyone has checked to see if he's alive. From where I sit, I can't be certain. A fly buzzes around his mouth and lands on his lip. The idea that I'm looking at a dead man settles uncomfortably in my gut. I set my donut down and glance in another direction.

Zeb and the girl with dreadlocks are busy inspecting bottles of a clear liquid and talking about doing some experimenting. I'm not sure what they're referring to and can't focus because the corpse on the beach is niggling my sense of right and wrong and tempting my moral responsibility to act. I glance over again and rise from the bench to make sure the man is at least breathing. The pestering gull is now interested in him as well, or more likely the empty food wrapper sticking out from under the guy's sleeping bag.

I stare at the man's chest watching for any sign of movement and imagining the worst. I honestly can't tell if he's alive. I'm chilled, to say the least, and my imagination begins conjuring images from every zombie movie I have ever seen. I notice movement inside the bag and the scenario is even worse than the imagined zombie apocalypse. I should have looked away, but instead, my gaze lands on his face, and my eyes meet his dead on. He stares back at me with bloodshot muddy eyes and I suddenly feel naked and exposed. Spinning around I plop back down on the bench with my back to the vagrant. My humiliation comes from the fact that the homeless man had been scratching his genitals, or at least that's what it looked like, and I had been caught watching him do it.

"Hey! Just because she's pretty doesn't mean you can choke your chicken right in front of her," Caspar barks from across the table.

She's glaring at the homeless man and brandishing what could be a blackened marshmallow on a long skewer.

"I was on this beach first." His voice is rough and full of gravel as he defends his territory.

"Screw you, dude. Stop jerking off or her boyfriend will come kick you in the nuts."

"What the hell?" Keel says and moves closer to me.

"It's nothing." I reach out to place my hand on his arm.

"Get out of here." Caspar snarls and points her weird weapon down the beach.

The homeless guy rolls over inside his sleeping bag and pushes himself up. His hands are grimy and black around the nails. The vision of where he just had said hands makes me feel ill.

Keel brushes me aside and steps forward. "You heard her. Get your ugly ass out of here." Keel makes a false lunge toward the man.

The man flinches, bumps into the concrete retaining wall, and tips haphazardly to the side. Fear shines in his eyes and my sympathy for him soars to new heights. *One fake charge from Keel made him cringe like that?* It's disturbing on so many levels.

"Keel, stop." I grab his sleeve to pull him back, but he shirks out of my grip and takes another threatening step forward.

The poor guy scurries the rest of the way out of the bag. He's dirty and rumpled and clearly making an attempt to leave. He reaches down into the bottom of his sleeping bag. I wonder if he's searching for his shoes or something, but we don't get a chance to find out.

"What the fuck, man? Get out of here! Who do you think you are? Do you want us to call the cops on you?"

Keel kicks sand at him and the man stumbles and trips over the folds of his sleeping bag. He catches himself against the edge of the concrete retaining wall and scrapes his forearm. Blood begins to flow.

He cries out in pain, and this seems to encourage Keel and the others. The band is now rallying at Keel's side.

"He was jerking off while staring at Tara," Caspar tells Saul and Demian.

"Gross," Saul says.

The homeless man cradles his arm against his body and shuffles off, barefoot, and dragging his bed behind him. I step around the group thinking I should go after him and apologize, but then I notice the stains on the back of the man's pants. Keel lays his hand on my shoulder. I spin around, disgusted, and almost to the point of tears. The whole situation is appalling, but I don't know how to respond. My tongue is all at once glued to the inside of my mouth.

Keel checks me up and down, and his eyes settle on mine. "Seriously. What a douche. You all right?"

I don't get the chance to answer before he turns to his band members and they all joke about the way the guy acted like he shit himself when Keel fake-charged him.

I take a seat and stare at my donut with no thought of eating it. I can't believe they think the situation is funny. It isn't remotely funny to me. I had no way of knowing if the homeless guy was scratching himself or jerking off. I didn't want to know. Either way, it didn't matter. I wanted to see if he was alive, that's all. His scraped arm and the fear on his face is my fault.

"So I liked what you did on stage last night. Are you a contortionist or are you just super flexible?"

I glance up and blink myself out of the mental fog of confusion. The heavily outlined eyes of Caspar watch me innocently. Her irises are a mix of green and brown and her mascara is layered on thick, just like the eyeliner. She has silver jewelry in her eyebrow and a near perfect beauty mark above her lip.

"I have some training." I look down into my lap and back up again.

"I can tell. Your movements are too practiced to be improvised."

"Thanks." I still feel shaken and try to mentally move on from the encounter with the bum. I glance down the beach looking for the man and his red sleeping bag, but he's nowhere to be seen.

"Did anyone tell you I'm Caspar?"

"Not really. I'm Tara," I say, introducing myself. My new name falls from my lips easier this time, and it spurs me into the present.

She smiles and laughs. It's a short quick sound that feels shallow. "I know, silly." Caspar rolls her eyes at me.

She tries to make it playful, not condescending, but I'm unsure how to take it, or her.

"So, Saul and Zeb asked me if I would show you guys what I do."

She fidgets with her fingers and shifts her weight from hip to hip as she talks to me. By now, I'm blocking out what Keel and the others are saying about crap-in-your-pants-guy, and I focus on Caspar.

"Want to watch?" she asks.

"Yeah." I nod and glance over at the bottle of clear fluid on the table that she and Zeb had been inspecting earlier. A thin multi-colored bag lays next to it. "I guess the stuff on the table is yours."

Caspar's smile widens, and she steps up next to me to lean across the table. She has exceptionally long legs and her hip brushes my shoulder. She backs up holding a small torch. I had already seen it and mistakenly thought it was a burnt marshmallow on a skewer. It's a torch, but I don't know what she's going to do with it.

"Listen up, boys," she says, flirting and batting her lashes as she commands everyone's attention. "The show's about to begin."

"She's going to teach me how to blow fireballs." Zeb places his hand on the bottle of clear fluid.

"I thought you only blew smoke out your ass," Demian says.

"Fire out the front door, smoke out the back," Zeb counters.

"Watch and you shall learn all my secrets," Caspar taunts and gives us a big cheeky grin. "Fill the cup like I told you, boyo," she tells Zeb as she lights her torch in the fire pit.

She proceeds to teach us how to hold liquid paraffin in our mouths and spit it out in a forceful spray at the burning torch. Demian and Keel aren't interested in putting the flammable fluid in their mouths. I'm not all that interested either to be honest. I've seen fire acts a thousand times. But Keel wants me to try it, so I do. I'm the last one to go and after watching Saul and Zeb learn, I pick up the gist of it right away. I practice spraying water out of my mouth first to make sure I can direct the stream away from my body and into the air without getting wet.

The way the morning is going, setting myself on fire isn't out of the realm of possibility. I blow a decent gush of flame on my first try. The flash of heat and surge of endorphins is exhilarating, and I want a second try at it to adjust the amount of fluid I can hold in my mouth and still spit with enough force.

Caspar says, "After you lose your virginity, you can't go back. Fire is addictive."

She hands me the cup with the paraffin in it, and I blow one more fireball. She's right. I could play with the balls of flame all day. I hand her the torch and rinse my mouth out with water. Brushing my teeth sounds like a better option, and I glance down the beach at the restrooms. The thought of a shower is even more tempting.

Music begins playing from someone's iPod and docking station on the table. Caspar starts dancing with a lit torch in each hand. I give careful consideration to her qualities and skills. It's quickly apparent she can only make so many different moves without burning her arm or setting her clothes on fire. Caspar spins around and circles her arms, dips low to the ground, and comes back up again.

"This is as good as what Tara does," Saul tells Keel.

I guess he doesn't care that I'm standing right here.

Keel nods but he keeps his face unreadable. "She's good, but how many venues are going to let us have an open flame on stage?"

"That's why she's multi-talented," Saul says.

My boyfriend's eyebrows rise with interest as he watches Caspar. Her finale is a flourish of teasing and taunting the flames with her mouth and her breath. She extinguishes the torches by swallowing the fire.

The guys bob up and down with approval and are grinning like she just tickled their fancies and their fantasies. I have to admit she's pretty good, and my standard for street performers is set fairly high since I grew up watching and training with professionals.

As she sets her torches down on the table, she somehow combines her movements to give a humble bow, a slightly flirtatious smile, and bat of the lashes, all the while sliding a set of devil sticks out of a bag.

The song switches to something harder with plenty of bass and drums and Caspar shows us how she twirls, flips, idles, and dances with the devil sticks.

"Yeah, I like her," Zeb says.

"She doesn't want any money. She told me she'll work for tips as long as she doesn't have to chip in for gas," Saul tells us.

"Caspar wants to go on the road with us?" I ask.

"She needs a ride up north." Saul keeps his eyes glued to Caspar. "What do you think, Keel?"

He glances at me, but not long enough to send him any secret couples-only messages with my eyes. I'm not sure what I would have said, but he doesn't give me the opportunity.

"She looks like she can use those things, so I don't see how her coming along would hurt anything." He straddles the bench at the table and takes a donut from the box.

Saul nods vaguely in agreement with Keel. He raises his voice. "If you're riding with us, we need to hit the road this afternoon."

Caspar flashes a glorious smile, all straight white teeth, and pointed canines. She whips the devil stick over her head in a twirling arch and dips low to her right to catch it and bring it back in front of her. It's a great trick she accomplishes with ease. She keeps the sticks moving and dancing in the air, and I turn away.

Pedestrians and tourists wander up and down the beach trying to avoid the joggers grimly determined to run the entire length of California. My gaze lands on a lady jogging with her dog, a retriever or setter or something. The dog's rust-colored hair shines in the morning sun. With tail held high, a prancing gait, and a wide grin on his face, the dog radiates joy next to his owner. It makes me think about Ollie. How devastated she was when I forced her to stay in my neighbor's backyard and told her she couldn't come with me. I knew she knew I was leaving and wouldn't see her again for a long time. Would Mrs. Fernandez take good care of her until I returned? The thought makes my chest ache.

I lean over to Keel. "I'm going to go shower."

He rises from the bench, half of a donut in his hand and sugar on his lips. He stretches and his broad chest expands beneath his shirt. "I need one, too. Meet you back at the truck."

"Okay," I say and leave.

He's apparently over the whole homeless guy incident, and I guess I am too.

Chapter Four

"Make it as awkward as possible so I know I'm still true to myself." — J. Pyrah

A: Public showers always smell funky.

B: The drains must be avoided at all cost. They're usually clogged with hair, someone's old band-aid, or a clump of something unidentifiable which makes you wrinkle up your nose and think, *ew*.

C: Showering at the beach is sort of like washing a pig inside its sty—except there's a lot of sand.

I put all the facts aside and go for it anyway. This early in the day the bathroom is mostly clean and private. The showers are inside the building, as well as outside, but there are no individual stalls. I came prepared for this and have my swim suit on. Call me paranoid, but standing naked in a spray of water in a public restroom isn't for me. I won't be caught on someone's camera wearing nothing but my body wash. All I want is to wash my hair, rinse off, get dressed, and get out of there with as little beach sand as possible stuck to me or my clothes—and no peep shows of Tara blasting the internet.

Caspar walks into the eight-person shower just as I turn on the water.

"Hey." She nods at me and glances around the empty room.

"Hi." I nod back and begin to wet my hair. My hair is long and thick. By thick I mean I could lose a brush in it. This stuff is a wilderness area with its own topographical map and a warning sign that reads, "Hazardous conditions may exist".

"Is your hair dyed that color?" she asks as she peels off her shirt.

"No. This is my natural color." I work with the pitifully weak spray of water to try to soak my hair down to the roots.

"If I had that color I wouldn't dye it either. It's gorgeous," she says.

Dark auburn isn't a very common color. I've been told my whole life how unusual and pretty it is. I like to think of the color as wet redwood bark, or the color of someone's coffee table. It's okay, I guess, but secretly I always wanted to be blonde like my sister, Evie. Do you know how easy it is to try any hair color you want when you're towheaded? I could have cerulean blue or forest green hair if I were born a blonde. Instead, I got my mother's hair, and while that may be interesting to everyone else, to me, the unruly mass is a hassle and a constant reminder of my maternal ties. It doesn't take to being colored, or permed, or anything. Believe me, I tried. I loathe the thick, unmanageable, and uncooperative pain in my butt.

"It's hard to take care of," I point out as Caspar tip-toes over to the shower head next to mine and turns on the faucet.

She's totally naked, and I wonder if she's ever heard of the internet and camera phones.

"Mind if I use some of your soap?" She smiles hopefully.

"Go ahead." I try not to stare or even look at her.

She bends down and grabs my bottle of body wash and then brushes up against my leg with her shoulder.

"I'm sure you hate talking about your hair. Like people always telling me what great legs I have—gets old after the millionth compliment."

"Pretty much," I agree as I begin to lather up my shampoo.

I can't help myself as I glance down at Caspar's legs. Yep, they are phenomenal, and now I know it. And I feel a little voyeuristic when that is exactly what I was trying to avoid. As an additional benefit, I'm massively aware of my need to shave my own legs even though they aren't bad, but they are developing a complex being in such close proximity to flawlessness.

"Sorry I brought it up. I have this serious disorder. It's screwing up my life a lot lately."

"Oh? I'm sorry." I wonder how she would take it if I walked out of the bathroom to shower outside.

"Yeah, it's called foot-in-my-mouth-syndrome. I say whatever the hell I want and make people uncomfortable. Last night I was reminded how much drinking increases my problem."

She sets the bottle of body wash down and then leans up against the wall letting the water wash over her.

"Yeah, I think I suffer from, do-whatever-the-hell-I-want-disease. There are a lot of similar side effects."

She laughs and splashes water at me. "You don't care that I'll be traveling with you for a while, do you? You're like the only other female, so I don't want to invade your country."

"I don't care. It's not my show. I need the summer off from some things, and Keel asked me to tour with them." I need to condition the ends of my hair, and I'm finding it strange being stared at by a naked girl, to stay the least. I try not to look at her and move on to the conditioner.

Maybe she senses my discomfort, or maybe she's finished, but she walks over to the bench where my backpack is and sits down next to her clothes. She never did ask to use the shampoo, and I wonder how she takes care of her dreads.

"Okay, well, I should tell you some things about me, so you don't think I'm trying to steal your boyfriend, or your money, or anything uncool like that."

"You don't need to make any confessions to me," I say through the tepid spray of water.

She goes on. "I won't lie. I'm nosy, and I want to know everything about you and the guys, so I'll be fair and go first. At least let me tell you the basics. I don't steal, so you don't ever need to worry about that nonsense from me. I'm trying to go to San Francisco, but if I can't find a place to share with some friends, I may be going all the way to Seattle. If Seattle turns out to be a mistake, I may be headed to Austin. Why?" she asks as if interviewing herself.

She's very animated when she talks. Her voice goes up and down a lot, and she likes to wave her hands in the air. I make the mistake of glancing over at her, and she still hasn't put her clothes back on.

"I was in this relationship and things were going pretty well. I got a street performer's permit to entertain on the pier and whatnot. The money has been decent enough to live on as long as I don't need to pay rent. Then I come home and find all of my stuff on the doormat and a note saying we're broken up and don't call."

"Wow, that sucks."

"Seriously. It does. My fuck-buddy fell in love with someone else, and I got kicked out with no warning. I've been working and staying with friends, but couch surfing gets old really fast. I'm ready for some new terrain. Umm," she pauses while I rinse out the conditioner. "Now I understand what it's like to be cheated on, so I wouldn't do that to anyone. What's your story?"

I shut off the water and walk over to my bag. Her skirt is strewn across it. I carefully pick up the skirt and set it aside trying not to drip all over it. Caspar doesn't seem to notice. She sits there with her legs crossed staring at me.

"Is there something wrong with your clothes?" I ask. *Is she a nudist?* I've seen stranger things on the road with The Show, but I'm not sure I'm ready for a few weeks of this. Especially if the guys think it's awesome and we should all go commando while we're on tour.

"I'm air drying. I didn't bring anything with me. Unfortunately, my stuff is inside Wiener William's car. Like I said, me and my mouth only get along periodically."

"Did you say, Wiener William? The guy from last night?" I laugh at the weird coincidence. "I was calling him Wanker William." I wrap my towel around me and start taking off the bikini and putting on my clothes using the towel as a shield. I don't think I'm a prude, but I grew up with circus boys who had a lot of free time to kill hanging around RV parking lots. Some of those boys thought spying on girls was a fun way to cause trouble. I mastered the art of dressing in public without showing my parts.

"Yeah. I thought he was all right at first. Paid for my drinks and willing to let me sleep at his place. We got a ride to his house because we were both wasted. Then he tells me if his parents find out I'm there I better sneak out, because if he gets caught with anyone in his room he's going to be kicked out for good."

"Lame."

"That's what I thought. The last thing I need is to be stuck in suburbia at three in the morning with pissed off parents chasing me out of their house, and no ride."

"What did you do?" I ask as I finish dressing.

"I had a cab drop me off back here. Weiner boy's car is still in the lot with most of my stuff inside. I either wait for him to show, or find someone who has his number so I can call him to come down here."

"I have his number, or Keel does."

"Want to text him for me?"

"I'll let you do it."

She rises from the bench and, thankfully, reaches for her clothes. The way she spins around gives me a full frontal. I also get a clear view of her nipple piercings. One pink nipple has a stud and one has a dangling star. *Jesus. I did not need to see that.*

"Ha," she snorts. "Don't want to get your hands dirty?" she teases as she slips on her skirt.

I collect my shower bag and stare at the exit. "I can't be involved." I force a laugh. "Keel thinks William may be a good connection."

"Whatever. I just need the rest of my bags so I can leave with you guys."

I move over to the mirrors and dig out my brush to start working on subduing the tangles.

Caspar comes up behind me and stares at me in the mirror. Her chin rests on my shoulder. "Thanks for the soap. Tonight, drinks are on me."

She's too pretty. Wild and wicked at the same time. I wonder how long it will be before Zeb or Demian tries to sleep with her. I swallow. "Great." I neglect to tell her I normally don't drink.

"See you outside." She waves and slinks out the door.

***

The text messages she sends to William go unanswered. Caspar doesn't wait even five minutes before taking a more hands-on approach to retrieving her clothes and bags from the backseat of William's junkie old car. The car is an innocent bystander in the whole affair, but the poor little sedan receives the majority of Caspar's wrath since its owner isn't present.

She hands me her phone.

"I'll be right back." She walks toward the street in front of The West Coast Nest.

She returns with a metal coat hanger in her hand.

"Did he message you?"

"Nothing yet," I say.

"What a wiener." She sneers reinforcing our desire to change William's name to something more suitable.

Caspar reshapes the hanger.

"Is that going to work?" I ask.

"I've done this before." She pries at the edge of the car window with her fingertips and the glass bends to her will. Actually, it tilts away from the doorframe and shakes as if it's going to shatter any second now, but it doesn't. Caspar slips the coat hanger in the crack between the seal and the door and begins fishing for the unlock button.

"Damn!" she says after a couple minutes. She sticks her tongue in her cheek and takes a break from sliding the wire back and forth inside the glass. "I can't put enough pressure on the button."

"Do you want to try calling him again?"

"No. He would've answered by now if he was going to. The asswipe is ignoring my messages because I wouldn't let him stick his pecker in my mouth. I don't sleep with someone just because they pay for a few drinks."

My eyebrows rise with this new information. I bite my tongue and keep quiet. Caspar seems frustrated as hell. I would be too if my stuff was right in front of me but I couldn't get to it.

"He made it sound as if I could crash at his house, but as soon as we were in the cab, he had his hand up my skirt and was drooling all over my face. It was disgusting."

"Sorry," I say.

She starts working at the hanger again, aggravation making her movements jerky and forceful. The sound of metal scraping against glass makes my skin crawl, and I step back.

"Some guy pointed at you from the street." I nudge her as the pedestrian leans over to tell the woman walking next to him.

Caspar looks up, waves and smiles, and then yells, "I locked my keys in the car!"

The lady says something like, "Oh, I hate when that happens. Good luck!" They move on as if completely oblivious to Caspar's blatant lie.

"Thanks for telling me. The last thing I need today is a bunch of cops asking questions."

"No problem," I say. I'm not looking for a shake down from the police either, and I'm sure Keel and the guys wouldn't appreciate it. I glance over at the beach, not expecting to see them, but more out of reflex. They said they were going to go check out some record shop down by the pier. I have no idea when they'll be back, but I know they won't be gone too long because we have a lot of driving to do today.

"This is total bullshit," Caspar says, walking away from the car.

I scrunch up my face and rub at my elbow not sure what to say or do. It doesn't matter, though. Caspar is in full control of the situation as she smashes the window of the car with a rock.

At least there's no alarm.

She unloads her duffle bag and a suitcase with calm efficiency and sets them aside.

"Did Saul say if you should load your stuff into the van?" I ask.

"I think so," she says as she digs into a purse.

"Is this everything?" I ask and move to pick up one of the bags. I'm ready to get out of here before anyone starts asking questions I can't answer truthfully, but Caspar seems intent on finding something in her purse.

"My torches and Devil sticks are already inside the van. Just hang out a second." She holds up a finger as she uncaps a tube of lipstick.

She twists the end of the tube, and red lipstick peeks out of its case. Caspar doesn't apply it to her lips, but instead crawls inside the car and begins to decorate the seats and the dash with penises and hearts.

I glance around at the deserted parking lot, but the people passing by on the street would need to be staring pretty hard to see her inside the small brown car. She backs out and stands next to the hood. In fiery red lipstick, she writes, "Willy the Wiener," on the windshield and draws a gigantic penis and his phone number on the hood. The lipstick runs out as she makes the finishing touches. She tosses the empty tube inside the broken window.

"Ready now?" I ask.

"I guess." She sounds a little down. "Do you have any spray paint?" she asks. A devil seems to wink at me from the depths of her hazel eyes.

Even if I had a can, I'm not sure I would hand it over. I shrug. "It's not something I carry around with me."

"Too bad."

Chapter Five

"Your integrity is your destiny – it is the light that guides your way." — Heraclitus

Two shows.

Camping.

Sex.

Struggling.

These are the highlights of the next week on the road.

How did it go? I can only relay the events in flashes. My memory is like lightning; sporadic, but brilliant. Memories come with perfect clarity at random moments—at other times, just bright lights followed by sound fading off into the distance.

The shows.

The first gig in Northern California lands us in Santa Cruz on an outdoor stage. We're told close to a thousand tickets were sold. Paradox is the opening band tonight. Supporting bigger names happens more often than not. We're mostly unknown, and we need to start somewhere. The hope I carry around for Keel and Paradox 21 to make it big is this enormous presence in my daily life. I want them to do well and share their music with the world. I'm sure we all dream about it. Otherwise, we wouldn't be able to do this together. The amount of work involved for little pay can only be sustained by dreams, desire, and intense dedication. They have it in spades, and I'm only adding a small piece of myself to their collective motivation. During the show, I dance and add more contortion and arm balances to my part of the act on the Santa Cruz stage.

The next night, we land in San Francisco and walk into a club called The Guard Shack. Maybe the name comes from the fact that Alcatraz is visible across the bay, but that's only a guess.

I take a look at the depth of the stage and the overhead rigging and go speak to the venue manager. My aerial silk is hauled from the van, and the stage manager is helpful and competent in helping me set up. Not much is needed to hang forty feet of fabric from a ceiling. My hardware is simple, a swivel, carabiners, and my rescue 8. I need to clip to support beams and have enough room to move, but that's all. The stage at The Guard Shack is perfect, and I hang from my blue silk behind and above Demian and his drum kit. Being able to use my muscles and perform to my ability is just what I need. My body sings along with Saul as I climb, stretch, twist and hang from the fabric.

The crowd falls in love with us. Paradox 21 is spot on. Tighter than ever. Caspar is fantastic and performs her fire dancing and flame swallowing after I come down from the silk. Caspar and I dance to the final song of Paradox's set.

Everyone seems to be complimenting each other. Caspar and I worked out a routine we like. Our combined energy during these last two shows is over and beyond what any of us ever did before, and it's exceeded our expectations.

The after show high makes me feel like I'm developing a new addiction. And one I never want to recover from. If every show is as successful as the one tonight, I can picture myself doing this forever.

Camping and Sex.

The decision to camp is communal. Camping sounds fun to everyone, and the two venues are only a couple hours drive away from the campground. We return to our campsite, excitement running high, and dreams of our future lofty. Everyone's mood is soaring. The fresh air, enormous redwood trees, and a wide clear river appeal to us all. We're saving a few dollars, which is also good. In my mind, it's crazy the gas tanks have priority over sleeping in real beds, but I haven't given up the dream that one day we'll have both money for a nice hotel room and our hundred dollar fuel stops. Meanwhile, we have sleeping bags and campfires, and that's not all bad.

Caspar decided San Francisco could wait. She said her friends in Seattle would take her anytime so she's in no rush to leave us. With the success of the previous shows, we're all happy she's sticking around. She's currently nowhere to be seen, but I thought I saw her wander toward the tents with a guy she'd met earlier at the show named Virgil. He caravanned into the mountains with us—I don't think Caspar will be making an appearance before morning.

"Mmm...make me another one." Keel kisses gooey marshmallow from my fingertips. No matter how much he nibbles my hand, not all of the stickiness will come off. He moves his lips to my neck and melted sugar transfers to new places on my skin. It tickles, and I turn into his body letting my hair cover part of my face and most of his. I'm not into making out in front of the guys. Everyone knows we're a couple, but that doesn't mean we should share our intimacy with them, or put on a show. A little is okay sometimes, like now, in the semi-dark of the night with only the tarnished-copper glow of the fire.

When Keel's palm begins traveling across my mid-drift, I not so subtly brush his hand away from exploring beneath my shirt. "Let me up." I climb off his lap to grab more chocolate and graham crackers for another s'more.

The heat of the fire warms my face as I toast marshmallows. They're divine, but I've eaten enough to coat my mouth with cotton and turn my blood to syrup. I'm not sure how Keel can keep eating them. The men seem to have no limit on drinking beers and eating blackened food from the fire, but I need to say when shortly after beginning.

Keel comes up behind me and wraps his arms around my middle. He takes my roasting stick and slides the half toasted marshmallow off the branch and holds it up in front of my lips. Overwhelmed with the sugar rush, I bite it in half and push the remainder toward his mouth. He eats the other half and sets the sick down against the fire ring.

He snuggles his hips against my backside. "Let's go for a walk."

I give him a surprised glance over my shoulder and then glance around the campfire at Saul, Demian, and Zeb. They're in the middle of a drinking game which involves flicking bottle caps into an empty pot while reciting song lyrics from nineties grunge and metal bands. The new game looks fun, and I wonder if they would let me play even though I don't have a beer or any bottle caps. One and a half beers had been my limit. I was high on my performance, and I could tell the alcohol would make me sleepy if I continued to drink. My slight buzz is enough to make me fuzzy and warm. The band doesn't even know we exist at the moment. Keel is aware of the fact, or he doesn't care and takes my hand leading me in the direction of the river.

"A walk?" I ask and lean into him as we meander down the trail.

"And maybe a swim."

I squint up at him to see if he's serious, but I can't read his face in the dark. He leads me straight to the small beach area I found earlier. There are boulders scattered along the riverbank like black holes in the night. Their hulking shadows provide a modicum of privacy, but there are campsites all around. He releases my hand and in the moonlight he begins to strip off his clothes.

"Seriously?" I ask. "You didn't want to swim earlier when I wanted to."

"Now I do." His shirt puddles on the gravelly beach. He shifts toward me and cups my breast. "I'm hot for you, Tara. I need to cool off. Undress and come in the water with me."

I swallow a laugh or maybe my nervousness. "There are people everywhere," I whisper even as I step out of my sandals.

He kisses the spot just below my ear. "All the more reason to be in the water. Once we're in, no one will see our bare asses."

"Well, when you put it like that..."

He unbuttons my shorts and leans in to capture my earlobe between his lips. His erection grazes my stomach. I swallow again and peer into the forest for spectators. Filtered moonlight falls to the earth in small patches between the trees and highlights the top of the tallest granite boulders. Ripples of silvery light flow downriver and disappear into the velvety dark. Everything from the waist down is concealed including the lower half of Keel and me.

I try to make a neat pile of my shorts, tank top, underwear and bra on top of my sandals, but it's an exercise in futility. Changing tactics, I attempt to leave them somewhere I can find them again in the dark. Keel splashes into the river and I try to hurry, but I'm on edge that other campers will stumble into us, and I'll be the hilarious topic of conversation on some stranger's lips for eternity.

As I slip into the water, I'm equally torn and tormented by my own mind. The rocks jab into my feet. I can't relax because I'm sure someone's looking at my naked body, and I'm terrified of biting fish or other mythical monsters that live in black water.

Where is he? I lost sight of my boyfriend. I stop moving when the water reaches my navel. I squat down to hide my chest like Keel suggested and grip the earth with my toes finding a spot with no sharp rocks or slippery moss or algae. I try to settle my nerves. There's virtually no current along this side of the river, and the temperature is nearly perfect, refreshing rather than cold. If I could let go of my insecurities, then this could be romantic instead of nail-biting.

"Keel?" I hiss into the dark. "Stop goofing around and come over here."

Pretending I'm wearing infrared goggles, I penetrate the night with the sheer willpower to see. My imagination betrays me, using fear instead of being helpful. My belly tightens, and breathing becomes difficult. Keel's round head and broad shoulders are nowhere to be seen. I hear muffled voices from the neighboring campsite and think there are elongated shadows of people coming toward the river.

As I'm about to dart toward the deepest shadow on the far side of the pool to hide, Keel tries to give me a heart attack. Something smooth runs up the length of my thigh and grips my ass. I flail, throwing myself toward the bank, screaming. It's impossible to move quickly or gracefully through waist deep water and in my attempt I fall and go under.

My swimming skills are decent enough that even panicked I don't suck in a lungful of water, thank God. Keel rises from below and somehow manages to lift me up with him.

"It's only me," he says laughing at my hysteria.

I try to push him away even as I cling to his heated body.

"Shit! That was...shit!" I try to catch my breath and settle my pounding heart. "So not funny."

He's shaking with hilarity at his own prank. "Totally funny." He pulls me in tighter against him.

"I'm not... just don't... I mean...." I'm far beyond speaking intelligibly. "Fuck." I finish and give into his strong arms and stop squirming with terror.

"That's what I was thinking."

We're only in thigh-deep water now, and Keel lowers his mouth to my chest. I suck in a breath when the heat of his tongue swirls around my cold nipple. I push his head away.

"You scared me," I say as both an accusation and complaint.

"I know. I can feel the goosebumps on your skin and your heart pounding against my lips." His voice sounds husky and thick.

He lowers me to my feet and runs his hands over my body. My nerve endings electrify and cause every hair follicle to stand at full attention. Keel's not grasping the situation like I want him to. His hands continue to explore. I edge toward the shore, but only manage to take one step before he cups the back of my neck and places his mouth over mine. I return the kiss because it's his way of apologizing. He deepens the kiss, groaning into my mouth, and pressing his pelvis against mine. He still wants me in every way.

"Not here," I say with a slight shake of my head.

He takes a deep breath. "Why?"

"Too many people around."

"I need you. No one will see."

"I—"

I don't get to finish. He scoops me into his arms again and takes me to the same place I had been looking at a moment before, the darkest spot along the river. The water rushes over my sides, and I cling to Keel's chest as he moves us.

"It's pitch black. Be with me, Tara. I need to be inside you."

He places me down in front of him. The river bottom is soft, and I'm grateful there are no rocks digging into my feet. His hands are urgent and exploratory as his finger dips between my thighs. He captures my mouth with his once more while guiding my hand to his erection. I'm half appalled, and half turned on. His longing for me is sexy as hell, but I can't do this in a river. I just can't. The thought of sandy, algae, fishy water inside me is more than unpleasant. I'll get an infection—or worse. I don't know what could be worse than an infection, but I don't want to find out.

I stroke him and wait for him to break the kiss. Distinct voices can be heard in the surrounding woods. We pause to listen, but the sound fades as if they're headed another direction.

Keel takes this as a sign to lift my leg and wrap it around his waist. Holding it in place, he presses into me.

"Not in the water," I say. "Let's go back to our bed."

"I can't wait that long. Don't you love me, Tara? I love you so much. Come on," he pleads into my ear.

I bump into the boulder at my back. I'm torn between wanting to keep him happy and getting out of the river. Why can't I just do this here? I do love him. Drunk, stoned, playing his guitar. I love him, and I love that he loves me. But, *excuse me*, I don't want fish water in my crotch, and I don't want to be watched.

"Move over here." I cave giving into his request and compromising my own.

We shift positions, and I climb onto a flat rock, fairly smooth from years of water running over its surface, and I'm at least out of the water. I lie back and let Keel enter me. The stone digs into my back, and I clench my teeth to distract me from the discomfort. Keel must feel me stiffen.

"It's too hard, isn't it?" he asks and stops moving.

"Mmm-hmm," I whimper.

"Tara, babe, sorry." He pulls out, turns over and sits down on the rock. "I'll be on the bottom."

I'm not positive this is the answer to my issue, but it must be better than having my spine bruised. I climb over him and settle into a better position. Being on top gives me a better view of the flowing river and of the surrounding woods. Apparently Keel likes it as he starts finding his rhythm while massaging my chest.

A nearby campfire glows, and the orange and gold flames shimmer through the screen of tree branches and bushes. Someone is standing on a moonlit boulder upstream. Her red and yellow dreadlocks are incongruous in the mountain setting. Caspar is watching Keel and I and appears unashamed about seeing us. One side of her mouth lifts as she sees me notice her. I shut my eyes and pretend she's not there. My heart skips a beat and then pounds in my temples. Blood rushes down my body and pools around my ankles causing more pulse points to throb. Embarrassment and shock are the cause, not lust or enjoyment. I turn all my attention to Keel, to help him finish so I can get off him, dress, and forget this ever happened.

Struggling.

Dear Evie,

I wish I had my own place. It wouldn't need to be anything special. A small apartment, maybe a tiny cabin in the woods. Would you come live with me? We could totally pull it off. It would be so much fun. Of course, Ollie would live with us too. I'm dreaming of the day when I can make it happen. If you don't want to live with me, that's fine. It's your choice. We all need freedom to choose what we want.

I guess all I'm saying is I need my own space. I don't think I even want to live with Keel today. That probably surprises you. Me, too. Last night proved sometimes it's a good thing to be alone. It isn't always necessary to be around others to find happiness. I think you already know. You never seem to need people to stay entertained. I like that you're as happy drawing or reading as you are playing with a friend. I think I've always needed someone around to talk to or keep me busy. It's one of my many faults. Just when I think I've figured out all my problems, I get slammed with another one.

I'm needy and have to make other people happy before I can feel good about myself. It's a sucky way to live, Evie. Don't be a people-pleaser. All it does is decrease your own well-being. Please believe me when I say you can't make others happy. It's as if I give pieces of myself away, again and again, hoping these people will treasure my gift, honor it, and respect that I cared enough about them to gift them a piece of myself. The truth is, most people don't recognize the importance of selfless giving and if by chance they do, they usually can't accept the honor unconditionally. Putting conditions on a gift are the perfect way to ruin it.

Don't give yourself away. I do it too often, and the consequences hurt. It hurts like no other pain in existence because it's a bottomless hole. I think the reason I'm suggesting we move away from everything, and everyone, is if I was alone maybe I could start looking for all my lost pieces. I imagine they're stuck in the bottom of the void inside me. Part of me wants to believe I can regain them, but I'll never get the chance if I keep surrounding myself with people who I feel the need to keep happy. It's a screwed up conundrum. I want you to live with me because I like to think I can save you from putting yourself in the same situations I've gotten myself into. I should know better, though. You were always smarter than me—I doubt you would make the same mistakes I have. Be yourself, sweet sister. It's the easiest and the hardest thing to do. Speak your truth, and for the love of Ollie don't compromise yourself to make a guy, or anyone, happy. Make yourself happy first, then share it with whomever you choose. The light of joy shines within you, Evie. It doesn't come from anywhere else.

I shut my journal but keep my hand securely wrapped around it. I take a deep breath. How can I see the truth so plainly but not be able to live it? What am I so afraid of that I continually push my own needs to the back of the line?

Keel pops the door open on the back of the truck and grins at me. "What are you doing?"

"Nothing." I refuse to look down at my journal. So far, he hasn't noticed it, and I don't want him to. I don't want him to notice its importance to me.

"We're taking off soon. Do you want to cook us some breakfast before we go?"

"Sure," I say and hate every cell of my being. I'm not even hungry, yet I won't tell Keel no.

I'm doing it again—the people-pleasing—and a piece of me disintegrates into that horrible, soul-destroying darkness.

"Thanks for last night." His eyes soften, and he gives me his sweetest face "I was so blitzed, but I still liked it. A lot."

He watches me expectantly as if waiting for me to say how much I liked it too or tell him what a sex god he is. I try to smile and think of what part of sex by the river was enjoyable enough to compliment him on. "I'll never forget it," I say like a lame ass.

My gaze shifts to my knee where the skin is still red, but the cut scabbed over. I have a small bruise on my other knee. Nothing major but the whole experience was uncomfortable. Keel sees me looking at it.

"Yeah, my ass is scratched too. Battle wounds," he says with a laugh. "Want to make some more before we go?" His eyebrows rise with hopeful anticipation.

I turn around, breaking eye contact with him, and slip my journal into a bag as discreetly as possible. *Battle wounds,* he says. *Were we fighting?* No. Just my internal battle against myself. But how does he not know that I'm upset? Doesn't he fucking have eyes? Can't he hear my voice? I set my jaw and speak through tight lips. "I don't think there's time. Besides, I wouldn't want to put on another show for Caspar. She was down by the river last night with us."

He's silent for a beat. "Oh yeah? Are you serious right now?"

"I saw her."

"That explains a lot."

"What are you talking about?" I slide over toward the door watching his face closely.

"Just something she said. Don't worry about it."

"You're not going to tell me?" I ask, incredulous.

"Nah. It's nothing."

"Keel, that's not fair. Tell me."

"It's nothing," he says, trying again to disregard it.

I slam the door on my way out and then turn around to face it again. I'm not sure I can make breakfast with Caspar watching me and knowing she saw us.

"Lighten up, Tara. She said something about Sirens on the rocks and drunken sailors. It didn't even make sense."

I close my eyes. That seems like the only way I can deal with Caspar spying on us. Shutting her out. Shutting out the world.

Keel steps up behind me and enfolds me in his arms. "Don't sweat it, babe. I think she thinks it's funny. And I don't care if the world watched us. Your sexy ass is mine."

He plants a kiss on the side of my neck and releases me. Maybe he's right. Maybe I should lighten up. Maybe my feelings don't matter at all, and I'm the one with unrealistic problems. Maybe I'm wrong to be upset. I mean, who cares?

***

Two days later.

The passage of time can be as thick as peanut butter or as thin as air—with no medium viscosity. This makes life a horrible challenge or a flight of whimsy. I'm pretty sure I'm swimming through peanut butter these days.

On our drive to the next show, I have another one of those weird moments where random quotes find me and niggle their way into my brain. Indiscriminate advertising seems to be speaking directly to me. *"Forever is composed of nows. – Emily Dickinson."* The billboard displaying these memorable words is divided into two sides. Two ads. The left side of the billboard with the quote is for some yoga/pilates studio. PiYo. *How wonderful. Inspirational. Possibly even motivational.* Except the other side of the billboard is for feminine hygiene products. Behold, the gigantic package of tampons—*"Forever is composed of nows."* Bitchiness and cramps, or inner peace and wellbeing? *Choices, choices.* I simply blink at the irony. *Laugh or scream?* I want to do both. Instead, I do nothing. I don't even point it out to Keel, who would surely provide comic relief over such poorly planned advertising—or did someone do it on purpose?

Evie,

Putting one foot in front of the other can be harder than you think. Getting out of bed and facing the day should be easy, but some mornings, or afternoons—depending on how late I stayed up—there isn't anything worth rising for. Days like these wrap me in a haze with no beginning or end. I suspect they aren't infinite, but the cloud of disillusion is as real as my head buried in the pillow. Even after I manage to wake up, the fog won't leave my atmosphere, hanging around like an uninvited guest with repulsively bad breath. God, I just want it to bugger off, but he isn't ready to leave.

Evie, last night was incredible. The show we put on couldn't have gone better. Everything flowed with ease, and the excitement of the crowd was almost overwhelming. I even got to meet one of my favorite bands. You've heard them, too. Collapsed Stars. The lead singer gave me an open invitation to come to any show in Scotland. That's where they're from. It may be a while before I can fly across the pond, but isn't that flipping fantastic! I wish we could go together, just you and me. We could find a haunted castle or look for the Loch Ness monster. I would love exploring Scotland with you. I hope we can take a big trip like that someday.

Everything that's happened so far this summer is amazing. I should be ecstatic, but instead, I want to come home and crawl into my old bed and read stories to you and your stuffed animals.

I probably shouldn't be telling you this. You don't need to know that even though I left home and got away from Geoff and his mad explosions, I still have bad days. This should be the best summer of my life, right? I hope in the future I won't remember the days I couldn't function because I got stuck on the far side of some emotional chasm. You know I'll snap out of it, don't you? This business of feeling sorry for myself never lasts long, so please don't worry. You shouldn't have to see how unhinged I can be. No one needs to witness the hole which burrows inside of me. I always thought I could tell you everything, but it doesn't mean you should know. I'm sorry. No one likes to be sucked into someone else's drama. That's another piece of advice I can give you. Don't take someone down your pity road. If you must buy a ticket to Depressiontown, go alone. Or pay a professional to listen. Okay, now I need to rip out these pages and go burn them...

See how easy that was?

Go alone.

***

The following Saturday.

Today I found a book.

We performed at three o'clock on the auxiliary stage of the Pacific Pastime summer festival. It was so hot outside. Sweat becomes the newest member of our group. He's overly productive, has an affinity for unpleasant odors, and is swampy all the time. Mr. Sweat is a selfish little prick who does what he wants whenever he wants, and he definitely prefers the guys.

After our show, I needed a break from sweaty band members and Caspar. The festival grounds have shopping booths. That's where I found it. I didn't buy the book and can't even remember the title. While perusing a table, I picked up the book with flying birds on the cover and opened to a random page and read, "I have come to the conclusion that always being what others want me to be will only lead to regret and deep sadness".

One simple line in some accidental book made me realize I'm not alone with my faults. And knowing someone else in this world is messed up the same way I am was all it took to shake me out of my funk.

I'm writing this down as a reminder to be myself, not what others want me to be. I can do it. My need to please people is harming me. I need to stop—now. Regret and sadness may always be a part of my life, but they won't rule me any longer. In the expansive range of my emotions, they only get one tiny little corner to brood in. Today, I'm finally able to recognize the beginning of something new. I like what I see.

Chapter Six

"There are three methods to gaining wisdom. The first is reflection, which is the highest. The second is limitation, which is the easiest. The third is experience, which is the bitterest."
— Confucius

Leaving isn't hard if you have something to look forward to. Saying goodbye to the west coast is unexpectedly easier than I thought it would be. In the rearview mirror, the mountains fade into the horizon, and I think of Evie and Jonah. They're hundreds of miles away to the south but venturing east across the country brings up my abandonment issues afresh. And as always, accompanying the memories of home is my stepfather. Geoff invades my head space and dominates my thoughts. His existence always reinforces my decision to leave home.

I haven't called Evie as much as I promised, but she understands. At least, I hope she does. Geoff's always there somewhere, and Mom hovers around our calls. Evie says she takes the phone to her room to be alone, but I can feel my parents nearby. I don't tell Evie everything I've been doing this summer with the band. I would like to tell her more, but the ties to that household are shredding. That's what I need, even if it means talking to Evie less.

So instead of calling my sister to tell her about all the places I've been and the amazing people I've met, I put on some music and sleep for most of the drive to Salt Lake City. When we arrive, we check into a hotel, grab some dinner, and go find the venue for our sound check. Running around in an unfamiliar city keeps us busy, and I use it as an excuse to ignore my phone, but I don't forget my sister. I will never forget about her. I need to remember to call her later.

After the concert, we're greeted by some fans, and a party commences—hosted by us.

***

Caspar promises the Irish Car Bombs will be life-changing. To be honest, the mixture of whiskey, Irish cream, and the frothy stout lager sounds pretty damn good. I know better, but the temptation is an alluring tease, and I fall for his good looks. Caspar's enthusiasm and the night's success on stage help persuade me to drink with everyone else.

I drop the shot of liquor into the pint glass and chug it, being careful that the shot glass doesn't slide forward and crash into my teeth. The rush of carbonated malt and liquor is almost yummy. My stomach, however, revolts after the second car bomb on top of the double shot of whiskey I swallowed earlier.

I take a visual survey of the hotel room and notice how drunk everyone is. The floor sways right and left beneath my feet. The last I checked we weren't in a floating hotel. I lurch toward the door of a ship I don't want to sail on.

"Tara, where are you going?" Caspar calls.

My stomach is an overfilled water balloon. The front of my shirt looks distended, ready to burst. I think walking might help ease the pressure—or possibly puking. Either way, I want to be outside.

"I need some air." I throw open the door. Fresh air isn't to be found. The night is warm and stale. The sidewalk and the two-story hotel are holding the heat of the day, even at one in the morning. Maybe it never cools down here this time of year. I swallow some of the rank hotel air and take a step toward Keel. *Where is he?* Between our band, and the fans we ran into, we got four rooms at a cheap hotel and an after-party that isn't going to wind down for who knows how long.

My hand slips from the door as I turn for the room where Keel most likely is. I want him to come with me. Wandering the streets alone, buzzed from alcohol, doesn't seem too intelligent.

"Wait up," Caspar says. "I'll go with you."

She carries a bottle in her hand, and the sight of it makes my stomach turn over. I put my hand over my mouth and take a steadying breath through my nose. "Keep it away from me," I warn.

"What? This?" She waves it in the air in front of me with a laugh.

I knock on the next door over and hope Keel's inside. It creaks open and a face I don't recognize stares back at me. The guy holds a can of cheap beer that does look familiar, and I'm pretty sure I found the correct room. I tilt my head to peer around him and see Keel standing on the bed. *What's he doing?* Someone's laughing, and music is playing. The guy steps aside leaving the door stand open.

"Hey," I say, and grimace. The noise inside the room swirls through my head, pounds on my temples, and clouds my tipsy perspective.

Caspar slips around me and leans against the open door.

"Tara's here," Keel drawls, grinning like a drunken idiot. He passes the beer bong in his hands to the nearest person and jumps from one bed to the other and then lands in front of me with a thump. He bends forward to place his lips on mine.

I step back. Nausea is so close to the surface. I can't even think about being touched, or kissed. I place my hand on his chest. "Come out with me."

"Where?" He frowns, looking confused.

"Just come?" My eyelids drift closed as if darkness can help settle the rising stomach acid. Unfortunately, it doesn't help, and I reopen them. "Please."

From the corner of my eye, I spot Caspar glancing around the room at all the people we don't know. I pull at Keel's shirt, dragging him outside. The streetlights cast a dingy glow over the parking lot but the darkness beyond calls to me.

"Tara's had too much to drink and needs to walk it off," Caspar says.

He tips my chin up and stares into my eyes. Keel is definitely not sober either. His slightly out of focus gaze and red-rimmed pupils match my own. But I can tell he knows how desperate I'm feeling.

"Let me grab my shoes." He looks around for them as he backs away from me.

I manage a weak nod and swallow a gag. Shaking my head brings back the floating boat sensation.

"Who wants to go on an adventure?" he hollers over the pounding music

Immeasurable minutes later we're walking down the street heading away from traffic, or lights, or any possibility of awake people. Keel and I are ahead of Caspar, Zeb, and two others named Aiden and Wyatt. They're so loud I keep expecting cops to arrive any second to ticket us for being drunk in public. I keep turning down darker streets and the night helps clear my head. Don't get me wrong, I'm still drunk, but the urge to vomit is lessening.

We're eventually buried in some neighborhood when we stumble upon a construction site. Its magnetic pull on us is as if we walked straight into a tractor beam. There isn't much of interest on the lot, which is probably why there's no fence. Mounds of dirt, ditches, and the beginning of a foundation are the highlights. Beneath the stars and the single streetlamp at the far corner of the block, it's a glorious, magical kingdom for six intoxicated fools with nothing better to do.

I stare hard at the closest house looking for spectators, but all is quiet. Not a single lit window or glow of television can be seen. I half wonder if the lot has been abandoned since there isn't any equipment sitting around. We climb the largest dirt pile and plop down on our butts. The bottle of whiskey is passed around, and the war starts. I scoot out of the way before being tackled and promptly remind myself I will never be king of this dirt mountain. Keel slides halfway down the mound and clambers back to the top and overthrows both Zeb and Aiden. His leadership over the dirt doesn't last very long, though, as the three guys retaliate and continue the battle.

Caspar appears next to my elbow.

"Children," I say, staring at the four drunken boys wrestling in the dirt.

"At least they're cute."

"True," I admit and stare at Keel thinking he's cuter than the others. It isn't just his sculpted face and muscles. The way he plays guitar is so damned hot. It gets me every time I watch him.

"Look at you." Caspar pinches my arm.

"Ow." I pull away. "What?" I say with mock defensiveness.

"You're drooling over that idiot."

I wipe the back of my hand to the corner of my mouth. I may be tanked, but I'm not drooling. "Who could blame me?"

"I'm cutting you off now." She tips the bottle up to her lips and finishes it.

"Too late. I don't want anything to do with that." My stomach clenches as I stare at the whiskey bottle with revulsion.

"But it's so good." With a wink and her sly devil smile, she swings her arm and flings the bottle straight for the moon.

It whirls, spins, and crashes back to the earth. "I like breaking things."

"Charming," I say, sarcasm thick on my tongue.

She laughs and bumps into my shoulder.

"Whoo!" one of the guys calls out in triumph behind us.

A porch light flips on two houses down, and across the street.

"Someone's awake," I note.

"Let's move out of the light," Caspar says.

I glance around dubiously. Shadows are heavy all around us. I doubt anyone can see our group, but they can no doubt hear Keel and the others.

Caspar starts dancing toward the back of the lot. She stops to hold her arm out to me. "Tara?" she whispers. "Tara, come over here."

I follow her because I don't like the sudden light shining from the neighbor's house and because clods of dirt are falling from the sky. They explode like bombs on the hard ground.

"Look! Can you believe this?" she asks.

"What? I don't see anything."

"I'm going over." She grabs my shirtsleeve to drag me along.

"What are you talking about?" I ask as I squint past her.

"It's a cemetery. I have to do this."

"Seriously?" I whine as she drops my shirt, jumps over a ditch, and approaches an iron fence separating the two properties.

"Tara?" Caspar calls. "You owe me. I just walked ten miles with you to play in the dirt. Now you're going to follow me into the land of the dead. I need corpses, and I need them now."

"What are you going to do with a corpse?" I ask.

"You'll see," she says.

I barely hear her as she wanders away and tries to find a way over the fence.

"Keel?" I whisper-yell over to the guys.

I can make out the shape of two of them lying on their backs, head down on the dirt pile. Someone else's silhouette summersaults down the mountain.

"Babe!" he calls back. "Come try this."

"We're going over the fence. Find us when you're done over there," I call as loud as I dare.

A muffled, "Okay," reaches my ears.

Leaping over the ditch proves unsuccessful. I misjudge the distance in the dark, and my right foot slips over the edge. Fear of the unknown is the greatest motivation for self-preservation. I collapse to the ground in a heap before I tumble fully into the ditch. Is it deep? Is it full of water or mud or worms? Weeds jab into my hands, and my knee is being stabbed by something hard. I scramble to my feet and look back at the ditch. It isn't nearly as scary now that I'm upright again, but I still can't tell if it's an abyss or a foot deep. I brush the dirt off my clothes and face my next obstacle. The fence.

"Where did you go?" I whisper to Caspar.

I plant my foot between two of the iron rails on the low horizontal bar and heave myself over. Crashing into the ditch must have sobered me some because jumping the fence goes much easier. On the other side, I press my hands together to ease the bite of the hard iron digging into my palms. While pondering the sensation, something grabs me from behind.

"Booga-booga-booga," she shouts as she bumps into me, knocks me down, and whirls away.

"You're freaking hilarious," I say flatly as I turn over and plant myself in the cool grass.

She comes gliding up to me and squats down. "Sorry. Couldn't help myself."

Caspar takes my hand and pulls me to my feet. I'm reluctant to move. The manicured lawn is thick and soft. There are no headstones nearby, and I want to stay where I'm at and pretend we're at a park.

"You're going to drag me into this aren't you?"

"Absolutely."

She sounds absurdly pleased with herself. I roll my eyes and let her lead me deeper into the cemetery. "Don't get us lost."

"We're lost, Tara. We're so lost. In a world that makes no sense. Where we bury the dead together in little plots of earth. People need each other. I thought I could do it alone, but I need people, too. I'm as weak as everyone else. In life and in death as well. Do you want to be my ghost bestie after we die?"

"I think I'll pass." Her drunk mumbling is half lost on me. I'm trying not to crack a shin on a grave marker or break a toe. For how much she's had to drink, she's amazingly stable on her feet. It's her incredible legs, I think with envy. Who gets legs like hers and a stunning face to boot?

"You're not weak." I toss the compliment out to soothe her and because it's what you're supposed to do, right? When someone is beating themselves up, you say everything to contradict their negative attitude toward themselves.

"Ha," she snorts. "We're all weak in some way, Tara. Keel's your weakness."

"No, he isn't," I say. If anyone, it's Evie.

She stops tromping over graves and approaches a mausoleum. Caspar places her hands flat against the marble and leans forward like she's about to kiss the stone. I change directions and put some space between us. Her face next to the polished stone in such an intimate way, it makes my skin crawl. A few empty plots are near the mausoleum so I sit back down in the grass and stare at my midnight surroundings.

"Do you hear them?"

I can't help but glance over. Caspar has her ear pressed to the wall.

"They're in there," she whispers.

"All I can hear is your crazy song playing. It's not pretty either. Kind of morbid, but mostly messed up with a lot distortion."

She giggles and backs away from the tomb. I lie back in the grass and stare up at the moon. Its morose light falls down over me and makes the goosebumps rise.

"You can't see it, but I do," Caspar says as she folds down next to me.

"I'm not interested in seeing any zombies or ghosts," I say with no enthusiasm. This place is just a place. The grass is comfy and the fact that there are decomposing bodies planted here is just an inconvenience. Real ghosts come back to haunt me on a regular basis. The kind of ghosts who visit dreams, causing doubt and regret. Most of my ghosts resemble Geoff, my mom, the cast of Farinelli World Circus, and my real dad.

"They're not out tonight. And that isn't what I'm talking about."

"I think the whiskey has addled your brains."

"For sure," she agrees. "But I don't need my brains. They only confuse everything."

"I still elect to keep mine," I say.

"Alcohol is the perfect preservative."

"Umm, did you ever see anything preserved in alcohol?" I ask thinking about the jarred specimens in my college science lab.

"I told you, I'm not interested in the dead anymore. Geez, Tara, get off it already," she feigns playful disgust.

I rip out a handful of grass and throw it at her and let my eyelids drift shut. Sleep suddenly sounds inviting. The thought of trekking back to my room almost makes me think staying overnight in the cemetery is a good idea. Isn't that ironic? We finally splurge on a hotel room, and I want to sleep outside. Something tickles my face. A lot of somethings. A blade of grass goes up my nose and makes me snort. I brush away Caspar's grassy retaliation and ignore her inebriated laughter. The effect carries me swiftly away from my fantasy of going to sleep.

"You know why Keel is your weakness?" she asks as she stares down at me.

"I already told you he's not. I love him."

"Do you even know what love is?"

"I know I feel it."

Her face was above mine, but now she leans back and glances skyward like I had been doing. "What do you feel?"

My brain searches for the words to describe my feelings for Keel. With alcohol stewing inside my bloodstream, I'm about to say something completely corny, but I don't get the chance to embarrass myself.

Caspar answers herself. "Love is different for everyone. I think it's all a lie. A big fat farce so we keep depending on each other for nothing."

"How can that be? Love is one of the only real things in life. Everything else is an illusion except love, Caspar."

"You sound so sure about it." Her tone drops to one of sadness. "You sound like you read some bullshit manual on life."

I ignore her bitterness and add, "I don't believe in very much, but I can't give up on that."

"You believe it, so it's true for you." She leans over me again.

Her face hangs above mine. Her dreads are tied back so I don't have to worry about them falling into my face. The glow of the moon forms a halo around her head.

"You really think love is a lie?"

"Most of the time. You wouldn't recognize my version of love because it's ugly, full of pain and misunderstanding."

"That's..." I pause. The last week hasn't exactly been peachy and perfect, but that's been my own demons messing with me. It doesn't have anything to do with my relationship. Does it? I hate that Caspar's reminder of pain and agony makes me question what I have with my boyfriend. "Then what do I have with Keel?" I ask, starting to fall into her absurd line of thinking.

"Lust."

I blink and close my eyes so I'm not staring straight up at her. Could she be right? My feelings for Keel run in the center of the deepest veins in my body. He's my life. He makes me happy and gives me a reason to wake up every day.

"You think you love him, which may be true, but he's in lust with you, and that's not real love."

"I don't think you know us well enough to say that." I'm defensive because it's all I can come up with to refute her observation. Surely, Keel loves me for more than the sex.

"Tara?"

"What?"

"Being in lust is okay. It feels fucking fantastic. He might love you back, someday. I'm having a similar problem, so I totally get it."

My eyes are still closed. I don't want to see the look on her face. The doubts swimming through me are treacherous, and killing my confidence in what I think is real.

I sigh. "You're in lust with someone? What's the difference? When it comes to Keel, I'm pretty sure it's more than lust for me."

"Lust is like...," she trails off.

The next thing I know, warm lips press against mine. The tip of her tongue darts into my mouth. Her hand brushes my cheek. I shove her away and scramble to my feet. Shock and repulsion fight for first place in the strongest emotion contest.

"Don't!" is all that comes out of my mouth as I swipe my hand across my lips. I taste earth and grass on my fingers, and it's exponentially better than Caspar's whiskey breath.

She reclines back on her elbows laughing and wearing an evil smile.

"You're uptight, you know that. I thought you wanted me to show you what lust feels like."

"That's not it," I say, appalled.

"It is for me. Do you think I would show you all my stuff if I didn't like you?"

"What?!" I say, thinking she might be referring to the first day in the shower at the beach, but I can't even be sure about that. Caspar is playing with my head, and I need to make it stop.

"Never mind," she says. "Here's why your relationship with Keel is a lie."

"Shut up." I turn to leave. "I don't sleep with girls. It's not personal. It's just not who I am."

"You'll do anything to make him love you. If he doesn't love you, you'll fall apart into nothing. You'll be nothing, and that's why your love is a lie. Why it's painful and ugly."

"You're drunk, and I don't want to talk about it anymore."

She climbs to her feet, stretches her arms over her head, and yawns. "Whatever. You're right. I'm stinking drunk. Keel's drunk, too. Here he comes, by the way. Just in time to rescue his sweet little fatal attraction."

Chapter Seven

Today's Sign
Danger: Enter At Your Own Risk
(Conveniently located on an innocuous gray door on the side
of the hotel.)

We're all hung over. The result of which looks something like this:

Trash cans are overflowing. Beer cans and bottles decorate every flat surface. Random clothes are strewn around the room. People appear to be in the process of mummification by being wrapped in hotel linens.

Everyone's in a bad mood and incapable of acting like functional beings. Zombie mode has been activated. I don't know the magic cure. We didn't need to visit the cemetery after all to find the undead. *Hmm...who knew?* It's just as frightening as it sounds, but not like horror movie frightening, more like, "This is your brain, 'show picture of whole egg in its shell.' This is your brain on drugs, 'show picture of carton of eggs being thrown at our heads and splattering into an enormous mess.' Any questions?" That kind of scary. My own brain feels damaged after last night. *So not worth it.* What's the difference between mummies and zombies anyway? Not much, if one were to gauge it on the look of Paradox 21 this morning.

As I gather my stuff and try not to speak or make eye contact with anyone, I notice Zeb stretched out asleep on the end of the bed wearing a bra. I do a double take to make sure it's not one of mine. It isn't. My eyebrow lifts at the makeup job someone gave him after he passed out. *Who the hell owns blue lipstick and glitter eye shadow?* I glance across the hotel room to the counter by the sink; my makeup bag appears unmolested.

"Zeb." I poke his leg.

The thought of waking him up to tell him he should take off the bra, pull out his pigtails, and wash his face seems like the right thing to do. When he doesn't stir, I let it go. Chances are good he's already been photographed and posted on every social media page in the universe.

"Hey." I poke him again because we need to get going.

We have a seven-hour drive today to make it to our next gig. It isn't ideal but the opening came up, and we couldn't turn it down. The venue had a cancellation, was desperate to fill it, and the owner is a friend of Saul's dad or something. We'll be paid well too, which helps motivate us to make the long drive. We just need to make it there in time to warm up and do our sound check.

"Err...," Zeb grumbles and rolls off the bed.

He kicks at the tangled sheet and his feet make an appearance. Someone, or more like multiple someones, graciously painted his toenails...and his feet...and his ankles. I stare at Zeb's multi-colored nails and reconsider my assumption of the use of nail polish. I'm pretty sure the variety of black, green, blue, and red is from markers, not paint. I squat down and gingerly pull the sheet away to inspect the nautical stars, pornographic stick figures, mushrooms, and of course, humping unicorns covering most of Zeb's lower body. You can't draw artwork on a passed out person without adding a unicorn penis or two. I'd laugh if I wasn't so tired and it didn't hurt inside my skull every time I think, let alone laugh.

"We gotta go, man. It's getting late." I shake him lightly. "I hope that's not permanent ink," I mumble and finish packing my overnight bag. The abundance of permanent markers that travel with our band gives me little hope for Zeb's future clean unmarked skin, but my well-wishes are all I've got at the moment. Maybe my makeup remover will help.

After putting my bags in the truck, I go back to the room. Keel steps out of the steamy bathroom, hair still damp from the shower. Zeb mumbles something incoherent and slips past Keel, slamming the bathroom door behind him.

The miscellaneous bra lays neglected on the floor. I wonder if it's Caspar's, but then I don't care. I don't want to think about her. I didn't tell Keel what she did, or said, in the cemetery, and I don't think I'm going to. Would he be mad? If another guy kissed me and he found out, he'd be raging. Ready to murder someone. Does it make a difference that Caspar is female? And what she said about Keel not loving me unsettled me, and I didn't sleep well because of it. Her words stung and I hate how much I let it get under my skin.

I'm glad she slept in another room last night. We need a break from each other. Weird discomfort and the need for personal space happens a lot when you travel, live with, and perform with the same small group of people night after night and day after day. We find our own ways of dealing with it. Ear buds are a necessity and learning to sleep at different times of the day helps a lot. I don't want to see or talk to Caspar this morning. She basically confessed to lusting after me, and it made the queasiness inside my stomach roil. I thought we were becoming friends. Female friends were sparse in my short life. I had a couple from growing up with The Show, who were like my sisters, but I haven't seen them since my family left. After we had settled in Crapville, I finished high school as a solitary participant. I felt like an island amidst the cliques and well-established groups of friends who grew up together. My two semesters of college went about the same way. Since I met Keel at a show, we've been hanging out ever since. Having Caspar to talk to made me realize how much I missed having a female friend. I'm entirely too tired and lousy feeling to be thinking so hard on the subject of female/female infatuation.

"We need coffee," I say.

"I'm starved," Keel complains.

Of course, he is. He's always hungry after a night of drinking. My stomach groans in protest at the thought of food. I only mentioned coffee because it seems like the most likely way I'm going to snap out of zombie mode. Getting a cup could be the magic potion we need. What I want is six more hours of sleep and some herbal tea.

"Did you see anyone else? We need to get moving," Keel says as he zips up his bag.

"Yeah. Saul was loading the van a minute ago."

"Good. We should go now and grab breakfast. They can do whatever. We'll meet them on the highway."

"Okay," I agree. "Will you go tell them and I'll meet you at the truck?"

"Sure, babe."

The morning flies by. Mostly because we didn't start until ten a.m. Funny how that happens, like an unintended time warp or something.

Keel suggests we grab sandwiches at about two in the afternoon. I had just awakened from a nap, and although groggy, I feel revived. The sleep had settled my mind like silt sinking to the bottom of a murky puddle, leaving it clear on top. As long as nothing comes along to stir it up, I know I'll be okay for the rest of the day.

Saul, Zeb, Demian, and Caspar join us at the sandwich shop and we decide to eat as we drive. I avoid Caspar, and she avoids me. Everything remains kosher. Keel asks me to drive after we order our sandwiches, and I agree. He wants to eat and I'm not hungry yet, so I take my turn behind the wheel. We need to keep moving if we're going to make it to Denver in time.

"I'm going to crash for a while," Keel says about five minutes after he eats his foot-long sandwich. "You doing okay?"

"I'm good." I keep my eyes on the road.

"Follow the van and you'll be fine."

"I know," I say. "You should sleep now while you can. We're going to have a late night again tonight. And don't worry, I do know how to drive," I add because he's acting reluctant.

He grabs the pillow I like to keep in the cab with us and tucks it next to his head.

The hours creep by. The drive is one long valley after another with an occasional mountain to climb over. We wind through a rock wall canyon of monumental gorgeousness and spend a couple more hours driving through the mountains. As we enter the metro area, the gas light comes on.

"Keel?"

"Hmmm," he hums and sits up.

"We need gas."

"How close are we?"

"We're on the edge of the city so we can't be that far."

As if right on cue, the traffic begins to thicken and rain begins to pelt the windshield. I slow down. Keel is quiet for a minute as if considering what to do next.

"Pull off at the next station."

"K." I focus on the traffic and the flashing red brake lights ahead of us.

Keel grabs his phone and calls the van. "We're getting fuel. How far is the club?" he asks into his phone.

There's a pause, and then he adds, "Don't stop with us. Traffic is getting heavy, and we're supposed to be there for sound check in an hour. We'll be right behind you."

Three or four miles closer to the city I finally spot a gas station sign. I take the exit, and as I make the right turn and merge into traffic, I hit the mother of all potholes followed by a string of her babies.

"Ahhh," I yelp with surprise. "Sorry," I apologize quickly.

"Damn it!" Keel says as the back tire drops into another hole.

"Sorry," I say again. "I didn't see it." I maneuver across three lanes of traffic to the turn lane for the only gas station in sight. My blood pressure is up, and my cheeks burn from the sudden stress.

"That sounded horrible. God, you probably bent a wheel on that pothole." Keel's gripping the door handle so hard I'm afraid it will break off.

I remain silent and pull up to a pump. I didn't see the stupid pothole because I was too busy trying not to crash into oncoming traffic. As soon as I stop the truck, Keel jumps out. I'm slower to open my door because I'm afraid of what I might find. I resolve myself to the fact that I didn't do it on purpose and climb out to inspect the damages.

"It doesn't look bad." Keel finishes running his fingers over the rim of the back wheel.

"I guess it felt worse than it was," I say.

He moves around to the pump and doesn't apologize for yelling at me. I take up residence in the passenger seat and watch the rain increase. When Keel finishes filling up, there are streams of water flowing across the gas station parking lot.

It didn't need to be said that Keel would finish our drive to the venue. Before he starts the engine, he opens the navigation on his phone and finds the club. He sets the phone down where he can see it and hear the directions, and we head back to the interstate. He's still not speaking to me.

The stress of the day, hitting the pothole, and being in a rush to reach the venue on time becomes its own entity inside the cab with us. I wish it would dissolve and leave us alone, but that's not going to happen until we reach the club and load in.

"Something's wrong," Keel says after a few miles down the interstate.

"What?" I ask.

"I'm pulling over."

"What's going on?"

He doesn't answer me as he puts his signal on, turns on the emergency flashers, and pulls into the breakdown lane.

"Do you know where my sweatshirt is?"

"In the back." I'm über aware of the sheets of rain falling from the sky.

"Fuck." He steps out of the truck.

I climb out after him heedless of the weather. I want to know what's going on or find his hoodie for him. I can't just sit.

The front passenger side tire is totally flat. The tire that took the biggest hit on the pothole. I press my lips together and make a dash for the back door of our sort-of camper. Keel lets out a few choice words as I jump into the truck bed.

He opens and closes the front door, then joins me in the back a few seconds later. I push the bedding toward the corner in a vain attempt to keep it dry.

"We don't have time for this shitpouch."

"I know."

He hands me the phone. "Call the guys and tell them what's up. Tell them we're going to be late and not to wait for us to warm up."

"Do you want me to call roadside assistance or something?"

Keel speaks through a clenched jaw. "Seriously Tara, we don't have time to wait on them. I need to change the tire myself."

"Can I help?" I ask meekly. I've never changed a tire, but this is my fault, and I want to help.

He rolls his eyes—I want to bury myself in the corner under the sleeping bags.

"I was looking for your hoodie. Do you still want it?"

Keel looks down at his soaked shirt and jeans. The rain blasting the cab over our heads is as loud as the thunder booming in the sky.

"No," he snaps. "Call the band."

His final words are as harsh as the raging storm outside. I make the call and tell Zeb what's going on. He says traffic is a plugged up twat, not to worry, and he'll see us whenever we get there. Zeb's cool response helps settle my overcharged anxiety for maybe fifteen seconds.

When I join Keel outside, sure I can help in some way, the decreased pressure in my chest blows back up as soon as my boyfriend speaks.

"What are you doing, Tara?" Keel asks as he rolls the spare tire toward its flat sibling.

The interstate traffic is thick and moving like a herd of slugs. The constant roar of motors and wet tires pushing through the rain is loud enough that I yell to be heard.

"Anything. Something. I'm sorry, Keel," I say as rain and Keel's anger beat me down.

Rain pours down my body and soaks through my clothes in seconds. Keel's clothes cling to him and rivulets of water pour off his head and run down his face.

"Go back inside." He throws the jack down to the ground by the wheel.

"Can I—"

He cuts me off before letting me finish. "Jesus, Tara. Can't you hear what I'm saying? I don't want any help."

I swallow and blink away the rain stinging my eyes.

"Zeb says he'll see us whenever and not to worry too much about being late," I say, making a final attempt to hold the peace, another mistake. Nothing I say or do is going to alleviate tension between us. Keel's never been this angry. I don't know how to fix this. Then I remember it isn't my job to make anyone happy. I bite my lip and take a step back.

"Zeb's not fucking here, so what does he know about it?"

"I think he's just letting us know a flat tire isn't worth getting all worked up about." I let Keel hear the new me. He can't talk to me like this. I'm a girl who says what she thinks and stops trying to make everything all better—All. The. Fucking. Time. My frustration reaches a pinnacle, and I teeter forward and back, not sure which way I'm going to fall. It's precarious and scary as hell.

Keel runs a hand over his head, pushing his hair and a wave of water back. "Sit inside, Tara, and let me get through this nightmare by myself." He squats down to set the jack in place.

I don't know why but I stand there and stare. I don't want to be ordered around. I obeyed more orders from Geoff than a soldier with a military career. Keel ignores me and the source of the cold seeping into my skin is equally divided between the icy rain and his attitude.

He begins to jack up the truck and my feet make the decision to move. My mind is blissfully blank as I park my butt on the back bumper and wait for nothing and everything. The rain turns to hail, and I suffer through every stinging ball of ice as it strikes me.

Eventually, I move so Keel can put the flat tire in place underneath the truck. Then I'm back inside the cab, and we're driving into the city.

Neither of us speaks. The voice on the GPS tells us we've reached our destination, and I snap out of my frozen state of mind. The clock says we have about thirty-five minutes until we're supposed to be on stage.

Keel parks near the van and gets out without saying anything to me. By this point, I'm beyond pissed he hasn't apologized for being a jerk. He hasn't made any effort to accept my apology, and I'm doubly pissed I apologized at all. The pothole was an accident. I grab my props bag as he digs out dry clothes, and we find the back entrance of the theater.

Chapter Eight

"If the moon smiled, she would resemble you. You leave the same impression. Of something beautiful, but annihilating."
— Sylvia Plath

"I was wondering if we were going to need to send the coastguard to retrieve you," Caspar jokes as we slog into the hallway backstage.

"Almost, but we made it," I say.

"Where is everyone?" Keel asks.

"Keep going down the hall. We're in the second room on the right. We're sharing with the members of the Gnarled Roots. There are birthday cupcakes, and a pony keg from some local brewery," she says with a smile.

Keel heads straight for the backstage lounge Caspar is talking about, but I need someplace to clean up and change. I haven't spoken to her since she kissed me, and this isn't the time or the place to rehash our drunken excursion. She's gorgeous, fresh as a summer peach, and ready to perform. I cringe and try not to look at her.

"Is there a bathroom somewhere?"

"Probably." She bats her eyelashes.

I swear if she could flip her hair at me she would. As it is, her heavy dreads make that flippant act impractical.

"What are you doing tonight? I got permission to swallow torches. Since you were so late, I decided we should do what we did at the last fest. You stay on the right, and I'll do my thing on the left. Saul knows."

"If I don't change like right now, I won't be on tonight at all."

She gives a shrug of indifference. I bite my tongue and decide to not respond. I head to the dressing room or lounge, or wherever Keel just disappeared into, and try not to dwell on Caspar.

"You might want to fix your hair, Tara. The wet dog look isn't really working for you."

She follows me, staying close enough that I can smell her strawberry and fire scent. About ten or twelve guys and a couple of girls are hanging out in the backstage lounge. After Caspar's comment about my hair, I'm self-conscious. Fortunately, everyone's preoccupied with beer and pre-show excitement.

Saul and Demian are near the door when I enter.

"Where can I change?" I lift my bag and peer down at my wilted clothes.

"Keel just went into the bathroom." Demian gestures with his head toward a closed door.

"Corban?" Saul calls to a guy talking with Zeb. They're standing by a table covered with snacks and drinks.

The tall twenty-something guy with trim black hair glances at us, says something to Zeb and comes over. His pale green eyes flicker over me. I take in his all black clothes and muscular physique. My awareness of my drowned rat appearance grows exponentially as he approaches.

"Tara could use someplace to change outfits in a hurry. Think you can help her out?" Saul asks.

He glances at me, then at the closed door where Keel is getting ready. My cheeks flush with heat from anger and also embarrassment, but at least I'm not quite so cold anymore. Sitting for an hour in wet clothes is chilling, in case you didn't know. If Keel and I weren't fighting, we could be sharing the bathroom.

"Hi, I'm Tara." I try to sound professional. "Sorry, we're running late. We had some minor car problems."

"I heard. Sucks about the weather. Come on. You guys are on in," he checks his watch. "Twenty minutes."

Corban moves toward me, and I sidestep out of his way, pulling my bulky bag to the side, and trying to keep my rain water and car exhaust aura to myself. He takes me down the hall and opens a door with his key.

"This is the office. There's a private bathroom over there." Corban points to the corner of the large office.

"Are you sure it's okay if I use it?"

"Yeah. Sure. Saul's a good friend of ours," he says as if this explains everything. He holds the door open, and I slosh past him. "When you're done make sure the door is closed all the way so it's locked."

"Of course," I say.

"Cool. See you out there. The house is packed tonight. Gnarled Roots are a local favorite."

I give him a weak smile, and he closes the door behind me.

Rushing through the process of getting ready isn't fun, but I manage and step out into the hall, hair braided, fresh makeup applied, and my outfit dry. I stash my bag in a corner of the lounge and look for Keel. He's not around, and it doesn't surprise me. I'm sure he's checking his guitar even though Zeb set up and tuned it. I find the stage and take a peek. The venue isn't huge but bigger than some of the clubs we've played. Capacity seems to be around eight or nine hundred and Saul mentioned the show is sold out due to Gnarled's popularity.

For our standards, the theater is gorgeous. The art deco elements add a nice touch to the building. Out on the floor, the crowd is whirring and chatty as waitresses buzz around with trays of drinks. I back into the shadows behind the stacks and stand near the gold velvet stage curtains. My breath is shallow and my chest tight. I force air to move down to my diaphragm and exhale slowly and repeat. There's just enough space around me to do some stretches and make an attempt to warm up. After the drive from hell and being soaked to the bone with freezing rain and pellets of hail, I need blood moving through my muscles before I can dance without looking like an uncoordinated robot.

While I bend and twist, the lights in the theater lower, the buzz of the crowd lessens, and Saul and the guys gravitate toward their instruments. My hamstrings battle with my quads on who is the tighter muscle group. They reach an impasse, and I breathe a plea for them to relax and let go of some tension. It doesn't help that Keel is still ignoring me. No eye contact. No "break a leg", or a kiss before the show. Maybe his fly is down, I think, and wonder if karma can be instantaneous. It would serve him right. Sometimes I check his zipper for him, just a glance to make sure he doesn't embarrass himself. And he gives me a once over to make sure every hair is in place, and I'm still the "hot girl" before stepping onto the stage. We're usually in balance like that, but not tonight.

I push the hurt aside and focus on what I need to do to make it through the night. This isn't my first performance where all is not shiny and wonderful in my universe. My thoughtful parents taught me how to suck it up, plaster a fake smile on my face, and go through the motions as if pain and discomfort don't exist.

Five years earlier.

"I can't go on tonight." I close my eyes for an extra-long blink so I won't see her first reaction.

"You're fine," Mom says. "You pick yourself up, put on your prettiest smile and go do what you're trained to do."

"It hurts, Mom. I'm not like you and Geoff. I can't ignore the pain. I twisted my knee during practice, and it's not getting better. It feels way worse now than earlier."

"You don't get a choice in this. If you don't go on in," she glances over at the clock on the side table, "sixty-three minutes, you're done. We're all done. I will pack us up and be done with the Farinelli Circus forever."

"You said we're leaving at the end of next season. What difference does it make if I miss one show?" It came out of me severely, as I meant it to. Full of spite and vicious as a feral cat attack. "Mr. Markovic never wants anyone to perform injured." I rub my aching knee.

"Get up and take ibuprofen. Then keep an ice pack on until you're on. The aerial routine won't make it worse. Be grateful you're not on the low wire, Jas."

"I'll never do the low wire again," I say through my teeth.

"Don't talk about my act like it's repulsive, you ungrateful little…"

"Little what?" A rush of blood scorches my cheeks. "I don't know why you're making me learn the low wire. That's your thing, not mine."

"Because you're good and family traditions should be passed on. You can take the low wire act with you anywhere."

"It's old school, like you." I don't care if I'm hurting her feelings anymore. My knee aches, and she's not even worried I may hurt myself tonight because I'll be compensating for the pain.

The door to our trailer opens and Geoff steps inside. He assesses us with cold, knowing eyes. "Is she still favoring the leg?" he asks my mother.

"No." She turns away from me and continues this conversation like I'm not in the room with them. "She's being stubborn and doesn't want to perform tonight. I say she should go on. We all have bad days. That doesn't mean we skip over them."

Geoff's gaze slides my way, and I harden my resolve to not lose this battle. They can't make me go on with an injury. I just need to tell Mr. Markovic, our manager, and he'll find a substitute. The problem is I have to do it soon, or I run the risk of upsetting the schedule for the entire show. Everyone gets cranky when the schedule is off. Precise timing affects everyone.

My stepfather walks over to the sink and turns on the water to wash his hands. He's silent as a tomb and just as dark. I saw that aura around him many times. My better sense is urging me to rise from the table and flee before he makes up his mind. Geoff's silence means he's contemplating on how he can win the asshole of the moment award—he always wins. It's not something to aspire to in case you were wondering.

He shuts the water off and places his dripping hands on the edge of the sink.

"I'm so sick of her whining. How did I end up with a daughter who can whine for two seconds and think she can just skim over her commitments?"

Mom's hugging herself and looks about as fragile as I've ever seen her. This pitiful helplessness is happening more and more, ever since she married Geoff. I stare at the table and consider listening to the tiny voice in my gut saying to lie and get out of the trailer before it gets worse.

"I told you a thousand times, if you're going into the business, everyone will be counting on you to show up. You can't miss. It harms your reputation, and it's bad for your ego. You train yourself to let your injuries and self-pity gain control over your actions. Your knee isn't bad enough to not perform tonight. The team is counting on you."

"Jesus! You're telling me my ego is controlling me? What in the actual hell does that even mean? My knee hurts. There's going to be a ton of pressure on it when I'm up in the silks, and you just say, take control? If I need surgery after tonight, it will be on you." I rise from the table and move to the door.

My mom's head is down, and her eyelids are shaking. I want to roll my eyes and tell her to stop acting so injured, but I know she's not acting. I hurt her again. Every breath I take moves her one more inch toward the cliffs of insanity. I'm pretty sure my very existence is what brought the crazies into her life in the first place. My real dad, Glen Jasper Pyrah, introduced her to the cliffs, and when daddy-o disappeared, she took up residence near the edge. At least this is how I imagine she became so unstable. It's as good an explanation as anything else. And, yeah, I was named after my father's middle name. *Lucky me.*

Geoff reaches his arm out, effectively blocking me from leaving.

"Autumn," he says.

His calm, centered tone of voice makes the small hairs on my body stand at attention. The door is a mere five feet away, and yet I'm not going to be allowed to exit until he lets me. The knowledge doesn't stop me from trying to preserve myself.

"I'm going on. I don't think it's the best decision for my knee, but I'll do it. The show must go on, right?" The crappy attitude just won't be smothered no matter how much danger I'm in. Why can't I turn it off? You'd think with the sharp-edged gleam in Geoff's burning glare I would know better than to provoke him, but alas, my teenaged mouth has to be heard one way or another.

His arm continues to hang parallel to the floor, so I'm unable to pass.

"Jasper and I need to talk about her mouth. Autumn, you go on and lie down, or see what Evie and Jonah are up to. I'll handle this," he says.

Mom doesn't need more encouragement to escape the confines of our trailer.

"Mom," I say, but I can't add anything. Her name. The simplest declaration that she is the one person in the world who can save me from Geoff. And by happenstance, she's also the only one who can give him permission to do what he wants with me by just walking out of the room. Can she hear the desperation in my voice or only the whiny, needy girl with too much rebellion and not enough appreciation for the screwed up life she's given me?

Autumn walks out and doesn't look back. God, I wish Evie and Jonah were in the trailer. Geoff is never as much of a Geoff when his own kid is in sight or within hearing range. Why is that? I secretly think he doesn't want his own offspring to see just what a fucker he truly is. Shame on him for being a two-faced prick-and-a-half.

He waits until the door is closed and then he waits another five seconds. I place my butt on a seat at the table and train my eyes on the window.

He breaks the silence. "Who do you think you are?"

Nothing I can say will help. I've been through this before. I dug my grave and now I fall in. Once he's made up his mind on how to "handle" me, I only make things worse no matter what I say—or don't say.

"Answer me," he says with a clear warning tone.

"Anything I say can and will be used against me," I say because it's the only truth I know at the moment.

"Your mouth is the problem here, Jas."

Tears taunt me with emotions I don't want. I hate him using my nickname. It's an intrusion into a personal piece of my life he's not invited to be a part of.

He leans back against the counter and crosses his muscled forearms. "What do you think we should do? You obviously don't give a damn how you hurt your mother. I saw you watching her. We could both see how upset you were making her and yet you continue to run your mouth like the little bitch you are."

I bite my lip and stare out the window waiting for him to finish. He'll just keep expounding until I'm drowning in his exhaustive sermon. A little sparrow sits on the roof rail of the trailer next to ours. The trailer belongs to Madam Reimer, the poodle trainer, and I wonder if Jonah and Evie are inside with the dog lady and my mom. Could I scream loud enough to let everyone, or anyone, know what's happening in here?

"Don't ignore me." He slams his hand down on the table.

I jump in my seat, and my heart lurches into my throat. The sparrow is equally surprised and takes flight leaving me with nothing beautiful. The skyline is as gray as old ashes, and only distant power lines cut the view above the roof of the neighboring trailer.

"I'm not ignoring you, Geoff. I'm going over my routine in my head and trying to figure out if there's any way I won't blow my knee out as I come out of the triple flip roll."

That did it. Geoff's trigger had been pulled. See? No matter what I say, it's never in my best interest.

"I'll fix you up for tonight." He nods in agreement with himself. He turns to the sink, and I scoot away from him, moving farther down the bench seat under the window.

"You'll remember this lesson one day," he says. "When you think you need to talk to us like we're your servants, you'll remember the taste and the feeling of your punishment. Now get up and come over here."

No force in the world can make me rise and embrace my penalty for talking crap to him and my mom. But I don't need to worry because he takes care of the force and yanks me off the seat and around the table. Before I can scream for help, or even react in any normal defensive way, he wraps the rolled up dish towel around my face, making sure to cover my mouth. He ties a knot at the back of my head. I reach up to rip if off, but he grabs my hands away and pulls them behind my back.

Thrashing against him does little to free my arms. He's a thousand times stronger than I am. I grunt and scream and work my jaw against the terry cloth and I'm rewarded with a glob of dish soap entering my mouth. The gagging starts pretty quickly, and the towel is blocking part of my nose. Getting air seems vitally important, and there isn't enough. This distraction holds all of my concentration, and I don't realize he's tying my hands together behind my back until too late. The towel is a thoughtful touch to ensure no one hears me. And the soap, well, washing out my mouth is memorable. Let me tell you, he definitely earns points for that detail.

"It hurts me to treat you this way," he says. "But your mother and I can't seem to make an impression on you that will help you learn to be more respectful."

"Furrck you!" I grunt into the cloth and kick my foot back and up at his crotch. My heel barely catches his shin, too weak to do any good. The frustration, anger, and fear finally take over my senses. Bucking, thrashing, and kicking make no difference. I'm sure he anticipated my panic. He squeezes me up against him in a full body hold rendering me almost paralyzed. The soap in my mouth is seeping down my throat, and the urge to puke and choke simultaneously sends burning tears streaming down my face.

The heat of his breath is in my ear as he speaks with measured control. "There you go again. The foul mouth. You can learn to behave yourself. I know you can. You're a smart girl." He forces me forward until I fold over the dining table. "Control your body, your mind, and your mouth, Jas. You're forcing me to teach you the difficult way. Why are you doing this to yourself? Tonight you will do your aerial act, and your knee will not hurt one bit. Do you know how I know?"

He answers himself, but I don't hear what the asshole has to say as I attempt to kick him again. I get him in the knee. The satisfaction isn't even close to enough, and it certainly doesn't stop him from the next round of torture.

"I'm keeping count. That's number eight since I walked in. I'll assume you had more exchanges with Autumn before I came in so I'm going to say an even dozen. Let's begin, shall we?"

And with that, I receive my punishment in the form of a whipping.

I vacate my body for an indeterminable length of time. Where does one go when being violated beyond comprehension? My space is blank—I wish it were full of stars, smelled of grape and cherry, and had endless fields of wildflowers—but the void I transport myself to is empty. There's only blind blissful silence. At some point, I return to reality, but reality shifts in moments like these, and uncertainty battles with certainty in the most perplexing ways. The light is different, foggy, yet clear. I don't know if I should wither and die or fight for my next breath of air.

The tool he uses isn't known until he unties me and I look over at the counter. I kind of thought it was the wood spoon, something used on me before, but part of me knew it didn't feel quite the same. Geoff likes bare skin. He also picks the part of the body so the bruises won't show in any of my costumes. In other words, I yank my shorts and underwear back up when he's done beating my ass. That's when I spot the frying spatula lying on the counter as if innocently waiting to flip pancakes.

And you know what? Geoff is right. My knee doesn't hurt anymore because my butt is screaming in agony...and I will go on tonight.

Smile.

Pretend.

All is frightfully wrong with the world, and yet nothing is the matter.

***

Thankful I saw the set list tonight, I know I don't need to be on stage until the third song. The stage lighting is adjusted, and Paradox 21 plays the first notes of the night. Keel hits it—he's as tight as ever. As I watch the band, I continue warming up.

Before the third song, *Overly Anxious*, Saul thanks the crowd for showing up and says, "We're Paradox 21. Who likes to dance, eh?" He takes a drink of water from his bottle, sets it down, and they start. After two bars of music, I step into the space reserved for me on the corner of the stage and begin to move. It's practiced and well-rehearsed, and I let go of the fact that my boyfriend is a jerk. I move to the music and try to stay focused on doing my best.

Paradox 21's music is full of luscious vibes and groovy nuances. I loved every note from this band since I first heard them. It isn't hard to enjoy what I do even if I'm butthurt, and life sucks. During a jam session in this song, I can add some of my contortion skills or whatever else I want. Tonight, I decide to dance, twist, and add a back-bending flip. I land perfectly to Demian's bass beats. The crowd gives Demian and I an appreciative whoop. The song closes and I slink back into the shadows to wait for Caspar to eat fire and have a bit of the spotlight during the next song. We'll both be on stage for the last portion of the set.

I bring my scarves out for *Meander* and return to dancing during *Waves of Atlantis*. The crowd is large, and I think we all soar on the loftiness of their combined energy. Saul is especially in top form and I smile as he tells a joke about living on the road with a bunch of punks and two beautiful women.

One song left, I tell myself, and I'll be free for the rest of the night. With the extra pep in the air, I let go of the stress from the last couple of days, and the music moves through me. Midway through the song my foot slips on the stage and shoots out from under me, twisting at an unnatural angle. I right myself with surprising ninja-esque reflexes. Adrenaline rips through my bloodstream, and I'm unsure of how bad my ankle is. I back up, leaving the stage as unobtrusively as possible, and trip over backward, landing hard on my right wrist.

Keel's eyes meet mine, but he turns away, not missing a note on his guitar.

Accidents happen all the time, but not to me. Humiliated and hurt, I roll over to pick myself up.

A stagehand helps—or tries to. "Hey. You all right?" he yells near my ear.

I nod, trying to appear confident and test my weight on the ankle. It's surprisingly strong, and only a slight burning sensation radiates through my muscles and tendons. The guy supports me by my arm and gives me something steady to hold.

I smile at him and yell, "Thanks! I'm good." Stepping away, a couple of people stare, and I keep my head low. Making sure I'm not favoring the ankle, I return to the backstage lounge and duck into the bathroom.

The door closes behind me, and I turn the lock. I slide down to the floor, and the tears collect and spill down my cheeks. My wrist is screaming in pain. I cradle it gently against my stomach and try to breathe through the stabbing agony. I landed just right to set fire to every nerve. Unable to accept what's happening, I test my wrist by carefully bending it forward and back. It's moving, and there doesn't appear to be anything catastrophically wrong. I take it as a good sign and get up from the unwelcoming tile floor.

Only three tears escaped, I tell myself. Three, I can handle. I brush them away like intruders and look into the bathroom mirror. My makeup is holding its place rather well, and I wipe a tiny smudge from under one eye.

The crowd cheers and Paradox adds an encore song, a short rendition of *All About You*. It'll be short because the opening act has to be off the stage by a certain time so they can break down and set up again for the next band. Not wanting to attract more attention to myself, I slip out of the bathroom, grab my stashed bag and a bottle of water from the buffet table and leave. The back door of the theater slams closed behind me and rattles my jangling nerves.

The night air hits me with the cool, saturated scent of the recent rain. I stare up at the cloud-heavy sky and thank the universe for stopping the raindrops. Even if for just a minute.

I park myself on a somewhat dry spot near the backstage doors and take a breath—and ten more. My mind replays the disaster over and over again. What did I slip on? A spilled drink is my best guess, but there's no telling. I should have seen it. I should have paid better attention. I would like to die from embarrassment.

Opening the bottle of water hurts my sore wrist, but I do it. I can't let a minor injury hold me down. The wrist has to get better. And thankfully, my ankle isn't too bad. The joint rolled over, but I'm walking. I can work with a sore wrist, but being off my feet would end my summer performances.

The stage door opens, and indoor light sweeps the sidewalk and then retreats. Someone's standing by the door. The stage crew and band members are often in and out during a typical night. Not wanting to make eye contact or inadvertently open myself to unwanted interruption of my sulking time I stare in the opposite direction. His boots approach my corner of the loading zone. I huddle deeper into my hoodie and will him to go away.

"Hey," he says.

Looking up I find a white package being held out to me.

"Here's an ice pack."

"Thanks," I say and take it. "My, umm, accident was that obvious?"

"Not at all."

I glance up at Corban's face after he says this. He squats down a couple feet away. He's watching me with cool assessing eyes and no other expression.

"How did you know I needed an ice pack, then?"

"I didn't. I guessed. You took it. We're all good. Unless you need an EMT. If so, I'll call one." He reaches into his pocket as if he's ready to pull out a phone.

"No. It doesn't hurt that bad. Please don't call the paramedics."

"All right," he says nonchalantly.

I wrap the cold pack around my aching wrist and realize this is just what I need. I'm mostly certain nothing is broken, but the ice will do wonders for how it feels later.

"I thought you hurt your ankle. Are you holding it to your wrist?"

I nod.

"Need a second one?"

"I don't think so. Are you like the ice pack hander-outer?"

"Yeah. Among other things."

He's holding a small paper plate with something on it. With his last words, he sets the plate down next to me.

"I bring Death Wish cupcakes too. This one's for you. Since you're injured and there were only a few left, I thought you might want it. And believe me, when I tell you that you want one of these cupcakes. They'll change your perspective on the night."

I glance down at the offered cake and the candy button sporting a skull and crossbones on top of the three-inch pile of frosting. Except the crossbones are guitars.

"Your look of skepticism is making me want to take it back."

"Oh no. I'm not skeptical at all." My doubtful expression deepens. "No take-backs. Once you offer a cupcake, you can't take it back. That's like a baked goods felony or something. I'm pretty sure it's punishable by law."

"Okay then." A hint of a smile cracks through his serious demeanor. "What's the punishment?"

His black clothes and boots match his punk attitude. The wallet chain hanging from his belt glints in the amber light behind the venue and a tattoo peeks out from under the sleeve of his T-shirt.

"Are you saying that depending on the severity of the punishment you're still considering taking back my cupcake?"

"I am. It shouldn't be wasted on someone who doesn't appreciate it. I'll take the firing squad if I can save the world from chocolate injustice."

I set the ice pack on my lap and snatch up the cupcake before he can. After peeling the paper, I take a bite, and it melts in my mouth like nothing I've ever tasted before. An ultra-rich satin-smooth filling tantalizes my tongue, and the frosting is equivalent to fluffy decadent chocolate heaven.

I may have moaned in ecstasy as I experienced the first bite. Corban's raised eyebrow would suggest I did something embarrassing. It doesn't matter. The chocolate orgasm is worth any strange looks.

"I guess my work here is done," he says as I savor another bite.

I swallow and ask, "Are you the runner tonight?"

"Yeah. You need anything else?"

"Do you have another dozen cupcakes in your pocket?"

He shakes his head and stands. "You might be able to grab another one before they're gone if you go now. My guess is you'll be too late. You're holding the last miracle in your hand."

"I thought you said it was a death wish?"

"The bakery is called Death Wish because it's what you'll wish for on your death bed."

"One last taste of perfection before you die." I nibble the edge of the whipped frosting. Corban's absolutely right. This cupcake will be my last wish before I go. I lick a tiny spot of frosting off my lip and let the dark chocolate melt on my tongue. "Maybe I'll choke and die, then I won't be able to make my wish." It's out of my mouth before I realize what I'm saying. *Suicidal thoughts happen, don't they? I can't be the only one.* Since I'm humiliated enough for a lifetime, I may as well make it worse. I don't take it back.

The side of Corban's mouth lifts. He glances down at the concrete loading dock and back up to my face. "I could think of a lot worse ways to go."

"Yeah," I murmur and take another small bite wondering if this will be my last. The image of myself falling off the stage and breaking my neck comes to mind. The crowd aghast as they circle around my broken body and wonder about their ticket refund. I picture myself strangled by my own aerial fabric. That would take real talent. The fabric is thick. The morbid thoughts are loose, and they're prolific, multiplying, and spreading like a disease. Luckily Corban distracts me.

"If you want to come inside, I'll set you up on the couch, and you can put your foot up. The caterers are good. You can eat something and chill out."

"I don't want to go in. I'm sort of ready to get out of here."

"Don't worry about tripping. Much worse things happen all the time. It's one of the reasons we keep a dozen ice packs in the freezer."

I bite down on my lip. I don't want to admit I never stumble. It's a total career fail for me. If I'm practicing something new in the gym, sure, but never during a performance. "I'll be fine out here."

He backs up and stares out across the small parking lot behind the theater. The crowd finally stops whistling and cheering for Paradox. With such a receptive audience, Keel and the others will be in a great mood tonight.

Corban says, "You're traveling with Paradox, aren't you?"

"Mhhh-hmmm." I tuck a stray hair behind my ear as the heavy feeling in my chest returns.

"They're planning an after-party at Tully's house."

"Tully is a friend of Saul and Zeb's, right?"

"Yeah. A friend of mine too. No one will get out of here until after Gnarled's set is over."

I sigh. "Sure," I say with no enthusiasm.

"I'll see you there. Until then, holler if you or the band needs anything."

"Okay. Thanks for the ice, and the chocolate."

"No problem," he says and heads back into the theater.

***

The door opens again a few minutes later. I recognize Keel's voice immediately. He's with Demian and someone I don't know. They're talking shop. I've heard it dozens of times. Things that could have gone better. Things that could have gone worse. Sound quality. The crowd. What's for dinner after the show, or will alcohol suffice?

"There you are," Keel says.

I keep my face neutral.

"Have you seen my sweatshirt?"

Is he seriously asking me for the same sweatshirt I offered him multiple times before and after he changed the truck tire? "It's still inside the truck."

"Oh right." He ventures closer to where I'm sitting with my ice pack and an empty plate. "Hey, what happened tonight?"

Tears threaten to make a reappearance. I'm not sure what part of tonight he's asking about. Our fight? His ignoring me? His shitty attitude? Me twisting my ankle? Or falling over and cracking my wrist?

He doesn't sit next to me. I stare at his shins and past him into the night behind the theater. Tires against the rain-soaked asphalt create a blur of sound. I'm focusing on any distraction rather than my personal problems with Keel.

He continues before I can answer. "We've been invited to stay the night at Tully's house. They're throwing the after-party. Everyone's planning on heading there after the show—cool, right? A house and a real shower. He says we can use the guest bedroom."

I don't say anything. Keel bends down and actually looks at me.

"We don't need to stay there if you don't want to." He seems confused by my silence.

"Sounds fine. I'm glad we have somewhere to go."

"Zeb says the house is big. There's room for all of us."

"Great." I look the other way.

"What's up, Tara?" He acts as if he has no idea what my problem could possibly be.

"Nothing." The need to roll my eyes is so strong they ache in their sockets.

"Do you want to come in? Gnarled Roots are supposed to be kick-ass."

"Go ahead. I need a few more minutes out here. You know how hot it gets on stage. I'll meet you inside."

Keel says something to Demian, and they go in without me. I'm not sure if I want to watch the show or go to sleep in the truck. The suckiness of this day needs to end, but it's not over yet. Not even close. After-parties generally go on until the sun rises. Oh, joy of joy. I can't freaking wait.

Chapter Nine

"The road to hell is paved with good intentions." — Proverb

Keel continues to act as if nothing is wrong during and after the rest of the show. I have to drive us to Tully's house because he's already started drinking. When we arrive, I track down Zeb to help me find our room. Keel's drunkenness is a good excuse to ignore him without him realizing what I'm doing.

The futon in the guest room is hard and lumpy. For bonus points, they have no blankets or pillows. I look in the closet and find it packed with miscellaneous boxes and some clothes on hangers. I don't want to interrupt anyone while they party downstairs, so I retrieve our bedding from the truck and attempt to make myself at home remaining as invisible as possible.

Everyone seems laid back and uncaring about how I use the house. It helps. Pot smoke is thick in the air as I slip into the kitchen for water before going up to sleep. I run into Keel on my way back upstairs. He blocks my path and stares into my tired eyes. He's drunk and stoned, and his pupils look out of focus.

"Tara, the hot girl, where have you been all night?"

"Avoiding you," I say honestly.

"I love you," he says.

I place my hand on his chest with the hope of pushing him out of my way. I only want sleep, not participate in a crazy mixed up conversation that smells of craft beer and burnt weed.

"You're drunk," I point out.

"You got hurt earlier, didn't you?"

"A little."

"Where?"

"Where on my body, or where did it happen?"

"D. All of the above." His words are slurred and run together.

I lick my lips and sigh. I wanted him to care earlier when my ego was still black and blue with fresh bruises. Now, hours later, I want him to know how angry I am. As usual, his timing sucks.

"It's nothing, less than a minor injury." I move to go around him and retreat upstairs. Someone turns the stereo up, and a new song starts. It's one of Paradox's songs. The voices of the people inside the house go up with the music. "I'm going to sleep." I inch farther away from him.

Keel reaches out and grabs my hand, stopping me from making my getaway.

"Ow," I say and flinch.

He drops my hand instantly. As bad luck seems to be the theme of the day, Keel grabbed my sore side. I cradle the aching wrist and force my face to not show the pain. I'm pretty sure I need a wrap or a brace, but it'll have to wait until I can go to a store.

His brows gather with actual concern. "I'm sorry, babe. Right there? Is that where it hurts?"

He takes my arm from me and lifts it gently into the air between us. Then he's crushing me against him in an awkward hug, with my sore wrist sandwiched between us.

"Jesus, Tara. You're not allowed to get hurt." He runs his strong hand down my back and sounds genuinely worried.

He makes a sound in his chest like a low groan, masculine, and protective. Some of the strain between us lifts as he holds me. Then he says so only I can hear him, "I love your boobs. I'm so glad you didn't hurt them."

"Super. That's so special." Disgusted, I push myself away from him, sore wrist forgotten.

He's laughing at his joke. "Don't be like that," he pleads. "I was kidding. No, I wasn't," he amends, being a total drunken ass and looking pleased with his stupid joke. "I'm coming upstairs soon. Wait up for me and I'll make it up to you."

I shake my head in disbelief and scurry away from him.

I'm asleep by the time he comes in. His weight shifts the futon, and it must wake me up. He wraps himself around me, and his hand moves straight to my chest.

"I'm too tired," I whisper.

"That's okay," he says. "I'm not."

He's unmistakably not too tired to fool around. His erection is hard against my side.

"I mean it," I say.

"Whatever." He rolls away from me.

His drunken snores reverberate through the room as I lie there guilty for denying him and wondering if this means we'll be fighting again tomorrow.

***

Dear Evie,

In my high school literature class my teacher, Mr. Elliot, made us memorize a poem and then stand in front of everyone and recite it. The kids got to choose which poem they would like to memorize, but it had to be from one of Mr. Elliot's books. I'm not sure why I chose the one I did. I kind of liked it, and it was short compared to a lot of the others. The words conjured images inside my mind. We had just moved into Geoff's house, and I knew our days of traveling with The Show had come to a stop. Our life had stopped. That's how it felt to me, and this poem talked about taking different paths when I desperately missed our friends and our lifestyle.

Last night I lay awake, and the words to Mr. Frost's poem spoke to me in a whisper and then louder in repetition. Here's what I told myself for hours last night when I should have been sleeping. (And of course the words are incomplete and chopped up, because it was four in the morning and I didn't excel in English Lit. Forgive me. If you get a chance, read the whole poem. It's worth it.)

The Road Not Taken

Two roads diverged in a yellow wood,
And sorry I could not travel both
And be one traveler, long I stood
And looked down one as far as I could
Yet knowing how way leads on to way,
I doubted if I should ever come back.
I shall be telling this with a sigh
Somewhere ages and ages hence:
Two roads diverged in a wood, and I—
I took the one less traveled by,
And that has made all the difference.
— Robert Frost

Choices and regrets, Evie.

I hope your choices never lead down the harried road to regret. I did something yesterday. I might be beating myself up for it later, but, for me, it was the road less traveled. Right now, I don't regret a thing. I need to keep taking the path of the unknown—it will lead me away from the familiar. My familiar causes pain, longing, desperation, and hurt. I'm done hurting. I'm done trying to make him happy. He either loves me for who I am, or he doesn't. How can either of us know who I am if I don't stand up for myself—speak up when I have something to say? I can't be a doormat forever. I can't shut down and push my feelings aside when I become uncomfortable. It's so hard, Evie. I'm struggling within every cell of my body, but for once I held my ground and didn't cave in. You don't need the details because I'm not ready to share that with you. By the time you reach fourteen, maybe fifteen, I'll give you the rest of the story. Can you tell how confused I am changing this one thing about my behavior? What if I change something even bigger? Will I lose myself completely? Would it be the worst thing that ever happened to me or the best?

This new me—the girl who speaks up for herself and quits trying to make everyone happy—is having a hard time adjusting.

I'm rambling, sweet sister, but I hope you can see I'm trying. I'm besieged by my own insecurities. However, I'm attempting to find myself and be a stronger person. I'm gathering my courage and repeating The Road Not Taken like a mantra.

I love you, Evie.

I love you wider than the whole sky and deeper than my most secret emotion.

I hope you're safe and having the summer of a lifetime.

Talk soon.

After getting virtually no sleep—again—I still wake up before Keel. It allows me private time to write to Evie, so I don't mind. I tuck the journal away. Evie will probably never read anything I write this summer. *Does it matter?* Should I rip out all the letters and mail them to her in one big package? Would Geoff steal her mail and read it before giving it to her? That sounds like something he would do. I push aside my thoughts and focus on getting ready for the day.

The slim pickings of clean clothes leave me with a pair of jean shorts and a tank top. I put on my last clean bra and wonder if they have a washing machine in the house. After dressing and brushing my teeth and hair, I follow the buzz of commotion drifting through the house and go downstairs to find out what's going on. We have a lull in our schedule for two nights, then we're supposed to be in Cedar City for another show Sunday. Off days often include a laundromat, grocery store, and some randomness to pass the time. I'm hopeful the laundry gets priority over the randomness, but it's a group decision.

When I pass through the living room, I notice a nameless body on the couch, and the runner from the club, Corban, burrowed into the loveseat. He's incredibly huge on the small sofa, but it doesn't appear to affect his ability to sleep. Following the sounds of clanking pots and rattling dishes, I enter the kitchen and find Saul, Tully, and another guy I don't know.

"Hey, Tara. Did you meet Tully and Seamus yet?"

"Yeah, I met Tully yesterday. Good morning," I say.

Seamus looks over at me from his pan of scrambled eggs. "What's up?" he says with an acknowledging lift of the chin. "Eggs will be ready in a minute. Saul, give her a muffin."

"Seamus is Tully's brother. They own the house together. Seamus and his girlfriend make baked goods infused with THC oil for the local marijuana dispensaries."

Saul pops open a container full of muffins and picks one. "He's testing a new flavor on us, Blackberry Hemp Haze."

Seamus flips the eggs. "Besides the THC, they're made with blackberries, hemp oil, white whole wheat, and have a hemp seed crumble top," he says.

"I ate one, and this is the perfect cure for any hangover. The marijuana settles the queasiness from last night's drinking." Saul hands it to me.

I smile dubiously at the muffin. "Thanks, but no thanks. I'm not hung-over."

"Really? The selection of craft brew was the holy grail of beers last night. You'll never find this much brewed excellence in one place again."

"Colorado is the Napa Valley of microbreweries," Tully says.

I shrug and take a step back from the offered muffin. "Sorry I missed out."

"We can try again tonight." Saul places the muffin back in the box. "If you need a sweet mellow high, eat a muffin, Tara. I swear it's the cure."

"Seamus will hook you up with whatever you like," Tully says as he opens the refrigerator door and pulls out a container of juice. "He needs as many test subjects as he can find. And we like to offer the products to our friends first."

"Thanks. I just don't think I can get high this early in the day. It sort of reduces my motivation to that of a slug."

"I gotcha. Well, later then. Whenever you're ready, there's a couple dozen muffins and some cookies too."

"Help yourself to the eggs." Seamus flips off the heat and moves the pan to the backburner, next to another frying pan full of sausages.

"Juice too. Glasses are in the cabinet, or in the dishwasher."

The two brothers make plates of food and take them to the table.

Saul grabs a plate from the dishwasher and moves to the eggs. He's always up as early as I am. We're kind of similar that way. I think he often has a lot on his mind and needs the quiet of early morning to think. He's wearing his glasses today, which isn't unusual. He saves his contacts lenses for when he's on stage. Saul is a walking contradiction in many ways. His skin is a deep olive tone, but his hair and eyes are light. He's mostly quiet and reserved until he starts singing. Then everyone is like, how is that sound coming out of him? His vocal range is ace. He's lanky and tall, but strong as a horse. When he's not on stage, he looks like a guy you'd meet at the library, not at a rock concert.

"We're invited to squeeze in another set tonight at The Gothic," he says.

"That's awesome." I consider eating a little with the guys.

"It is. They obviously liked us last night. So, are you doing okay this morning?" he asks, taking a forkful of food.

"I'm fine," I say.

"What happened? I didn't get a good look."

"She tripped," someone says as he enters the kitchen. "It was no big deal."

Corban walks into the kitchen and heads straight to the food.

"I, umm, twisted my ankle. There was something slippery on the stage. It's better now." I purposely don't mention my wrist. It aches when I bend it backward, but way better than last night.

Corban's head reappears from behind the cabinet door. "You need a plate?"

"Sure." I almost begin to think this guy is my secret unpaid personal assistant.

He passes it to me and turns to the eggs and sausage.

"You think you'll be able to perform tonight?" Saul asks. "People were stoked about you and Caspar after the show. It'd be good if you were with us, but not if you're injured or anything."

"I'll be good by tonight. I should stay off the silks, though." I switch places with Corban to serve myself before the food is gone. "We were so late yesterday, I didn't have a chance to check if there was a place to hang them up."

"Cool," Saul says, moving to the kitchen table. "We'll skip your aerial act. You and Caspar nailed it last night—without flying in the air. And, I'll double check the stage for spills before we play tonight." He grins and tosses a wink at me, then focuses on his breakfast.

"We should have another party here after tonight's gig." Tully leans back in his chair and pats his stomach. His plate is clean, and his brother is nearly finished as well.

"Does that mean we'll be here all day and another night?" I ask.

"Yep," Saul says. "Laundry day, right?" he asks as if he knows what I'm about to ask.

"Yeah," I say and take my first bite.

"I may not make it to the laundromat. It's the muffins. They need me to stay here and guard them," Saul says.

Seamus grins. "The new recipe needs a disclaimer."

"Hell yeah, it does." Saul strikes a pose, angling toward the muffins. "Warning: Blackberry Hemp Haze is an amazing motivation blocker. Eat one and be doomed to lethargy and gluttony."

"Hey, that's not going to sell my muffins."

"Sure it will," Corban says.

"What about truth in advertising?" Saul asks.

"Doesn't exist," Tully says.

Corban and I eat our eggs in the kitchen and listen to the debate on what the package should say for the new muffin recipe. I drink a glass of water, wash my dishes, and exit the kitchen without interrupting the discussion on capitalism and marketing from a stoner and musician's point of view.

As I pass through the living room, Caspar perches on the arm of a chair by the fireplace. She's talking on the phone, and I overhear her. "I'm headed back to—" She cuts herself off when she sees me.

"I'll talk to you later," she says into her phone and ends the call.

The stairs are in her direction. I lower my gaze and pretend she's not there as I make my way closer. A guy is still asleep on the couch and out of courtesy I don't want to wake him.

"Good morning, Tara," she says.

"Find someplace to crash last night?" I ask even though I'd much rather go back to ignoring each other.

Caspar doesn't want to continue the silent treatment. "I was wondering if you got hurt last night, but you look as beautiful as ever."

I give her a blank stare and bite the inside of my lip. Her compliments hold a whole new meaning for me now. She slides off the arm of the chair and glides over to me. I'm about to tell her I need to get upstairs, but she speaks first.

She tilts her head as if inspecting me on an angle. "Are you still upset with me?"

"No," I lie.

One eye narrows. She knows I'm not being truthful. The barest hint of humor plays with the corner of her mouth.

"I'd kiss you again when we're both sober. Would that make it better?"

She leans in close as if inviting me to take her up on her offer.

I move back and sidestep closer to the stairs.

She laughs. "I'm totally messing with you. You make it so easy." She rolls her eyes and smirks. Her gaze slides over to the couch at my back, and I turn toward what she's looking at. Sleepy Guy is sitting up and looking at us.

Caspar glances back at me and her eyes travel down my body and back up again. "Play along," she taunts. "He'll appreciate the show," she says with a quick glance at the dude.

I don't know how to take her this morning. Is she joking or is she screwing with me?

She takes another step forward, and I back into the wall—cornered. Her hand lands on my hip, and she whispers, "I'm sorry." She tries to kiss my cheek, but I duck out of the way.

"You're acting strange, Tara," she calls after me.

Me? I'm the strange one? She's making things exponentially worse, and she calls *me* out. *What the actual fuck?* When I open the bedroom door, Keel is tying his shoes. He looks up at me, then back at his laces. The tension between us is thick enough to cut with a chainsaw. I want to tell him about the weird exchange with Caspar, but I hold my tongue and wait for him to say something. When he doesn't speak, I fill the space with meaninglessness.

"I'm going to go find a laundromat. Do you want to go?"

"Not now. I have a raging headache." He sits back and glowers at me with dull eyes and a hardened set to his jaw.

"Seamus made pot muffins. Saul thinks they're a miracle cure."

"Perfect." Keel rises from the side of the futon and drags himself to the door.

"Water might help. I have some ibuprofen if you need it, too."

He says nothing and I'm not sure he even heard me.

And so goes the entire day between Keel and I. Awkward small talk. Disconnection. My hurt feelings. My self-esteem plummeting, and my inadequacies soaring with every passing hour. Caspar steals glances at me and pretends not to. The Road Not Taken gets replaced by ear buds and my playlists. Keel takes the truck to find a tire store and doesn't invite me to go along. Laundry is put on hold.

I call home.

"Hey," I say.

Mom says, "You mean you remember us?"

"Is Evie there?"

"Can't you spare a minute to talk to your mother?"

"How's everything?" I ask. Her tone is dull and yet accusing. To be honest, when she sounds like this, I don't want to talk to her at all, but I make an attempt to keep things peaceful. My good intentions promptly blow up in my face.

"Geoff is on the rampage because he says I forgot to put in the order at the store, and now we're short on about half of our best-selling items. It's his damn fault. He told me he was going to do the order this week, but he doesn't remember telling me. Now I have to listen to him bitch and complain about pissed off customers and he thinks I'm to blame."

She's ranting, and I couldn't care less what's happening at their liquor store. I stay silent, and she continues.

"Your brother and sister are driving me crazy. All they want to do is go to the pool and the mall and the skate park. I'm done with those two. They won't give me even a second to myself. You wouldn't believe how horrible they've been since you left."

My jaw stiffens, and my spine goes rigid. I was the one in charge of keeping Evie and Jonah busy with things to do. They were my responsibility more than hers and now that I'm not around my mom has to be the mom and participate for a change. I knew she'd fail in this department, and it's part of the reason I feel so guilty. Evie and Jonah are on their own more often than not. During summer vacation, they don't even have school to keep them busy.

"Is Evie home or not?" I ask, interrupting her complaining.

My mother huffs into the phone. "What's that tone of voice for? You're the one who asked how I was."

"Mhh-hmm," I make an agreeable sound because I don't want to fight. "So, is she home?" I try again.

I'm awarded silence, and I think I've been hung up on. Just in case, I hold the line. My sister answers a minute later.

"Hi!"

"Hey there!" A smile brightens my life when I hear her alive on the other end of the line.

"Where are you?"

"Colorado."

"Wow. Really? How cool. Do you like it?"

"It's going okay." I don't want to involve Evie in my latest mini-crisis. "Have you seen Ollie?"

"Umm, sort of. I think she was howling the other day when some sirens went by."

"Yeah, she likes to howl along with them." My joyful smile is replaced with a sad one as memories make me melancholy. "What are you doing?"

"Actually, I can't talk. Geoff is out back waiting for me. We're working on the trampoline a lot now. He thinks I need to practice my flips. He's teaching me some new stuff."

"Like what?" I ask. Evie's skills are superb. Geoff likes to push her, and it makes me anxious. She's always been a quick learner, but she's still a kid.

"Forward triples with a half twist and a new backflip. I think you've seen him do it before. You know the one where you arch and then tuck right before you land?"

I did know—I also know how difficult it is. "How's it going? Can you do it?"

"Not quite yet. I'm a little sore, but he wants me to keep trying until I can do it perfectly."

"Do you need a break? Just refuse to do anymore if you're getting tired. He can't make you jump."

"I know. I'm okay. I gotta go. I just heard the back door slam."

I know what's going on, and it makes my skin itch with invisible mites. And coupled with what Mom said about Geoff's bad mood, her training session is going to be brutal.

"I love you. Don't forget to take plenty of breaks and drink a ton."

"I know," she says. "I wish you were here to spot me. I miss you."

"Miss you too," I say.

"He's calling for me."

"Okay." I'm reluctant to release her back to the wolves. Wolf, I correct. *Damn it.* "I'll call again soon."

"You better," she teases and hangs up.

Even though she's going to face our stepdad alone, she still manages to keep her sunny and warm personality. I can't even think or talk about him without the clouds of depression moving in. *God, I love that girl. Why can't I be more like Evie?*

Later that night, our performance goes better than expected. My wrist is healing fast and causes me little discomfort. I don't slip, trip, or fall, except for a million times inside my mind. Slipping backward to question everything I said or did with Keel over the last forty-eight hours. Tripping over my emotional baggage, and falling into a battle with myself over nothing and everything.

Hell.

Life is hell even when it's not.

***

More partying. Drinking, smoking, loud music, and fangirls—and fanboys.

This scene is starting to become a cliché in my life. Nevertheless, I'm grateful I'm not working some other mindless low paying job. I stick my party face on like a mask and try to have a good time. It could be worse, right? I could be on the side of the interstate during a hailing thunderstorm changing a flat tire.

Chapter Ten

"Don't assume it can't get worse." — J. Pyrah

We have another day to kill and a whole night off. We're supposed to be in Cedar City, Utah tomorrow. It's an eight and a half hour drive, and since we have a free house to sleep in and friends to hang out with, everyone agrees to stay at Tully's for the third night.

Sleep and I become reacquainted. I would even venture to say he's returned to my life like the best friend I've never had. Waking up alive and restored sets my attitude in a much better place and I begin to think about doing something fun on my day off that doesn't include beer or pot.

Keel isn't as motivated as I am, but with a good night's sleep fueling me, I make my best attempt at bridging the broken space between us. By midday, I realize everyone is hung over, and no one wants to go out and do anything. I offer to do laundry and shopping for the entire band just to be out of the house and see a little of the city before we need to leave. The guys never ask me to be their personal runner, and they're grateful as they hand me some cash. I take off for the afternoon in Keel's truck and breathe in the rare alone time.

With fresh air in my lungs, clean clothes, and bags full of groceries, I return to the house almost like life isn't trying to shove me under the bus today. A change in perspective can change everything, I realize.

Demian and Saul help me unload the laundry and sort the groceries. Some of the supplies will go into the van, and mine and Keel's food will stay in our truck. Leaning against the counter, my wrist barely twinges when I twist open the cap of a super berry smoothie. I drink half of it and wonder where Keel is. I set my bottle down on the kitchen counter and head upstairs with thoughts about organizing laundry and packing, so we'll be ready to go first thing in the morning.

When I open the bedroom door, Caspar is riding my boyfriend like the fair queen of Whore County. By all the whooping and screeching going on, I guess she thinks she's a champion bareback rider on top of her prize-winning stud. In my opinion, she looks like an amateur.

Too shocked to claw her eyes out, or my own—some things can never be unseen—I turn and run from the room and keep running until I'm breathless and hollow inside. I collapse against an unfamiliar wall of some dingy building on an unknown street.

"Tara!"

I don't want to talk to anyone. I can't. I'm incapable. I bury my face into the crook of my arm and wonder if I can suffocate and die before having to 'talk about it'. The thumping of his boots comes to a stop somewhere to my left. I keep my face hidden, but I can hear his labored breath.

"You run cross country or something? Shit. I knew you could dance but...shit," he says again between panting breaths.

My chest aches and I'm still trying to catch my own breath. Apparently the Mile High city is lacking the typical oxygen supply found at lower elevations.

"Listen, Tara—"

I cut him off. "My name is not fucking Tara!" I've had enough of being called Tara. Keel and Caspar have been using my road name, and I never want to hear it again. I am so done.

"I know it's not Fucking Tara. You're way too fucking sublime to be called anything with the word fucking in it."

I peer over my arm at him and narrow my eyes. *Why did he follow me?* I turn back to the dirty wall and rest my incredibly heavy head against it. I close my eyes. When did my skull become a two-ton block of stone? The weight of it is like an elephant sitting on my shoulders. Somewhere nearby there's a loud bang like a door slamming closed. Traffic drones on in the background like an incessant intruder.

The longer I stand there, the more I see my life falling apart. I can't go back. Keel was screwing that bitch! I don't want to see him. The tour is over. Traveling with Keel and Paradox 21 would be a bizarre atrocity overflowing with pain and awkwardness. Does everyone in the band know? Has this affair been going on for a while? *Why would Keel do this to us? I'm such an idiot! Where am I going to go?* I kick the wall in front of me and my foot screams in pain. I don't care. I kick the wall again. *He doesn't love me. She was right.*

"Come on," he says.

Corban takes my elbow and begins to pull me away from my wall of solitude.

I yank my arm away from him.

"We should get out of here," he says.

"I'm fine." I plant my heels in the asphalt.

"You're not, and you shouldn't hang out behind here by yourself."

"I don't care." I compose my face and wipe away the stupid tears trying to stain my cheeks.

"This place is a strip club." He tips his head toward the building. "And not a classy one."

I glance around, taking in my surroundings for the first time. The filth in the cracks and crevices of the alley become more apparent the more I look. Not wanting to appear as even a bigger fuckwit than I already am, I set my shoulders back and walk out of the dirty alley and back toward the street. I turn in the opposite direction from Tully's house.

"Mind if I walk with you for a minute?" he asks.

"You don't have to." I don't want his sympathetic kindness.

"You don't know this side of town very well, do you?"

"Does it matter?"

"It could," he says.

My feet tramp down the sidewalk, and I try to ignore the poverty-driven, high crime, bars-on-windows, type of neighborhood around us. I stop at the corner and look up at the street signs. Left on Syzygy Street, or right on Crooked Lane? I'm on Astronomy Parkway, looking at Crooked Lane's dead end sign. Dead end sounds like where I'm headed anyway, so I turn that direction and Corban steps in front of me.

"I can give you a ride somewhere if you need one, but I'm due to work in about an hour. Would you like to come to the theater with me? I'll take you wherever you want after my shift is over."

"Don't you work until three in the morning?"

"Yeah, but I may be able to take off around one."

"You don't need to give me a ride. I'll figure something out."

He stares at me—I look away. Traffic whizzes by, innocuous and impersonal. Who are these people? Millions of anonymous people in a city I don't know. *Where am I going to go? Can I find a hotel room? And then what?* Keel and I are done. The tears threaten to fall again. I keep moving.

"I don't know you very well, but I know what it's like to be cheated on. My offer is open. No one will care if you want to hang out at the theater until you decide what you're going to do. My parents own the place so it's cool if I invite someone in."

"That's nice. I... I just," I stumble inside my mouth. "I can't think. All I know is, I need to go back and get my bags. I don't want to, but I can't get a room until I get my wallet."

"Let's start walking that way," he suggests.

I stare down at my shoes and press my fingers to my temples for a second. No matter how much I want to get my stuff out of Keel's truck, I can't make myself face him.

As if reading my thoughts, Corban says, "Maybe they won't be around."

They being Keel and Caspar. That thread of hope is so flimsy it may as well be made of cobwebs. I grab a hold of it anyway and drag myself around. One step back toward the house where my cheating boyfriend failed us, and I'm propelled into the street. There must be some awareness of traffic and my life coming to an abrupt end, but I'm not conscious of it. I just run. The screeching brakes, the yelling, the blaring car horns don't deter me. Let fate decide what happens next.

After dashing across four lanes of traffic, I take the next side street and don't stop until the din of chaos is drowned by silence.

"Are you done running? Because let me tell you, that was messed up back there."

I blink at Corban. I hadn't realized he followed me. Part of my brain wants to yell at him. *He could have been killed!* But if I say it out loud, I would be yelling at myself, too.

He watches me with little to no expression on his face. My chest heaves and begs for air, but otherwise, I'm numb. I'm so dazed I'm not even sure I can tell what numb is anymore.

What did he say? Am I done running? Another question with no answer. Admitting the truth means looking deeper into my life. I stare at nothing and find only nonsense. Life is suddenly blurry and unfocused. Nothing makes sense. Even the street signs are confusing.

Aphelion Drive and Syzygy Street.

"Are you in there?" he asks.

I shake my head and keep reading the signs like the words will magically translate into something I comprehend.

"They're astronomy related," he explains. "There's an old observatory and planetarium up the road from here, over there at the top of the hill." He points down the street.

All I see is a bunch of trees. I glance at his face. When I finally make eye contact with him, his silvery-green eyes are searching mine. Pale eyes with hair as black as Caspar's soul. I shudder.

"Did you just make that up?"

"Yeah. I mean, why wouldn't I want to mess with you when you're already screwed up in the head?"

"Right." I start walking again, away from Corban.

"Jesus, I'm kidding. Yes. All the road names in this neighborhood have to do with astronomy."

"And you know because you're an astronomy major." I roll my eyes.

"Nah. Just a minor. Physics comes first."

"Of course, it does."

"Don't hate me because I'm smart, and I won't hate you because you're beautiful."

"Seriously?" I ask, thinking, is this guy for real?

"For Christ's sake, don't jump off the deep end here and think I'm hitting on you. It was just a way to say, hey, I'm using my brains to better myself, and don't judge me for it. And I won't judge you either."

"You can study the mechanics of dog shit for all I care."

"Great idea. I'll put it in the suggestion box at the school for the up and coming science programs."

I keep my gaze trained on the distant horizon as I pound down the street. *Aphelion Drive,* to be more precise.

"And this is how you deal with your anger?"

"I'm not angry," I say.

"Your sadness?"

"I'm not sad."

"What are you then, Fucking Tara? Some kind of emotionless drone?"

"Why are you following me?"

"Can't in good conscience, let you loose on the world in your condition."

I glance up at him. No matter how fast I walk, or run, or stop, he continues to shadow me. "I don't have a condition."

He raises a dark brow at me. "Seriously?" He mocks me with his own version of my word.

"I'm fine," I say.

"Fucked up, insecure, neurotic, and emotional. It's my mom's definition of F.I.N.E. She uses it sparingly."

I keep moving, dimly aware of the once prestigious neighborhood, now almost ruins. Its vintage beauty is buried beneath overgrown gardens, fallen fences, and layers of chipped paint. The Craftsman and Victorian homes are all in different states of decay; I think it was amazing once. This neighborhood is the perfect simile for what my relationship with Keel is turning into—a memory of what once was fine.

"I'm fine," I say again. "I need to take the roundabout way to Tully's. That's all." *I have to go back. I can't. I have to. I can't.*

"Okay." He runs a hand through his hair.

"You don't need to stay. I heard you say you're scheduled to work."

"I can't leave you out here alone. I probably shouldn't have followed you in the first place, but I did, and now I wouldn't feel right if I left without knowing you're safe."

"Oh, my hero." I fake swoon and place a hand over my heart and flash him big doe eyes.

"Girls." He shakes his head with annoyance or disgust. I can't tell which.

"Listen. I don't want you following me."

"You do want me to. You just don't know it."

"Wow. It almost sounds like you're hitting on me again."

"You're something, Fucking Tara."

"You're talking into a mirror."

"We've reached an impasse. I'm sticking to your side. If I leave and you wind up getting hurt, I couldn't live with myself. I'm following you for my own selfish reasons. Got it?"

"Whatever."

"You should thank me for my service as your guard."

"Are all bodyguards self-righteous swines?"

"Thank you."

"You're welcome."

We keep plodding down the sidewalk. The relative silence is a ghastly lingering presence wedging itself between Corban and me for the next block. The hum of the city never ceases in the background, and I yearn to return to camping and stillness and silence in the middle of the night in a forest far away. The memories come flooding in and drown me with their clarity. Pine-drenched nights snuggled next to Keel in our sleeping bag and falling asleep to the crackle of the campfire. Nights where I knew he loved me, and I dreamed of living with him in our own place. I fantasized about what it would be like to marry him and live our perfect life together. I'm hit with the image of drunken sex on moonlit rocks with Caspar watching us. The clenching ache inside makes me hunch over, arms wrapped around my middle. Vomit splashes into the gutter. Berry smoothie splatters all over the concrete curb and the tips of my shoes.

When the memory assault passes, I find myself squatting down close to the ground, holding my hair back with one hand while keeping the other one clenched over my stomach. I spit the sweet, rank acid from my mouth and wipe the back of my hand across my lips. Tears drip from my eyes so I swipe them away as well.

God, I want to curl up in the dirt and leave the world. I begin to tip over and give up fighting for some sort of a happy life, but Corban takes my arm.

"Come on." He escorts me away from my mess.

He doesn't talk and after another block lets go of me. My feet continue to move and the urge to lie down and die passes, for now.

"What is it?" I force my thoughts to focus.

"The absurd reality that male chivalry is still alive and thriving."

"I'm not talking about your stalker personality."

"You could try being more specific."

"What is aphelion and syzygy? Did I say that right?"

"You said it fine. Aphelion is the point in the orbit of a planet when it's the farthest from the sun."

I absorb the definition for a long minute.

"Syzygy is when three astronomical objects are in straight-line conjunction, like the Sun, Earth, and Moon."

I picture the definitions in my head. Then I say, "Syzygy is like me, Caspar, and Keel. And, I think I'm at my aphelion. My farthest point away from the sun."

"Not really," he says blandly. "If you're talking metaphorically, maybe. Besides, how can you be sure you've reached the final point in your orbit?"

"I don't know." I realize even though this feels like the darkest, coldest, point of no return, it could be the beginning. "But this better be the end, because..." I can't even finish the thought. *How can things get worse than this? No boyfriend, no job, no friend, and nowhere to go.*

We turn down another street, and the neighborhood is starting to become familiar. I think we've made a gigantic loop, and Tully's house is approaching.

"It can't be the end until you're ready to embrace it."

"I'm not ready," I whisper and my steps involuntarily slow down.

"I'm sorry your boyfriend is a jerk. You don't deserve this shit."

"You didn't deserve it either."

He shrugs, not admitting guilt or blame.

"I would suggest you go inside and don't let it show how bad they've hurt you," he says.

I swallow and visualize the pain going down and down and down until nothing anyone says or does can bring it to the surface again. "Thanks." I'm suddenly grateful he stayed with me after all. *Don't let them see how painful it is when your heart is broken and pulverized.*

"Do you need a ride? My offer still stands."

I pivot on my axis and look up at Corban. In my current mental state, he seems to tower over me. "Are you sure you don't mind taking me to a hotel? I don't want to hang around your work. That's not cool. I have a lot of stuff, and it would be uncomfortable."

"Either way is okay. Hotels are expensive around here."

I cringe at the thought of using my savings to sleep in a strange bed, but I don't have much choice. "I owe you huge."

"You don't," he says.

"I'll make this fast." I force myself to open the front door and step inside.

***

"Keel's not here," Saul says.

I'm standing at the edge of the living room, feeling like the biggest outcast in the world.

"I just came back for my stuff."

"I think he's out looking for you," Zeb says from the couch. "He and Demian left in the van shortly after you ran out the door."

"Well, he didn't find me." I pause and swallow again. The hurt wants to rise and announce itself, but I like Corban's advice, and I won't let it show. "What about her?" I ask them both. I'm sure they're fully aware of what went down. You don't live in close quarters with each other and not know what is happening moment to moment.

Zeb stares at the coffee table.

Saul answers. "I don't know where she is. I'm sorry, Tara."

I nod in acknowledgment. Of the three band members, at least Saul has the balls to say something kind to me about this bullshit. I honestly wasn't sure if any of them would even care. They sleep with whoever they want. Saul tends to remain single. Keel is the only one with an attachment. Or he was. Now that I think about it, I'm surprised we lasted this long. Girls are always hitting on him. Some of them right in front of me. As far as I know, he's been faithful. That is, until today. Maybe I've been lying to myself. Maybe he's been a cheater since we met.

I head upstairs to our room. The same room Caspar and Keel were screwing in.

The door is ajar, and I take a steadying breath before entering. *Collect my bags, clean out the truck, and be gone. Simple, right? I can do this.*

With my hoodie thrown on and my backpack shouldered, I grab my duffle and make a visual sweep of the room. Caspar is in the hallway outside the door.

"He's a good lay. You would've been better."

"You fucked him because I wouldn't do you?"

"I tried to tell you he was only in lust with you. Lust is fleeting." She waves a dismissive hand in the air like she didn't just ruin my life.

I try to slip by without any part of me touching her, but she's blocking the way to the stairs with her "perfect" legs.

"Move," I order.

"You're so pretty, Jasper. Is that why you're together? The gorgeous couple. I know you're not that shallow even though he is."

I wish I could shoot venom at her with my eyes. My blood is boiling so hot I don't even notice the name she called me.

"That's right. Keel told me all kinds of stuff about you, including your real name and how horrible your family is to you." She crosses her arms over her chest. "Your boyfriend treats you just as bad, and I proved it today. It took me less than an hour alone with him before he let me go down on him."

"Shut up!" I close my eyes and will the pain to stay buried.

"It's sad you still love him after this. He even thinks he loves you, but he doesn't. He uses you."

"Why are you doing this?! Move out of my way," I say through clenched teeth. My nails dig into my palms and cut deep.

"You deserve so much better. Someone who respects you and knows how sweet and thoughtful you are."

I shove her out of my way, knocking her to the side, and fly down the stairs. Her laugh trickles down the stairwell.

She calls out, "I told you. I like breaking things."

***

"This is fine," I say in my current state of deadness.

The shroud of fog returns, worse than before. The cocoon of oblivion is my only salvation. We're sitting beneath a vacancy sign of one of the cheaper chain hotels.

"I'm sorry I made you late for work. Please don't wait for me. I promise I'll go straight in and get a room."

"It's okay. I called work to tell them I had an emergency to take care of."

"I'm not an emergency."

"I disagree."

I pull the door handle open and start to climb out. "I feel bad enough. I'll text you later and let you know I'm still breathing."

He doesn't respond to this pathetic promise. He reaches to turn off his 4-Runner. "Are you sure this is what you want to do?"

"Corban," I want him to stop helping me. "I'm sure. Thanks for today, but you need to go to work. I don't want you to come inside with me," I add as a final push to make him leave.

His hand moves away from the key to rest on the shifter. I grab my things and close the door. After I enter the lobby, I glance back and watch his black SUV drive out of the lot.

There's a short line at the desk. It's awkward standing there holding fifty pounds of clothes and gear and my other burdens. I realize I left my aerial silk behind. It's in the van. Not that I could haul it around with me without a vehicle. Carrying fourteen yards of fabric is cumbersome for anyone. I haven't checked into a hotel room alone before, and it seems too grown up, too adult, and too out of my realm.

When it's my turn, I take my card out and lay it on the counter. "I need a single room for one night, please," I tell the desk lady.

"I'm so sorry. I sold our last available room to the gentleman before you."

I blink and look down at my fingers resting on my debit card. I glance back up, not wanting it to be true. "I just got dropped off here because your sign said vacancy. I don't have my own car. Are you sure there isn't even one room left?"

"We're clear full," she says again. "I checked my computer for cancellations, and there aren't any."

"Are there any other hotels within walking distance?" I ask, trying to think of what to do next.

"The Travel Inn is about a mile down the road," she says.

"Which way?" I ask.

"Go out the front door and take a left. You can't miss it."

"Thanks," I say and gather my bags.

***

114

"You can't miss it," should have been my tip-off. Did the desk clerk flat-out lie? The way today is going—the way my life is spiraling down the shitter—it wouldn't surprise me. My only other guess is The Travel Inn must be a figment of her imagination created to dispose of unwanted travelers.

I walk for another thirty minutes after already walking for an hour with no sign of any hotels whatsoever. It's getting dark, and my bags are iron anvils. You know Wile E. Coyote ACME anvils. I picture one landing on my head and the accompanying sound effects to go with it. My shoulders and back need a break so I sit down at a bus stop. Corban dropping me off at a hotel isolated from any other hotels is a problem which never occurred to me. How was I supposed to know there was only one hotel in a three-mile radius? Did I walk three miles? Five? Am I traveling in circles like a lost child on a bad television show?

With my perspective changing as quickly as the sun setting behind the mountains, I dig out my phone to begin an online search for a room. My phone isn't the greatest; Keel and I use his for everything. His parents pay his bill, and his phone is overall a thousand times better than mine. But having absolutely no service on my stupid phone isn't what I expect to find. I power it down, then back on again, refusing to believe in the middle of the city I can't make a call or access the internet. There's still no service. I stare at it, baffled. I'm doing a lot of blank staring lately.

The urge to launch the phone into the street like a professional baseball pitcher is strong, but I hold my temper at bay for another minute. The realization that my phone is dead provides a modicum of hope this is the real reason Keel hasn't called or texted me. Not that I want to talk to him... but I do want to talk to him. But I haven't tried to call him, which places a medal of honor for self-control right over my heart. This is the new me. The girl who stopped making everyone happy except herself. Too bad this supposed happiness is so damn devastating.

Since I can't do anything else, I dial the service number on my phone. A robotic female voice says, "Your account has been temporarily deactivated. You must enter a valid form of payment before your account expires in thirty days. Dial one to make changes to your account now."

What? I stare at the screen like it should answer all of my unasked questions. Instead, I faintly hear the robot say, "Goodbye."

My phone is set up to automatically charge my card every month. That's over two years of service based on the balance in my bank account. My heart leaps at the thought of Mom or Geoff cleaning out my account. *They wouldn't. They couldn't.* I took my mom off my account as soon as I turned eighteen. *How the hell is this happening?*

I redial the customer service number and fumble through the menus until I get to the right one for reentering my card number to turn my service back on. Dusk turns to night around me, but I'm helpless without a working phone. I re-enter the debit card number and am promptly told the card is expired. I squint at my card in the dingy yellow glow from the buzzing streetlight and the card expired two days ago, on the last day of the month.

I drop my face into my hands and let it sink in for a long time.

Desolation. Isolation. Tears. Aphelion. The farthest point in my orbit away from the sun. This has to be it.

When I'm done considering how screwed I am and how far I may or may not be from Tully's house—where I might be able to get some sympathy and use a telephone—I realize I don't even know which direction the house is from here. I was too distracted by the things Caspar said to notice where Corban had driven.

My entire life feels like a gross error. Everything I've chosen to do since I left my mom's house has been a terrible mistake and now I'm paying for my poor choices. Isn't that what Geoff would say? Be a whore and you'll ruin your life. Do drugs and you'll ruin your life. Slack off and you'll ruin your life. I listened to him insult me for years, and now it seems his predictions are true. I ruined my life.

A car turns the corner. I wished it would be the bus. Unfortunately, I spent most of my cash at the store earlier, but I should have a couple of bucks left for a bus ride. I could at least get on and ride around the city, maybe even pass the neighborhood where Keel and the band are.

The car slows down as it approaches the bus stop. I get a grip on my bags in case I need to bolt. In a strange city, in an area that feels isolated, I'm not willing to take any chances.

The window rolls down a crack, and I rise from the bench.

"Excuse me," the voice calls.

I only see eyes and a forehead. I bite my lip. He sounds innocent enough.

"Which way is North Street?"

"I'm sorry. I don't know," I say.

The brake lights flicker. Then the window rolls down further, and I see his face and the gun he's pointing at me.

"Give me the phone. And your wallet."

I've never had a gun pointed at me before. Someone doing something truly violent toward me never crossed my mind. Well, that's not true. I mean, I do watch TV and I traveled around the U.S. for most of my life. I experienced some horrible things in my past, but I'm careful, and the reality of first-hand random violence isn't what I imagined it would be.

"Bitch. Do it, or I'll kill you right here."

The car door cracks open. Part of the driver is visible now, and he has another gun, also pointed at me.

I raise my hand very slowly to pass the dead phone over to this monster. I react without thinking and hurl my phone at his pistol.

It hits the target and makes the gun flinch. I don't know exactly what happens next because I'm too busy running for my life. The car door flings open and someone curses, but no gunshots.

It doesn't take him more than a second or two to catch up with me. My duffle bag is ripped out of my hands, and I'm screaming for the entire world to hear. The ground comes rushing up to me, and I collapse on top of my other bag. Before I know what's happening, something crashes into my head. I'm kicking and clawing backward and trying to roll over so I can beat the living shit out of this guy. My foot must hit a sensitive spot because he grunts and my back smashes like he tried to break my spine, but he's not trying to kill me because I'm still breathing and not shot.

The fight for my life is a riot of sound. Beside the thunder of my heart, I hear cars and yelling. Lots of yelling.

"Hey! What's going on over there?"

"Get off of her!"

"Call the police!"

The weight is lifted from my back. My bag is yanked out from under me. Night air blows over my body like a cold caress. I scramble from the sidewalk and sprint toward the nearest buildings.

The sky whirls overhead. The fences stream past me in a blur of splinters and chain links. I stay in the shadowy places and run into garbage cans, and god knows what else. I keep moving without any real sense or reason.

When I find a house that appears occupied, I'm about to run up to the front door and beg for help, but I realize the people inside could be the same people who jumped me. That stops me cold. I turn away from the lit porch light and search for the darkest place to hide.

***

"Mommy! Someone's under there."

The child's voice is whiny and high pitched. My nerves are raw, ragged, and searing from the unbearable night of anguish. I'm not sure if I should hold still and hope they go away or disentangle from my hiding place on the playground and reveal I'm only a girl and not some evil villain.

I consider how much dried blood is on me, and I don't move. I could terrify the kid, and I would never want to do that. My hair must be a disaster too, and I ripped my pants and shirt when I was fleeing through fenced yards. It hurts to swallow, but my sandpaper throat isn't my only pain. The bruises are coming to life now, and they're crying.

I hear the mom's voice. "Hi," she says from not too far away. "Can you come to the park by our house? I'm here now, and I don't like the look of this." A pause. "No, I'm not in any danger. Just come over. Thanks."

Then, "Jack. Let's go, sweetie."

"No. You promised we could play at the park today."

"I'll buy you an ice cream," she says.

"Ice cream! Yay!"

Then silence.

Time to leave, I think, and then revise, giving them a minute to depart before crawling out of my hole beneath the playground equipment. The awareness of having spent the night hiding, shivering, and praying for a new reality hits pretty hard as I prepare to face the day with nothing but bruises. It hits me again and again. It's not that I blame myself for being mugged, but on the other hand, I do blame myself. The nightmare that was yesterday gets worse and worse the more I think about it. I pry myself away from the powder-coated and plastic playground and see the whole park in the daylight for the first time. The mom and her kid are well across the other side of a green lawn.

I reach back into the space where I had stayed and grab my sole surviving bag. Somehow, I managed to hang on to one of my three pieces of luggage. As I limp away, I realize I'm down to one shoe, the other probably fell off while running, some of my stage clothes, and my journal. Everything else is gone; my phone, wallet, ID, debit card, clothes, and toiletries.

Having only one shoe is ridiculous on top of the other mile long list of humiliations, regrets, and fears. I kick it off, pick it up, and drop it into a trash can. My elbow and forearm are crusted with dried blood, and I'm not certain it isn't broken. When I fell, my elbow took most of my weight. The swelling is pretty spectacular. There's a lump on my head and my back hurts. I trudge in the direction where I think there could be a store and maybe a payphone, or a kind stranger.

Two minutes after I begin limping down the sidewalk, a cop pulls up behind me and orders me to stop walking and keep my hands visible.

Chapter Eleven

"Be kind, for everyone you meet is fighting a harder battle."
— Plato

Cops.
Shelter.
Counselors.

What to do with Jasper Pyrah?

It seems to be the question of the day.

Jasper Alexia Pyrah is my real name. I guess I could lie about who I am, but looking into the compassionate blue eyes of the officer, I'm optimistic for some help. And I'm done with the name Tara. Tara was a mistake.

As far as cops go, Officer Stuart is as ace as they come. Sure he treats me like the playground villain, but this only lasts a few minutes. I mean, I did freak out his wife and kid at the park so he could have been much worse. When I break down and become a sobbing mess in his patrol car, he waits patiently for me to calm down enough to talk to him in a language that doesn't sound like, "Wha-wha, wha-waaaa. Sniffle, sniffle. Blither blubber. Bad guys." He gives me a tissue and a blanket.

At the station, he lets me clean up in the bathroom and buys me some food from a vending machine. He tells me the incident was reported the previous night by whoever happened to drive by and see me being assaulted. He's clearly upset I didn't contact the police earlier. I explain I was lost and couldn't find a phone. I felt trapped in a maze of foreign houses and closed businesses. I was unable to find my way out of the nightmare and hid in the playground equipment and pretended not to exist anymore.

He gives me a stern eye for the briefest of seconds, sets his jaw, and doesn't press the issue. I finish giving my statement and am told the jerks who robbed me had gotten away.

When it comes time to call my family, I can't make myself dial Mom. Or Keel. My stubbornness and elephant-sized shame won't allow me to call either of them. The thought of having to explain what happened, where I'm calling from, and how humiliated I am won't let me reach out to them. No matter how much sense it makes, I can't do it. I search for my Aunt Summer on Officer Stuart's computer and find her number.

She doesn't answer. Officer Stuart offers to take me to a shelter where they will give me some food and clothes, and let me use their phone. It's the best he can do other than letting me wander the streets. I take the ride and dismiss the nagging voice in my head to call Keel. He can't find out about this. And besides, I don't ever want to see him again. I'd rather be homeless and helpless than ask for his help—the cheating prick. On the drive, we follow behind a truck with a tailgate covered in bumper stickers. Three of them stand out as my signs of the day:

All is well.

I love haters.

I hate bumper stickers.

Oh but the irony is sweet.

***

The shelter.

Joy doesn't radiate from the walls or the floors of Serenity House. It's sad before I even open the door. Sadness smells like pine scented soap, dusty ventilation, cafeteria food, and the ancient plumbing of the three-story seen-better-days building.

The room where I get to sleep has five beds, one window, and a lady with stringy gray and blonde hair. She glances over at us as I'm shown which bunk is mine to use for the night. The growing sensation of voluntarily walking into some sort of jail won't quit tickling my better sense. I try to breathe through the urge to run out of this weird place, but my lungs are uncooperative. The constriction is making it hard to breathe, almost impossible to speak.

My tour guide is going over more rules of conduct and etiquette for the house, but I only hear about one in every thirty words. Aunt Summer still isn't answering her phone, and I'm starting to think she's either out of town or changed her number.

"What?" I ask, and do my best to pay attention to the counselor.

"Did you hear me say your appointment is at eight a.m. tomorrow morning?"

"Right. Yeah. Downstairs, by the office. Eight o'clock," I mumble.

She seems to accept my tongue-tied babble as good enough and gives me a final send-off for the night. "I know you said you won't be staying with us very long, but please know you're welcome here, and the staff is here to support you. If we all follow the rules, there won't be any problems during your stay."

The confusion on my face probably seems rude to Bethany, my intake counselor, but the twisted expression has nothing to do with her and everything to do with my disbelief of how I ended up in a homeless shelter.

"I'll be gone by tomorrow. I just need to touch base with my family."

"Okay." She wears a kind smile.

Do I imagine the disbelieving look in her eyes? Does everyone who walks through these doors say the same? *I'll only be here a day. I don't need your help. I'm not homeless and begging for a pair of shoes.*

"Sleep well." She leaves me alone with the other homeless woman.

As soon as Bethany is gone, I'm panicked about being by myself in this strange building. Not that I know Bethany from Adam, but she walked me through the intake process, helped me pick out some shoes and clothes, and talked with me for a couple of hours. She currently seems like my only ally in the whole world. My stomach clenches with fear, but I don't call her back. *It's just one night*, I tell myself over and over again.

"The others will be coming in soon. If you don't check in by nine, you're locked out for the night. The showers will be real busy after nine, too," the stranger on the bed says to my back.

Turning, I check out my roommate more closely. She's mending a pair of pants with a needle and thread.

"Thanks." My voice is dull.

"Sure, hun."

I grip the bag of free toiletries tighter in my hand. The soap, shampoo, toothpaste, toothbrush, cheap flip flops to wear in the shower, and a few other miscellaneous items are the gems of my worldly possessions. The house rule—residents must stay clean or risk getting a write-up—reinforces the feeling of being in jail. I swallow hard and try to be thankful for the soap. The scum and grit of the last thirty hours need to go. *Is it only a day now? Can someone age a lifetime in twenty-four hours?* I glance briefly at the woman with the needle and thread. The wrinkles on her face and the protruding bones of her back, shoulders and elbows confirm my thought. Aging rapidly can happen. She was probably beautiful once, too. *Don't look in the mirror Jasper*, I warn myself. *Not until after you take a shower. Maybe not even then.*

The soap is only a little less valuable than the toothbrush and toothpaste. I've never been so thrilled to possess either item before tonight.

Sleep is elusive, haunting, and full of paranoia. I'm paranoid about moving around too much on the thin mattress because the frame creaks. I don't want to keep anyone else up. I'm paranoid about losing the few belongings I have left even though they're locked inside my designated locker. I'm paranoid about being surrounded by strangers. Even though everyone here signed their life away on the intake forms and promised there would be no fighting, no violence, no weapons, no alcohol, and no drugs, I'm still uneasy. The rules are a mile long. The variety of women in the room is wide and diverse. Rules or no rules, I can't trust these people. After trusting Caspar, I may never be able to be close to another female friend again.

The snoring and shifting of bodies becomes a nightmare. Sleep transforms into this ghoul hanging over my bed taunting me incessantly through the dark hours. When he fades for the slightest respite, all I can do is think about how and where I'm going to go next, and what happens to me afterward. Every time I consider calling Keel a wall of unyielding strength gets thrown in my face. *Am I choosing Serenity House over him?*

It's only one night.

The images of my life don't help me relax. In fact, if all thoughts were this repulsive and depressing, the suicide rate would be a lot higher. No conjured vision of my future seems bright. The only reasonable idea I can come up with is joining The Circus of the Sun and traveling with them around the world. Since this is pure fantasy, it doesn't help. Besides, the other side of the globe isn't far enough away from Keel. I could join a troupe headed to Pluto, and that wouldn't be far enough either.

I envision going back to the Farinelli World Circus, and this seems the most likely place for me, but it's not an immediate answer. It'll take time to get in touch with Mr. Markovic, see when they're auditioning, and then figure out a way to get to Florida where their headquarters are located. This plan could take months.

Why is the mind capable of examining every negative aspect of one's life, then playing the clips on a never ending loop—but only between the hours of midnight and five a.m.? *What the hell?*

Wake up call comes, but I don't think I ever fell asleep.

***

Counselors.

My counselor bulges over the confines of her desk chair like a can of busted biscuits on wheels. The name on her badge says Lucille Mei-Xing Choo, but to speak with her, you wouldn't tie in her Chinese last name with her appearance. Her skin is as dark as anyone's I have ever seen, and her accent is as thick as the humidity on a summer day in Georgia, which is where she sounds like she's from. Regardless of her African American appearance and her Chinese name, she comes across as more of a military commander than a professional counselor.

"Are there any medical issues that'll be stopping you from working?" She tilts her large head down to peer through her bifocals at my paperwork. The tripling of her chins swells impressively as she reads my file. I stare at my lap so I don't start counting the rolls around her neck as I tell her I have no medical problems.

"You into drugs?"

"No."

"Gang member?"

"I think I would need a few tats or a bigger attitude problem for that."

She gives me a one-eyed amphibian glare.

"No," I answer again, this time without the snark.

"You into any weird shit? Satanism, Voodoo, cannibalism?"

"Umm, no." I hesitated, not because I'm lying, but because of the absurdity of this interrogation.

"Don't you give me that uppity look. I've seen it all, and I want a good look at your skeletons right now. Show your cards before one of us pulls the Joker."

I promptly erase my face, or at least make an effort to, and swallow in an attempt to moisten my dry mouth. "I'm in town because—"

"I ain't finished." She cuts me off. "You'll get your chance to tell me all about it in a minute. It says here, you're only nineteen years old. Any living parents or relatives?"

Did I mention my mouth is dry? I lick my lips. "My mom's alive."

"Does she know you're here?"

"No." I hadn't thought about it until now, but I wonder if Keel called her. Is he looking for me, or did he go to Utah with the band? Canceling a show is bad PR. Really bad. It takes an emergency to call off a gig. Would they consider me an emergency? Should I call him and tell him I'm not coming back? That I won't be touring with Paradox 21 ever again? Would he call Mom and Geoff to check on me? Is my mother searching for me right this minute? Mrs. Choo interrupts my head space.

"Did you sleep last night?"

"No."

"Neither did your mama."

"I—"

"Ehh," she makes a sound deep in her throat letting me know it's still not my turn to talk. Her hand is poised in the air as if she might slap it over my mouth if I continue. "I don't need every detail about your life to figure you're on the outs with your family. I can see that. I've seen a thousand cases like yours. It don't matter if your mama is three sheets to the wind or battier than Count Dracula. No mama sleeps well if she don't know where her baby is and whether or not she's alive or dead in a ditch. You keep it in mind as you toss and turn at night."

"Yes, Ma'am." I surprise myself as I don't think I ever use the word ma'am, like *ever*. I wasn't raised anywhere near the South. I just know from traveling there the use of ma'am is as common as sweet tea and Jesus.

She turns her hairy eyeball back to my intake forms, takes an enormous breath, and lays the paperwork down on her cluttered desk. She frowns up at me and pushes her chair back with a protesting groan. Reclining against the backrest, she crosses her stout legs and stares down her nose at me. She takes her glasses off and lays them on the open folder. The chair whines and screeches in agony as she rocks forward and back. Serious doubt the chair is going to survive the day crosses my mind, but I keep my mouth shut because doubt for my own survival is also in the air.

Mrs. Choo massages the bridge of her nose where her glasses had been resting. "Don't matter how you got here, Miss Pyrah. Now you gotta let what's happened to you slide off your back, like water off a duck. Just let it roll. You're young and healthy. Those bumps and bruises will heal quickly. Good things happen to bad people, and bad things happen to good people all the time. I think you're a perfect example of the latter."

"Thanks?" Did she just say she thinks I'm a good person?

"Tell me three ways you're gonna get back on your feet today."

"If I can use your computer and phone I can contact my bank and request a new debit card. Then I'll buy a bus ticket out of this town." I hope my plan counts for her requirement to list three things.

"Very well, but in the meantime, you will be given chores to help keep this house spic and span. Did you agree to the rules of conduct to be staying here with us?"

"Yes."

"Well then, my staff will add your name to the cleaning schedule, and you can start tomorrow."

"But I just said, I'll be leaving as soon as I can access my savings account and get a bus ticket."

"Yes, you sure did," she drawls. "And I've been at this long enough to know snags in the system are about as common as fleas on a dog."

***

After my rather eye-opening and uncomfortable meeting with Lucille Mei-Xing Choo, I go online for my bank's contact information. When I call, the lobby isn't open yet because of the time difference between Mountain Time and the west coast. While watching the clock, I'm informed if I don't want to be written up, I need to get the hell out. Well, the security officer didn't say hell, but he may as well have. Everyone gets kicked out of Serenity House at 10 a.m. We're not allowed to come back inside until 3 p.m. Unless you're like my sewing roommate. She's disabled, and some kind of phenomenal seamstress. Being handicapped or having a doctor's note, or some other acceptable excuse means you can stay in the building during the day. Everyone else leaves. My excuse that it's Saturday and if I don't talk to my bank before noon California time means I'll be stuck waiting until Monday doesn't mean diddly squat to the guy holding the door open. I consider asking Mrs. Choo for a pass to stay inside today but her husky and thunderous voice is chewing someone out about smoking cigarettes upstairs, and I tell myself I'll figure something out on my own.

I collect my sole remaining backpack and follow some of the other women outside to a fenced patio with some picnic tables for "loitering". This is the only place on the premises where we're allowed to hang out. The day is already warm, and the concrete patio, security fence, and faded tables aren't overly inviting. The thought of sitting back here for five hours waiting to be allowed back inside to use the phone sounds about as appealing as drowning in quicksand. Almost everyone wanders through the back gate, and I follow.

The alley leads to a neighborhood street, and since I don't know my way around, I go with the herd. The herd being a couple of clusters of women from the shelter. A few blocks later there's a city park where I can kill time, and maybe even find a nice citizen who will let me use their phone.

Desperate times call for desperate measures. Not really, but the point of desperation is long past, and I would do just about anything within my power to get my life back under control.

"Hey," I say to a bunch of kids hanging around at a picnic table by the small lake.

"How's it going?" a guy says. He's wearing a black leather jacket, cargo pants, and unshaven scruff around his jaw.

The group of six or seven of them, plus one black dog, appraise me with cool stares. They seem to be around my age. I make eye contact with the only female in the group, but she turns away. Their lack of baggage and level of cleanliness suggests they aren't homeless, but they're somewhat scruffy, so I can't say for sure.

I'm cautious to stay a few feet back from their circle. I don't want to intrude and start something I'm not prepared for, like a fight. Two of the guys, including the dude in the leather coat, step forward. I plaster a hopeful smile on my face and pretend they're fans after a show.

"Sorry to bother you," I start.

"No problem," a cute guy with shaggy medium length hair and wearing a hipster flannel shirt says. "What's your name?"

"I'm Tara." I slip right back into the habit of using my road name. "Do you guys live around here?"

"Sure. Lived here all my life."

"Not me," the other one says. "I'm a transplant from Kansas City. I'm only up here because this is where the scene is at."

Okay. I'm completely ignorant as to what "scene" he's referring to, but I keep going like it makes perfect sense.

I don't want to tell them too much, like I just broke up with my asshole boyfriend, got mugged, and now I'm homeless, but a little sympathy might be beneficial. "I'm in town for a short time and just my luck, a whole pile of unbelievable nonsense landed on top of me."

"That sucks." Leather coat guy raises sympathetic eyebrows.

"Yeah, it's been hell. Anyway, I'm not trying to dump my sob story on you or anything. My phone was stolen, and I'm wondering if you would let me use yours? If you have one. It's okay if you don't want to let me use it. I just thought I could ask."

"Sure, you can use my phone," he says.

"Really?" I say in stunned disbelief.

"It's just a phone call, right?"

"Yeah. Maybe two calls if you don't mind. I won't use your data or anything."

"Cool. But this is my new phone, and it cost a wad of cash, so you won't mind if I hang around kind of close. Not that I don't trust you, but I don't know you." He reaches into the inner pocket of his jacket and hands over his phone.

"Oh my god, thank you. And no, I don't mind at all. I'd keep my phone in view, too, if I were letting a total stranger use it."

The cute one says something about leaving soon to go to so-and-so's house and moves away from us. The rest of the group starts laughing, and someone begins playing the bongos.

"Come over here where it's not so loud." He walks toward a picnic table about twenty feet away.

"Thanks." I appreciate his thoughtfulness all over again. I couldn't talk with all the noise right next to us. "What's your name?"

"Lucas."

"Nice to meet you." I lean against the end of the table.

Lucas hangs out a couple of feet away looking relaxed and patient as I stare at the screen looking for the right icon to make a call. When I don't see it right away, I glance over at him and catch him checking me out.

It happens. Guys look. I notice, but don't make much of it. Being stared at is part of The Show. I don't like it, but I don't hold it against him. I tell myself they're watching me because of my talents, not because of my bra size, or whatever it is guys like to look at. Besides, I was noticing how cute his friend is. Lucas isn't ugly, but he oozes a skeevy aura, and it isn't attractive.

"Can you get me to the right screen?" I ask.

"Sure. Sorry about that." He takes the phone.

Sitting down at the table I dig out my journal and open it to the page with all the important numbers on it.

Lucas takes the opposite side of the table with his back to me and stretches his legs, giving me a minimal amount of privacy as I dial the bank. The teller is extremely helpful—except she's not. My new debit card is being issued right away which means it will take about three to five business days to show up in the mail—to my mother's address. When I ask them to mail it to another address, I don't know what to say. Without having talked to Aunt Summer, I'm reluctant to give her address, and I'm not going to give the address of the shelter; there's no way I'm going to be here for another week. I hang up with the bank and call my aunt yet again. There's still no answer and no voice mail.

One of Lucas's friends comes over and asks him if he's ready to leave.

"In a minute," he says.

The phone beeps in my hand, and I hand it back to Lucas to check the text or answer the alert. He's busy for a minute and turns around, straddling the bench. "I couldn't help overhearing you. So, you're staying at the shelter until you can get your money?"

"Yeah, I am. My stuff was stolen, and I'm not from around here. The police thought the shelter was better than sleeping on the street."

"That blows hard."

"Definitely."

"You don't have any friends here?"

"No. I mean sort of, but I don't think I could find their house again, and all my contact information was lost with my phone. All of it. But I'm fine. I'll figure it out."

"Do you need to make another call?" He places the phone down on the table between us.

"Sort of, yeah. It'll just take a minute." I sound a little pathetic even to my own ears.

"Go ahead." He waves his hand toward the phone.

"Are you sure you don't mind? I think your friends are waiting for you."

"They can wait. Besides, I want to invite you to come with us after you're done."

"Really?" I say.

"Sure. We're going to a friend's house for a cookout. Make your call first. Then I'll tell you more about it. You can come with us and use my phone or my friend's computer. I'm sure he won't mind."

I smile, perplexed and somewhat happy about the unexpected invite and meeting some cool people. I don't answer him yet, but I do pick up the phone one more time. Lucas unthreads his leg out from under the picnic table and turns back around so I can talk without being stared at.

The hesitation to make the next call is felt all the way from the tip of my dialing finger to the pit of my soul. I suck it up and dial the number. A backyard cookout? After this call, I may not be capable of functioning around other human beings at all.

The conversation goes like this.

"Hi, Mom."

"Jasper, where are you?"

"Still in Colorado."

"Christ, Jasper. Ever consider calling your mother more than once a month?" she demands.

"No," I say truthfully. Not to mention I spoke to her like two or three days ago, not a month. "Listen, I can only talk for a minute before I have to go."

"If you don't have time to talk to me, why should I bother answering?"

She must have taken a double dose of bitch pills today. It's bad. I barely said anything, and she's already on my case.

"Mom, my debit card was stolen. A new one will be coming in the mail sometime next week."

"Stolen? How? Where?"

Now I have her full attention, but the crazy tone of her voice isn't subsiding. "It doesn't matter right now."

"Jasper, what's going on? Are you coming home? Where's Keel?"

I skirt around the questions I don't want to answer. "I'm not going back to Geoff's house. We're staying on our tour schedule. You know how it is. Can you mail my card to Aunt Summer's? We're headed that way in a few days, and I think we can stop by and pick it up."

"So you'll go see my sister, but you won't come home."

I lower my voice and duck my head so Lucas won't catch every part of this awful conversation. "Mom, please. I told you where I'm at and why I can't come clear across the country for my card. Will you please just overnight it to Aunt Summer's?"

"I don't know, Jas. First, you take off without telling me, and now you're demanding I do a favor for you. I don't think I can support your erratic behavior. How do I know you're not buying alcohol or drugs with your money? I can't contribute to that."

"That makes absolutely no sense. You know I don't drink."

"But you smoke pot with your boyfriend. I've smelled it on you."

"I don't anymore, and besides, you can't pay for pot with a debit card," I say. This conversation is going nowhere but straight to Crazy Central.

"Marijuana is legal in a few states, young lady. I watch the news. And I know plenty of lying drug addicts. Are you lying to me?"

"Fuck," I whisper out of sheer frustration. "Just send my card to Aunt Summer's so I can eat." I refuse to tell her about Keel and everything else. If a simple request to mail my card to her sister's house goes this well, I can only imagine the magnitude of insanity that would follow if I told her the truth about my current situation.

"Keel doesn't have food?" Her tone is disbelieving, snippy.

"He does. I need my own money, too. Will you please tell me Summer's address and phone number? I think this is the wrong one. Did she move or something?"

"I don't know, Jasper," she huffs. "Let me check. Hold on a minute."

In the background noise, I hear her moving around. I mouth an apology to Lucas for taking so long. He stands up and looks around the park, fingers drumming against his thigh.

My mom comes back on the line and gives me the address and phone number. The number I write down is different than the one I had been dialing. She says, "You owe Geoff and me an apology."

She sounds calmer, but sometimes the calm is much scarier than the pissed off. Sometimes the calm means a new level of irrational behavior is taking hold of her and is just waiting for detonation.

"I don't have time for this."

"You come home and apologize to Geoff and me for what you did to our family, and I might give you your bank card."

"I didn't do anything."

"Is that what you believe? Your sister is a wreck and denial is another sign of drug abuse. What are you on?"

"I have to go." I hit the disconnect button and hand Lucas his phone.

"So, what do you think? Beers, food, music, free wi-fi? Want to hang out? We're walking across the street. You can see my friend's house from the park." He points to the far side of the lawn at a row of houses.

"Umm, yeah. Sure." I shove to my feet.

The conversation with my mom spins around and around, and I'm not paying much attention to Lucas, his band of friends, or anything else. Would my mom refuse to mail my card? Should I call my bank back and ask them to send the card to the shelter? Does the bank offer overnight shipping in the case of an emergency? I'd still be stuck until at least Monday. Can I handle the homeless shelter for a few days? Gah! The thought of another night tossing and turning—actually—refusing to move at all because the creaky bed makes me want to go back to the sandbox on the playground makes my whole body shudder.

I make noises which sound like introductions with some of Lucas's friends. They seem indifferent to me, and I start to fall behind as we cross the park. I stumble over a tree root and collide with a green steel cage housing a trash can. I'm partially shaken back to reality with this not so graceful move. Lucas slows down and gives me a look of mild concern mixed with hilarity.

"Oops," I say. "I didn't see it there."

"Yeah, trashcans are pretty shifty. You better start walking with your eyes open."

"Right. Pretty sound advice. I'll keep it in mind," I say.

As I'm trying to forget how embarrassing that was, we're attacked by a flurry of canvas and burlap, and a very long stick.

"Remove yourself from thy blessed realm of the Governor's Park, ye who are not worthy of walking upon hallowed ground."

The stick swivels, twirls, and comes crashing down between Lucas and me, almost taking my nose off. Jumping back, I follow the length of the seven-foot-long staff with my eyes from the ground to the man wielding it.

"Scum of the earth shall not molest the innocent. Remove thyself immediately!" the stranger says. His eyes are fierce as he lifts his weapon and steps between Lucas and me.

The man wears a billowing jacket that sort of resembles a duster, or a cloak. I can't quite tell as the multiple shades of layered brown and black fabrics all blend together. He's tall, barrel-chested, and has a head full of bushy white hair.

"Get out of my face!" Lucas shouts.

I move to the side, putting space between me and the lunatic wizard, and look for Lucas's friends. We need some backup over here. The eccentric looking man is rather intimidating with his staff, and it's freaking me out.

Before I can scream for help, he speaks to me. "Fair maiden, make a dash to the far side of the loch and report to the crown's guards you have been accosted by this most heinous enemy of the governor."

"I don't have time for this shit," Lucas says. "Tara, tell this dirtbag, you're a friend of mine so he'll back off."

"Take one more step toward the lady, and I will leave my mark upon thy villainous face."

The man does a swift maneuver with his staff that involves a flip and a jab and results with the end of the staff stopping about an inch from Lucas's ear.

Lucas dives to the side and calls out, "Mike! Cal! Vincent's back!"

"Leave us alone," I say and start looking for help. There are plenty of people around, and it doesn't make sense no one sees this. I realize the looming shade trees block the view where most of the people are. This maniac picked this spot on purpose.

"Be away. Find the guardsmen. They are near the motorized carriages," he says to me. "Tell them to make haste as the vagrant will make his escape to the east."

"What do you want?" I clench my fists in preparation for... God, I don't know what. A fist fight? I'll protect myself again. I mean my arm and elbow are still scabbed and bruised from my previous attack, but I'll ignore it.

"I'm out of here." Lucas jogs away to catch up with his friends, who didn't hear his distress call.

Blood pounds in my ears. I can't believe this is happening—again. What does this guy want? My toothbrush and shampoo? My hideous new shoes? The rush of adrenaline hits me hard as I search for my escape. The wizard is blocking the most direct path. There are two large trees in the way and a lake at my back. I'm about to scream bloody murder and run into the bushes when he turns and speaks.

"Are thee injured, fair maiden?" He adjusts his staff so it looks like a walking stick at his side and he even moves, giving me a much wider escape route.

"Who are you?" I ask as I take a wary step away from him. I saw how quick he was. He could cut me off before I can blink. "Lucas is going to go find the cops," I say as a totally false threat.

"Bah! He calleth Sir Vincent a dirtbag. He is the scum upon which the scum grows in the bottom of yon turd pond. Are thee a true friend of such a loathsome scoundrel?"

"No. Not exactly," I stammer and take a couple more steps.

"The honesty in the lady's eyes and upon thy lips is most refreshing." He bows gracefully. "Vincent. At your service, milady."

"I need to leave." I wonder if my eyes show lies as well as truths.

He rises and watches me with a crystal blue stare. The whites of his eyes are tinged with a fair amount of yellow and red. His cheeks display the puffy, mottled appearance of someone who drinks a lot or has health problems.

"Flee whilst the angels still watch over thee, maiden of Governor's Park, and let it be known I advise thee to speak with the guards before thy final departure."

"What guards?" I ask—just three more steps to take before I have a clear path back to Serenity House, or at the very least, to the street where traffic is flowing steadily.

"Your mighty force who wear the star of honor upon their breast."

"The cops?" I'm confused.

"Cops. Yes. Lucas and his band of ruffians are wanted criminals. They dishonor the land and the people of this mighty city."

"Uh-huh," I say slowly and am about to bolt when we're interrupted by a familiar voice.

"Uncle Vincent! Hey. What's up?"

"Ah. My good nephew returns," he says with a wide grin full of stained teeth and turns to someone approaching from the lawn.

Chapter Twelve

"The two most important days in your life are the day you are born and the day you find out why." — Mark Twain

Corban enters the emerald shade beneath the trees and is smiling at the crazy knight in canvas armor. He notices me in the next second and does a double take.

"Tara? I mean not Tara." He squints into the gloom and shakes his head as if clearing the fuzz between his ears.

"He's your uncle?" manages to dribble out of my mouth. I realize I never told him my real name. I only told him it's not Tara.

Corban glances at his uncle and back to me for the third time. "Am I interrupting? Uncle Vince, you look like you're ready for battle."

"Another fine day protecting the land of God. Thy fair maiden was about to be taken by Lucas and his men. I arrived just in time to preserve her honor."

"Lucas Hensley?" Corban asks me.

"You know him?" I ask. The pieces of this ludicrous situation don't fit together. I'm struggling to make sense out of any of it. But Corban just walked into my life again, and it helps calm my frazzled circuits. Seeing Corban is like finding a life raft in a sea of hungry sharks. *God, please don't let Corban be a shark.* After the last couple of days, I'm willing to admit my assessment of people might not be spot on.

"Indeed," Vincent says. "Lucas was leading thy friend into the bowels of debauchery and sin."

Corban's attention flickers back and forth between us. "I know who he is." He answers my question.

Corban walks up to his uncle and hands over a bulging grocery bag. "I brought provisions. Would you mind if I speak to the Lady alone for a minute while you take inventory of the goods?" he asks.

"I believe she is without a chaperone, young Corban. Is it well understood you will protect her honor if I step away to tend to the shipment?"

"Of course, Sir."

"Let us meet by the castle, near the gaming."

"We'll be right there," Corban says.

Vincent is a whirl of dense brown fabric as he takes his leave. The scent of patchouli and camp smoke washes over me as he stalks off through the tall brush near the water's edge.

"He's not that weird once you get used to him."

I cough. "By weird you mean crazy, right?"

"Oh, no, he's crazy," Corban assures me in a backward way I wasn't in any real danger. He continues. "But, he's harmless. Uncle Vincent needs to be this noble knight character most of the time. It's easy to accept after you've spent some time with him."

"Does it fluctuate? I mean, does he ever act normal or closer to normal?" I ask thinking of my mom. I swear she's sane sometimes. It can be so hard to tell the difference because what I think is sane may be her version of crazy. And what if when she's totally flipped her wig is when she's the sanest? I don't understand mental problems, but it's hell living with someone who is never the same person day to day.

"It does. Sometimes he shows up at my parents' house, and he has almost no accent. All the thy and thines are gone, but he's usually depressed without his knight archetype. He's always been in my life so I guess it's hard for me to see him the way outsiders do. He must sound nuts to you."

"Pretty much." I grimace. I don't want to call anyone's family member crazy, but Corban asked, and I'm not going to lie. "I thought he was going to kill me, or that guy, Lucas. He scared the crap out of me with the way he uses his staff."

"Yeah, he's a phenomenal fighter. If the law would let him, he'd carry around a sword, but he knows he'll get arrested for that. I'm glad he stopped you from going with Lucas and Mike. They're a bunch of losers."

I swallow hard at the thought of a sword in Vincent's hand instead of a long stick. He could have taken Lucas's head off, or mine. I begin walking away from the trees toward the sunshine on the path. "What does loser entail?"

"He's a pusher. Heroine, from what I hear."

"Shit."

"It's bad for your health. Not a recommended lifestyle choice," Corban says as if he's talking about smoking cigarettes and not mainlining street drugs. "Hey, check it out." He points across the park toward the side street.

Cops, or the guards as Vincent kept calling them, are working Lucas over. He's currently spread eagle and receiving a pat down. I want to keep staring at the proverbial car wreck where I could so easily be getting searched right alongside him, but I force myself to turn away. I'm not over there. I'm right here thanks to Sir Vincent—and Corban.

"You would be okay," Corban says as if he has a direct connection to my thoughts.

"Yeah, after they looked through all my stuff and run my name in the system."

"True, but there isn't a warrant out for your arrest or anything, is there?"

"No. My record's clean. I was at the station yesterday, but I don't want a repeat visit."

Corban's brows gather, and he stares at me as if he's trying to further tune into my brainwaves.

"Can I please borrow your phone to make a call?" I ask instead of explaining why I was at the cop shop yesterday.

He reaches into his pocket and hands me his phone. As I extend my arm, his gaze lingers on the cuts and bruises on my arm and my swollen elbow.

"Are you still staying at the Quality Lodge?"

I shake my head in answer as I dig out my journal with my phone numbers. We walk down the sidewalk until I stop at a bench and park myself on it. I dial the number and pray the bank is still open. I go through the bits of my story again with a new teller and ask them to change the shipping address to my aunt's apartment. They'll expedite the card, but it's still going to be a few days because of the weekend.

Corban sits down next to me and takes his phone back after I'm finished. I had to send my bank card somewhere besides my mother's. *Why was she such an unreasonable rag? What did she say about Evie?* It doesn't matter. I need to find a way to get to Aunt Summer's.

"So other than being rescued by an eccentric old guy, what are you doing in the city park? What happened last night? And what's wrong with your arm?" His iced peridot green gaze lingers on me, and I shiver despite the heat of the day.

I stand and sling the strap of my bag over my shoulder careful to not pull or tweak any of my sore muscles. "Hey," I say softly, glancing over at Corban for a fleeting second. The crease of concern between his dark brows deepens, and I stare at the shimmering water on the lake's surface instead of his worried face. "My real name is Jasper, okay?"

I can't look at him. He responds with silence. I shuffle the toe of my free shelter shoe around on the concrete sidewalk. The pink daisies and yellow smiley faces printed on the canvas make me want to vomit. These are the most ridiculous shoes I have ever seen. Free vomit-inducing shoes are what every homeless girl needs, right?

"Jasper?"

"Yep."

"Are you joking?"

"No. Why?"

"Nothing," he says.

From my side-eye, I see him looking down at the ground. One of his large hands grips the back of his neck, and his other hand is jammed in the pocket of his black cargo shorts. A white T-shirt and leather boots complete his outfit.

"I'm Corban Duran. It's still nice to meet you whatever your name is." He rises from the bench and continues to rub the back of his neck.

"Tara's my stage name. It seems kind of silly now, but..." I don't want to talk about all the reasons I had for using an alias. It would take too many words to explain it all. The need for a new identity. The anonymity. The fact that I never liked having a boy's name. I'll just bore the crap out Corban, and he's so helpful. I don't want to scare him off.

"I know tons of people with stage names so don't worry about it. If I shared my alias with you, then I'd have to kill you."

"Secret identity, huh?" A smile tugs one side of my mouth.

"You know too much. My position is compromised. This is bad, Tara. I mean Jasper. You might want to start watching your back."

I laugh and bite down on my lip to keep the rest of my emotions from gushing out. I need a little lightening up after everything. "Thanks," I say. "I wanted to tell you my real name. Especially after I yelled at you for calling me Tara." I return to staring across the park, then back down at my cheap canvas shoes.

He leaves a noticeable beat of silence before he asks, "Are you all right?"

"No."

"Because you lost your credit card?"

"Yeah, and the whole mugging thing. It hasn't been a fun forty-eight hours."

"You were mugged?"

"Sort of attacked at gunpoint, but yeah."

"What the shit? I hate this town." He scrubs a hand through his thick black hair.

I glance up from the mocking smiley faces on my shoes when he brushes his hand against my arm.

"When did it happen? Is that why you're not staying at the hotel where I dropped you off?"

"Let's walk." I start moving again. My body needs to be doing something other than standing around like a societal reject.

He matches my pace and gently brushes my shoulder with his, but he doesn't keep the contact for more than a split second. He shoves his hands into his pockets. "Are you feeling the need to run another marathon?"

"Just walking this time." I let out a heavy sigh. "After you dropped me off, I was told the hotel was full. The lady gave me directions to a different one, but I couldn't find it. I sat down at a bus stop and my stuff was stolen by this thug. Then I hid on some playground for the whole night because I got scared. A cop found me the next morning. I guess that was yesterday. Serenity House is letting me stay there because I'm broke, and I can't reach my family." *Jesus.* It sounds horrifying when I say it out loud.

"Why didn't you call me? I gave you my number for a reason, Jasper."

"I lost it. My phone was stolen, but it was dead. I was going to call someone when I realized I was lost, but my service had been shut off. Everything is a fucking mess." I force the tears to stay out of sight.

Corban takes my arm—not the bruised one—but his touch is rougher than necessary. My insides flinch. I can't handle any more trauma. He sees my fear, or feels it, and the pressure of his grip eases. He reels me in and wraps his arms around me. He smells of sunshine and summer and something unnamable but devastatingly familiar. Tension cables replaced the space where my body used to reside. I'm rigid from head to toes, only I didn't know it until this moment. With human arms around me, the comparison between us is night and day. He's strong, but pliable, and warm. I'm weak, fragile, and cold. I resist him, but he won't let go.

"What are you doing?" I ask with mild panic in my voice.

"Letting you know it's not okay. You can't be nearly killed and think no one cares."

He's trembling. I'm trembling. His hold on me grows tighter.

"Fuck…," he says under his breath. "I shouldn't have left you."

"You don't even know me," I whisper and grip his T-shirt in my fists.

"I don't care about that. You matter, Jasper. I know you well enough to know you fucking matter in this world. This shouldn't have happened."

He's ripping off the blindfold and forcing me to see it all afresh. *Do I matter?* I couldn't even tell my family what happened. My mom and Geoff would somehow manage to twist it around so it was my fault. They would point out I was all alone in a city I don't know by my own doing. That I'm screwing up my life, and there's no one to blame but myself. *Shit.* I almost took off with a heroine dealer. My eyelids shake as I cling to Corban and sort through my uncertainties.

I don't know how long he lets me use him as an anchor to this world, but eventually, I choke out the words, "I can't do this."

He loosens his hold and backs up a half step, but he keeps his hands connected to the tops of my shoulders. Corban's wicked eyes are the color of sun-washed daydreams. They're molten green gemstones, lively, and full of depth. They give him an air of wisdom and understanding. It unnerves me, but I can't look away as he stares into my heart.

"You're taking this better than anyone I can imagine. How are you this strong?"

"What other choice is there?"

He shakes his head ever so slightly like he's either in disbelief or disagrees with my perception of isolation.

"There are always choices. We do our best, and it's all we can do. Don't doubt yourself."

I finally turn away from his crazy-intense eyes. I stare at the wrinkles in his shirt. I had been gripping it hard enough to leave lines like cracks in glass.

"My best is pretty awful lately."

"I doubt that. Come on. You like to keep moving." He drops his hands from my shoulders, and he reaches into his pocket. Just the left one. He moves around me and starts walking.

"How do you know that about me?" I ask as I stumble behind him.

"I pay attention." Corban stops and removes his closed fist from his pocket. He lifts his hand up as if he's going to hand me something. "I, umm…"

"What?"

His hand disappears back inside his pocket. "Never mind."

Whatever he was about to say gets shaken off, and he adds, "You said you're having your debit card sent to Chicago. Do you need a ride?"

"It's at least a fifteen-hour drive."

"Yeah. So?"

"So, I was going to call my aunt and ask her to buy me a bus ticket."

"You can call if you want, but I'll drive you. Then you won't need to wait for a bus, which may not be heading to Illinois until who knows when. And you're strapped, so how will you eat?"

"There's food at the shelter, and they're willing to let me sleep there until I work this mess out."

Corban slides a glance over to me from the corner of his eye. "Has anyone ever told you, you're stubborn? Like over-the-top hard-headed. I mean your skull is so thick, I think it's a solid mass."

I lick my lips and work them back and forth for a few seconds as I try to find the answer I need without sounding even more immovable. "I like to do things my way, but it doesn't mean I'm stubborn."

"Bah...humph." Corban makes this double sound of disbelief that is half snort and half groan. "I'll drive you to Chicago. I have the next three days off from work."

"I can't let you do that, and I don't even know you. What if you're worse than Lucas, and I'm making another potentially horrendous life-altering error in judgment?"

He gives me an assessing look and a half-hearted shrug. "I guess that's fair. I can't prove anything about who I am other than what you see standing next to you. And what I've done to help you out. But if you want to stay at the shelter and wait for a bus that's up to you."

"Honestly, I was considering hitchhiking. It would be faster than taking the bus." A red Frisbee skids over the sidewalk and into the rubber sole of my shoe. The words, 'Peace & Love', and 'Ultimate Freedom', are printed in bold white letters on the top of the disc. I bend down and pick it up and the word 'Freedom' miraculously changes to 'Frisbee'. I blink at the message a few times and take a second to wonder if all signs and messages are oddly skewed by what my brain wants to see rather than what is really there. A little girl runs up to me to retrieve her disc.

"Sorry," she says and skips off across the Kelly-green lawn.

"Hitchhiking with a complete stranger is a way better idea than riding with me." Corban lets the sarcasm roll off his tongue.

Snapping out of my mind funk, I blink back into the previous topic. "I said I was thinking about it, not that I was going to do it. Life just slapped me down, and I'm not thinking as clearly as I should be."

He stuffs his left hand in his pocket and raises a wary brow.

"If I get a ride from a stranger heading in that direction, there's no guilt about bothering someone. Does that make any sense?"

"No. There's no guilt, Jasper. I'm offering to drive you to your aunt's house Scott-free. I don't want anything from you in return. It's a completely free ride. Take it or leave it, but if something else happens to you when I could ensure your safety, I'll be living with the guilt for the rest of my life."

I swing my arm and lightly smack his stomach with the back of my hand. "I thought you just said there would be no guilt," I say with a roll of my eyes and a bemused smile.

"I said you shouldn't feel guilty for mooching a ride from me. It's entirely free for you. I'm saying if something else happens to you after crossing paths with me again, I'll have some serious culpability sitting on my shoulders."

"You think we've run into each other again for a reason. Like a higher power at work or something?" I ask.

"There are no coincidences. You need a ride, and I own a vehicle, and I'm not working until Tuesday night. The only higher power at work here is the universe fulfilling the never ending supply and demand."

He pauses as I digest his philosophy about the universe.

"Still think you're going to wait for a bus?"

"I think I need to call my aunt before I answer you. I haven't talked to her yet."

Corban whips out his phone and passes it to me. "I need to spend a minute with my uncle. He's over there." Corban points with his chin toward some people playing chess and other table games near the wood castle playground. His uncle is sitting with a group of shabby-looking men who are busy eating and drinking the food from the grocery bag Corban brought.

"Take your time," he says.

"Thank you." I wish my overflowing gratitude could be felt by his heart as well as heard by his ears.

Corban jogs over to his uncle leaving me alone to make my call.

Chapter Thirteen

"Open my eyes and let me see the truth in all things."
— J. Pyrah

"Hello?"

"Hi, Aunt Summer. It's Jasper."

"Your mom called me a little while ago. Are you okay, sweetie? She was pretty upset."

"I broke up with Keel." It darts out of my mouth like a slippery fish, gone in a flash. Out into the waters of Lake Can't-Take-It-back.

"She didn't tell me," Aunt Summer says on the other end.

"She doesn't know. Please don't tell her."

"I won't," she assures me. "She said you were planning to come see me. Is that true? Where are you?"

"I'm in Denver. I, umm...got mugged. Pretty much everything I had with me is gone."

"Oh my god. How awful. Are you hurt? Was anyone with you?"

That's a lot of questions, but I don't mind answering my aunt like I do my mother. It's different with her. She won't use what I say against me in the future.

"I was alone. I think I'm okay. It's been hectic, but I'm okay," I say it again like repeating myself might make it true.

"Well, what can I do to help?" she asks.

Her offer deflates some of the anxiety. "Can I stay with you until I figure out where I want to go?"

"Yeah, of course. I'd come pick you up, but Finn took the car until next week. He's working a job in Atlanta. I've been riding my bike or taking the L."

"Hmmm..." I murmur. "If you can buy me a bus ticket, I'll pay you back."

"Ahh, the bus," she says as if this is a good second option. "I can get you a ticket after work tonight. It won't be until late, though. I just got here, and I'm working both shows, then I carpool home with a friend around midnight. Can I call you at this number after I check the bus schedule?"

"Actually, no. This isn't my phone."

"Are you staying with friends?"

"No."

"Where can I reach you? Or, do you want to call me in the morning? I'm sure I can find a ticket by then, and all you'll need to do is get to the station."

I glance over at Corban. His eccentric uncle Vincent circles his arm around Corban's neck in a chokehold and he's more or less giving him a noogie. Corban is all smiles, and he laughs as he pulls an expert-looking move on his uncle by twisting out of the hold and jumping over a table to escape Vincent's incredibly quick reflexes.

"You know what, Aunt Summer, I think I can get a ride. Forget about the bus."

"Are you sure?"

"I'm sure. Keep this number, though, okay? It belongs to my friend, Corban. He'll be the one driving me. I'll call if anything changes."

"All right. I can do that. Oh! Gotta go, Jas. I'm at the theater, and someone needs me. You know how it is."

I do, and I know how hard my aunt works for the company as head of the costume and wardrobe department. "Okay. I'll leave you a message when I know what time I'll be there."

"Be safe and I'll see you soon."

Corban sits down across from his uncle as I approach the table. The staff rests near Vincent like an innocent walking stick, but I notice it's within reach of Vincent's hand.

"Thy fair maiden graces us once more with her lovely presence. What say thee regarding thy plans for traveling east?"

"I say," I hesitate and watch Corban's face as I tell him my decision. If he looks regretful, I'll take it back. "If you're still willing to give me a ride, I...umm could really use it."

"Yeah. Sure," he says.

A smile is hidden somewhere in his full lips, and there's a hint of excitement behind his faceted silvery-green eyes as if the sun were reflecting off his irises. His gaze shifts, breaking eye contact with me. He's staring across the acres of lawn at my back. I'm about to tell him to forget it and seek out the bus station when he refocuses on me and gives me an actual full smile.

His phone buzzes in my hand, and I pass it over to him. He glances down at the screen and says, "I can take you tonight." His sparkle seems to diminish ever so slightly. "But I need to take care of something this afternoon before we leave."

He rises from the bench and comes around the table, stuffing his phone in his pocket.

"Tonight's fine." I'm hoping to ease the sudden stress on his face.

"We could go now, but I have a commitment. It's..." He shakes his head and doesn't finish the sentence.

I shrug. "No problem. If you want to skip the road trip, I understand."

"I want to go. I just need to take care of this thing first."

"Sir Corban hath fulfill his noble duties to the lady whom—"

"Who needs me for a few hours today." Corban cuts off his uncle.

He turns around to face Vincent, and also conveniently hides his expression from me.

"We can leave whenever you want," I say.

"You can hang out with Uncle Vincent, and I'll be back as soon as I can." He turns back around and takes out the phone he just stuffed into his pocket and places it in my hand.

I'm reluctant to take it, but he wraps my fingers around it. "If you need me before I return, just call my mom. She's in my phonebook under Mom. She knows how to reach me."

I can't help myself. "Your mom?" I smile at how easy it is for him to turn to his mommy.

"Yeah," he says with an unembarrassed grin. "She's cool. Her name is Jili. She can find me anywhere."

"I'm not sure I should take your phone," I say, holding it out to him.

He steps back. "Keep it. That way you know I'm coming back to pick you up."

I glance down at the expensive-looking smartphone in my hand and think about all the things that can go wrong if I'm being held responsible for it.

"You might need it. The battery should be charged," he says in a way which somehow reflects back to what happened the last time he left me alone.

Corban moves to his uncle's side and leans in close to his ear. Words are exchanged between them, but I can't hear. He stops next to me again before leaving the park. "In case I'm delayed, I'll call you. And Vincent will keep you company, all right?"

I try not to look too dubious at the prospect of spending the afternoon with a middle-aged medieval knight in canvas armor. No words come to assist my reservations.

"My uncle's a good guy. I swear it. I'm sorry I have to leave. This appointment's been scheduled for a long time." He seems regretful.

His left hand is stuffed inside his pocket again, and I can't help but wonder why he keeps doing that. Is it a nervous tick or something?

"Don't apologize. You're helping me out, and I appreciate it. I'll be fine." I hold up the phone to reassure him.

Corban catches his bottom lip with his teeth for a second, then gives a sharp nod of agreement. He takes off toward the parking lot.

"Would milady prefer to stay and observe court or would thee enjoy an outing by the water?" Vincent is on his feet with his hand over his heart.

With a sigh of resignation, I walk over to the table and sit on the bench. "Court looks entertaining. What's everyone playing?" I ask as I contemplate the men and their card game.

"Tis' a game of wit," one bearded, crusty-looking man says.

"And a bit of luck," his opponent adds.

"It's Ninety-Nine, and if your memory is as bad as Dallas here, you'll never win a hand."

Vincent sidles up next to me. "After a round is played a new rule is added. Therefore, the game usually ends when we no longer recall the beginning rules. We argue over who is the biggest bootless beggar and call it a day."

"We're in round seven now, and Clark already forgets you can't draw a new card when you play a four," Dallas tells me.

"I'm quite a worthy opponent for a game of Ninety-Nine. Would you care to play the next round? My acquaintances and I welcome a lady such as yourself to the table."

"I think I'll watch for a while before I decide whether I can handle playing a memory game."

"Very well." He takes a seat at the table with the other three players.

The men take turns laying down a card on the table and calling out a number. The number ascends and they don't go above ninety-nine. Then the round is finished. The third man grins in triumph as he is the last man standing—so to speak—since his buddies had to drop out because of going over the ninety-nine total.

He says, "The next rule is, if you play a queen, you must compliment the lady in the manner of Sir Vincent here. No modern peasant English to herself."

The groans equal the laughs. Dallas mumbles under his breath a list of complicated rules. "Play a two and take two turns. Threes change direction. Fours don't pick up a card. Nines say a Spanish curse word. Jacks change direction again. Queens medieval compliment. Black Kings add twenty points. Red Kings subtract ten."

The number of rules staggers my mind, and I watch in anticipation to see if the players can pull it off. The game is simple and complicated—if that's possible—and lively entertainment. I'm treated to one, "Milady is as lovely as a rose in her majesty's garden," and a stammering Clark tells me he is, "most humbled to be in the presence of such a beautiful and delicate young lass on a fine summer day such as this."

His compliment earns him a smack on the back of his head by Vincent. "Are ye' brain boiled, you dirty scoundrel? You do not address the fine lady as lass. I call him out. He's broken a rule."

The others share looks of amusement, but they consider whether or not Clark broke a rule by not getting his dialect quite right.

The blush warming my cheeks flares hotter when the third man—I didn't hear his name—says it's my call whether or not Clark gets to continue playing.

I swallow hard. "Leniency shall be granted," I manage. "Can you eliminate the other queens from the deck?" I add. *How did I wind up in the middle of this?* I think to myself even though the game is helping take my mind off my other problems.

"Absolutely not," Vincent says.

Thankfully, no more queens are played for this round, and as they approach a total of ninety, the arguing starts over who is forgetting what rule and by the end they decide the game is over. They start from scratch and play a couple of rounds while I watch.

Afterward, the men lean back, stretch, and begin packing up the leftovers from lunch. They clean up the trash and stash away their water bottles and other belongings inside their packs.

"Thank Corban for the chicken, would you, Sir Vincent?" Dallas says.

"Aye. He'll be along next Saturday, and you can tell him yourself," Vincent replies.

"I will. And let's play rummy tomorrow. Ninety-nine scrambles my brains."

"An egg scramble does you well, sir."

He shakes his head. Whether to clear his brain or in disagreement with Vincent, I can't say. Dallas turns his focus to me. "Nice meeting you."

"You too," I say. It's either Dallas's red shirt or his twiggy straw-colored hair, but I'm suddenly reminded of the homeless man on the beach back in San Diego. I should have stood up to Keel and checked if the man was okay. Letting the past lay still and silent, I shake off the memory.

The men disband and soon it's only Vincent and I and the chatter and giggle of the children on the nearby playground. The squeak of swaying chains on the swing set, the occasional scent of sunscreen wafting over from attentive parents and the heat of the day provides a soothing summer atmosphere. On any other day of my life, this combination would be the ideal recipe for chilling out and relaxing—and watching Jonah play. Only today I can't begin to reach that state of mind. The Frisbee told me Peace, Love, and Freedom but all I can think about is what's needed to put my life back in order.

I take a deep breath and stare at Corban's ominously black and silent screen. *When is he coming back?* Waiting is becoming fingernails on the chalkboard of my existence.

"Innocence is a lovely state of being. Those young ones are in the midst of their innocence, and yet they know not what they have," Vincent says from his side of the table.

"Until it's gone," I add my own ending to Vincent's observation.

"Ah. Milady's keen mind compliments her gracious manner."

I raise a doubtful brow. "You're very kind, Sir. Vincent. I doubt I deserve such high praise."

"Verily you do and more. You are still but young and know not who you are. There comes a time in every life when innocence falls away and searching for the truth becomes your mission. Perhaps milady hath breached the walls of the kingdom within but still dares not cross over them."

To say speaking with Sir. Vincent is rather strange would be putting it mildly, but in for a penny in for a pound. I go with it and follow where this conversation leads. It's not like I didn't grow up around a cast of characters. Being surrounded by the weird and unusual is more normal than not. Why I find today's company surprising at all is rather presumptuous. "I may be walking the top of the ramparts and don't know which side I want to be on," I admit.

"Knowing yourself is the beginning of all wisdom. You stay on the ramparts, milady, as long as it takes," Vincent says from his corner of the table.

I glance over to my knight in homeless attire, and he's staring at me, or maybe through me.

"Does it take long?" The question spills from my mouth.

"Does it take long? Bah!" His tone is somewhat condescending. He scratches his rough beard. "Do you know who spoke those words?"

"No."

"The fine and memorable, Aristotle."

"I haven't studied him," I say.

"'Tis a shame, indeed. He had a valuable mind, well worth examination. Perhaps studying the masters will help you find your way? But, as he said, knowing yourself is the beginning of all wisdom. The search continues as long as there is blood beating in thy heart and breath passing thy lips."

"Hmm." My response is noncommittal.

"Corban speaks of recent troubles crossing your path."

"They have." I'm wary of where this conversation has turned.

"Life doesn't fall into place one picture-perfect scene after another. There is no painting of life hanging on a wall inside the castle for you to mimic, milady." Vincent picks up the playing cards on the table and slips them out of their box and into his thick hands. He turns around on the bench and hurls them across the lawn.

A flurry of black, white, and red numbers and symbols scatter in all directions.

"That chaotic disaster is your life. It is everyone's. You pick it up because no one will do it for you the way you need them to. You must take one step at a time as you build a tidy stack in your hand again. Maybe you trip over your own foot—perhaps someone else's if you are careless—and the cards become chaos over the ground once more."

He snorts, then wipes the back of his hand under his nose. Not deterred in the least by this, he rubs the smudge on his not-so-clean pants. "This is what life is. Order within the disorder, circling around and around. The frown upon thy face is uncalled for. For, you see, it is a beautiful cycle."

I watch Vincent for a long, penetrating moment, then look back at the disarray of playing cards on the grass. A sudden breeze blows the cards across the lawn tumbling them like leaves in a shifting wind. It isn't beautiful to think the cards of my life are under the control of an unseen force. That I can suddenly be picked up and tossed aside at any second. Surely life can't blow me down on a whim—when I pull myself back together, I'm only preparing to fall instantly apart again.

"Being scattered wherever the wind blows isn't the life I choose."

"Is that so?" he asks.

Do I detect a hint of disdain in his words? "Are you telling me I have no control over my future?"

"You maintain complete control as you restack the deck."

"But I lose control when someone knocks me aside." I'm trying to understand his point of view.

"I admit there are forces stronger than us. Perhaps, milady, I am but suggesting you do not hand over your deck of playing cards to just anyone who comes along, but keep them for thyself."

I screw up my face for a moment, letting the thought sink in.

"Every person finds a time when trouble and heartache rule the happenings of daily life. It is so. In thy present as it was in thy past. The circling of the sun has not altered much over the last thousand years."

"Do you pick up your cards and make yourself whole again?" I ask.

He chuckles and licks dry, cracked lips. "Oh, but I do. You are witness to myself in the stage when I travel with the winds. 'Tis the most surreal place I've ever been. If you never reach the bottom how will you know what the top looks like? Be grateful, Lady Jasper. You're visiting the pits of hell while you're young. It is far easier to pull thyself up when there are not so many creaks and aches in thy tired, old bones."

I stare at the trees growing by the lakeside and their branches swaying over the water. Vincent is giving me advice I can understand, but not wholly comprehend. He isn't so old, is he? It's hard to say if he's in his forties or fifties, but living on the streets can make anyone appear older than they are. I move from the bench and retrieve the cards before they're lost. He thinks repairing a life while you're young is easier than when you're older, and he's probably right, but at the moment, nothing about my damaged life feels easy.

When I hold a neat stack in my hands, Vincent says, "It is the mark of an educated mind to be able to entertain a thought without accepting it."

"Aristotle?" I venture.

"Indeed."

***

Hanging out with Sir Vincent is bizarrely eye-opening and not unpleasant. He's somewhat gruff, but sincere. By evening, I need to check in at Serenity House. I also need to notify them I'm leaving.

Vincent walks me to the fenced patio behind the shelter and bows over my hand. It's all very formal and strange, so I wait for him to rise and give him a quick hug and thank him for saving me from the drug dealer in the park.

"Farewell, Lady Jasper." He spins around, coat billowing and strolls down the alley, staff in hand.

Inside, I make all the necessary arrangements, say goodbye to Mrs. Choo, and go sit outside to wait for Corban. He said he'd return by evening, and it's now a little past seven. After forty-five more minutes and no phone calls from Corban, I start to worry—like for real. A staff member eventually steps outside and tells me they are locking the doors for the night, and I should come in.

I glance down at the screen on Corban's phone and wonder if it's working. My trust is about as flimsy as gossamer, and my hesitations are even more wobbly. How well do I know Corban? Hardly at all, and yet I was willing to believe he would be back to pick me up.

I haven't eaten since breakfast, and my stomach constricts at the smell wafting out of Serenity House. It reminds me of school cafeteria food, but it's one hundred percent better than nothing. I rise from the bench and shoulder my bag, reassuring myself he's on his way. He's just running late. And what's the worst that can happen? I wind up sleeping at the shelter for one more night. A near panic attack almost sends me running down the alley when another woman trudges her miserable-looking self into the building. *What if*

I'm saying those words every night for another week? Don't panic, I tell myself. This is temporary. One minute, one hour, one day at a time. I'm not homeless, I'm just picking up a card.

I grip the door and stall out. The other stragglers disappear within the confines of Serenity House. *Breathe Jasper. You can make it through another night. When you make it to Aunt Summer's, you can rest.* I glance back toward the alley and over at the parking lot. There's no black Toyota 4-Runner.

To the dining room, I go. The walls aren't closing in on me, and the floor isn't falling. There are no haunting playing cards blowing down the hallway, and I'm not courting depression or even asking it out on a date. I'm simply walking numbly through my current life and wishing reality would bend to my will.

"There you are, Ms. Pyrah. I was just coming on back to find you." Lucille Choo waddles toward me. "There's a visitor for you at the front desk. And we're kicking him out in exactly," she pauses to look down at the watch strangling her chubby wrist. "Well, missy, in fact, right now."

"I better see who it is," I say and hurry down the corridor.

For the most fleeting moment, I imagine Keel waiting for me. He used to meet me after school or come pick me up at home. Those moments when I would anticipate seeing his face after a long day, or need him to be there when Geoff was completely unbearable, used to get me through the week. I would picture him waiting for me, all arrogance and guitar-wielding sexiness, and every shard of stress would fall away. Those daydreams of Keel kept me going more times than I like to admit. The warm caress of hope-filled memories passes in the next second as I find Corban waiting for me at the front entrance.

I'm relieved to see him and also scared shitless. Here's another boy in my life, rescuing me. If hell is a downward spiral of the same mistakes wearing a different face, I don't want the express ticket. I don't want to be saved by a cute guy every time I'm in trouble. Yet, here he stands.

I smile at him, but I know the look on my face is pathetic, wary, and cheerless.

"Hey," I say and hand over his phone.

"Are you hungry?"

"Yes." This time, the smile is genuine. "I'm starved."

"Good. I am too. Are you ready to go?"

"No."

His eyebrows dip with concern.

"I'm sorry," I say quickly. "I meant, yes. I'm so ready to get out of here." *He's not rescuing me. I'm saving myself this time.*

Chapter Fourteen

"We heal by remembering. And the memories are as potent as the incident which created them." — J. Pyrah

Corban takes us through a drive-thru.

We eat fast food and drink milkshakes while cruising down the interstate at eighty miles an hour. Exhaustion jumps on my bandwagon joining the carbs and sugar, and a nap pulls me under...

Sometime in early spring:

In the middle of an exceptional plate of spaghetti—one of the few meals my mom cooked well enough that everyone gorged themselves on it—my mother's husband decided he would like to prove for the thousandth time what a gargantuan prick he is.

Let me go back to the spaghetti and why Geoff is my mother's husband and not my father, stepfather, dad, or any other name by which to associate myself with the king of all the worthless assholes running around in this world.

So, yeah, I was high from smoking pot with my boyfriend twenty minutes before I sat down to eat dinner with my so-called family. This is in part why the homemade sauce, the recipe for which has been passed down through generations of tomato sauce-obsessed women, slathered over a heaping pile of steaming pasta was so extra extraordinary. It tantalized my taste buds and fulfilled every munchies-induced fantasy brought on by my syndrome, otherwise known as being stoned.

Geoff sat at the end of the table barely touching his food because he didn't care much for "red sauce". It always annoyed the crap out of me that the man couldn't call it spaghetti, or tomato sauce like the rest of the known universe, but I sort of figured it was his ignorant redneck side peeking through, and he just couldn't help himself. To annoy me further, he wasn't even eating pasta with the rest of us. His spaghetti sauce was on top of sautéed squash. Because, you know, carbs make you fat and blah, blah, blah. In all honesty, his health food lectures ultimately made me want to eat more junk food. Looking back, I wish I had just inhaled dinner and gone straight to my room, or better yet, taken the next space shuttle to Venus rather than sit there and attempt to eat civilly. It was the only meal my mother had cooked all week, and I wanted to eat it. My mouth watered the second I walked in the door. There was even a heaping pile of garlic bread, and I was so ready to indulge in a real dinner.

We sat at the kitchen table. The three kids, Evie, Jonah and I, Geoff and Mom. I was trying my hardest to not appear high. I didn't talk much and tried to avoid pissing off Geoff or arousing suspicion from my mom. She never seemed to know when I smoked, or if she knew, it didn't bother her enough to talk about. I kind of assumed that she's so caught up in the drama of her own life she doesn't notice the subtle changes in me and my siblings unless blood or screaming is involved. Screaming would be involved shortly. I'll get to that part in a minute.

I was half aware of Evie's nervousness. The way she kept throwing wide-eyed covert glances at me, but I didn't want to think about how bad it had been while I was out with Keel.

Then good ol' Geoff said something like, "Someone better shut that damn dog up."

Being engrossed in my spaghetti, I didn't even hear Ollie barking until Geoff mentioned it. There were always dogs barking in our crammed tract-home neighborhood. Ollie is a nickname for Olivia, my pure white Husky. My mom let the three of us keep her after we found her as a stray and no one ever showed up to claim her. It was right after we moved into Geoff's dead dad's house. Ollie was still a puppy back then, and I think even my mom couldn't resist her sweet kisses, soft white fur, and howling songs when emergency vehicles drove by. Geoff was against having a dog, but we were four against one, and we actually got to keep her. Ollie bonded with me more than anyone else in the family. I can't say why other than I loved her more and she knew she was my savior.

Olivia was not made to live in the desert heat, so I kept her inside the house with me as much as possible. When I left for school or went out with Keel, I never knew what Ollie was up to. Geoff liked to tie her up to a cable in the backyard which is where she currently was barking as if an intruder was trying to break into the house next door or some other shenanigans which might simply involve a rogue squirrel. My dog isn't a barking machine. She howls occasionally, but she only barks when it's serious. Apparently, squirrels and rabbits are serious business when you're a dog. I never held it against her.

I rose from the table to peer out of the kitchen window into the backyard. I tried to see what was making her so upset. I squinted across the yard, the marijuana-induced fuzzy coating running through my bloodstream, and wished I could finish my spaghetti before it got cold. It was hard to see Ollie around the trampoline and the platform for the low wire, but there was plainly a new hole in the yard because of the fresh dirt scattered on top of the trampoline. Stoned as I was, I stood there trying to picture how my dog had managed to toss dirt up that high in the air when I heard the screen door slam open.

Before the resounding crack of the door closed, I glanced at the table and saw Geoff missing. Running outside after him, I went straight for Ollie forgetting that only a second before I was thinking it was going to be funny whatever she had gotten into.

"Stop!" I screamed as Geoff stormed around the trampoline to where Ollie was tied by the storage shed. "Don't touch her!"

I knew it was going to be bad before he said or did anything. It was a feeling in my gut like ropes twisting beyond their limits. His fury was obvious in the set of his jaw and the way the muscles of his shoulders were bunched into hard lumps. An explosion was about to happen.

He ignored my screams, so I ran to get between him and her. Ollie barked at the shed, fixed on getting her point across. A mound of dirt sat in a heap next to where she had dug the hole. Loose gravel and earth covered the back of the yard. I think I saw the damage to the shed about the same time as Geoff. The wood trim above the hole in the ground had been clawed at and gnawed until there was a gash in the small building.

Ollie remained oblivious to my panic as we approached. I had to get to her before Geoff. It was her only hope. I'd seen my stepfather angry more times than I could count and I know when to duck and run, but I wouldn't abandon my dog to his wrath. He was going for her at full steam ahead.

My dog is only a dog, and she couldn't turn off her hunting instincts just because Geoff didn't want to hear it. Olivia ducked her head into the hole beneath the ruined trim on the shed and started tearing up the ground and sending fresh sprays of dirt flying across the yard. Her tail wagged furiously as she tried to get to some animal or some other enticement. Maybe she was having a spaghetti moment. She looked about as happy as I had been only minutes before when I scooped steaming sauce onto my plate. But all Geoff saw was the damage, and all he heard was her loud incessant woofing.

"Ollie! Stop!" I said as I ran between her butt sticking up in the air and my enraged stepdad. "Don't!" I shrieked at Geoff before he said or did anything. "I'll fix it!" I defended. "Don't touch her!"

I swear his eyes became the windows to hell. A black vengeance resided inside him, and it didn't matter what I said or did. He was going to kill Ollie for tearing up the yard and destroying the side of the shed.

I turned to grab my dog and pull her away, but as I reached for her, Geoff's muscular hand swatted me away like an annoying gnat and left me on my ass.

I cried out more from shock than pain, but then I screamed in horror as Ollie was flung through the air by her cable. The yelp of surprise and hurt that came out of my dog caused a piece of me to break. It was only a small click somewhere inside my chest as my faith in mankind cracked.

Geoff wasn't done. I scrambled to get to Ollie, but she was on the far side of her cable, and he was between us. Before I could take her next punishment for her, he closed the few steps between my beautiful husky and himself. She was cowering at the end of her cable shaking with fear. He bent down and grabbed her by the throat and squeezed.

"Shut up, you worthless piece of shit!" he roared.

She lay on her back and pee trickled out of her terrified body. Her eyes bulged from the pressure. I wanted to murder him, and I think I would have tried if I had a weapon in my hand, but I felt as helpless as Ollie, and all I could do was scream hysterically.

He released her and turned to me. "You're getting rid of this damned animal, or I'll bury her in the hole she dug."

I couldn't look at him. All I could do was lean over Olivia and offer the comfort of my voice and my hands. She started seizing a few seconds later. Her body convulsed and neither of us could make it stop.

That's the last time I ever smoked pot and also the last day Ollie lived at our house.

***

I wake from the dream, which was a memory, or a dream of a memory. I turn my face into the seat. My cheeks are wet, and my body trembles. I squeeze my eyelids shut as tight as I can. It's painful, but I refuse to let up. If I squeeze out the world, maybe it will cease to exist. Maybe Ollie never lived in our backyard, and I never had to give her up to the neighbors. Maybe I'm not flying down the interstate toward a destination unknown. I don't want to look at Corban because I don't want to answer any questions. What if I cried out in my sleep? Crying in my sleep isn't the impression I want to leave on him.

***

Corban is different than other guys. It's a serious turn on. He's hard to describe, but he doesn't fit into any box. Plus, I don't need to act any certain way around him. It disconcerts me, and I was used to playing the concert in a certain way. A familiar way. He is unfamiliar. His style makes me curious, but also on edge. Have I been around dysfunction so long I can't recognize a normal person when I meet one? It's a possibility which definitely has possibilities.

He looks at me, and I want to hide, but I also want to dance.

"That good huh?" he asks.

My insecurities are making me put up shields. My mouth betrays me and clams up so I can only mumble something incoherent. I'm surprised he hasn't given me a w.t.f. stare and made up some excuse about how he has to go home and floss his pet turtle's teeth.

Do turtles have teeth?

Corban would know. He's intelligent like that. My community college education, all two semesters of it, is most likely severely lacking compared to his university experience. Maybe my community college offers an introductory course called *Basic*

Abilities and Necessary Skills to Act Less Asshat-ish In Public. I should have signed up for that class before today.

I don't make eye contact, but I can tell he's keeping his eyes on the road. Swallowing before I answer takes some work, but I manage. "It was just a dream," I lie.

"Sort of like this is just a quick drive across town to a friend's house."

"Yeah, like that."

"Cool," he says, and that's the end of it.

No pressure to explain the tears or anything else I said or did in my sleep.

"Sleep it off and try not to worry about it."

I recline the seat back, turn on my side and follow his suggestion. A minute later something soft is laid over me. My eyes crack open, and I see Corban's sweatshirt. The extra layer of warmth is welcome and so appreciated. I tuck my hands under my cheek and slip into a thankfully dreamless sleep.

***

"Where are we?"

"The circus for miscreants of misnomers," Corban says.

In my current state of being half asleep, I don't fully comprehend what he said. I try again. "What are we doing?" I ask, blinking my tired eyes into focus. The clock on the dash reads 11:11. The multi-colored lights of a carnival flash and bend reality for a few seconds too long. I look over at Corban and shut out the distracting disco lights outside of his SUV.

"I had an idea. This should only take a few minutes." He checks his phone.

"Where are we *really*?" I ask again.

"The Scarberry Carnival."

"Do you need your fix of funnel cakes and whirlygigs?"

"Not exactly." He stops texting and levels his gaze on me.

A twitch of amusement plays with the corner of his eye, but he otherwise doesn't elaborate on why we're here.

"Want to come with me, or would you like to wait out here?"

I run my hands down the tops of my thighs. "I'll come," I say. "I need to walk around and stretch."

We've been on the road for a few hours and moving around should help ease the sense of confinement inside the SUV. But a simple walk around a street carnival won't get me far enough away from the memories of Geoff and Ollie.

Corban pops his door open, and I do the same. We walk up to the main entrance and stop by the gate. Scarberry Carnival looks like the classic traveling carnival. It's the kind of transient entertainment that takes up residence in an undeveloped city lot or unused parking area for two or three days and then disappears as if they had never been there to begin with. I understand this kind of life all too well, and the smell of popcorn, corndogs, asphalt, and mechanical grease is a reminder of my home before my life broke.

"Do you have a lot of nightmares?" he asks without explaining why we're hanging out in the shadows of the main entrance.

"No." I push the toe of my hideous shoe around on the lot. Should I explain more or should I leave him wondering?

"Were you being swallowed by a giant venomous snake?" he asks. "That's what my nightmares are about."

"No," I say again. "Why snakes?" I ask.

His shoulders rise and fall in a shrug. "I don't think we choose our nightmares. Otherwise, I'd dream of being swallowed by a giant wormhole filled with down feathers to an alternate universe."

"Do alternate universes exist? Because if they do, I'm coming with you."

"Sounds like our next road trip." He stuffs his left hand in his pocket.

I smile and hide my eyes below my lashes, purposely avoiding looking down at my free shelter shoes.

"Corban," someone says, walking up to us.

"Hey, what's up, Terryn?" Corban steps forward into the ring of light cast by the ticket booth.

"Marjorie sent me out to walk you in. She's dealing with some work thing and couldn't come herself. Come with me." He waves a hand for Corban to follow.

"I brought a friend," Corban says.

"Sure. Whatever," Terryn says.

Terryn walks ahead of us and doesn't say much as he takes us inside the fence, through the midway, and past a few rides. We walk around the fun house to an appendage sticking off the back. It looks like an office trailer. There are three steps leading up to the door and a small lit window to the right.

Raised voices drift out of the open window, and Terryn stops by the stairs.

"Let me see if she's ready for you," he says.

The office is so tiny I wonder if we will all fit inside.

"I can come back later," Corban offers.

"Nah. She'll be done yelling in a minute. Maxim's just getting his nightly ass chewing. No big deal."

"If you say so," Corban says.

Terryn jogs up the steps and pounds on the door. "Hey, Marj, Corban's here."

His radio begins spewing a frantic message about power being off in the fried cheesecake booth.

"That's my department. Catch up with you later." He nods at Corban and trots off in the direction of the food booths.

A second later the door flings open and a bald Hispanic-looking man with tattoos all over his arms and neck stomps down the stairs. "Besame el culo!"

"Bend over pendejo and I will! I'll kiss your lazy ass with my boot!" the person inside the office yells back.

Maxim waves his middle finger in the air toward the window as he exits stage left. I take a few wary steps back and wait for whatever's coming next.

"Corban, I know you're out there. Get in here before I drag you in by your bootstraps."

Corban hops up the steps, light on his toes, and stands in the doorway. "Marjorie, your hostile timbre is music to my ears. God, I've missed your sultry Hispanic curses."

"Quit slinging the shit shovel in my face and tell me why you're two hours from home pestering me."

"Didn't you miss me?" Corban sounds hurt. "Never mind. Maxim's giving you a run for your money."

"He is," Majorie's voice drifts out the open door softer now but still loud.

I edge closer to the stairs and peer into the glow of the office. Around the side of Corban, all I see is her long muscular arm and the cut off sleeve of a flannel shirt.

"Fucking cara de culo."

"So, I take it he's your new guy," Corban says.

This is followed by a loud and rather masculine laugh. "Yeah. I love that bitch. He'll be back in a minute to make up with me."

"Don't let me keep you, Marj, I just stopped by to say hi and ask you about your brother. My friend is with me too. We're headed to Chicago."

Marjorie rises from the desk and walks over to the door. Corban steps out on the landing at the top of the steps, and Marjorie follows him outside.

"Bob's doing great," she says to Corban as she clunks down the stairs wearing heavy work boots.

She extends her hand to me before even finding the pavement. "Marjorie Scarberry. Nice to meet you."

"Jasper Pyrah." I smile into her beseeching brown eyes.

"Pyrah? Related to Autumn Pyrah?"

"Umm, she's my mom? She's Autumn Holsteen now, and Mr. Pyrah hasn't been around for a long time. Do you know my parents?" I ask with prickles of caution raising gooseflesh down my back.

"I've seen her perform. It was years ago. She was good enough to leave an impression on my bad memory. I'm sure you're talented if you share even a hint of her blood."

Without overtly assessing my body, I can tell Marjorie has already looked me over and passed her judgment. It's not as if I didn't do pretty much the same thing to her as she took the three steps to stand in front of me. Although I might be justified in looking at her. Marjorie's manly outfit of jeans, flannel shirt with the sleeves cut off, tattoo arm bands, and work boots weren't all that notable, but her beard just wouldn't be ignored. It's close-cropped, full, well-kept and quite striking on a six-foot tall woman.

"I perform. I don't know if I'm as good as my mom, though."

"Is she still in the business?"

"No. She quit a couple years ago. She's remarried and lives in a real house without wheels."

"Too bad. I guess it happens to most of us eventually."

"Maybe." I wonder how in the world Corban has managed to bring me to someone who knows my family.

"Anyhoo, if you're a friend of Corban's then you're a friend of mine. But as your friend, I'm going to warn you, he's quite the shyster. You watch out for this one."

She winks at me, and I find her gruff manner mixed with kindness and sincerity captivating.

"Hey. Don't give away my secrets. She thinks I'm a nice guy," Corban says.

Marjorie lets out another one of her man-laughs and turns up her palms. "I kid you. Corban's all right most of the time, but don't let him tell you he's a bouncer. This boy belongs behind the sound board and nowhere else."

"Did you used to work together?" I ask.

"Sure did. His father is my cousin. We worked at the theater in Denver together for a few seasons."

"We better stop this conversation before we find out we're all related through some fourth cousin five times removed on my second great aunt's grandmother's line," Corban says.

"Could be, Corbs. It's a small world we live in."

I smile at their easy relationship.

Corban asks again about Marjorie's brother, Bob, and I hang out and only half listen as she catches him up on current news.

There's a slight tang of a full garbage can in the air, but the sky is clear and bursting with stars. The Midwest town we're in must be small because the light pollution is minimal. Wrapped in the carnival smells and sounds, I let the night pull me in close and hold me in its embrace.

When someone shuffles around the corner of the fun house, I tear my eyes away from the Milky Way and peer into the dark to see the return of Terryn and Maxim. Marjorie glances over her shoulder at them.

"That was fast." She crosses her arms over an ample chest.

"Forgive me, sweetheart. I know not how to control myself when I'm near you," Maxim says.

"I guess you're forgiven," she says.

He grabs her waist and snuggles her to his five-foot frame. She towers over him by almost a foot. I give them some space and a little privacy by stepping farther into the shadows of the office. Lights from the Ferris wheel sparkle crimson, amber, blue, and green, and reflect from Maxim's shiny bald head.

"I love our tiny battles, Max." Marjorie bends down to meet his lips.

"And I love your long legs wrapped around my waist, you giant hairy hunk of woman."

I swallow hard, and my cheeks burn. They clearly don't care who overhears them. I tip my head toward our exit and hope Corban takes the clue. He clears his throat. It doesn't stop the lovebirds from their passionate embrace. We both shift farther away from the couple.

Terryn saves us. "You guys want to grab a smoke with me before hitting the road?"

"Yeah. Later, Marj," Corban calls over his shoulder.

I make the mistake of glancing back to see if she heard Corban. Maxim is grinding his hips against her and whispering something about what he's going to do to his hot baby. I duck my head and book it around the fun house and back into the carnival crowd.

"They're a trip," Terryn says. "Sorry you had to see that."

"To each their own," Corban says.

Terryn pulls out a pack of cigarettes and shakes one out of the package. He offers the box to us. I shake my head and try to hold in the inappropriate laugh that wants to burst out of me. Seeing a muscular, bearded woman make out with her lithe and tiny, bald, tatted-up lover was the last thing I would ever imagine on this warm summer night.

"They don't bother me," I say and clamp my lips shut.

Corban flashes me a perplexed look and then the side of his mouth twitches.

"Yeah, it's fun and games until they catch you laughing at them. Then they'll invite you to join their freaky foreplay fiesta and act pissed off when you don't take their offer seriously," Terryn says with a knowing and serious tone.

Corban declines the cigarette. Terryn's unamused and equally alarmed look is enough to break Corban's passivity, and he rumbles with laughter.

"How long did it take to get back on her good side after you turned down the *foreplay fiesta*?"

"Too long. I think they finally know now, that's one ride I won't get on."

My shoulders shake with the wonder and hilarity of it. "Anything goes behind the fun house?" I say before I can stop myself.

"You got it. Corban, what were you thinking, bringing this girl to meet Marjorie?"

"She's cool, man. She's lived with The Farinelli Circus most of her life. Besides, she wanted to come inside with me."

Corban nudges me with his elbow.

"I think they make a cute couple." Another wave of laughter rises inside me.

Terryn eyes me with doubt as he takes a drag off his cigarette. "Hey, who am I to question love?"

I smile at Terryn's response. He's right. Love is individual and doesn't need explaining.

Corban sort of snorts and says, "What is love?"

His tone is dubious and somewhat cynical.

"It's when we're entwined." The words slip from my lips before I can think.

Corban's footsteps stall for a half a beat. I glance over at him. His eyes connect with mine, and I glimpse a new depth inside him I didn't see before. Then he's walking toward the exit and the moment is lost.

"You guys headed to base camp?" Terryn asks.

I wait for Corban's answer, having no idea what base camp is.

"Yeah. I think so."

"Well, have fun. Wish I was there."

"You going anytime this summer?"

"Not until our season's over."

Corban nods in a manly way which doesn't need verbal communication.

He turns to me, and I think he's about to tell me where we're headed. Instead, he says, "Can you hang out for a minute? I need to make a pit stop."

I take pit stop as code for using the restroom. "I'm good," I say.

Corban veers off, and I'm instantly sideswiped by Terryn's next statement.

"So did you guys find a sitter for the baby? Congratulations, by the way," he adds as an afterthought.

"Baby?"

He peeks down at my stomach and back up to my eyes. "Shit." He rubs his face with a work-roughened hand. "You're not Gabrielle are you?"

"Umm...no."

"My bad. Sorry. I should shut up now." He sounds more than flustered.

"You don't need to apologize." I try to ease his discomfort over saying something that perhaps he shouldn't have. "I'm just a friend of Corban's. We're not dating or anything. We just met recently."

"Well, mysterious lady, I'm sure if we ever meet again, you'll find my foot will still be wedged neatly inside my mouth."

"Sounds uncomfortable, but if that's how you roll, I'm all for it."

Terryn grins around his cigarette. Corban appears from around a vendor selling glow-in-the-dark neon trimmed rockets, hats, and necklaces. "Guess we better get going. Good to see you, Terryn."

"Yup," he says, dropping the cig to the asphalt and crushing it beneath his shoe.

Chapter Fifteen

"'Tis the privilege of friendship to talk nonsense, and to have her nonsense respected."
— Charles Lamb

"Whose yurt is this?"

"It belongs to my family."

"This is cool." The round tent-like structure is full of shadows, but I can see well enough to make out the lattice walls, domed skylight, larger pieces of furniture, and feel the rugs beneath my feet.

Corban shines a small flashlight across the round room, and I see it more clearly. He sets his backpack down on the futon by the door and walks over to a small woodstove. The stove squats on its hearth like a little troll ready to wake up and share its stories with us.

"I like the yurt. Since no one's using it, I thought it would be better than sleeping in the 4-Runner. And, the property is close to the highway, not too far out of our way."

"I don't mind your truck."

"I noticed." He bends down and opens the iron door of the stove with a clank. "I was starting to worry you had slipped into a coma."

"That's about how I felt, too," I admit.

"I'm not going to start the generator since it's late, but I want a fire to warm it up in here and give us some light."

"Thanks." I move deeper into the yurt and take a seat on an oversized chair. "I don't need electricity or the fire if you want to go straight to sleep."

"I need to unwind for a while after all the driving," he says, wadding up paper.

The crinkling of paper is followed by the groan of a metal hinge. Corban's silhouette moves through a patch of silver moonlight. The white light of his flashlight shoots across the yurt and settles on a stack of firewood near the stove.

"Can I help with anything?"

"You can take the role of upper management." He begins stacking kindling wood inside the stove.

"What does the management do for this operation?"

"You're doing it," he says.

"Yeah, I'm not really manager material. Got any other positions for me?" As soon as I say it, I'm aware of the sexual connotation charging the words 'positions for me'. The darkness hides the blush creeping into my cheeks. *Thank God.* I didn't mean it that way, but my libido won't be ignored. How can I even consider these thoughts when I'm still hurting from the devastation of breaking up with Keel? *What is wrong with me?* Did Corban hear the innuendo? Does he think he can make a move on me since we're all alone in this secluded little yurt? Is he going to pull the whole, 'There's only one bed, so I guess you can have it'. I say something like, 'Oh no, I couldn't let you sleep on the floor. You can lay up here next to me.' Then we'll make out in the dark because, well let's face facts—he's hot. And I'm weak and needy. Things will be unbearably awkward between us in the morning?

"I guess if you really want a job that bad, the janitor position is still open," he says.

Earth is such a better place to reside than the delusional landscapes of my imagination. However, even when I crash back to the present, the lingering thoughts still exist in the miasma of my brain. I push them deeper into the mist.

"Janitor or supervisor?" I ask aloud, and weigh them out by holding my palms up like scales. "I'm pretty used to having a lot of crap in my life, so I'm more qualified for the custodial job." This time, I remember to avoid the word "position". But of course, once you consciously try to ignore something, it roars in your face. My brain conjures images of Corban on top of me, behind me, side by side. *Damn it, I need therapy.*

"I don't know if I agree." He lights the crumpled paper inside the woodstove.

The orange flames blend with yellow, blue, and green. The colors of burning ink on paper hold my gaze. They make me think of cauldrons brewing magical potions. Is there a potion to fix codependent females? If so, I need to chug it like right now.

Corban continues his thought as the snap and crackle of burning kindling adds depth to the midnight atmosphere inside the yurt. "Supervisors have a lot more shit to clean up than the cleaning crew."

"You sound like you know something about it," I say.

"Yeah. I help run The Gothic Theater when my dad needs extra shoulders to carry some of the load."

"Either way, I'm not supervisor material."

"All right, but you get to clean up in the morning."

"Sounds like a deal." I realize Corban hasn't once hit on me or acted in any way inappropriate, or even the slightest bit interested. If only I could get out of my own head and *stay out.*

Corban nurses the fire for a few minutes and then rises to his full height. In the soft flickering glow around the yurt, I notice the kitchen area and the bunk beds. He walks over and disappears behind one of the only dividing walls inside the yurt. I rest my head on the back of the chair and stare up at the round ceiling, watching the roof poles flicker and sway with the firelight. My nap on the road helped considerably because even though I'm tired, I'm not passing out like I was earlier.

"I lit a candle in the bathroom so you can see. It's an incinerating toilet, so just close the lid and push the button when you're done. There's a jug of clean water by the sink for washing and brushing your teeth. I can check the water tanks in the morning if you need to shower and stuff."

"I'm fine, but thank you, and since I'm the janitor, just tell me what dirty job needs to be done, and I'll do it."

"Right. Jasper the janitor." He sinks down on the futon and leans forward to untie his boots. He slips them off and rests his heels on the coffee table.

Geoff always liked to tell me I'd be lucky to scrub the piss off the toilets one day, and now I picked my new janitorial title willingly, and happily. I almost wish I could shove the irony down his throat, but I let it go. Geoff's not here, and if it's up to me, I hope I never speak to him again.

Listening to the fire becomes almost hypnotic, and I realize my first impression of the stove had been eerily accurate. There are stories leaking into the room. I'm not sure what the popping and crackling of the wood is saying to Corban, but it draws me into its tales, and I'm not opposed to listening.

Corban's husky voice infiltrates the murmuring fire. "Since you're my guest, you get first pick of a bunk or the futon, and I'll sleep somewhere else."

"Okay." I pull myself out of the chair. "How about the bottom bunk?"

"Anywhere you want." He rises from the futon and adds another log to the fire.

In the glow of the candlelight, I use the incinerating toilet—it isn't as weird as it sounds—and wash my hands and brush my teeth. As I stretch out on the lower bunk, I'm swaddled with soft cotton quilts and down pillows.

I'm still relishing the bliss of a real bed when Corban comes out of the restroom and climbs the ladder to the top bunk. He's up above me, and I smile to myself, not only because my earlier fantasy of him on top of me was correct—only in a completely different way—but because it's been a long time since I had a sleepover.

"Thanks for being cool about the yurt," he says.

"This is one of the best places I've ever been," I say with sincerity. "And I've traveled to forty-nine of the fifty states." I snuggle deeper into the warm fluff of the bed clothes and release a deep sigh of contentment.

"It's one of my favorite places, too. Not only sleeping in the yurt but the rest of the property."

"I got a glimpse of the river. Is there more?"

"Yeah there is, but it can wait until morning."

"Are ya messin' with me, mon?" I ask in some version of a Jamaican accent.

"Err...no. I'll show you around before we take off tomorrow. It's not a bad place we've landed."

"Hmm..." I hum, wondering what lies outside the door of this round canvas house.

"Tell me something," he says from the top bunk.

"What's up?"

"Are you a morning person or a night owl?"

"I'm more of a chameleon? You?"

"Night owl," he says.

"Why do you ask?"

"How can you be a chameleon?"

"I've worked at night for so long I can stay up late when I need to, but through the fall and winter, I woke up early and went to my morning classes, and it didn't bother me. I think I like being awake in the morning."

"What do you like about it?" he asks.

"The newness of the day. The air is clean, cool, and renewed. I always imagine the moon and stars going to sleep for the day." I shrug beneath the blankets, a little self-conscious. I've never told anyone about waking up before.

"You're definitely a morning person," Corban says.

"You probably think a lot less of me now."

He gives a half-laugh which drifts up to the ceiling. "I wouldn't judge someone for the time of day they prefer to live their lives. But I'll ask you to show me the same courtesy in the morning when I'm functioning and speaking like a dim-witted ghoul."

Now it's my turn to laugh. "You got it. There's no judgment on my end. I'm just grateful for the ride—from a ghoul or from a university student."

"Yeah-yeah, I know what I'm good for." He lets the sarcasm tumble out of his extremely cute mouth.

He shifts around on the mattress above.

"Why do you think there's such a huge difference between morning people and night people?"

"Balance," he says with hardly a pause. "We spend half of our lives in the dark. If everyone were one way or the other, there wouldn't be a balance."

"So you think there has to be balance?"

"There is a balance at all times and in all aspects of creation. You can see it in the simplicity of a circle or in the complexity of physics."

"Balance is why cruelty exists," I say.

"Because kindness is its polar opposite." He completes my thought.

"And people tend to only see one side of things, but the opposite still exists even when we don't acknowledge it." I think about the awful things that happened to me recently. It makes sense, but at the moment, it's difficult to accept that faithfulness and generosity are abundant in the world when I was cheated on and mugged.

"The light of day is still happening when we're surrounded by the dark of night," he says, reiterating my previous words.

I pause, creating the image in my mind and savoring the feeling that goes with the picture of the world as half dark and half light. I store this away like a keepsake somewhere where I can revisit it again later. I ask, "Do you think a person would recognize the light if all they ever knew is the dark?"

"I think the person would know it was there, and it would be painful at first. A brave person would step forward and question whether or not this new bright object was worth investigating. Someone who is full of fear would run and hide in the dark because it's what they are comfortable with. People always tend to gravitate toward what they know, even if it's not in their best interest."

I ponder that for a second. "What would you do?"

"Run straight at it and see if it responds."

"And how would the light react to a sleepy ghoul university student?"

"I'm sure it would open its arms and take me under its wing."

His confidence and the new image forming in my head makes me smile again. "We have weird conversations."

"Nah. It's more like an intellectual vacation."

"Same thing."

***

When I wake up, I roll over to find Corban sitting on the floor, leaning his back against the end of the bed, and holding my shoe in his lap. He has a black marker in his hand, and the arrangement of his body seems odd at first. Then I realize why. He's left handed.

"I thought I was the morning person," I say.

"Not sure what happened, but I'm awake."

"How late is it?" I feel like I slept through an entire century. There's not a lot of daylight filtering in through the windows, but I'm pretty sure that's only because of the overcast sky.

"Not late." He tips his wrist over to peer at his watch. "Ten-thirty."

"Hmm. Late enough." I scoot to the edge of the mattress to inspect his handiwork.

Corban's decorating my gaudy canvas shoes. The flower and smiley faces are being replaced with a black ink design.

"Do you always seduce girls into your yurt and graffiti their shoes while they sleep?"

"Wouldn't you like to know?" He doesn't look up.

I slip out from under the covers and scoot over until I can reach my other shoe. Corban glances over just long enough to see me looking at his artwork. The shoe is slightly damp from all the ink. I check out the fresh new look of my chintzy shelter shoes as the tart scent of permanent marker wafts off the canvas. I don't shy away from the vapors. It reminds me of coloring with Evie. When she was younger, we used to color together all the time. Evie always wanted markers over crayons. I liked the crayons because there were more colors to choose from, but Evie didn't care about that. She only wanted to draw and color with the bright saturated colors of ink. My left shoe is sporting a black sun with wings. Corban used scrollwork and tribal elements to cover up the rest of the cheesy print. When I flip the shoe over, the bottom reads, "That which does not kill us".

Corban tosses the right shoe to me. This one has the moon, nautical stars, and more tribal elements. They're better than phenomenal and instantly become my favorite shoes of all time. I trace a finger over the outline of the crescent moon and revel in the details.

"These are horrible." I attempt a look of disgust. "I thought they were bad before, but you ruined my new shoes." My smile is aching to be released, but I hold it in and wait for Corban's response.

"I know. I suck. I'm a vandal at heart. I couldn't take all those yellow happy faces looking at me. They needed to die."

"Those cheery little faces were keeping me going. Now, I'm not so sure I can hold it together." I'm still playing along.

"Give them back and I'll black out the whole shoe. Black I can handle. Those pink flowers were ruining the ambiance inside my truck." He holds out his hand waiting for me to pass my new art shoes back to him.

I hug them to my chest and turn away from him as he leans over from his spot a few feet away. His hand is a bit too grabby. The black marker in his other hand flicks back and forth as if in anticipation of covering up what he created.

"That's okay," I say. "I'll just learn to live with this sentimental reminder of balance and the yin and yang of life. I'm sure I need it more than flowers and smiley faces anyway."

One eyebrow rises in a look of barely concealed impatience.

He's too damn cute, my brain informs me. I turn all the way around and place the shoes on the bed admiring his artwork again.

"I did it for me, remember?" he says.

He shoves to his feet behind me and walks away. I let the suppressed joy of this unexpected gift rise, and a huge smile spreads across my face. I turn the right shoe over and read what it says, "makes us stronger". I flip over the left shoe and line it up so the whole quote reads, "That which does not kill us, makes us stronger". I give the moment pause and breathe in the scent of permanent marker.

***

"Before we go, I want to show you something. Are you in a rush to get to your aunt's?"

I give him a questioning look. So far, Corban is über-polite, considerate, and selfless. He's raised the moral bar so high it's my civic duty to tease him. "I knew you were too good to be true. This is the part of the road trip where you expose your inner weirdo and tell me besides stealing women's shoes, you collect bellybutton lint and earwax and make tiny voodoo dolls out of it. Am I right?"

"You're onto me. I knew we connected on a higher level." His dark, piercing gaze could almost fool me into believing he has a secret freak buried inside him. "I already made your doll. Would you like to see it?"

"Seriously, no. And stay away from my ear wax."

"Too late. I scraped it out while you were sleeping."

He waggles his brows with seductive pleasure, and I laugh.

"So what's next? You let me stay in your amazing tent house. Is there something better than this?"

"It could be better." He turns off the creepy stalker face and turns on his normal cuteness. "I'm not sure what you'll think, but we're here so, you may as well check it out."

I make an inquisitive humming sound and tap my chin with my index finger. "Okay, I'll bite, but is there a fire escape?"

"There is. Just yell fire and we'll escape."

"Cool."

Outside the yurt, we walk down a private road following the river deeper into the property. We pass a few small log cabins and another yurt and end up in a large gravel parking lot next to a huge metal building. The building is nondescript, but the outside is tidy and clean, with no sign to indicate what type of business this is. A few miscellaneous vehicles are parked in the lot including a colorfully painted old school bus and a matching trailer, but there are no people around.

Corban opens the door for me, and we enter a hallway. The only sign is a sticker that says, S & D Inc. There are some offices on the left, but he opens a door to the right, and we enter.

"Is this base camp?" I stare across the enormous gym and training facility.

"Have you been wondering since last night what Terryn and I were talking about?"

"Sort of," I admit.

"You could ask."

"I didn't want to insert myself where I'm not invited."

He gives me a look. I'm starting to recognize the "Corban look" even if I can't fully interpret it. He just looks back at me like he's searching for answers I'm not openly giving away.

"If you're with me, you're invited." He's very straightforward and direct. He shifts his gaze to the open gym. "This is the main training building for about a dozen different companies. Performers, acrobats, dancers, and anyone who needs the facility and the grounds can lease it for a day, week, or months. A bunch of performers use the gym regularly, and others come and go throughout the year. There's more out back if you want to see it," he says.

"So, what is S & D Incorporated?" I ask, thinking of the decal on the front door.

"Scarberry and Duran," he says.

"That's your family?"

"More like my extended family," Corban explains. "My parents own about twenty-five percent of the property, but they don't manage it. The Scarberrys are more involved in running and managing this facility."

I stare at a man and a woman practicing on the vertical poles in the far corner of the building. The air conditioning is on even at this time of the morning, keeping the air temperate for hard working athletes. The aerial silks are about mid-way down the length of the enormous steel structure, but I don't let my gaze stray to my favorite activity for more than a few seconds. I'm still not sure how I feel about abandoning my silk with Paradox 21.

The low wire is set up about forty feet to my left. I almost whimper with the need to feel my feet grip the cable. Wanting to practice the low wire is the last thing I would've thought I needed, but the intense focus sounds more than a little enticing.

"I'm...I can't believe what I'm seeing." I try not to gawk. "I haven't been in a real gym for a long time. God, it even smells good in here."

Corban flashes me his grin. "I thought you might like it. It reminded me of you somehow."

He pauses and his chest rises and falls with a deep breath.

"You can use anything you want."

"How? I mean what about liability and stuff?"

"Don't do anything that requires a spotter or trainer, or the hospital, and you'll be good. I thought you might want to practice or warm up or whatever it is you do before we start driving again. I've lived with enough artists to know how much your sanity depends on regular practice."

I lean over and kiss him on the cheek, light, friendly and full of thanks. "You're so right." I twirl away from him, heading toward the nearest floor mats to stretch.

"I'm going outside to find a friend. I'll be back in a few."

With only two others in the gym with me, I'm practically alone and let myself relax and concentrate on nothing but waking up my body. Corban must secretly be my angel in disguise, but even those thoughts I put aside to think about later.

My hamstrings, quads, lower back, and neck need the most attention in regards to warming up. I move through my routine and breathe into my tension-bound muscles. My elbow is getting better, but I make adjustments for it. When my blood is moving through every cell and muscle fiber, and Corban still hasn't returned, I climb on the low wire and test my balance by sitting on it and trying out a few moves without my suede foot wraps.

After a few more minutes pass, I climb down and practice my low wire routine on the padded floor. There's a painted line the same length as the wire for such purposes. Someone left a balancing fan behind, and I pick it up. Three steps forward, dip right foot, left foot, right, spin one-eighty, three steps, and jump. Bring knees to chest and land perfectly centered.... As I move, muscle memory takes me through most of the tricks I know. My focus is so complete, it isn't until I reach the point where I would normally be hanging down below the wire to tease the audience with the possibility of falling that I realize Corban has returned.

He's watching my performance from near the wall with a group of guys. I set the fan back down and trot over to where I left my shoes and slip them on before joining him.

"I wish I had my shoes for the wire, but I don't." I shrug.

A tall man with extraordinary thick, black eyebrows watches me intently with his sapphire blue eyes. There are two other guys with them. One is medium height, with an average build, sporting a buzz cut, with a half dozen facial piercings, and covered with tattoos. The last guy seems normal and unremarkable in almost every way. He's not unattractive, just nondescript with his peanut colored hair, brown eyes, and pale complexion.

"Feeling better?" Corban asks.

"That was great. I needed to work out more than I can say." I turn to the strangers. "Hi, I'm Jasper." I smile, and it feels natural and not at all forced. Corban was absolutely right—sanity and even a little happiness are a lot easier when an artist is able to be in their element.

Corban does the introductions. "This is Tink." He gestures to the tattooed guy. "And this is Marc." The guy in khakis and a polo shirt. "And this is Bob Brows Scarberry. You met his sister, Marjorie, last night."

I shake their hands. "Nice to meet you," I say. "Are you training here?"

"Not currently. We're camped here temporarily because we're holding an audition," Bob Brows says.

His manner isn't warm, but he's not cool either. His blue eyes are intense, to say the least, but his tone of voice is neutral.

"Our fly girl is taking an early maternity leave. We need someone to fill in for her, or we reinvent a majority of our show."

"Fly girl?" I ask.

"Sasha," Tink says. "She's Marc's wife and stage assistant for his mind manipulation act. She has her own danger act as well. Her doctor thinks it's best for her to put the knives and bows and arrows aside until after the baby hatches."

"Oh." I tuck a stray hair behind my ear. "So, are you like a traveling sideshow or something?"

"The Circus of Misfit Marvels at your service," Bob Brows says with a small flourish of his hand, a sly smile, and a bow.

He's the perfect ring leader, I think as he rises and settles his jewel-tone gaze on me. Bob's eyebrows are outrageous, and I picture them coming alive and skittering away off his forehead. Apparently, the Scarberrys have an overabundance of facial hair.

"Are you here to try out for the position?" Tink asks.

"Me? No. I just happen to be passing through with Corban."

"She's being modest. I've seen her dance now a couple of times. Jasper is world class. She told me how The Show is all she's ever known." Corban's gaze lands on me. "She was born into the Farinelli World Circus."

Raised eyebrows of interest, all but Marc's, focus on me. Blood rushes to my face, and I'm unsure of what to say. I'm not ready for an audition.

"I liked what I saw when we came in. Can you do the same routine on the wire?"

"I can. I also belly dance, and incorporate gymnastics and contortion, but I'm not...." I let my words trail off. I was going to say I'm not looking for a new gig, but the truth is, I'm jobless and homeless. If I don't figure out something soon, I might end up back at my mother's, and that's the last place I want to be. I clear my throat. "Besides low wire, I specialize in aerial silks and I do trampoline routines as well."

Corban says, "Jasper was touring with the band, Paradox 21 until last week. She's been working shows and festivals this summer."

The door in the corner of the gym begins to open and close as people trickle into the building.

"I think they're looking for us." Tink glances in the direction of the gathering crowd. "I liked what I saw too. Give Bob your contact information if you're interested in our troupe." He leaves us to meet and greet the newcomers.

"Okay," I say.

"I'm in need of a new assistant. I prefer a female, but we're pressed for time, so I'll make do with who we can get. We travel all over the country and sleep in a bus. Someone with experience would be welcome," Marc says.

He offers me his hand, and I shake it before he joins Tink.

This is the first time he's spoken, and he has a strong, clear voice with a very slight accent I can't place. He's sort of unremarkably odd, I realize, and I don't dislike it. All three of them have an uncommon edge about them that I haven't been around since leaving Farinelli. Keel and his band were goofballs and partiers most of the time, but these guys remind me of my childhood home.

"Marc is correct. We want someone with experience and someone who is willing to travel almost every day until the end of October. It is a paying job with a contract. Would you like to interview?"

"I'm not prepared today. I don't have my gear." I avoid the subject of my stolen luggage and my sore elbow.

"I understand. However, I saw how you move, and Corban wouldn't bring up your resume if he didn't recognize your talent. We can talk more if you're serious. We're back on the road next week. We average four to seven shows a week. Sometimes more."

He pulls out a business card from nowhere. I smile at his sleight-of-hand trick. Had I been expecting it, I probably still wouldn't have seen where the card appeared from.

"I'll call you. Soon."

The corner of his mouth lifts a fraction of an inch. "I look forward to talking with you, Jasper."

He struts across the gym to join the others, and I stare in disbelief at his card. Bob Brows' soccer shorts, trainers, and tight-fitting jersey shirt make him look right off the soccer field, but the added suspenders and newsboy cap make the outfit really stand out. Corban interrupts my observations of his cousin.

"Didn't you say you were looking for a new job?" Corban asks.

"Yeah, but I didn't expect one to land in my lap."

"Well you don't have it yet, but if I were you, I wouldn't turn my nose up at the chance if this is something you're interested in."

"I'm pretty sure my nose is to the ground in a humble tribute to the universe... and you."

"I didn't do anything. I had no idea Bob would be here until Marjorie mentioned it."

"So the physics major, runner, nice guy is also humble?" I tease.

He shakes his head in dismissal. "We should get back on the road," he says with a tilt of the head toward the door. "We still have hours to go before Chicago."

***

Corban pays for breakfast, and we eat pastries and drink coffee on the road. Since all I was capable of doing last night was sleeping, today we talk about everything and nothing as the miles of farmland pass us by. The nonsense and hilarity inside his SUV make time fly, and it's the most entertaining conversation I've had in possibly forever. I notice neither of us breaches the wall of our personal lives. He never mentions the name Gabrielle or talks about his baby.

I wonder if Terryn was mistaken when he dropped those names at the Scarberry Carnival, or if Corban purposefully remains silent on that part of his life. Likewise, I stay far away from the subject of Keel or my parents.

Hours later, we stop for gas, and I'm about to get out and stretch my legs, but change my mind and pull my journal out of my bag to jot down today's sign:

"Are you lost? Follow the signs to..."

(On an old billboard which appeared to either have been neglected for the last decade or a storm had ravaged it and made only part of the message decipherable.)

Follow the signs to where?

Where am I going?

Is it possible to find my way without a map? Are some people born with a better sense of direction than others? Where was I when these life skills were handed out?

Why do I take every wrong turn before arriving at my destination? A to B should be a direct path. Of course, I like to mix things up. I add a lot of unnecessary C, D, E, F and Zs as I climb over mountains of my own making. How can I stop being my own worst enemy?

To whom it may concern,

Please let this trip to Chicago be the right direction. Could you let this be the beginning of a new, happy chapter in my life? I'd really like to begin writing down all the positive things I want to remember.

I glance up and see Corban walking out of the gas station holding drinks in his hands. He smiles at me, and I shut the journal.

He takes his seat behind the wheel. "Need anything before we go?"

"Nope. I'm good." Then I notice I'm still holding the journal in my hand. Corban notices too, and I don't feel like I should hide it like I always did around Keel.

"I bought an extra bottle of tea if you're thirsty." He sets the two bottles in the cup holders.

I lean down and place my journal on top of my bag.

"Thanks. I love peach tea."

"I had a feeling you couldn't resist," he says and shifts the 4-Runner into drive.

I twist the cap open and smile when the fresh sweet scent of peaches fills the air.

My new chapter begins with the smell of peaches.

***

We pull into the parking lot of my aunt's apartment building, and Corban shuts off the engine. Leaving can be so awkward. I don't want anything to be awkward between Corban and me, but it seems unavoidable, sort of like life in general.

Without speaking, he opens his door and steps out. It's abrupt, so I grab my bag and follow his lead. Corban's next to my door by the time I step out and I belatedly realize he was going to open it for me.

He gives me room to close the door but stays in my personal space. "Don't take this the wrong way, okay?"

"What?" I ask. Something in the tone of his voice or the sudden softness around his eyes has me wondering.

"Goodbye, Jasper." He wraps his incredibly strong and warm arms around me.

I'm taken off guard as he holds me tight against him. My feelings for Corban scare the crap out of me. I'm consumed by the loss of Keel and what I thought we had together, but Corban is tempting me to love someone else. Loving him would be spontaneous, combustible, and tragic. It's too soon to fall for someone new. He holds my head with one hand and my back with the other.

"My mom does this to me at the worst possible moments. I used to hate it, but eventually, I realized it sort of makes everything better. You deserve better, Jasper. Take care of yourself."

"I will." I attempt to memorize his warm sun and clean laundry scent, and the way my head rests against his chest.

"Thanks for the road trip."

"Anytime," I say.

He squeezes me tighter, then releases me, a quiet smile on his lips. His eyes are penetrating and mystifying. I don't understand what he sees in me. He's perplexing yet intriguing. Mysteriously thoughtful and surprising.

"Thanks for...everything." My simple declaration of gratitude falls short in every way.

He gives me the guy's way of saying "no problem", a simple bob of his chin. I hear or sense movement from over my shoulder and glance up.

"Is that your aunt?" Corban asks.

"Yeah," I say.

Aunt Summer is standing on the upstairs breezeway by the apartment doors. I wave up at her and turn back around. Corban's climbing into his 4-Runner. And he's gone.

Chapter Sixteen

"The face of love is often unrecognizable." — J. Pyrah

Aunt Summer gives me a huge hug, maybe even bigger than Corban's. Two hugs in two minutes. I should feel loved and wanted, but the truth is I just want to disappear.

"I'm glad you made it. Sorry again for not being able to come pick you up."

"It's fine. It all worked out. Corban was amazing."

She watches my face, and I detect the slightest inquisitive lift of her eyebrow when I mention Corban.

"Your friend should come in. I can cook him something or give him some gas money."

"Please don't worry about it." A cloak of guilt wraps itself around me. Everyone is doing something for me, and I can't repay their kindness. I'm a leech. A blood-sucking parasite on perfectly innocent unsuspecting people. "He needed to head back to Colorado for work."

"Well, next time you talk to him, please tell him my offer stands to repay him for his time and gas expense. I can mail him a check if he wants one."

"Thanks, Aunt Summer," I say as we enter her apartment.

The guilt cloak is also covered with a Vaseline-like coating of numbing solution.

"You can sleep in our spare room." She walks me down the hallway to the first door on the right. "It's our multi-functional space, but the daybed is comfy."

This is the first time I've ever been to her new apartment. The last time I visited, she lived in a caretaker's house in Winnetka near the lake. Before that, she lived closer to downtown, where the streets were crammed with cars and the brick buildings were even more jammed together. It doesn't matter where she lives. Aunt Summer is always the same. She overflows with excitement for Evie and me to experience Chicago. Since we were little kids, Aunt Summer kept us entertained by taking us to parks, swimming, and the zoo, but she always found a way to add some kind of real art whether it was pointing out different architectural styles, listening to live music in a cafe, or visiting a museum. Schooling us in culture ranked high on her list of priorities. Visits with Aunt Summer were adventures stamped into my memories. I'm sure this visit will be memorable as well, but nothing like our past family vacations.

"You probably need to rest. I set some clean towels in the bathroom, and you can help yourself to anything in the kitchen. I'm going to give you some space now, Jas."

She places her hand on my arm. Her touch is so light, I barely feel it. I stare at the office/workout/sewing/guest room and my walls begin to crumble. There are yoga mats, straps and weights on the floor, and rings hanging on straps bolted to the ceiling. Her makeshift gym takes up one corner of the room while the bed and a tiny desk hunker against the other side. The rest of the space and an overflowing closet are crammed with sewing machines and fabric. Her income is dependent on her seamstress and wardrobe skills and work often follows her home from the theater. Gorgeous posters of scenery from around the world and framed affirmation art cover the walls with images that remind me so much of my aunt's personality.

"I'm around if you need me. You're welcome to stay here forever," she says.

Aunt Summer doesn't wait for me to reply as she closes the door and provides me with everything I need—a quiet space and time to process. After placing my bag on the desk, I sit down on the edge of the bed, and the realization of my landing in a safe zone deepens. My recent traumas raise their voice and come out of me in wracking sobs. I fall over onto my side and let everything tumble out of me. Boulders of despair, chasms of fear, and the stabbing agony of heartbreak crash into the pillows.

Sometime later—after an undeterminable length of time—Aunt Summer lays a light blanket over me. She sits down and rests her hand on my side. The warmth of her palm penetrates through the blanket. She says something about a glass of water on the desk. I can't reply. My throat aches. My head is somewhere between the first level of hell and a nightmarish dreamland. I can't shake it, so I just lie there.

"I told your mom you're here."

This brings me closer to the second level of hell, and I focus on the buzzing between my ears instead of facing reality. Her next whisper slips through the air and disappears before I can catch it. I want to think she said I was justified in leaving home. Then I return to sleep and hope for a silent and desolate dreamland.

My wish isn't granted. I'm engulfed in memory nightmares.

***

The bones in my body are miniature. Thin arms, thin legs, flat chest and every part of me is hot. My insides are fuzzy and overheated. Moving is a chore, and all I want is to sleep. Evie isn't there. Looking around I notice her clothes and toys don't exist inside our room. It dawns on me the reason I'm so small is I must be five or six years old, and Evie hasn't been born yet.

Mom pulls off my purple nightgown and wipes my mouth and face with a cool washcloth before tugging a dry shirt over my head.

When I lie back against the pillow, I realize I'm ill. The trashcan next to the bed splattered with vomit, confirms it. She pulls the sheet up over me, and I kick it off. It's too hot to be covered.

Mom says, "I know you don't feel good, baby, but you have to eat something. Be right back."

She grabs the soiled laundry and the trashcan and walks out. I watch from the bed through the open door on my end of the trailer as she takes care of the mess.

Singing softly under her breath she ladles chicken noodle soup into a bowl. Mom brings the soup and a small cup of 7-Up and tries to get me to eat, but I don't want to. She's smiling her beautiful smile, but her eyes are shadowed and tired. When I refuse to eat again, she begins making up a song about eating soup while she shimmies her shoulders and sort of half dances to make it fun. Her light mood, happy smile, and encouragement helps me eat half of the bowlful and sip the soda. She says I can nibble some saltine crackers or eat some canned oranges if I want them, but I tell her I'm full.

Mom sets the dishes aside and grabs one of my favorite books from my shelf. She climbs into the bed next to me, snuggles up close and begins reading. My tummy is actually a little better, and I'm getting super sleepy, but I want to keep listening to the story more than I want to sleep. The book is about a baby circus bear who gets lost in the woods and goes on an adventure to find his way back to his parents. My mom's voice is soothing as I listen to the part about the bear and the porcupine's disastrous hot air balloon ride. But I can't keep my eyes open any longer, and I drift off to sleep and miss the end of the story.

***

I'm suddenly awake, and my pillow is wet with the fresh tears of longing and bittersweet memories.

My first night at Aunt Summer's continues on like this until the sun rises. Not only does my childhood torture me, but then my mind goes right into my fallout with Keel and Caspar. Eventually, I push myself out of bed and find the shower. I end up at the kitchen table wondering if I'll ever resemble a normal person or if I'll always be plagued with my past and sleepless nights. Aunt Summer sets a glass in front of me containing a questionable pond-scum green beverage.

"Drink it," she says.

I eye it warily and decide to try it. Who cares if it's poisonous? My life can't get much worse than it already is. As I taste test the green nutrition drink, she begins setting out what looks like the entire contents of the refrigerator and pantry. A bowl of hummus, dolmas, carrot and celery sticks, some sort of marinated salad, strawberries, cut up melon, an apple, pita chips, tortilla chips, crackers, nori, kale chips, cashews and almonds and a few other things cover the entire table.

"Would you like something to eat?"

"Not really."

"You should eat. Look at all this food. I think I went a little overboard at the store."

"You think?" I wonder if she bought all this stuff because of me.

"Finish the mega greens and then I'll bring you a cup of tea."

"Okay, sure." I don't want to be rude. I take a berry from a bowl and bite down. My stomach decides it can handle food. To be honest, I wasn't sure at first, but as the sweet juice soaks in, I realize I didn't eat much in the last few days.

Aunt Summer returns to the table, places a mug in front of me and sits down. She scoops some hummus with a carrot.

"Are you ready for a talk?"

"Ready as I'll ever be. Which is never."

"Okay, well, I'll start and if you don't want to go there just tell me."

"Sounds fair enough." I chug the rest of her green bionic mystery juice.

"What do you want to do with your life, Jasper?"

"I don't know." I reach for a chip. "I can't stay with Mom and Geoff anymore."

"I understand why you left. It's not entirely different than why your mom and I left our father's nightmare house. What I'm asking you is what do you think you're going to be doing in ten years? Have you given it any thought?"

"It's not like I haven't thought about it at all." I place my elbow on the table and rest my forehead against my palm. "I don't see my future. It's like I can only go from show to show and if I try to think about what I want or what I may be doing next year, I blank out. God, that sounds pathetic." I groan.

"You're not pathetic. You're young, you can do anything you want."

I scoot back in the chair and lay my cheek on the table. "I don't know," I say again. "My freshman year of college is over, but I don't even know what I want to study."

"You don't need all the answers right now. I'm not trying to add any pressure to you, but you should at least have a general direction. Something to motivate you and keep you going. A spark of hope to chase."

"I'm spiraling toward a great fat nothing. A hole with no end. I'll be performing on the street for pennies until I throw myself into the ocean with dirty change stuffed inside my socks to weigh me down."

"Stop," she says but puts compassion in her order.

A weighted silence is sitting in the room with us. I wonder if the bubble popped, would I be crushed by my own self-pity. What would it look like? Me, being smashed by doubt, hurt, and victimization? Would it be red, shiny, overbearing, huge and suffocating? Like being swallowed by a giant blood-red latex balloon. It's closing in on me. I'll suffocate because of my own misery.

Aunt Summer interrupts my delusions. "Here's some homework for you. I want you to think about what makes you happy, and I want you to do a little bit every day. You don't need to do anything major. Go for a walk, watch a funny show, or dance to your favorite song. No matter what it is, you have to do something that makes you feel better. Then I want you to picture yourself in ten years still making yourself happy. Can you do that?"

"I guess so."

"Good. Now get up. We're going out."

"Where?"

"To buy you a new phone."

"My debit card hasn't shown up yet."

"That's all right. You need a phone, and you need to go outside today."

"I can't let you pay."

"You can, and you will," Aunt Summer says, and begins cleaning up the smorgasbord which we've hardly touched. "Go get ready, or go as you are."

I glance down at my dirty T-shirt and Aunt Summer's shorts and rise from the table. "I think I'll go change." I grab the mug of tea and force myself to move.

She hums a song under her breath as the food disappears back into the fridge and cabinets. They both like to sing, my mom and Aunt Summer—not a trait I inherited.

***

My lovely, petite, unconventional Aunt Summer drags me to a bike shop instead of a cell phone store. I don't say anything until she walks up to the door and enters, her head held high and a sense of purpose on her shoulders.

"Are you buying a bike?"

"No. But I am going to rent a couple."

She doesn't elaborate, and I don't question her. When the bike salesman tells us to meet him outside so we can pick a bike, I ask her what's going on.

"We're taking a ride." She walks out the door.

"These are good bikes." She inspects the racks of red or blue rental bicycles. "Which one would you like?"

I don't answer.

"You look like you need a medium frame," the bike salesman says as he looks me over and then gestures to the middle rack.

Aunt Summer grabs a red bike and wheels it away from the others.

"I don't feel like riding," I say.

"I need you to do this with me, Jasper. It won't kill you."

I suck in a long breath and stare into the chaos of a hundred bike frames, black tires, chains, gears, and handlebars. The sales guy is waiting for me, but I'm having a hard time with basically everything today.

Finally, I step forward and grab the closest bicycle.

"Bike riding? Really?" It's my final redundant complaint. She ignores it.

"It's great. You'll see." We situate ourselves—seats adjusted, helmets buckled—and set out.

Aunt Summer leads us away from the crowds along the sidewalks and the busy street. She rides down the alley behind the bike store, turns left and then I see she's taking us to the lake.

Without hurrying and without small talk, we pedal along the bike path around the lake. It must be a popular thing to do because we pass dozens of bikers. I stay focused on not wrecking or crashing into anyone and pretty soon I'm beginning to notice the water lapping against the shore, the warmth of the day, and the way the air smells different by the lake compared to one block over by the bike shop. Families of all shapes and colors are out enjoying the day. I listen to the flapping of birds' wings as they fly over my head.

When my aunt pulls off the main path and starts heading toward some shops, I follow behind and enjoy how easy it is to breathe and move, and I get a rush of gratitude for being alive. That hasn't happened in longer than I can remember. When I was at the S & D gym with Corban, I felt better after moving and getting my blood pumping, but I didn't attribute that to being grateful for my life. Today may be the first time I've ever felt happy about my existence.

Aunt Summer takes me into the cell phone store, and I pick out a cheap phone with a pay-as-you-go plan. Then we park the bikes outside a frozen yogurt shop, and we pick out our favorite flavors and toppings. Personally, I like blackberry and coconut with a little caramel drizzled on top and a lot of whipped cream. Aunt Summer eats strawberry vanilla swirl with fresh strawberries on top. We sit outside on a deck overlooking the lake and soak up some of the hazy Midwestern sun. A seagull competes with a courageous sparrow for crumbs on the wood planks of the deck. The sparrow holds its own against the larger bird, and I silently cheer for the little underdog.

Aunt Summer and I compare our desserts and chat about everything that doesn't include mom, Keel, being assaulted, work, or the future. The breeze off the lake ruffles my hair and provides relief from the heat. We tilt our table umbrella to stay beneath the shade and catch up with one another like life couldn't be any better.

***

The thing about grief is, it comes in waves. Ebbing and flowing and sometimes turning into a hurricane without any forewarning. Then the bastard disappears for a while, and I almost forget he exists and holds a mean grudge. Out of nowhere he reappears and overpowers you, once again leaving you wrecked on the shores of Lake I-Don't-Want-To-Be-Alive. About twenty-four hours after my bike ride and frozen yogurt break, Sir Grief barges in and commandeers the helm of my ship.

How miserable do I need to be before I actually do something to change things? This is what's carving grooves inside my skull when Aunt Summer throws a glass against the wall, shattering it into blue shards like frozen rain inside the apartment.

She laughs like a lunatic and turns away from the mess to walk back into the kitchen. I check myself for slivers of glass but don't find any. My aunt is singing as she moves around in the other room. I can almost place the lyrics with a song title, but it won't come to me. The strawberry flavored almond milk dripping down the wall, and puddling on the floor has my mind preoccupied. The clink of ice in a glass and the sound of the refrigerator door slamming closed makes me want to follow her into the kitchen to find out what she's doing, but I can't make my feet unglue from their spot under the dining table.

Crazy genes run in my family—no, really—it's true. At least to my untrained mind we have plenty of crazy running around. Besides my mother, my grandfather could out-crazy the worst of them. But I always considered my aunt to be the most dependable regarding mental stability. I haven't seen her in a couple of years so I could be mistaken. Perhaps she's reached her breaking point. Sort of like my mom did after she married Geoff and left the circus for good. Some part of me was counting on Aunt Summer to remain sane so I could pretend to have a rock to shelter under if need be. Like now, when I'm homeless and desperate. She's supposed to be my rock. Yesterday, she seemed sane, but who am I to judge?

"Aunt Summer?" I say, but so feebly I can hardly hear my own voice, so I doubt she can either over her off-key singing.

Did I make a mistake coming here?

I walk around the end of the table toward her galley kitchen. I suck up my apprehension and step into the kitchen just as my pixie-ish, questionably nuts aunt walks out, and we almost collide.

"That felt incredible! Here." She thrusts a tall blue glass filled with ice water at me. "Try it. You won't regret it."

I step back and refuse to take the glass from her.

"What?" she asks. "I'm serious, Jas." She inches forward brandishing the glass like it's vital I take it from her. She takes a drink from the mug in her other hand.

A small pink smear decorates her upper lip after she lowers the mug.

"I love strawberry milk. It's my weird vice right now, which is why you can throw this instead. I'm too addicted to keep wasting this on the wall. Take it."

"I can't." I stare at the mess of pink liquid and blue glass across the room.

"You certainly can and you will. Shit, Jasper. I waited months for something dramatic enough to justify smashing these glasses. You showing up with your life drama is the perfect excuse. Now go ahead." She slams the glass down on the table next to me.

I swallow and slant my gaze at the glass making sure it didn't just break. Water sloshed on the wood, but the glass is intact.

"This isn't going to help anything."

"How do you know unless you try?" she counters and places her knuckles against her bony hip.

"Aren't you going to get in trouble with your landlord?" I say, wondering if almond milk washes off walls.

"Probably, but you can see how much I don't care." She turns and walks back into the kitchen still talking. "Why are you hesitating? Picture the wall as Geoff's face and have at it. I know you need to release some anger, and the smashing sounds are brilliant."

"Aunt Summer, this is bizarre. I can't hurt your apartment and then feel better for doing it."

"I live here, but this isn't my apartment. The owner will get over a dent in the wall. He lives to fix stuff around here. Don't think about it. Think about how you were forced to do a million things against your will. How you've had to live with unreasonable, ridiculous rules that don't make any sense. How Geoff has been controlling your life without your permission. Think about how he's made your mom into a submissive, weak, distant, and manipulative person!" She stands in front of the freezer and the ice cubes clink as she rants.

Aunt Summer's words taunt the pain of my dysfunctional home life. I thought I was handling my emotions like the way some people punish young children. Stick them in a corner and make them hush until they learn a lesson. My aunt is acknowledging she understands how terrible it was to live with a controlling monster. She totally knows what it's like having no control over the basic necessities of life. To always have worries and threats to your well-being shadowing your every breath. The stifling, suffocating fear of always doing something wrong, and of being punished for always being the wrong person in their eyes. She says her father treated her the same way.

The glass sits motionless but calls to me, waving a welcome sign. The urge to throw it at Geoff's face makes me ball my fists with need. *I will not pick it up. I will not pick it up.* I'm not allowed to flip out and let my rage show. I can't scare Evie and Jonah like that. They can't see me lose my mind. The glass holds my sanity and if I voluntarily shatter it, how will I survive after it's broken?

Aunt Summer scoots around me. "Follow me. I'm not giving you a choice about this. Bring the water too."

At this point, I'm afraid to pick up the abandoned missile. I want to kill Geoff, and I might try if I touch it. Aunt Summer is chipping away at well-constructed emotional barriers, and I don't know what to expect if those walls come down.

She heads for the door to her apartment with a medium sized cardboard box in her arms. She pulls the door open and throws a final glance over her shoulder at me. "Grab it and let's go. If you don't, I won't make you the strawberry shortcake I promised you."

Confusion burps through my brain for a split second. She never said anything about shortcake, but boy, she has a real thing for strawberry flavor.

I snatch the glass off the table and rush after her doing my best to ignore the cold, fragile thing in my hand. "Where are you going?" I call after her, but she's two apartments down by the time I step outside.

She's singing again. Not as loud as before, but loud enough—this time I know the words, and it's not helping. My mom used to play the CD in the trailer when I was little. And I used to love singing along with her, but *De Do Do Do, De Da Da Da* by The Police is annoying the ever-loving shit out of me.

Aunt Summer stops walking when she reaches the end of the building and the end of the balcony. She sets the box down next to the railing and belts out the lyrics to the song.

If she didn't sound like a keening Basset Hound, the singing might be tolerable, but she does, and I'm struggling to cope as it is. *She's killing me.*

She flashes a diabolical grin that makes me halt about four steps from the end of the balcony. I return her look with one of doubt and hesitancy.

"Are you all right?" I ask.

She answers with more wailing and lyrics from a different Sting song.

"You better stop singing, or I'm going to jump." I seriously consider this a viable option. Her off-key notes are torturous.

Aunt Summer rolls her eyes and doesn't give into the next line. Instead, she tromps toward me and takes my arm, the one holding the glass of water. She drags me to the very edge, and we peer down at the far end of the parking lot where no cars are parked. This is where the dumpsters are sitting by the fence waiting for their weekly rendezvous with the trash truck.

She starts to hum next to my ear and damn if she hasn't put an earworm in my head and left me singing to myself next to her. Except, now *De Do Do Do, De Da Da Da* is in my brain instead of Sting's more romantic lyrics. I slant my impatient gaze her way. At the moment, I can't even handle the humming.

Her look is priceless. I wish I could laugh this off, but I'm incapable of laughter.

"What?" I ask.

She grips my wrist harder and before I realize what she's going to do she wings my arm out over the end the railing.

"No!" Condensation on the glass makes it extra slick. It slips from my fingers and soars straight down to the black asphalt like an anvil. Shards of blue glass and ice cubes explode in every direction.

"Yes!" She cheers like I just made the perfect game-winning goal.

Unamused, I press my lips together and step back. She bends down and pulls another tall glass full of ice cubes from the box at her feet.

"Another one. And this time, throw like you mean it."

"This is absurd." I start to go back to the apartment.

"You wouldn't do it inside, so I brought everything outside. Jesus, Jasper. You need this."

"I think you need it, not me."

She shrugs. "You're right. I do." She spins around and throws a fast, powerful pitch straight at the dumpster. The crash of glass and echoing against metal ricochets off the side of the building and the privacy fence. Aunt Summer's joy and satisfaction radiates from her whole being even as I see it in her eyes.

"That was phenomenal!" she says, a whoosh of excited breath leaving her lungs.

Looking around I check to see if any of the neighbors are peeking out of their doors yet.

"He made your mom become an accountant. He forced you to run away. He made you get rid of your dog." She takes another glass from the box.

"He didn't make me. I chose to do those things."

"But he was the catalyst."

Swallowing is suddenly difficult. Geoff had become this nightmare of fantastical proportion. Part of my brain wants to blame him for everything. For every hardship in my life. I hate his guts, and I detest the awful goatee on his horrid face.

I take the glass from Aunt Summer's hand and step up to the invisible plate. I stare at the open dumpster and picture all the crap I want to throw away from my life. Then I hurl the glass straight into its depths. When it bursts, I picture my anger, frustration and hatred blasting into minuscule bits. Pieces so small they can't exist in the physical realm any longer.

Aunt Summer goes right back to singing lyrics with maniacal joy.

"Oh my god. Stop," I plead.

She hands me another glass full of ice cubes, and she continues with the lyrics.

"I can't do this if you're going to sing like that."

"What?" she asks innocently. "I'm contributing to your delinquency while making you a better person."

"Just no more singing."

She shrugs, but with a twinkle in her eye that has me worried and rightly so. As soon as the glass makes contact with the dumpster she starts howling again.

I suck in a deep breath and let it go. At least if a song is going to be stuck in your head, Roxanne is better than De Do Do Do.

My aunt reaches for a glass and prepares to throw. "This is for the night my car broke down at three in the morning, in the snow, when Finn was out of town!" She let fly, and I follow with round number four.

"And this is for having my stuff stolen when I was already homeless!" I scream and hurl the glass down to the ground, not even caring if it hits the dumpster.

"Hey," we hear behind us, and we both spin around in surprise.

"Finn!" Aunt Summer cries and tosses the glass over the railing before running toward my uncle. "You're back early!"

"Thought I'd surprise you." He envelops her in a tight embrace.

I take the last glass from the box and stare at it in contemplation. What is the last thing in life I would like to smash? Breaking sounds remind me of what Caspar said. She liked shattering things too. This one is her. One for one. We'll be even now.

Before my last pitch, I close my eyes and let myself breathe. Then I throw and listen to the tinkling music of transformation. Relief and exhilaration are all wrapped together. My eyes begin to water from the emotional release, and then I'm aware of Aunt Summer and Uncle Finn talking to me.

"Let's go. Finn says there were cops down the street." She's urging me to move while Uncle Finn picks up the empty box and tosses it toward the dumpsters.

***

Back inside the apartment, we close the door and let silence engulf the room. I think we're straining to hear through the walls and waiting for the cops to come knocking and asking questions. At least that's what I'm doing.

"Well, if you get a ticket, you deserve it." Uncle Finn presses a kiss to my aunt's lips.

"It'll be worth it," she says while wearing her heart on her sleeve. Her happiness over Finn's early arrival shows on every square inch of her body.

"Here you go. I checked the mail on my way up, and this was in there for you."

Uncle Finn hands me an envelope. I plop down on the couch and find my debit card inside. I pick up my phone from the coffee table, and a voicemail message is waiting for me from a number I don't recognize. I hit send and wait for the prompts. I'm mildly stunned when Bob Brows Scarberry invites me back to S & D Inc. and asks me if I'm interested in joining their troupe.

Aunt Summer and Uncle Finn meander into the kitchen catching up on all sorts of domestic issues. They smile and listen to what the other has to say like it matters. Their body language, touching a shoulder, resting a hand on the other's hip, or laying a palm on a back or stomach, is all so loving and beautiful. I couldn't be happier for my aunt, but I reflect on how different my mother's marriage is. Tension is always running high in our household. Whispering behind Geoff's back so no one pisses him off is a common occurrence, and little or no open affection is shown toward each other. Aunt Summer and Uncle Finn are the exact opposite. I stop comparing differences and take my phone to the bedroom to return Bob's call and give my aunt and uncle a little privacy.

Chapter Seventeen

"Life is the greatest illusion of all." — J. Pyrah

Audition Number Two.

Bob Brows sits with me on a bench outside the gym at S & D Inc. The interview isn't what I imagined it would be. I mean some of the questions he asks are normal, like my U.S. citizenship and if I'm an adult and don't need parental permission. *Do I seriously look that young?* But mostly we chat about the inconsequential weather, and venture toward the more existential, such as, does life exist in other galaxies and why or why not? He also asks if I'm a sports fan, and what sport reigns supreme.

Bob Brows offers his opinion. "Soccer rules over other major league team sports while individual sports such as cycling and downhill skiing are rated on a different scale."

"I don't follow any sports teams, although hockey would be my first pick if I had the time. And to be honest with you, I'd take a live concert over a game any day."

His stunning blue eyes give nothing away as he listens. I don't know how this interview is progressing until he asks, "Would you like to demonstrate your talents to the gang and me?"

"That would be great," I say.

We step inside, and he gestures to the practice floor as if I have the entire place to myself. Which apparently I do since no one else is around.

"I need a few minutes to warm up, and then I can show you what I do on the silks or the low wire."

"It's your choice today, Jasper. I'll go and grab Marc and Tink."

"Let's do this." I slip out of my favorite Corban-exclusive shoes.

Bob leaves me alone to stretch and returns ten minutes later with the other members of The Circus of Misfit Marvels. The variety act puts plenty of vids online, and I did as much research as I could before the audition. They certainly have an edge to their acts reminiscent of classic sideshows of the historical traveling circus variety, but they incorporate their own uniqueness and style which makes them stand out by today's standards. I wasn't sure if my aerial silk routines or low wire would be enough, but I had to at least try. Before making the drive to S & D, I did what I could in my aunt's apartment to practice, but it's not the same. Aunt Summer also took me to a gym in Chicago, so I could work out, and it helped a lot, but I'm mainly counting on my muscle memory and determination to carry me through. I want to perform on the silk rather than the low wire. The low wire was never my passion even if I'm pretty good at it and enjoy it occasionally.

I shimmy up the silk and find my starting position. It feels right in every cell of my being. There isn't any music to move to, but I've done this set a thousand times, and I can hear every beat inside my head. I set up and wrap the fabric, then I add the spins, twirls, extensions and hanging tricks. My closing exercises hit the counts perfectly, and I swing down to the mat, smile, and take a bow.

"I've seen enough," Bob says as I jog over to the three of them.

"Good job," Tink says.

Marc remains silent.

"Take your time to cool down and step into the office so we can finalize an agreement."

"So, I've got the job?" Hope radiates out of my every pore.

Bob looks at Marc instead of answering me. He nods his approval and walks out of the gym.

"Congratulations. I believe we've found our newest member," Tink says and follows Marc out.

"Meet me in the office," Bob Brows says.

I'm left alone as the world shifts below my feet. Can I join this troupe of guys I don't even know? Did a job just fall in my lap? Am I too stunned to think clearly? I guzzle some water, slip Aunt Summer's sweatshirt over my head, and gather my bag. A few minutes later, my hand is shaking as I fill out paperwork for my new job.

Marc comes in as we finish going over my very first contract of employment.

"Can you start training today?"

"I can." I remind myself my aunt and uncle said to take my time and not worry about returning their car today.

"Meet me out back when you're finished with Bob."

***

"Life is about illusions. Your mind sees what it thinks it knows. I create illusions for an audience, and the people see what they want to see. It's entertainment and magic, but for the most part, it's a mirror of reality."

I nod, and Marc does a stellar sleight-of-hand trick by producing a dog biscuit from seemingly nowhere. He lets out a high-pitched whistle, grabbing the attention of a small black dog with a white star on its chest. Marc tosses the dog treat into the air, and the animal catches it without hardly trying.

"Meet the magnificent, Twix. He belongs to Bob and the dog goes everywhere Bob goes. His keen mind and house elf fugly good looks outweigh his propensity for outlandish flatulence. How's your sense of smell?"

"Good?" I ask while trying to grasp all the words flowing off Marc's quick but precise tongue.

"That's unfortunate. Twix can run us out of the bus on a good day. He's allowed a handful of these herbal biscuits every day. My wife Sasha swears upon Maya they help with the gas, but I haven't seen the benefits. Sasha creates an illusion within the bus. She keeps the tin box of dog biscuits at the front of the bus near Bob Brows. Twix likes his treats and Bob is his person. The worst of the odor, therefore, stays near the front. Bob, in turn, likes plenty of fresh air when he drives the bus and, therefore, has his window open. It's an illusion, you see? To think the dog treats have sole responsibility for the lack of foul air coming from the dog's rear end when in reality it's a combination of factors saving us all from suffocation and the befoulment of air quality inside our vehicle."

Marc produces another dog treat before my eyes and tosses it to Twix's back. The dog whips around and snatches it out of the air before it touches the ground.

"You're basically telling me Twix is a valuable member of the troupe, but he's also silently trying to kill you guys with noxious gas?" I say.

"Precisely, but it's the combination of factors that creates the illusion. You're the extra factor I need to make my illusions work in front of an audience."

"And you think I'll be a suitable substitute for Sasha even though I've never been an apprentice to an illusionist?"

"Ahh," A gleam shines within the depths of his liquid brown eyes. "You have stage presence and experience as an entertainer. You may not be familiar with the routine, but you draw the eye. This fact alone, Jasper, is a valuable asset. Your part in the act is simple yet essential as long as you are willing to try your best."

"I can do it." Being around performance artists, showgirls, clowns, and acrobats of all varieties, it was easy to recognize how they all had their own mojo. The variety of personalities was astounding, and I like to think I learned from all of them. Evie and I lost our biological father at a young age, and I believe the members of the Farinelli Circus thought it was their collective duty to look out for us and raise us as their own. All the kids were treated like a big family. Marc seems to think highly of my stage presence, and although it's hard to agree with him one hundred percent, I'm sure I can do what he needs me to. "I'm eager to learn everything you want to teach me."

"Very good," he says, and we begin.

Illusions are powerful manipulators of the mind. Marc spends the next three or four hours proving to me what you see with your eyes is not reality. Sasha, his pregnant wife, joins my training, and she's sweet and helpful as can be. Plus, she provides comic relief, making jokes about her mishaps with knife juggling and shooting arrows into Marc on accident. I can't tell if she's exaggerating or not, but she helps me understand what I need to do to assist her husband.

Marc's mastery of his chosen art is apparent and even though he confuses me repeatedly, I'm excited to work with him on stage. To be honest, I'm also scared. I know that, too, is another illusion of my own making. Fear and nervousness will keep me vigilant and anxious to always do better and be a more adept performer. Marc, although hard to wrap my mind around, is going to be my best boss ever—or at the very least—the most intriguing.

After eating a homemade superfood bar—that resembles one of Twix's dog biscuits—with Sasha and Marc, I meet back up with Bob Brows and Tink. They show me the bus we'll be living in while we're on the road and talk about what they do.

Tink hangs ridiculously heavy cookware and tools, like circular saws and bowling balls, from his body piercings. He also performs amazing and dangerous feats of human oddity using his body to balance huge items on his chin, forehead, toes, and other parts, the likes of which I've never seen before. It's one thing to watch it on the internet, but a live demonstration, sort of warps my brain. And don't get me wrong, I like the distortion. He tries to describe his human pulley system, but I'll just wait and see that part of the show another day. Bob Brows tells me Tink manages a majority of the marketing and scheduling for the troupe. I watched a lot of Bob's performances on the computer so he doesn't need to demonstrate his act today. Spidey is the last of the Misfit Marvels to meet before I'm officially their new cast member.

As we're walking away from the bus, Tink and Bob Brows tell me how it has been converted to run on vegetable oil and the exhaust often smells like French fries. They did most of the work for the biodiesel conversion and they definitely like explaining the benefits and low environmental impact of their bus.

"When we first converted the engine, biodiesel wasn't as widely available as it is now so we added the extra tank to hold the veggie oil." Tink points at the multi-colored oil drum on the roof of the bus.

There's a substantial-looking roof rack and what appears to be a platform on the entire roof of the bus along with a small hoist to lift things up.

"Who painted the bus?" I ask.

They share a look of camaraderie, and we all gaze at the wild painting on wheels.

"Sasha designed the logo and banners. Then she, Spidey, and a few artist friends did the actual painting," Bob explains.

I smile with appreciation at the colorful bus and the trailer behind it. The images have a classic sideshow aesthetic with lots of vibrant colors. The design makes me think of hyper-realistic folk art with surrealism thrown in for good measure. Caricatures of Bob Brows, Tink, Marc, and someone who must be Spidey are painted on the side. I can't help but chuckle at the faint cloud of painted green gas around Twix.

"It's uh…" I stall out as I search for the best adjective. "One of a kind. It's the most amazing tour bus I've ever seen."

"The other side is even better," Tink says.

"I'll be sure to check it out," I say.

We begin walking back to the main building when the door opens, and a short younger guy steps out. He closes the door and walks into the parking lot, head lowered so he doesn't see us.

"Spidey! Over here, man," Bob Brows calls.

He glances up, looking somewhat forlorn and withdrawn. He gives a tiny nod of acknowledgment and shuffles in our direction. He's wearing black jeans and a faded black T-shirt, Converse, and thick black-framed glasses.

"This is Jasper Pyrah. I told you about her," Bob says.

I hold my hand out, but Spidey doesn't shake it.

"How are you?" he asks, and his vibe comes across as uncomfortable and out of place.

"I'm good, thanks. How about you?" I say because small talk fills the absence even though it's impersonal and somewhat weird for everyone.

"Are you like those other girls?"

"I'm not sure what that means."

"I don't know what I mean either. I'm sorry." He looks away, his farsighted gaze trained on something beyond my left shoulder.

"Don't be sorry. I'm not like other girls when it comes to, you know, everything. Being normal never worked out well for me."

"Good." He pushes his glasses up the bridge of his nose. His focus shifts, and he's staring at me again. "That should help."

"I hope so." I don't know what helps what, but whatever. A small smile tickles the corners of my lips. Spidey is completely awkward and uncomfortable talking to me. Yet, I instantly develop a soft spot for him and feel like slugging him on the arm.

"Spidey is his stage name although it's the only name anyone calls him. Tell her why everyone calls you Spidey," Tink says.

"I have a lot of spiders. And snakes."

"I saw the picture on the bus." I gesture across the parking area toward the painting of the guy wearing glasses. There's a large boa constrictor around his neck and shoulders and a tarantula on his head.

"That's Madame Pauline. She's the largest of my pets. Gram is the friendliest. You'll see her the most."

"Gram is a Chaco golden knee tarantula. You may or may not want to see her too often," Bob Brows says.

I try not to grimace. "We travel with tarantulas and snakes?"

"We do. It's all right if you don't like them, just don't take it out on them. They can't help what they are." Spidey stares down at his Chucks.

"I'm good. They don't bother me." I try to convince myself and ignore the vivid images inside my head of escaped tarantulas and snakes aboard the bus...while I'm trying to sleep.

"Gotta go now. See you later." Spidey shuffles off without further ado.

"He's always nervous around new people," Bob Brows says.

Bob is calm and straight forward, but something about him exudes distinction, and it's more than his expressive and overgrown giant wooly caterpillar eyebrows. He's calm but intense. Both he and Marc are totally unique and authentic. While I value those qualities in people, they will take some getting used to.

"I can relate," I say.

"Spidey won't shake hands with anyone," Tink says. "Not because he's rude, OCD, or what have you. It's because he's always messing with his pets and they carry salmonella and the tarantula hair can be irritating to some people's skin. He also handles a lot of feeder bugs and other things that gross people out. If he's keeping his hands to himself, he's just being courteous."

"Oh. Well, thanks for telling me."

"He's an awkward little troll most of the time. It's part of his way. There's a good but thoughtful weirdo inside of him. Kind of like the rest of us. You'll get used to it."

"I think I already have." I feel a small tug somewhere deep inside my chest for these people who I barely know but feel comfortable around.

***

Dear Evie,

Don't be alarmed if you forget everything I write to you. You can always come back later and read it again. That's the greatest thing about these letters. They'll mean something different to you every time you read them because you're never the same person twice. It's an enigma, Evie. It's one of the great paradoxes—everything is the same, and nothing is the same. The thought that everything exists inside also exists on the outside makes me shiver and want to dance. This is why I can go up in the silk or out on the stage and lose myself in the movements. I'm sure there is beauty somewhere inside of me, and I try to let it show on the outside. I close my eyes and let life move through me. All the training becomes important then. I can't just stand in front of a crowd like a bumbling idiot. So for the sake of a decent performance, I'm grateful to Mom for what she taught me. She's a beautiful performer, and I think the two of us inherited some of our talents from her. Even to Geoff, I can be grateful sometimes. There may be a lump of lead where his heart should be, but he made me practice when I didn't want to.

Today, my years of forced practice paid off, and I have a real job. The news is still sinking in, and of course, I wanted to tell you first. I tried to call, but Mom didn't answer her phone.

Thinking of you today brought up old memories. Do you remember the bliss of playing on the lot in whatever city we landed in for countless hours? I don't know what we found so fascinating about carving channels in the mud and watching the water trickle by, or watching ants carry insanely heavy loads, but the experience of being together without any expectations is what life is about. I loved creating our own ribbon dances and practicing them in some farmer's field. Find those moments as often as you can. I found one today with total strangers. Listen to the song of your heart, Evie. You'll be happier for it.

***

After returning to Aunt Summer's apartment, I collect all the letters and notes I wrote to Evie since staying here, except for this last one. I'm not ready to be rid of it. The remaining pile of miscellaneous wrinkled, ink blotchy, soul-destroying papers needs to go away.

I wish I knew where my journal was, but wishes and dreams aren't fulfilled on a whim in my normal everyday life. Corban hasn't answered my text messages about whether or not my journal was left in his SUV. I'm positive that's where I lost it. The complex I'm gaining by thinking about him reading my private thoughts and letters to Evie easily explains why he won't tell me if he has it. I wouldn't admit to reading about someone's psychoses either. I'm pretty sure my complex is developing a complex over my misplaced journal.

I step out on my aunt's balcony and set the letters on the barbecue grill and stab them with the tongs as their edges curl to black and the words catch flame.

"You okay now?" Aunt Summer asks.

I don't answer at first. The embers hold me, hypnotic. *Am I okay?* Is that the million dollar question? "Are your neighbors scared of you?" I ask.

"Why? Because I break things when I need to and barbecue letters instead of ribs?"

"Yeah." I continue to concentrate on the grill.

"In case you didn't notice, I don't care what anyone thinks about me." There's a hint of challenge and a lot of humor written on her delicate and feminine face.

"Must be nice."

"You'll get there, Jas. I know you will. The only opinion about yourself that matters is your own. Don't ever forget it."

I head back inside the apartment and straight to my bed clutching my letter to Evie. Aunt Summer's faith in me helps sleep come a little easier, but I still have a rough night of dreams and anxiety.

***

Two days later.

"I need to do this." I'm trying to convince myself as much as her. Aunt Summer shuts down the engine of her car and turns to face me in the passenger seat. We're in the parking lot at S & D Inc., and I'm supposed to hit the road with my new troupe today.

"You don't. You could stay with Finn and me and take the rest of the summer off. You can start college classes somewhere near us. I'm sure there's a school that will accept your credits. We're happy to have you for as long as you want to stay."

"We've been over this. Your offer is tempting, but if I don't try to make it on my own, I'll regret it for the rest of my life. Does that make sense?"

"Completely. You need to forge your own trails. I get it. I've been there, but if it doesn't work out, you can always come live with me."

I lean across the seat and wrap my arms around her. "Thank you. Thank you for everything. And I love my new costumes. You're the most amazing seamstress in the world."

"I know I am." She flashes a smug grin.

I take a deep breath. "I might take you up on your offer when we're off-season."

"You better call me like once a day. I don't know who these dudes are. I mean, just because they're on YouTube doesn't mean they're not a bunch of freaks. Well, you know what I mean." She shrugs since they are exactly that—a traveling freak show.

My new job is the best thing that's ever happened to me, but prying myself out of the car is difficult, to say the least. The imagined challenges of starting a new job, and living with strangers, are keeping me from opening the door.

"I know what you mean," I say. "They're new to me as well, and I don't know what to expect. I'm scared," I whisper.

"Good," she whispers back. "If it weren't scary, it wouldn't be worth doing."

I place a hand on the door handle and gnaw my lower lip.

Aunt Summer starts singing Bob Marley's *Three Little Birds*.

I close the car door with Aunt Summer's uplifting, albeit strained, voice dancing inside my head. Bless her thoughtful, caring soul, but my aunt cannot carry a tune.

Chapter Eighteen

"Do not judge me for where I stand today,
until you know how far I traveled to get here." — J. Pyrah

"She thinks you are on the run from shadows and invisible demons." Spidey holds Pubes, the tarantula in his hand.

"I'm not running away from anything. Bob Brows and Marc hired me, so here I am," I say in defense to the obscure observation.

"She says if you don't stop running you'll never see what's chasing you."

"Who knew giant blue spiders could also be oracles." I pull my knees up to my chest to hug myself as Spidey handles his creepy pet.

"She's insightful when the time is right."

My nerves tingle as if Pubes and her fellow tarantulas are running up and down my back. I don't like the direction this conversation is going. Spidey is usually a quiet guy, and I had moved to the back of the bus in hope that the air would be fresher for our long drive to Santa Fe.

The last three days included three performances. One show in Oklahoma City and two in St. Louis. It had been a mental and emotional trial as I became accustomed to the new routines and habits of my troupe mates while trying not to mess up anything. For the most part, I did all right, but I need to improve the flow of my transitions when assisting Marc. He made some minor suggestions and told me I was doing great. I don't feel great. I'm exhausted.

"How come you don't always bring Pubes on stage with you?" I ask as I lean back against a cushion and stop reliving the previous shows inside my tired mind. The spiders aren't my favorite part of traveling on the bus, but I accept them for what they are, just as Spidey recommended I do on audition day.

"I call her Sarah when we're not performing." He gazes down at her with admiration and what I think seems like infatuation. "They're fragile animals. Sarah can be skittish. Much more than Smithi and Gram. If I get a negative vibe from the crowd, she stays at home."

"Huh." I wonder if choosing Spidey's side of the bus was a mistake. I remember how repulsive Twix's gas is at the front of the bus and how Spidey's cages have little to no scent. The black dog is snorting as he rubs his back inside his dog bed behind Bob Brows. The dog's a gas bag today, and the more he squirms in his bed, the more toxic the air in the bus becomes. Despite the nearly constant warnings not to, someone slipped him some people food, hence the terrible odor.

"Why call her Pubes? Sarah's a sweet name. Tink told me it was because you dyed your pubic hair the same neon blue color as her legs."

"You can check if you want to," Spidey grins sheepishly down at his crotch.

He doesn't look up at me when he says this and his cheeks flare with embarrassment, but it didn't stop him from making the comment. I look out the window at the passing desert and speculate about how many hours it will be until we arrive in Santa Fe. Thinking about my fellow performer's pubic region needs to go out the window with my gaze. Spidey starts talking again, so I don't need to turn down his offer to confirm the hair color inside his boxers.

"Their names are short for their scientific names. Sarah is a Greenbottle blue tarantula, *Chromatopelma cyaneopubescens*. Gram is a *Grammostola pulchripes*, a Chaco golden knee And Smithi is a

Mexican red knee also known as *Brachypelma smithi*. A name can give a thing an identity, but identity is different than personality. Pubes is her identity to the outside world. Sarah is her soul's name."

"Spidey is your stage name, right?"

"It's a nickname I couldn't get rid of. No more, no less." He places Sarah inside her terrarium with the careful and practiced ease of handling the delicate creature on a regular basis. He picks out what might be the remains of a cricket from her cage and retracts his hand. I eyeball the dead bug parts and try not to look too grossed out. "She's extremely sensitive to too much moisture in her environment," he explains as he wipes his fingers on the inside of a plastic trash bag near the cages. "You can't leave carcasses in her cage. It could make her sick. My real name is Brandon. I never asked anyone to call me anything else. Everyone on the road likes to change their names. I understand, but I don't think it's necessary." He throws me a questioning look behind those thick lenses of his and waits for me tell him my real name.

"My real name is Jasper. Jasper was my father's middle name. I gave up my stage name, and I'm trying to just be myself."

"If you want, I'll give you a professional name after I get to know you a little better."

"Can't wait to hear what you come up with. You know, because Pubes is so freaking inspiring."

That earns me a hearty smirk.

"Should I start calling you Brandon?"

He snickers again, and the corner of his mouth stays turned up. "If you do, everyone will think we're dating."

"Let's not go there. No offense or anything. I'm just off a bad breakup. I don't need any new rumors or even a hint of involvement with someone."

"No big deal. My arachnids are a turn off to you—and everyone."

"Sort of," I admit.

"Some girls are into the snakes, so I'm holding out for the right woman. She has to be okay with Sarah and the others, too, or she's not the one for me." He focuses on his collection of glass and plastic jars and terrariums full of spiders, bugs, and snakes.

"Absolutely," I agree as I try to picture Spidey's future wife. "Wait for the perfect girl, Spidey. I'm sure she's out there."

"You're much more optimistic than I am." He places his hand on top of Madam Pauline, the boa constrictor's, cage.

He acts as if it's already settled in his mind that his creepy-slithery pets are likely to be his only source of female connection for a long time coming.

"They're misunderstood in all the right ways," he says, pushing his thick-framed glasses up the bridge of his nose.

"Why do you say 'the right ways'?"

"People are afraid of what they don't understand."

"And they shy away from what scares them," I add.

"They do. People's reaction is not what interests me. That's more or less predictable. I want to figure out why these creatures hold so much power over us. I can spew out facts about any of them all day long. My logical side tells me they're nothing more than reptiles and arachnids and a natural part of our environment. They're instinctual and perfect examples of nature at its best, but it doesn't explain Madam Pauline's ability to captivate an audience, or why she lets me do what I do with her on stage and never acts with aggression toward me. I want to know everything I can't see with my eyes. I need to understand why the spider weaves a web, or the snake sheds his skin in one piece. I'm not talking about the literal explanation, Jasper. Science is only the beginning of what we know."

"Well, we need to start somewhere." I try following whatever the hell tangent he is suddenly on.

"Ahh, a good answer from someone who doesn't know what direction they're headed."

"I'm not on the run." I circle back to where this conversation started. "Where do you start?" I ask.

"Anywhere I want. Sometimes at the end, sometimes in the middle, and sometimes at the flat bottom."

"Back up a second. Are you telling me if you want to learn why the first spider ever wove a web, you assume you know the answer and work backward to the question?"

"No. I assume nothing. There are no answers. Only the questions matter."

"You lost me."

"I have not. You're asking and seeking, which is my point. Seek the truth, Jasper. Don't ever stop looking for answers. If you think you know something, you've failed. You know nothing, just like I know nothing. The wisdom is always in the question."

"I'm not wise. I'm tired." I look over at my empty bunk.

"We all are," he mumbles as he organizes and double-checks the lids on the jars and cages to make sure each one is securely fastened. "We're all tired of living a lie. We're all tired of searching for answers without any meaning. The global consciousness is tired of the bullshit of society and feeling like our spirits are being buried under a mountain of consumerism and greed and the pointlessness of it all."

"Is this why I came back here to sit with you?" I ask as I start to move toward my bed.

"See there." Spidey gives a knowing nod. "The answer is in your question. You learn quickly, grasshopper," he says with a bad Asian accent.

"I learned you're sort of a freak." I stick my tongue out at him.

"Why do you think it is said, it takes one to know one?"

He's keeping up the cheesy Asian accent. "Shut up now before I find Tink's staple gun and use it on your mouth."

"A strong spirit, she is. The snake charmer likes it, he does."

"Oh my God." I roll my eyes toward the sky and laugh. I lie down on my mattress and shake my head at the silliness of the shifts in his personality from bombastic guru to Chinaman to Yoda in the span of a few seconds.

"My insights are master level but do not put me on your pedestal, grasshopper. I am but only a man."

"Staple gun," I say as a final warning.

Out of the corner of my eye, I see him break character and laugh before turning away to hide his face. I close my eyes and listen to the drone of the road noise, and I'm thankful for the smile tickling my lips and the warmth in my heart of having someone to joke with.

***

What happens when a stage artist messes up on the job? The answer is doubt.

Crushing doubt and haunting demons.

I hit my head on one of Marc's props during his act tonight. The dizziness is instant, and I sit down right there on stage, well, more of a sit/fall down, but still, it definitely isn't a planned part of the show. A heckler guffaws and makes a comment about ditzy bimbos. Marc recovers immediately while I sit behind a prop waiting to black out. Bob Brows gathers me up and escorts me off the stage while Marc goes on. I'm ready to get back on stage a minute, or even seconds later, but Bob won't let me.

Tink squeezes my shoulder and asks if I need to go to the emergency room. I decline.

Spidey says, "Shit doth happen to us all. Sweat it, you will not."

After refusing professional medical attention, Bob gives me his own medical assessment and won't let me stand for the rest of the show, or help pack up the trailer and the bus afterward.

Bob Brows drives us to the campground we booked for the night, and I exit the bus to brood over my inadequacies. Brooding is obviously one of my favorite pastimes. I picture myself living with Aunt Summer and Uncle Finn until I decide my life would be better spent at the bottom of Lake Michigan.

When I return from my walk, I'm not ready to board the bus. My head is fine, and the small bump doesn't even hurt, but facing Marc will. Marc walks out of the trailer holding one of the tents, and I move out of sight to avoid talking with him. He hasn't spoken to me either, and I'm taking it as a sign that my job is over. I park myself near a tree and try to make up my mind about shutting myself in my bunk or sleeping on the ground. There are more tents, and I consider borrowing one for the night. The clement temperature, a clear sky full of stars, and no wind is ideal for sleeping outdoors.

Twix skips by me and stops by the back corner of the bus, looks up, and barks. The hoist we sometimes use to load heavy gear on the roof swings out and the winch cable begins to lower down. A small flat-bottomed hammock is attached to the end of the cable, and I watch as it reaches the ground. Twix noses his way into the hammock and lies flat on his stomach. The lift system goes in reverse and Twix is lifted up. I glance up to the roof of the bus and see Bob watching his dog being raised through the air. When Twix is level with the platform, Bob reaches out and swings the hoist around so Twix can join him on the roof.

Bob peers over, and I'm caught staring at the strange pair. "Come on up," he calls.

I drag myself away from my tree and over to the ladder and climb up.

The view is stunning and reminds me of every memory I have of being on top of the trailer when I was a kid. My mom, sister and I would always sit on the roof to watch fireworks, or adjust our satellite dish if we couldn't get a good signal. The roof was always the best place to find a different perspective. Apparently, it's also the place to lose one's job.

"I can leave tomorrow," I say as I approach Bob Brows and Twix.

They're camped out on top of Bob's sleeping bag. He's got a lantern, a book, his banjo, Twix's dog bed, a thermos, and some food, by his side and seems more than comfortable.

"Do you have no respect for your contract?"

"Isn't it null and void after tonight?"

"Absolutely not."

"But I..."

"What? Had an accident? Are you experiencing any side effects?"

"No. I'm fine," I say.

"I thought so. If you were unwell, you wouldn't take such a long walk."

I chew my lip and try to breathe.

"Take a seat." Bob gestures to the platform.

The outdoor carpeting adds a decorative touch to the roof deck and provides a little cushion as I settle down.

"You're not fired."

"But Marc hasn't said one thing to me since I ruined his show."

"He's a man of introspection. He's likely focused on what happened, but not in the way you're thinking. Matter of fact, he told me he learned something new after he had his impromptu rush to continue alone on stage. He always goes silent when he's working hard on something."

"But the crowd. Did you hear their gasps and the guy yelling at me to get off the stage?"

"Let go of all your blame, shame, and guilt. These are not real things, Jasper."

"They feel real. I may not be able to work with Marc again. I'm so embarrassed." I keep my voice low because Marc is probably somewhere nearby setting up his tent and I don't want him to hear me.

"Your feelings are real, and they are powerful. But the force charging your emotions is only a collection of false thoughts."

Bob sits cross-legged scooping crackers into a can of tuna and eating it. He appears not the least bit disturbed by my announcement that I should leave before I ruin everything The Circus of Misfit Marvels has created.

"My thoughts are making me crazy today," I admit.

"It happens to everyone." He places his food to the side.

Twix's ears perk up, and his nose begins twitching in the direction of the cracker box.

"Not for you, dog," Bob says, and Twix lays his head back down.

He's silent for so long I begin to think our talk is over. The roof is surprisingly comfortable and knowing I'm not fired is even better, but I'm not sure if I should sit here or say goodnight. I shift around as if I'm about to leave.

"What does your soul long for, Jasper?"

Surprised by the question, I glance over at Bob, but he's staring at the western horizon. "What is a soul?"

"The part of you that never gives up."

"What if I've given up a thousand and one times?" I stare at the sliver of a waning crescent moon.

"That wasn't your soul."

"How do I find it?" I ask, sliding my gaze over to Bob and Twix.

"You don't."

"I don't understand."

"Shut your eyes and stop thinking. The nothingness inside you is the tip of your soul," he says.

I pause.

"Are you doing it?" he asks.

"I don't know."

"If you're thinking about it, you're not doing it."

"It's there," I finally say.

"Now hug it."

"That's dumb." I smile and a silent laugh bubbles inside me. He doesn't reply. I modify my insult. "Sorry. You're stupidly charming. Is that better?"

"Maybe."

"Well, you're not stupid... but definitely interesting."

"That works. Now, keep your eyes closed, Jasper. Do you sense the emptiness?"

"Yes."

"Hold it, but *don't* think. When you're ready, move past the point of no return and take in your landscape. If you get distracted, take a breath, and glide smoothly back to where you were. Are you ready? Now get set... and go." His voice fades with last words. "Your soul wants you to remember who you are."

From the roof of the bus, I picture myself leaving my body behind and joining the heavens. The stars are showing off their full glory tonight, and I wish I could be one of them.

How long am I lost to the vastness of nothing and everything all at once? Time escapes me.

"Do you know who you are, Bob?" I ask, not even knowing if he's still with me on the roof.

He says, "When I don't know anything, that's when I'm closest to my true self."

"Is there clarity in that space?"

"Perfect, immeasurable peace."

I can't even hear him breathe. The stillness of his body and soul is equally unnerving and calming. Even Twix seems to be part of our experiment and is completely silent—and not gassy.

"Is this the time of day when you imagine your performances? Do you see yourself on stage being the total badass you are before you do it?"

There's a slight movement somewhere to my left, or perhaps just a whiff of air leaving Bob's lungs.

"If you're asking whether or not I use visualization and meditation techniques to help my act, the answer is yes. Do you also put to use mental powers?"

"Me?" I say with doubt. "Seriously, Bob, I'd love to say I do, but I'm more of a plan-at-the-very-last-minute-and-hope-it-goes-well kind of girl."

"Everyone has their own way, Jasper. If we could all learn to accept ourselves and stop comparing and judging, the world would spin around much smoother."

"I'd like to try this meditation thing some more. I think I use dance and practice time on the aerial silk to bring me to the place where I am now. If I can be in a better state of mind before I step on stage, maybe I'll screw-up less."

"It does seem to go that way more often than not."

"Do you mind if I come up here again? Next time, I'll wait until you come down," I promise.

"Join me anytime. The roof of the world belongs to no one," he says.

Even though Bob offers me a place to sleep on the roof, I decide to climb down and borrow one of the tents to sleep alone with the window flap open so I can see the sky. I fall asleep listening to the tinkling twang of Bob's banjo, and I'm content with my life.

Chapter Nineteen

"The privilege of a lifetime is being who you are."
— Joseph Campbell

The text message I send to Corban on our drive from New Mexico to Colorado reads, *Hey. I'll be in Boulder with the Misfit Marvels for a couple of days. Can I buy you lunch or breakfast or something? You know, to thank you for driving me to Chicago and getting me a job.*

Corban: Sure. Tell me when and where. I'll bring your journal.

My journal may be resurrected, after all, I think as we cross the border between the two states. When Denver approaches, I send another text to Corban.

Me: I'm almost in Denver. When can we get together?

Corban: Are you proposing now? I wasn't ready for a long term commitment, but if it's the only way I can see you, I accept.

Me: Proposing? You should get over yourself. After completing that monumental task, how about meeting me at the venue? We'll be at The Anti-Gravity Bar from 5 'til — late. Whatever works for you.

Corban: I'll be there. Enjoy Boulder. Humidity not 9001% like it is in the Midwest.

As we pull up, The Anti-Gravity Bar might be the smallest venue we've been to since we left base camp in Illinois. Looks aren't always deceiving, and when we enter the club, I check out the small stage and realize I won't be performing on the silks tonight or tomorrow. The ceiling isn't high enough above the stage, and I can't see any type of support beams.

Bob Brows and the manager discuss the details of our needs while the rest of us finish looking around.

Tink informs me, "The owner is a friend of Bob's. The club is well-established and has a faithful following who appreciate oddities and alternative forms of entertainment. Our three shows are sold out. Plus Bob's friend will let us stay at his house while we're in town."

"Any idea what I'm supposed to do instead of my aerial act?"

"I thought you were a contortionist?"

"Not really," I say.

"But you have other skills. You'll come up with something."

"I guess I need to talk to Bob. Do you know if we can add people to the guest list? Can I put Corban on it?"

"He's already on it. And go speak with Bob. I'm sure there's a plan in place regarding the low ceiling."

Regardless of the silks having to stay in the trailer, the night goes on without mayhem or discomfort. Tink was right in that the crowd is small, but their enthusiasm is felt throughout the club. Their silence as they concentrate on Marc's illusions is equaled with cheers and whistles after he melts their minds and makes them question their own existence. Bob Brows is spot on as he swallows an ungodly long sword and other items which don't belong down someone's esophagus. He shows off his crazy-good upside down foot juggling skills and finishes by playing a song on his banjo while standing on his head. I assist him by placing the banjo in his hands once he's upside down, and the weirdest part is—I mean it's all a bit odd to be quite honest—the banjo is right side up which means Bob plays the thing upside down and backward. Bob asked me to stay in the background and dance to his song and place the banjo back on the stand when he's done. Since the club is small and the audience respectful, Spidey finds his element and does a smashing good job of creeping out the crowd with his spiders and snakes. It's a night to remember, and I can't wait to jot down the highlights in my journal once I have it back.

So when we take our final bow of the evening, and I spot Corban standing to the side of the stage, I'm all at once happy and content on every level.

After a shower and change of clothes, I meet Corban outside and try not to be too anxious about the return of my ridiculously missed journal.

I bump my shoulder into his and smile.

"Great show." He shrugs. "If you like that sort of thing."

"And I suppose you don't. It's not your style, is it?"

"Not really," he says, indifferent. "I'm more into spending my nights watching old recordings of eighties televangelists with their wives. Man, I can't get enough of Jim and Tammy Faye. They were one hot couple. You know, that or listening to Country-rap with Uncle Vincent."

"Shut up." I shove him playfully. "Just tell me how The Circus of Misfit Marvels is the best live show you've ever seen."

He holds his hands up like an innocent bystander. "Can't. My heart belongs to Jim and Tammy."

"You're bizarre on a whole different level. And where's my book?"

"Thank you. And I uh…"

He jams his hand into his pocket in true Corban style. It's always his left side pocket, and I find myself noticing his habit more times than I care to admit.

I eye him speculatively. Is it a nervous problem? He doesn't come across as nervous at all. An oddity? Maybe.

"Your journal," he states as if he's going to make an announcement.

I lift inquisitive brows and wait for him to either produce it from nowhere—I may be getting too used to being around Marc and Bob—or to tell me where it is. He said he would bring it with him, but the doubtful expression on Corban's face isn't reassuring.

"I forgot it." He stares down the street outside of The Anti-Gravity Bar for a long moment, then makes eye contact again. "Sorry. I don't usually forget things. I thought I grabbed it, but when I got out of the 4-Runner, it was nowhere to be found."

Now it's me who turns away. There's no point lamenting something out of my control and yet I need about four seconds to let it soak in and move on.

Four, three, two, one... "Don't worry about it." I smile because he appears wrecked over the missing journal. "Will you still let me buy you dinner?"

He sucks in a huge chest expanding breath. "I'll get it to you as soon as I can. I swear. Tell me where to send it, or I can scan every page and email the words to you. Whatever you need."

"Corban, I'm serious. Don't give it another thought. It's just a book full of nothing, and you don't need to stress out about it."

The look on his face says he's not buying my line of B.S., but I don't want him to worry anymore.

"Let's walk. I don't know my way around, but there's got to be a decent restaurant nearby."

We're both in the mood for Asian food and Corban suggests a tiny hole-in-the-wall Asian fusion restaurant on Pearl Street. My taste buds quiver in ecstasy over the pot stickers and sushi rolls, and when the meal is over, they want to sit back down and start again from the beginning. I tell them they're going to wait at least a day before sampling culinary bliss once more.

We stroll down Pearl Street, moving away from the most populated bars and late night restaurants until virtually no one else is around. I'm not ready to call it a night. Corban doesn't seem ready either. I decide to take a break from walking and sit on a bench next to an overflowing flower bed. Whether this is a city beautification project or Boulder's way of thumbing its nose at water conservation, I can't say, but the lush flowers are beautiful, and they perfume the air, even at night.

Corban settles down next to me and his pocket chain clinks against the bench. He leans back, resting one arm on the armrest, while keeping his left hand in his pocket.

"Do you want to play a game?"

"You're up to something, Jasper. I can sense it."

"A simple yes or no would do."

"I'm not sure you want to play a dangerous game with me."

"Who said it was dangerous?" I ask, plastering innocence to my face.

"Okay. Yeah, I want to play. What's the game?"

"Truth or consequences." I flash my most tempting and devious grin.

"Like you ask me a question, and if I don't want to answer I pay the consequence?"

"Yep, and I get to go first."

"Meaning you want to answer the first question or you want to ask the first question?" He leans away and peers down his nose at me.

My smile broadens. "I'll ask first."

He doesn't appear overly enthusiastic about my idea. I forge ahead before I lose my nerve. "What's inside your left pocket?"

His body goes unnaturally still. "Wait a minute. I didn't fully agree to the rules yet."

"Come on. It can't be worth the consequence. Just tell me, or show me." I stare at his unmoving hand inside his pocket and wonder if I'm about to have my mind blown by Corban's weirdness.

A crafty devil expression escapes from his oddly colored pale green eyes. "Aren't we supposed to state the consequence if we refuse to tell the truth?"

"Okay. Well, if you won't tell me you have to answer an even worse question."

He considers my terms.

"Fine. That's your consequence. Mine is if you don't answer me truthfully you let me buy you a drink."

"Seriously? That's not a punishment."

"Ah—" He holds up a halting finger. "You chose yours, and I chose mine. We're agreed. Now hold out your hand."

"What? Why? Do you want to shake or something? Don't you trust me?"

He shakes his head with impatience. "Hand please."

I lick my lips, raise my palm, and wait for his next move.

Corban extracts his left hand from his pocket and holds his closed fist over my hand. His knuckles brush my open palm as he uncurls his fingers and places something very warm and very hard in my hand. I instantly bring it up close to my face so I can see it better. He lets me study it in silence for a moment.

"Bloodstone jasper," we say at the exact same time.

Our eyes lift from the small polished green stone streaked with blood-red to find each other in the glow of the street lights. I'm smiling, but he's staring at me making one of those faces I can't read.

"People were always giving me pieces of this when I was a kid. You know, because of my name. It's such a pretty stone. I have a huge collection at my mom's house. Nothing extravagant or anything. Mostly small polished pieces like this one."

"Were you named after it because it's your birthstone?"

"No. Not at all. My birthstone is Amethyst. Is it yours?"

"Kind of." He stares at the sidewalk instead of making eye contact with me.

"Kind of?" I ask and am suddenly dying to know what month's birthstone is bloodstone.

"I was born in March and bloodstone is the old birthstone for that month. It's what my mom told me. She says she likes these better than aquamarines which are what March is supposed to be now. I guess. I don't pay much attention to that type of thing."

"Except for this?" I curl my hand around the smooth rock.

"It's a boring story." He leans back again.

He doesn't ask me to return it or even looks at my hand.

"If it's that bad, I have to know."

I listen to him take a breath before beginning.

"My mom gave the bloodstone to me when my grandfather passed away. I was sort of messed up. Mom handed me that rock and told me it was a worry stone, and I could put all my problems into it when I needed to. It felt good to hold, and I've been carrying it around since I was eight years old. It became like this lucky talisman or something." Corban pauses, glances over at me and then looks straight ahead. "God, that sounds lame. What kind of game are we playing here?" He scrubs his hand over his face.

I hold in my giggle at his discomfort and tuck the stone inside the edge of his pocket. "Corban Duran: Punk, bouncer, sound guy, runner, astronomy and physics student, and he carries around a worry stone from his mom. It's just so... I don't know... sweet and innocent. And surprising."

A low grumble that sounds a little menacing moves through his chest. It only makes me laugh.

"Your turn. Tell me something bad that's happened to you and how you got over it? And don't say Keel and the mugging because I already know about that."

The smile falls from my face and shatters on the concrete. I don't want to ruin the night, but he asked a really hard question. "I choose my consequence," I say quickly.

"That's it? You're going to end our game? Come on, I told you something no one else knows. And here's more embarrassment. When you told me your name wasn't Tara, but Jasper instead, I had this fucking crazy déjà vu moment where I was sure I was carrying around this rock for fourteen years because I was waiting to meet you. The girl named Jasper. Like I couldn't forget you even though we hadn't met yet. Now you know, I completely lost my mind." He rubs the back of his neck, and his left hand is back in his pocket.

I digest this last declaration with infinitesimal slowness. Unsure of how to respond to that, I blink and begin telling my part of the game. After all, I'm the one who started it. "I've had more crap happen to me than most people I know. I don't like to talk about it."

"I know. I can tell because you have unending empathy for others, and you don't judge people like everyone else does. It's why I want to know one thing that makes you the person you are. What caused your crazy resilience and strength?"

The list of wrongs and undeniable heartache in my childhood is so disturbing it should never be grouped together into a single recollection. No one person should experience that much garbage in so few years. My dad leaving stands out in my memory garbage dump. So does the day I found out he died in some freak accident, and my mother decided to not take Evie and me to his memorial service—or even tell us until months after the fact. Being whipped by Geoff on multiple occasions isn't pleasant either. Each occurrence is a lasting memory and a story with no logic or justification. Mom telling me to hide Evie from made up danger and leaving us for hours on end, only to find out she was sick of dealing with us and wanted us out of her sight is unfathomable. Yet it happened. "I'll take a chai tea or whatever you're buying."

"I think it's partly because you're so beautiful."

"Shut up." I'm joking a little, but I'm also uncomfortable.

"I told you my mommy story," he says with comical disbelief. "The least you can do is be equally prickled."

I clear my throat, glance up, and let loose on the innocent night a story I've never told anyone. "All right, fine. When I was twelve, our circus decided to try something new and stay in one location for an entire season. The economy was horrible, and we were on the verge of shutting down for good. Everyone was stressed out, so all the execs, managers, and senior performers thought we could try bringing people to us to cut our traveling expenses. They arranged a deal to lease a piece of property for nine months, and we would all stay, stick it out, and hope for the best.

"I knew it was a big change, and everyone was on the verge of losing their jobs, but I was secretly so excited to be in California for most of the year. I could go to public school for the first time ever. Show kids are always homeschooled with each other since we travel all the time. My mom didn't want me to go because she said it would mess up our schedule and whatever shitty excuses she had. I begged and cried and promised going to a regular school wouldn't change my practice and training.

"I started seventh grade at Washington Middle School and was too excited for my own good. It didn't take long to make some friends. Most of the kids were super friendly and curious about me and what it was like to live at the circus.

"I felt special and like I was different than them, and it bothered me. I wanted to be the normal kid in class, but I also wanted to make new friends.

"About two or three weeks after I started going to public school, I was approached by some eighth-grade boys after school. They were cute, and I was interested in getting to know them. They asked me if I wanted to hang out with them and I was like, sure. I was supposed to be back at Farinelli for practice, but I couldn't say no to two cute older boys. They said they wouldn't leave the school property, so I didn't feel unsafe or anything.

"It was all great at first. They were into climbing on fences and jumping bushes and just boy stuff. Since I was good at anything athletic, I tried most of the things they were doing. They were older than me and a little taller so I couldn't do some of the jumps, but I tried to impress them. We were on the far side of the building, and the one kid pulled out a cigarette. He said we should hide behind the dumpsters so no one would see him. I didn't want these cool kids to get in trouble for smoking. I hesitated and thought about leaving. I couldn't be sure how late I was, but I knew I was in huge trouble for not going straight home, so I decided to stay a few more minutes.

"He smoked the cigarette, but the other boy and I didn't. The smell was bad enough. There was no way I was going to put it in my mouth. They brought up the circus, and I answered the same old questions. They started talking about my little sister and how cute she was. And I was like, wait a second, how did they know anything about Evie? She wasn't going to school or anything, and I thought it was weird they even knew her name. I was standing there trying to puzzle it out when the one bigger kid grabbed my arms and pulled them behind my back. He kicked the back of my knees, and I went down on the asphalt. I cried out, and he was hissing in my ear to shut the fuck up. I was so confused at first. I don't think I even fought back.

"The other kid pulled out his penis and shoved his hips toward my face. He grabbed my hair and pulled and started ordering me to put it in my mouth, or he was going to kill my little sister and bury her where no one would ever find her.

"There was so much happening all at once that I was frozen with fear. Until he said, he'd kill Evie. I started freaking out. My shoulder felt like it was being dislocated, but I couldn't get free from them. I was in horrible pain, but Evie's safety mattered more. I think I was about to do what they said when we heard someone coming.

"My arms were released, and they were off me before I even realized what was happening. Some man lifted the dumpster lid, threw in a bag of trash, and he noticed us. He asked what we were doing, frowned, and told us to go home. The boys left together, and I walked all the way back to the circus grounds. Since I didn't take the bus home like I was supposed to, it took me a couple of hours. I told my mom I missed the bus and got lost. Geoff was there. They weren't married yet, so he didn't punish me, but I saw him looking at my scraped knees. Mom made me clean the truck and trailer inside and out for an entire month. I never went back to the school, and I didn't let Evie out of my sight until we left California almost a year later. And maybe not even after that."

The telling sounds surreal to my own ears. That day changed me in so many irreversible ways. I lived with those changes for so long they'd just become part of who I am. I lost so much naiveté that day, but I also gained a new perspective on how and why I need to protect myself and my sister. I learned to be more discerning and pay better attention. And I realized, yes, there are bad people in the world.

"Fucking hell. I knew you'd floor me, but damn..."

"That was way more than you needed to know?" I venture.

"Life is shitty and complicated." He drapes an arm over my shoulders and presses me in close to his side. "I wanted to know. You didn't have to tell me, but you did."

"I'm definitely prickled."

"Truth and consequences should include shots of whiskey."

"Probably," I say.

He squeezes my shoulder and removes his arm. Corban's type of friendship is new to me. He's been like a brother or a good friend, and it throws me off. Guys generally want to hook up if they're paying me any real amount of attention. This was a fact in my life since forever. Corban flirts a little with me, but he hasn't hit on me. Although him spilling the truth about his déjà vu moment throws a new twist into our friendship. And I still haven't forgotten about the mysterious Gabrielle and his unmentioned baby. The Misfit Marvel's troupe was the same. Marc's married and ultra-respectful, but I haven't gotten even one sexually interested vibe from Tink or Bob Brows. Spidey is in his own class of strange and although he joked about us being a couple, he hasn't been even one ounce of inappropriate. They've been just what I needed.

Somehow I'm lighter, free from unseen chains, after telling Corban my crazy screwed up memory of my attempt at public school. He interrupts my thoughts with some of his own.

"Being beautiful means you get your own set of twisted horrors."

"I don't know if that's how I would describe it." I never considered my looks having any real impact on my life.

"There's some truth to it. Life's not easier with a pretty face. The constant judgment from people is like having a sword shoved in your back all the time. Expectations can never be met, but disappointing everyone is easy."

"I'm not that pretty. If I were ugly, I'd still disappoint my family."

"Oh, come on. Take a look around you. You stand out."

"I don't want to. I never want people noticing me."

"Yet, you're on stage bending yourself backward every night."

"I do it so I can eat. I need to live on my own and not be dependent on anyone."

"You could walk into a store or restaurant and get a mindless job anytime you want. You wouldn't have to be on stage."

I stare down at my fingernails, then I don't even want to see that small piece of myself. Is he right? "The Show is all I've ever known," I say. I wonder if it's the only reason I continue to perform.

"You're as beautiful as the ocean, Jasper. It's not only the surface. It's more about what's underneath. Don't hide any of it."

"I'm trying to stop hiding so much, but I'm uncomfortable when I notice people noticing me."

"All I'm saying is, denying who you are and hiding from yourself has absolutely nothing to do with your body. You possess a genetic dream cocktail, and it doesn't make life easier. It makes it just as complicated as anyone else wandering around on this planet. I suspect a little worse for you because you are also living in denial."

"I'm not in denial. De-Nile is only a river in Egypt," I say as a deflection from this subject. Even the skin of my teeth feels irritated by his picking me apart and analyzing things I don't want to examine.

"How do you know you're not in denial if you're in denial?" he tosses back at me and continues on before I can answer. Of course, there is no answer to such a sublime question. "I say you're fucking perfect."

"Perfectly screwed up."

"It's the same thing," he says. "Look at this."

I take a chance and glance up at him. Corban leans over the back of the bench and plucks a daylily from the large plant growing behind us.

"It's beautiful, right? It was created to be exactly as it is."

"Man is the only creature who refuses to be what he is." I'm quoting something I read in a book and liked enough to copy it down in my journal.

"Albert Camus, the Nobel prize winner," Corban adds.

I shrug. "I like his writing."

"So do I."

"Orange isn't my favorite color." I divert my attention back to the flower in Corban's hand and away from the reminder of the quotes inside my misplaced journal.

"Fine. Pretend it's cyan blue. Would that be better?" He makes an unconcerned gesture at the flower with his free hand to denote the color isn't the point.

I raise an eyebrow at his color choice. "Cyan blue? Is that like aquamarine or turquoise or more like cerulean?"

"Yeah. One of those," he says.

"Let's be clear on what color I'm supposed to be imagining. I'm at an impressionable time in my life. This could irrevocably alter the pathways carved by my firing synapses."

"You're improbable."

"Impossible to deal with and a pain in the ass. I've been told so many times, my soul adopted it as its true name."

"I said improbable, not impossible."

"Well, my dream gene cocktail, as you say, is sadly missing the main ingredient in case you didn't notice."

"Which is?"

"Brain cells. They're obviously missing in vast quantities."

He shakes his head with dismissal and waves the daylily between us. "You're not missing brain cells. If anything, you have too many. Intelligent and easy on the eyes. You're pretty much destined to suffer a ton of hardship in your life."

"How is that different than anyone else?"

"Being smart enough to recognize and change what you don't like about life is hard. Now back to this flower. It's perfect." He drops the bloom on the ground and stomps it. He raises his boot, and we stare at the crushed petals. "Don't be fooled. It's still perfect."

"Why did you say cyan blue?" I ask again.

"It's a color other than daylily orange."

"Is that the only reason?"

He bends down and peels the flower off the ground. "I don't know. It makes a nicer image for the mind than carroty-orange."

"When I was ten, a friend of my mom's said we could stay at his condo in Oahu. He offered to fly us there, so we went. My sister and I spent the entire week playing on the beach by this small lagoon while my mom partied with her 'friend'." I make air quotes around the word friend. At the time, I didn't know the reason she wanted me to babysit Evie the whole week was so she could screw around and party with this guy. "The water was this incredible shade of blue. All sky and gemstones and dreams rolled up into these salty swells of warm silky water. Lagoon-blue is my favorite color."

"All right, if it matters to you, picture lagoon-blue instead of cyan blue." Corban holds the bruised and flattened flower on his palm. "This is perfection with a story, not broken or damaged. It's anything it wants to be."

"It's a dead flower you killed." I point out the obvious.

"Yep. And so much more." He stares at the flower for a silent second, folds the bedraggled daylily in half and places it in his mouth. He chews and swallows. "Now it's transmuting itself into fuel for my body and my mind."

"You did not just eat that."

"I knew you had some delusions about reality, but you can believe your own eyes, can't you?"

All I'm currently capable of doing is staring at him while I attempt to process and deduce the level of freak I'm hanging out with.

He coughs. "Afraid I stepped in something unsavory." He runs his tongue around his mouth and swallows hard. He grabs his boot and lifts it up so he can see the bottom. There's something dark stuck in the tread.

The grimace on his face makes me snort and gag.

I lean as far away from him as I can. "Yuck."

"Not my favorite condiment for daylilies," he admits.

I can't help but bubble with laughter as he rises from the bench and spits in the grass beside the flower bed. He sits back down, hands flat against his thighs, apparently over his ordeal quicker than I would be.

"Am I fuel for your mind?" I ask.

"No more than I am for yours."

I like his answer. My mind can't help but ponder over how much I would like to be fuel for his body too. Heat creeps into my face, and I stare at the ground between my feet. Why did my mind go there? I'm not interested in a new relationship, especially with flower-eating-from-the-bottom-of-his-dirty-boot Corban. He's cute to be sure. I'm too aware of the tiny white scar along the edge of his dark eyebrow, and I was checking out his five o'clock shadow earlier. I may be missing vital components to a life of balanced well-being, but I know I don't need another emotional debacle so soon after Keel. Yet here I am, wondering if his chest is smooth and muscled and pale like the sliver of ankle I saw when he lifted his boot to stare at the bottom.

He shifts on the bench next to me. I see a flower in my peripheral vision.

"They're pretty good without the stale dog crap. Would you like to try one?"

The laugh resurfaces, and I put up my hand to stop him. The gag in the bottom of my throat is competing with the giggles. "I spent plenty of time cleaning up the yard after my dog, Ollie. The thought of what's on your shoe puts any ideas of food far from the realm of enticement."

He tucks the flower into my hair and rises. "Let's go find that drink."

I feel slightly ridiculous with the large bloom stuck on the side of my head, but I stand, touch it gingerly with my fingertips and leave it in place. Departing the emotional rollercoaster is such a good idea. I stretch my back and take a look around. The street is deserted save for the stars watching over the two of us.

Chapter Twenty

"The mind once enlightened cannot again become dark."
— Thomas Paine

After our shows in Boulder, we move on to Grand Junction. We get most of the day off, so I decide I should check in with Evie. It's been a while since I called and I miss her.

Mom answers the phone, and my world rotates one-hundred and eighty degrees in about three seconds.

"You can't talk to her. She's been in an accident and isn't up for phone calls now," Mom says.

"What do you mean she's been in an accident?"

"If you would've been here, Jasper, this wouldn't have happened."

"Don't start with the guilt trips, Mom. Please put Evie on the phone."

"She's sleeping."

"Tell me what happened."

"You should've been here to spot her."

"Seriously? Fuck," I curse. "Well, I'm not there. Just tell me what happened."

"Don't cuss at me. I'm trying to tell you."

"Mom! You haven't said anything."

I lean my head against the side of the bus. She's carving her guilt-edged initials along my spine. It hurts, and it makes me angry. I want to slap her and make her look into a mirror until she sees how wrong she is. Why does she turn every situation around so it's my fault?

"Evie was on the trampoline, and she fell off. She hit her face on the corner of the low wire platform."

"Where the hell was Geoff?" Evie's summer-blue eyes framed by her sun-bleached lashes are clear in my mind. I don't wait for Mom's answer. "How bad is it?" I picture my sister with a massive black eye. All black and purple and swollen shut.

Mom lets loose a weighted sigh.

"Mom?"

"She has seven stitches."

"Shit-balls. No..." I hit the off button and cover my face with my hands.

It takes maybe three seconds for her to call me back.

"You watch your mouth, missy. You can't speak to me like that. What is the matter with you?"

My throat feels stuck closed. I can't speak. The processing going on inside my head isn't ready to accept this. It's trying hard, but the news needs to bake for a few minutes before I can taste test it on my tongue. And holy fuck, it tastes like pure excrement. It also happens to be sugarcoated with blame and guilt.

"The doctor doesn't think she damaged her eye permanently, but we'll need to wait for the swelling to go down before she can get a more thorough exam."

Her voice crawls into my ear and spins a nest of eggs, like a spider. They'll hatch at a later date and torment me for a long time to come. I grip my chest above my heart and knead my flesh. Squeezing and pinching myself to feel something other than the numbness that wants to suck me under.

"Jasper. Are you coming home now?"

"When can I talk to Evie?" I finally say.

"When you come see her. Where are you? Do you think you can take off and not tell me where you're living?"

"Yeah. I can."

"No, you can't. Do you have any idea how worried I've been about you? This is your fault, you know. If I hadn't been so distracted by worrying about you, then I could have been outside with Geoff and Evie."

"That makes no sense at all." I try defending myself even as I'm inwardly blaming Evie's accident on my absence. I'll never admit it to Mom, though.

"Really? Your selfishness is tearing this family apart. How could you do this to us? Geoff's been a total jerk since you took off."

"Because he wasn't one before?" I practically yell it into the phone. "Stop blaming me for your problems!"

"I'm simply trying to tell you what happened since you decided to leave with your boyfriend," she says.

She's starting to get all poor me; I hate it even more than the guilt trips.

"I know I'm not perfect, but I'm doing the best I can, Jas. Can't you try to understand?"

"Your best is manipulative and destructive. Which is why I can't live with you anymore."

Her tone instantly flips from poor-me to angry and defensive. "You have no idea what I go through and put up with. Don't tell me I'm the destructive one in this family. I haven't done anything to earn that. Are you coming home to see your sister or not?"

There's no point in arguing with her. She'll only keep twisting everything I say around and around until I'm as knotted and tangled as she is. "I don't know. I'll call later to talk to Evie." I jab the disconnect button.

Have you ever wanted to bang your head against a wall so hard stars explode and the sky swallows you whole? I'm convinced it would be more productive and produce a more satisfactory result than the conversation I just had with my mother.

Why is she so maddening? The wall is looking more and more like the answer to my problems.

***

Later.

I dial Mom's number and wait for an answer.

"Hello?" I say.

Silence lingers like a freshly risen zombie who hasn't yet figured out he's awakened from the grave.

"Hello?" I say again knowing someone answered. The open connection between the two lines hums in my ear. Am I imagining the shuffling sound of somebody moving around?

"Evie's been taken to the hospital. She's asking for you."

Geoff's asshole tainted voice hits me like an acid bath on exposed nerves.

"What did you say?"

"Your sister took a turn for the worst. She had to go to County Memorial last night."

"What do you mean? What happened?"

"Sometimes when a person hits their head the injury goes into the brain, and it can cause swelling and complications," he says slowly as if he's explaining something to a two-year-old.

"Are you telling me Evie has a concussion?" Panic rises just under my skin. I take a deep breath to help me endure this conversation without exploding.

"I'm not a doctor, Jasper. I'm only telling you what I heard from your mother. Your mom could use your support right now, but she told me you're too busy to be bothered with our problems."

"Where is Mom? And why do you have her phone?" I ask, searching for answers.

"Think about it, Jasper. Do you think she might be busy with your sister?"

His condescension crawls over my skin and takes hold of my hair by the roots. *Prick.*

"Tell Evie I'm coming to see her."

***

Dear Evie,

I'm writing this in my head since my journal is gone. Stupid isn't it? I should just buy a notebook or something, but I haven't. Well, I did scribble a few notes down, but I burned them. I was afraid of letting anyone read my private thoughts. Besides, the chances of you ever reading my letters are slim to none anyway. The secret I hold, even from myself, is the journal is for me, even though I want to share my ideas, feelings, hopes, dreams and nightmares with you. Now I'm sure I never will, even if I get my journal back. I hope you can understand. I hope you have a secret place to hold all your most delicate and most explosive life-changing thoughts and dreams. And most of all, I hope your ideas are safe.

Here's what I need you to know.

I'm on my way to see you.

I bought a ticket, left my new job, and I'm on a bus.

In the rain.

Not the kind of rain we had in Hawaii, all warm and tropical and full of green smells. We played outside in the rain like we were taking an outdoor shower with our clothes on. I loved that day. And all the other days, playing on the beach in the morning and dancing in the rain in the afternoon. We ate the best pineapple in the world. Do you remember the fried Spam sandwiches? What was Mom thinking? Did she think we could live on Spam and pineapple for two weeks? I guess we did it, but I haven't had the canned, salty, delicacy since. I doubt you have either.

Did you know rain has multiple personalities? Outside the rain is playing a game of cat and mouse with the fog. The lightning is in on it, too. Lighting up the sky in brief flashes, then disappearing again. The wild lights, the mist, and drizzle mixed with moments of pelting rain make me want to get off this musty smelling bus and run right into the chaos. You would understand. We both like watching storms. This time, I want to be right in the middle of it. Would the lightning find me? Could I withstand the ear-shattering claps of thunder? God, I want to find out, but I want to see you more, so I'm staying on the bus.

Ever since I spoke with Geoff on the phone, I can't stop worrying about you. I hope he told you I called. Mom's not answering her phone, and it's driving me insane. Evie, I'm coming as fast as I can.

Please be all right.

I say this to myself every few minutes like a prayer, a wish, a mantra. Anything, if it will help. What I know for certain is if you're hurt and in the hospital, I'm going to do everything I can to make sure you recover as quickly and painlessly as possible.

Hang in there, sweet sis.

I'll see you soon.

J.

I fold the imaginary letter and stuff it in an invisible envelope to make it go away. Outside the bus window, I peer into the fog and pretend there's no glass between me and the mist. Pressing my fingertips to the window, I let the chill seep into my bones. I can almost feel the rain spattering my face and running down my arm. A brutal slash of light brightens the field and then disappears again. In some twisted way, I wish it had hit me. It would save me from my horrible plaguing thoughts. Mainly that if Evie is in a serious condition when I arrive in California, I'm going to murder Geoff.

Chapter Twenty-one

"Home isn't a physical place." — J. Pyrah

Where's Ollie?

Standing on my neighbor's front porch, I wait with anxiety for someone to answer the door. *What if they got rid of my dog?* I can return to Crapville, and I can suppress my emotions, but I can't do it without Ollie. I need her by my side as I walk into Geoff's house.

Open the door.

No one's home, my inner voice says.

Shut up. I need her.

Why?

Because the magnitude of Ollie's unconditional love will hold me up. She's the silent friend who stands with me no matter what happens. *This is your punishment for giving her to the neighbor and leaving,* my demons inform me. Now she's gone. Could I let myself into the backyard to check? Her whole body will wag with joy when she sees me again. I would be smiling with my tail, too, when I see her—if I had a tail.

What if they don't have her anymore?

I knock again and lean my forehead against the door, ears straining for any movement inside the house. They're not here. The car's not in the driveway.

Evie is waiting for me. I can't stall any longer.

Ollie won't be by my side.

***

"What do you want?" he asks as I enter the kitchen.

Geoff leans against the counter holding a glass in his hand. The shake is thick. The pitcher for the blender sits nearby, streaked with the remains of his health drink.

I grimace. He's already starting with the shitty tone.

"Good to see you too."

"Right." He gulps down the shake.

"Where is everyone?"

"Why are you here? I thought you were off seeing the world and proving you don't need your family anymore."

"You're not my family." I hold my ground.

He blinks with rapid fire. The bulge of tightening muscle along his jaw pulses at me. Geoff turns to the sink and begins washing the glass and the pitcher. "Your mother and brother aren't here."

My eyes rotate around their sockets. "I figured that part out," I say as calmly as I can. The bullshit in this house is suffocating me with its reek. Traveling across the country to see my sister doesn't guarantee he'll be pleasant for even one minute. He's purposely screwing with me. Aunt Summer called his behavior toward me "control dramas". Geoff has to be in control, and if he feels threatened, then Jasper gets to take the brunt of his threatened manliness. *What a weakling. Well, Jasper can handle one screwed up conversation with her stepfather. As long as Jasper keeps referring to herself in the third person. Seriously—this is weird even for me.*

"Why can't I get a hold of Mom? You told her I was coming didn't you? Do you still have her phone?"

"Slow down." He dries his hands on a towel.

I keep a wary eye on him. I'll never forget the time he stuffed the soapy dish towel in my mouth. He's all at once calm and sounds sort of rational. I take a protective step back. His mind games cannot be rivaled. Part of me desperately needs to challenge him and let him know he can't mess with me anymore. Part of me needs to flee via invisible jetpack and rocket right out of this smelly old house. Part of me needs Ollie's reassuring warmth sitting on my shoes and being my protector. None of these things come to my aid.

Geoff hangs the towel on the oven door handle. "Jonah is at a friend's house today, and Autumn turned her phone off. She needed time to process. I'm screening all the calls here at the house."

"Why are you screening her calls?" I cross my arms over my chest.

He tilts his head and stares at me with lifeless eyes. What a cold, uncaring bastard, I think, and refuse to look away. *Jasper can stare evil in the face, and it isn't allowed to hurt her anymore.*

"We found out this morning your sister had another seizure at three-thirty caused from an intracranial hemorrhage. It's a shame we weren't with Evie in the end, but I know she's at peace now."

My gaze slides to the wall so I won't have to see Geoff's burrowing glare and his hideous goatee. The paint begins to crack and fall to the floor in white shards. I think I can smell it, crumbling, decaying breakdown. Tin chalk, mercury ashes, and powdered dreams plummet to the floor and disintegrate. *Will Jasper collapse through the floor and join the rest of the souls in hell, or will she rise through the splintered rafters and fade into the infinite atmosphere?*

At this point, I wish for either.

Currently, I'm trapped in concrete with his eyes boring into me.

"What?" I mumble into the suddenly echoing kitchen. My ears begin to ring. The internal workings of my body are shutting down.

"Evie died today, Jasper. It's too bad." He shrugs. "I liked that kid."

I find my voice. "You fucking asshole!"

"Don't start with me." He narrows an eye to pinpoint his glare more effectively. "Your sister caused her own accident. I did everything I could to make sure the yard was secure and safe."

"What!" The thought that Evie's accident being Geoff's fault hadn't even pinged on my radar. I'm too busy trying to comprehend the incomprehensible. He's a bastard because of his indifference and lack of feeling... and now his self-serving defensive tone! How can he stand there like nothing happened?

"You heard me. This won't be put on my shoulders. Accidents happen all the time. An accident killed your father, and now your sister." He oozes past me and exits the kitchen.

The floor shifts below my feet, and I will free fall in the next second.

Welcome, Jasper. Hell awaits you, my demon whispers.

Nope. Not going there.

I force my body to come back to me and go through a quick checklist. Heart beating, blood pumping, limbs moving. It's all still there, but the trembling of my soul is what seems to carry me out the front door. I'm unsure if I weigh nothing or a hundred tons. The curb meets the soles of my shoes, and I stop. The concrete seems to be swallowing me one centimeter at a time into its murky viscous depths.

How did I get outside?

Where's my mom?

I shake off the momentary madness and find my phone to dial her number. It rings into eternity. I need the news from her, not Geoff. I need Evie's voice. I need to scream. I need to bury myself in the ground with a blanket of earth over me because if Geoff is telling me the truth, I'll die along with my sister. There's no way I can live without her.

Does Aunt Summer know?

I should call her.

My phone chimes in my hand. There's a new text waiting for me. I think my mom is responding to my urgent need for her.

Wrong. I should know better. When has Autumn ever been there for me when I needed her the most?

The number looks familiar, but I can't put it together with a name in my current state of panic. I push the button to read the text.

Hey, Tara/Jasper. You still alive? I need to know if you're okay.

The phone number registers like plugging my finger into an electrical outlet. Keel! I nearly drop my phone to get away from him. He hasn't texted me in weeks. How did he get this number? I want to text him back a giant, WTF? But I stop myself. I stare at his message. *I'm not okay. When have I ever been okay?*

If I had to guess, Keel still doesn't know what happened to me after I left him in Denver with Caspar straddling his crotch.

My heart aches inside my chest, and I hunch over in pain. *Breathe. Just breathe.* A magnolia tree grows next to the sidewalk between Geoff's house and the neighbors. I always considered the spot no-man's-land as it's impossible to decipher who the tree belongs to. No-man's-land is the perfect landing place for me. I stumble over to it and slump to the ground leaning into the trunk.

I type, *I'm pretending to be alive. It's not working very well* and hit send.

The next text is almost instant. *Where are you?*

Me: *At my mom's.*

Keel: *Stay there. I'm on my way over.*

Holy hell's bells. What does he mean? He's coming over? *Here?* I stare at the messages until the screen goes black.

Time stands still or flies by. I'm unsure which, but it's definitely moving against the realm of normal. When I become aware of a vehicle moving down the street, I glance over and see Keel's truck. I rise from the ground and stare at the mirage.

It's not my imagination at all and Keel parks in front of me. A minute later he's standing a few feet away. I hug myself and refuse to believe my eyes.

"Hey," he says.

Silence.

I glance down the street to the Fernandez house and decide to let myself into their backyard to retrieve Ollie. I'm sure Mrs. Fernandez will understand when I tell her what happened and how I needed Ollie back. My body starts moving in that direction when a hand touches my arm.

"I'm sorry," he says.

Then I'm totally aware of Keel. His body heat. His strength. The calluses on his fingers from playing the guitar. He's still hot, but his looks don't overshadow the cheater in him. Which is ugly.

I yank free of him and stare at my arm to see if any of his residue is left.

"What's going on with you? When did you come back to the valley?"

"My sister—" The rest gets cut off inside my throat, like my vocal chords have been severed by a straight razor. Tears spring forth, and I close my eyes.

"What about Evie?"

I shake my head and take another step toward the neighbor's house. He takes me in his arms, and I collapse against him. His smell is familiar, and he's here. He's a body when I don't want to be alone. The tears stream down my face, and I refuse to look up at him. Keel steers me to his truck, opens the door, and sits me down. When I'm unable to lift my legs inside the cab, he does it for me. The door shuts, and I huddle against the seat. Then Keel is next to me and his hand is on my leg, reassuring me he's near.

After a while, he says, "Is that your stuff in the yard?"

I manage to look over—my bag is sitting in the driveway where I left it before going inside. "Yeah," I think I say. The words could have been, *I don't fucking care about anything, so say what you want and don't expect me to answer coherently,* but I'm pretty sure it came out as yeah.

Keel leaves the cab and returns with my bag.

"Let's get out of here. I saw your stepdad watching us from the window."

A violent shiver races through me and freezes my insides.

After miles have passed us by, Keel says, "Is Evie all right, Jasper? I'm freaking out over here until you tell me what happened."

"I don't know." I force myself to swallow the obstructing boulder in my throat. It lands in my gut like a... a boulder.

"Can you talk about it?"

"Not really." I can't say it aloud. If I do, that means it's real. It can't be real. Evie can't be dead.

"Okay, well let's hang out and stay away from Geoff. He gets to you too easily. Do you want to go to my place and chill out? I promise not to bring up your sister until you're ready to talk."

I shift my focus over to Keel. He's acting like the boyfriend I fell in love with. Kind, caring, unselfish. I nod and bite the inside of my lip.

He pulls into the driveway at his parents' house and turns the key. The engine quiets and we sit in the relative silence of suburbia.

"When did you get back?" I whisper. My voice is hoarse and it hurts, but I should say something and at least pretend I'm not a lobotomy patient.

"Yesterday."

I stare at his gorgeous stucco mission style home. "What happened? Why aren't you on tour?"

"It's over. I drove straight home after the last show. I'm done with hotels and campgrounds. It's all good, but I needed my bed, and you know—something other than living on the road."

I nod again. It's hard to believe Paradox 21 had reached the end of their first official tour. How had the time gone by so quickly? *Oh right, it didn't.* I was recovering, healing, and learning my new job.

"Jas, I need to say something."

Our eyes meet. His sorrow can be felt...or maybe he's only my mirror. Either way, the heaviness is palpable.

He continues. "I miss you. I don't expect you to forgive me, but I know I made a horrible mistake. Caspar lied to me about everything and I was stupid enough to believe her." He's facing forward, gripping the steering wheel, and his knuckles are banded with white and red. Where there was sadness surrounding him before, now there's anger.

"Yeah, she does that," I murmur with regret tingeing my voice.

"She told me so much shit about you. God, I was an ass to believe it. Then she offered me X, and that's when I seriously screwed the pooch... pun intended."

My stomach heaves with the mention of him screwing anything. He didn't have to go there. Not now. I don't want to think about it. Any of it.

"I'm sorry," he says again. "I just want you to know I didn't mean to do it. To hurt you. To hurt myself. I fucked up really bad."

I swallow again. The lump keeps returning. How many rocks can my stomach hold before the weight exceeds capacity and crashes through me? Instead of answering, all I can do is continue to wipe the tears away.

"This isn't a good time. I see that now. Sorry," he apologizes again. "You can have the spare room for as long as you need and I'll leave you alone."

"Thanks," I say in a state of disbelief and follow him inside.

Chapter Twenty-two

"When a man is denied the right to live the life he believes in,
he has no choice but to become an outlaw."
— Nelson Mandela

When am I ever going to quit making life-altering mistakes? Perhaps I can get an alarm installed to ring every time I'm approaching the no turning back zone. Maybe a shock collar or something. It needs to be obnoxious, annoying, ear piercing, and can only be removed by someone who holds a degree in common sense and healthy decision making.

Do I know anyone like that? I'd be wearing the collar for the rest of my life. Note to self: Search online for a self-actuating alarm system against stupid choices.

Here's how my latest absurdity goes down:

I send my mother a text message begging her to tell me Evie didn't die this morning.

She doesn't reply no matter how hard I stare at my screen. By sheer force of will, I cannot make her message me back or call. Her phone no longer exists, I decide. I dial Aunt Summer and leave a message on her voice mail. She must be busy with work because she doesn't pick up either. I don't say much on the message. A quick, I'm back safe and did you talk to my mother? Leaving a message about the unthinkable isn't something I could do to my aunt. Certain words can only be spoken to a living person, not to a recording. Maybe Mom is screening my calls. She wouldn't do that to Summer, though. Even at her worst, my mom wouldn't shut out her sister. I groan and stare at the clock on the phone. It could be hours before Aunt Summer calls me back.

I need to get to the hospital, I decide, and slide off the guest bed to find Keel. When I reach the door, I change my mind and call the hospital instead. Even if Keel owes me for what he did, I don't want to take advantage of the situation. I don't ever want to rely on him again.

The hospital tells me Evie Pyrah is not in their system as a current or recent patient. I wrack my brain and try to think of anywhere else she could be, but the other hospitals are much farther away. Even so, I try the number for the next closest hospital and get the same results. My sister doesn't exist.

Where is she?

I curl up on the bed, defeated, heartbroken, panicked, and desperate. I tend to stay numb when I reach this stage, but I'm trying to do things differently. Although part of me wonders why I should bother. Numb is comfortable. Numb allows me to keep breathing even if I'm not aware of the air moving in and out of my lungs.

The tears begin once more, and they anger me. Tears mean I'm still feeling something, everything, with acute stabbing pain. I cry myself to sleep with the phone clenched in my fist.

Keel is sitting on the edge of the bed when I open my eyes. Did he wake me up, or was he sitting there for a while? He answers my unspoken question.

"Sorry if I woke you. I thought you might need something to eat." He motions to the nightstand. He lowers his hand, and I think he was going to rest it on my leg. I follow the motion with my eyes, and he withdraws before touching me.

I bite my lip and stare across the room at the only window. Night came and brought with it the blackness of my heart. A soft yellow glow warms the corner from a lamp on the desk. He had been thoughtful enough to leave the overhead light off.

"My parents are away for the night. They're at a work conference. I told them you were here with me. They're cool. They don't know what happened in Denver. I couldn't tell them I screwed up so bad. They'd probably disown me. They always really liked you, Jasper."

I swallow and wonder where he's going with this. "Next time you talk to them, will you say thank you for me?"

He nods as he stares out the bedroom door instead of looking at me. Vanity nudges me like a bothersome fly. How puffy and red are my eyes? How horrible is my hair? Did Keel notice my shoes from Corban? Why am I thinking about any of that? The only thing that matters is, Evie is dead. The tears threaten to spill again at the thought, and I turn my head to stare at nothing.

"Anyway, I brought you a muffin, an orange, and some juice. You always like that stuff, don't you?" He sounds pretty unsure of himself.

It's weird seeing him like this. Keel's always full of himself. Confident, sometimes too much so. Cocky and arrogant are his signature. I thought I liked his self-assurance. He knows what he wants and how to make things happen. Now I'm not sure it's attractive. Seeing this other side of him makes me think he's flawed like the rest of us and willing to acknowledge it.

I reach down and lay my fingertips on his thigh. *The alarm bell should ring right about now. A siren. A shock collar. A bloody freaking taser!* Instead, I say, "Yeah. Thank you. I haven't eaten in a long time." Honestly, I'm having serious doubts I can eat anything at all. Not until I find Evie and then possibly not after that.

Keel glances down at my hand but doesn't take it in his. If he touched me, I wouldn't have said what I say next.

"Lie down with me, Keel. Please." *Riiinnng! Buzz! Zap! I'm oblivious.*

I let him see the pools of tears in my lower lids and my trembling lip.

He drops his gaze, shadowing his eyes from me for a second and then he's stretching out by my side. I inch in close to him and lay my head against his shoulder and simply breathe and let the need to be held swallow me whole. One breath at a time. *I'm not numb.* Air moves in and out of my lungs. Life continues. *I continue.*

Keel's scent is familiar. His cologne blends with the smell of his skin and the soap he uses. He enfolds me in his arms and holds on, reminding me of the months we spent together. The countless nights we made love and I stayed with him in his bed until I had to go home. His warmth is a haven in my deluded mind. We don't speak. Where I felt completely lost and adrift a moment before, I find in his embrace the physical comfort I need. Being in Keel's arms may be an escape, but it keeps me rooted in the physical world, even if it's only temporary.

I slide my hand along his chest. He stiffens almost imperceptibly.

"I'm not sure what I'm doing, or what I want, but you feel good."

He relaxes. His body softens against my palm. "I missed you every day since you left. I'm sorry a million times. I want to make it up to you."

He begins to rub my back. He sounds like he's suffering for what he did.

"Don't." I place a finger over his lips. "I can't think about it now. I don't want to think about anything." My hand lowers from his mouth, and I let my fingers trail down the side of his neck and brush across his collar bone. Then I'm kissing a similar path over his skin and re-familiarizing his body with my hands.

"Jesus, Jasper. I need you. I promise I'll never fuck up again."

We're both different now after the tour, the summer colors, and the passing chaos. And yet we're still the same. Lying in bed with Keel is new and old, but not uncomfortable.

I don't trust myself enough to answer him with words. My hand moves below his belt and between his legs. He's ready. He's always ready. A small moan rumbles through his chest. He takes my prompting as a cue and rolls me to my back. His mouth locks on mine and I let him kiss me. His hunger for my body is startling. I kiss him back, and my tongue wraps around his. The motions are automatic as we quickly fall into our prior routine. Keel is nearly crushing me with his weight, but he doesn't seem to notice. Every ounce of his focus is on kissing me while fondling my breasts.

I let out the expected sigh of need mixed with desire and arch my back into his hand.

I'm using him. I'm letting him use me. I'm acting. It doesn't matter that I'm hurting on the inside. Hurting about my family. Hurting over what he did to me. He's acting injured too. I don't think he knows pain the same way I do. It's screwed up, but I'm a messed up person. How can sex be anything else with me?

He breaks our kiss and goes down on me. There isn't much finesse. After unhooking my bra, without removing my shirt, he kisses my breasts. Keel strokes my stomach before unbuttoning my pants and just like that, he's inching my jeans down over my hips and kissing me between my thighs.

The sensation is distracting enough that I moan and lose myself for a few minutes. Maybe less. Time needs to abandon me and leave me in a void where nothing changes. Somewhere absolutely nothing exists would be so much better. I feel the release happen and know I don't deserve it.

Keel rises over me and leans down to kiss my neck. He works on removing his pants, and I wonder if he'll want me to return the favor. It was our past custom. He does me and then wants me to put my mouth on him next. He can't get enough oral sex. I can't say I blame him.

The pulsing in my most sensitive place continues as he slips his pants and boxers off. He rolls me on top of him, and I start to slide down his body taking my time and focusing my attention on his chest. His nipple. His abs.

My phone chimes. I try to shirk off the intrusion. Keel needs me, and I want to be distracted by him. I don't want to know that anything else matters.

The phone chimes again like a nag. My breasts brush along the length of his erection as I move lower. *Where is my phone? Is it lost in the covers, or is it on the table?*

I pause to consider whether or not I should find the stupid phone and turn it off. Keel groans and raises his hips. He brushes his hand across my head and lightly pushes me down.

That's when I realize how horribly stupid I'm being. My lapse in judgment hits me so hard I want to vomit. I roll off him and turn my back.

"Are you all right?" He places his hand on my back.

I pull away from his touch. "I don't feel well." *That's the understatement of the year.*

"What's going on? Are you sick?"

"I can't do this. I'm—" I cut myself off. I refuse to apologize. I refuse to put my mouth on him and give him pleasure in any way. What in the land of absurdity am I doing?

"Come over here, Jasper. If you're not ready, I'll wait."

"No." I pick myself up, gather my discarded clothes, find the phone, and walk out the door.

***

Humiliation. Repulsion. Regret.

They are the shadows that hunt me down and slaughter me. Every. Single. Time. Any direction I turn, there they are and here I am. I wish I could be normal and hate them for everything they did to me, but it's not Keel, it's not Geoff, and it's not my mother. I am the beginning of every path taken and the source of every emotion felt. I want to scream about how much I hate myself. The self-loathing sits beside me, and on top of me, and oozes from my pores. I hate myself to the point of complete desperation. I think I shall collapse in a sorry heap and never get up. But I won't under Keel's parents' roof and not in front of him either.

His keys are sitting on the counter, and I pick them up, leaving the house without thinking about asking to borrow his truck.

Retching, ugly sobs overcome my entire body as I drive away. Why did I think I could ignore everything that happened? Life has no on or off switch. It's brutally stuck in the on position until it isn't. I look east to the mountains. It's dark, but they're over there somewhere. Would I have the courage to drive off the mountainside? Would ending my life be a gazillion times easier than suffering through one more harsh and foul breath?

Evie would help me answer the question. Evie would give me the right answer in three seconds flat. Evie wouldn't even need to answer. She would roll her eyes and giggle at my drama. Everything would be okay again.

I sniffle and wipe the back of my hand under my nose. I glance down at the passenger seat and see my phone lying there. Text messages are waiting.

I can't even look, but I have to check for my mom's reply. The two messages are from Corban. I drop the phone on the seat and ignore them. He doesn't need an inside look at my torment. Besides, if I drive into the mountains tonight, I don't want him to know his messages were the last ones I read before killing myself.

Before I realize where I'm headed, I pull up in front of Mom's. Her car sits in front of the house, and I'm not sure if I'm relieved, frightened, or pissed. Why hasn't she called?

My key still works in the front door, and I let myself in. Geoff can go fuck himself if he doesn't want me here. I need to see my mother. She heard the door because she walks into the family room before I wake her. Mom's wearing her robe, barefoot, and bedraggled.

"Jasper? I was hoping you would be here today. It's late. I could have picked you up from the station." She looks extra tired, and that's being kind. She seems like she's been battling dragons and losing.

"Didn't Geoff tell you I was back?" I ask. "I was here earlier." I try to sort through the confusion as quickly as possible.

"No. It must have slipped his mind."

Yeah. Right. "Where's my sister?" I whisper. I need to ask. I need to hear it from someone else other than Geoff. Does she look like hell because her daughter died today? I need an answer, but I can't take the news if it's what *he* said. My heart stops as Mom's face contorts.

She drops her gaze to the floor and then back up again. I swear I'll do it. I swear if Evie is dead I'll end my own life. I can't... I can't be here without her. She was injured because I left and I wasn't there to spot her like Geoff claimed.

"She's in her room. She got to come home today. We must have just missed you. What time were you here?"

I run to our bedroom at the back of the house. The light shatters the room as I flip the switch and there's Evie in her bed. I throw myself down on my knees and lean over her. The bandages on her head are frightening, but I can handle anything as long as her chest moves and her heart is beating.

Life.

It couldn't be stolen away from her by lies. I hate him. I do. I thought I hated myself for being weak and making bad decisions, but I hate Geoff like no other fury in existence. He deserves to die. I would make it happen if I could will him to choke on his own balls.

"She needs her rest, Jas," Mom says from somewhere behind me.

"I tried to call. I even called the hospital," I say, drenching the room with my need to blame someone or something for the lack of communication.

She shrugs her shoulders. "I didn't have my phone. I don't know why the hospital didn't put you through to our room. Did you ask for Evie Holsteen?"

"Evie is not a Holsteen." I let the venom pour out of me.

Tears should be cleansing. They should drain the hurt away and leave a person empty so they're ready to be refilled with hope and promise. Tears should cleanse and restore, but mine are like liquid fire, burning a path down my cheeks and scarring me indefinitely.

"Geoff told me she died," I scream in a whisper over my shoulder.

Mom gasps and places her hand over her mouth. "Why would you say something like that?" she says around her fingers.

I turn away from the bed to stare directly into her eyes. "Because it's true," I say through gritted teeth.

"You just heard him wrong." She wears her all too familiar mask of denial.

"I didn't," I say as I take a step toward the door. She always takes his side. My intentions at the moment are riddled with revenge and destruction. I'm pretty sure I'm about to stab Geoff to death or bludgeon him with an appropriate household item. He deserves worse.

It's a good thing Evie wakes up and redirects my attention.

"I knew you'd come home today." Her tongue is thick with sleep.

"I wish I could have gotten here sooner." I kneel back down to kiss her cheek. "How bad is it?"

"Not bad. I just wish some of the other symptoms would go away."

"What symptoms?"

"I'm dizzy. It sucks to move around much. I'm kind of stuck in bed until more of the swelling goes down."

"Oh my God. I'm so sorry. I should have been here." A new wave of tears rises up to drown me again. Geoff was so right, and it's my fault I wasn't here for her. "I'm sorry," I say again.

"No. I just miscalculated and had a bad landing. It happens to everyone."

She's too brave for a twelve-year-old. She's breaking my heart, and it leaks out of my eyes.

"And I look like a wannabe mummy. I'm not going to school with this on my head."

"I already told you, baby, by the time school's back in, all the wrapping will be gone," Mom says.

"Bah," I huff and wave my hand in dismissal over the mass of bandages. "Mummies are awesome. Way cooler than zombies. I wish my head were wrapped up too."

"You do not." She tries to shake her head.

She winces with pain from the simple act of moving an inch, and the tears burn fresh tracks over my face.

"I do too. I'll wear the gauze with you until you can take it off. How does that sound?"

"Silly." A tiny pleased smile lights up her face.

"I'm doing it," I say with conviction. "Now make some room. We both need to sleep."

I ease myself into the bed next to her, making sure she doesn't move at all. I cuddle up to her side, barely hanging on the edge of the mattress, and absorb her sweet sisterly goodness. Even injured, it radiates from her.

"I'm glad you made it home safe," Mom says.

I can't answer. Nothing I say will come out right. I'll spew out a long tainted string of obscenities about Geoff and how she is to blame for everything because she married him. I decide everything I say or do is a reflection of myself, so, this time, I choose to be silent, still, and present for Evie.

***

Morning comes in a blink.

I stumble out of the bathroom and into a wall of Geoff. His arms are crossed. He reeks of manipulation and malice. Any purity and warmth I found with Evie shrivels and disappears as Geoff eyeballs me.

"Sleep well?"

I hold my tongue. Staying silent worked with Mom and I attempt to use the same tactic with him. My shoulder brushes the wall as I slide past him. He grabs my arm and whips me around, his fingers digging in. I set my jaw and lift my gaze to stare back at him with defiance.

"I'm talking to you," he growls in my face.

"I'm not talking to you," I say through clenched teeth. He won't see my tears, I tell myself as the bruising begins. It's not like the bruises on my arm are going to be any worse than the ones he's left inside me.

"What did you say to your mother about me?"

"Let go of me," I say.

"Shut up before you wake everyone."

"What do you want? First, you ask if I slept well. You're pissed when I don't answer, and now you're telling me to shut up when I do say something. Make up your fucking mind or leave me the hell alone."

A small thump sounds from behind Mom's bedroom door. *Is she awake? Can she hear us in the hall? Will she actually step up and say something?*

I know what's coming before he does, and I duck. His fingernails scrape the wall behind where my head should be. I think a laugh actually escapes from my mouth. I avoided being slapped for the first time ever. The suicidal joy doesn't escalate because survival takes priority. I yank my arm free. He doesn't let go. I kick his knee and scream.

"Let go of me!" The whole neighborhood should have heard.

"You disrespectful little bitch!"

I'm crashing into the wall instead of flying to safety. My legs won't cooperate, or maybe Geoff bowled me over. It all happens so fast. The blur of a thousand cases of abuse collide into a single moment.

Mom's bedroom door opens, and she stands with the morning light shining behind her. "Jasper! What is going on?"

She yells at me. Not her husband. Geoff grabs me by the hair and the scruff of the neck and yanks me to my feet. Murderous screams tear a path out of my throat as I kick and fight back. He pushes me down the hall.

"Jasper!" Evie screams.

The tears can't be held back any longer when I hear her voice.

"Evie!" I yell back.

Geoff hauls me across the living room. I thrash and scratch and kick at him, but he's a vice grip squeezing the life out of me, and I can't break his grip.

"Mom!" I yell in desperation. "Get him off! Do something! Please... he's hurting me," I sob. *Why won't she help me?*

She begins to wail, but there's still no relief from Geoff. Then she tells Evie to go back to bed.

He pauses by the front door and twists to the side, making room to open it. Jonah stands at the end of the hall in his nightshirt. His eyes are glued to us. Fright and pain mask his little face, and my heart breaks again and again as I realize I can never erase this image from my brother's mind. He will always remember this example of how a stepfather treats a daughter. Jonah should never see anything like this. How can Geoff do that to his own son? The seething rage explodes inside and brings me to a new understanding. I'm all at once calm, and I stop fighting back. I catch a glimpse down the hall behind Jonah; my mother disappeared once again.

He shoves me out the door, but just as he lets go, I grab his shirt so I don't fall on my ass. He swipes at my hand, and I stumble backward but don't fall.

"Get the hell out of my house you ungrateful whoring tramp."

"You're a lying bastard, and you know it. You told me Evie died, and I told your wife the truth about you and nothing more."

He disregards my accusation.

"Don't ever come back." He swings the door closed in my face.

I hear yelling and screaming and doors slamming from inside the house and then silence. The calm of the storm moves in as I stand on the front step as if inside the eye of the hurricane. I'm not fooled, the chaos isn't over. It surrounds me, murky and destructive even as it holds its perimeter and waits for me to reenter. If I need to stay in the center then so be it. I won't let it suck me back in. Geoff will never control me or hurt me again.

Standing beside Keel's truck, I begin devising plans to get back inside the house to collect the truck keys so I can leave. My phone and shoes would be nice as well, but ya know, when you find yourself homeless—again—perspectives change and shoes are overrated, or not rated high enough. I want my Corban shoes. I want to say goodbye to Evie and make sure she knows none of this is her fault. I head across the lawn toward the side of the house where her window is. I'll break in if necessary. I should call the police too, but my phone is inside. Before I scale the fence Jonah's bedroom window slides open. *Is Geoff watching me?* No. It's Jonah on the other side of the glass. I hurry over to him. He's frowning, but his eyes are dry.

"I found your stuff and packed a bag for you." His voice is just above a whisper.

I reach up and take it from him. "Thanks." A sad smile passes between us.

"I'm sorry Dad won't let you stay here anymore."

"It's okay, Jonah. I'm sorry you had to see him like that."

"He's an asshole. We all hate him." He uses a grown up voice.

It kills me to hear him like this. How many victims can Geoff leave in his wake? This is so unfair to Jonah. I close my eyes and search for the words that will help my brother, and not leave more scars.

"He is, but all it means is that you learn to be better than him. Don't grow up and act like your dad, okay Jonah? You know exactly how *not* to treat people."

"Don't worry about me. I'll never act like Geoff. He's the stinkiest turd in the cesspool."

"You're so right. And you know what? You're the best brother I could ever have. Thank you for this." I hold up the bag. My shoes are sticking out of the top, and my phone and keys are tucked in the side pocket.

"I tried to grab everything. I almost missed your shoes, but Evie said something."

The tears trickle down my cheeks as I watch Jonah in the window being helpful and acting more mature than I had ever seen him. "Is she all right?"

"No. Mom's with her though and trying to calm her down and make her stay in bed."

I swallow hard and bite the side of my lip. "Will you tell her I love her, and I'll talk to her soon?"

"Yeah, sure. Where are you going? It's pretty early."

"I have a job. It's a good one."

"Oh, well that's good." It's his kid way of agreeing but not really understanding the importance behind the words.

"I better go before Geoff comes into your room and you get in trouble."

Jonah glares over his shoulder, and his frown turns to a scowl.

"Give me a hug, little man."

He leans out the window and hugs my head.

"Love you."

"Love you, too." He backs inside and sniffles like he might start crying.

"Here." I hand him my cell phone. "Give this to Evie. You can use it, too. I'll call every day."

He takes my phone, and his eyes widen with disbelief. "I get to use it?"

"Yes, but Evie's in charge. I don't think Mom and your dad will take it from her."

"Right." He shoves it under the front of his shirt to hide it and keep our secret.

"Talk to you soon," I say.

He nods, and I stare at him for one more second, taking a picture with my mind of how he looks with sleep rumpled hair and his precious golden brown eyes. This may be the last time I see him for a long time. Then I hurry over to the truck and climb inside before I kidnap my little brother and take him with me.

***

The truck guides me two doors down and across the street. The man who answers my knock is definitely not Mrs. Fernandez.

"Hi. Is Mrs. Fernandez here?"

He shakes his head at me. "Not home," he says in broken English.

"I'm Jasper. I need to pick up my dog, Ollie."

He continues to shake his head at me with confusion. "Que? Senora Fernandez not home."

"My dog. I need my dog." I can't believe this is happening. On top of everything else, this inconvenience is the cherry on top of my shit sundae. "Umm...perro blanca?" I try again, but my Spanish is rustier than an old iron saw blade.

He frowns but waves me inside.

Moments later, I'm being embraced by a wagging, jumping blur of white fur, pink tongue, and claws.

Ollie is alive and well. And she's coming with me!

Ollie and I drive down Geoff's street, and I'm foolish enough to look in the rearview mirror. How can one place hold my heart in its cupped palms while simultaneously crushing it? It's unfathomable, yet I feel it acutely. I never thought saying goodbye would be such a hard and terrifying part of life, but it is. I've done it so many times this year, and it never gets easier. Feeling your heart being torn out of your body and watching it shred before your eyes is torture. This place was never my real home, yet the people who live here are— and I'm leaving them behind.

Now isn't the time to fall apart. *When is it ever the time?* With one hand on Ollie's soft back, I stuff what's left of my heart back inside my chest where it belongs and let it twist, turn and struggle unseen.

***

"I tried to call you," Keel says.

He's pissed, but handling it relatively well. If he really wants to get back together, he won't let his frustration rule this conversation. It's a test that doesn't matter, but I still notice what he's doing and what I'm doing in response to him.

"I'm sorry. I needed your truck for a few hours. I should have asked, but I had to get to my sister."

"How bad was it?" He's referring to my home life that isn't my home life any longer.

"Worse than normal."

He flinches.

I try not to think about the new bruises.

He shoves his hands in his pockets.

"I meant it when I said you can live here with us."

"I know you did. But I don't feel right about staying with you when we're never going to be a couple again." There I said it.

His eyebrows shoot up for a second and then draw together. "You're turning me down just like that?"

"It's not just like that. You broke my heart when you slept with Caspar—"

"And I told you it was a mistake that won't happen again," he interrupts me. "I want to make it up to you, Jasper."

"You can't, because what I found inside my brokenness is more than I ever found by loving you."

Keel stares into my eyes and he appears more shocked that I won't take him back than he does hurt. He pauses, shakes his head to clear confusion or some other cloudiness. "You're with someone else already, aren't you?" he accuses.

"I'm not."

"I don't understand why you can't forgive me. I messed up, and I'm sorry."

He messed up, and he's sorry, but he doesn't say he loves me. I drop my gaze and stare at the asphalt. I glance back up and say what I feel. "I don't want you anymore. While we've been apart, I fell out of love with you. And I don't think you know what you really want, because if you wanted me, you wouldn't cheat."

"Well, if that's how you feel about it..." He sounds defensive.

"It is. Goodbye, Keel."

Chapter Twenty-three

"The true value of a human being can be found in the degree
to which he has attained liberation from the self."
— Albert Einstein

The Misfit Marvels' bus picks Ollie and me up near Keel's house. Keel had my aerial silk and some of my other gear from the tour with Paradox in the back of his truck. Having it back feels like the final strings of attachment to him are severed. It's a relief like no other.

Marc, Spidey, Tink, Bob and Twix greet me unceremoniously, but are enthusiastic about Ollie joining the troupe, another good sign all will be okay with my new life. Luckily, I only missed two performances in Las Vegas, and no one seems bothered I had to take care of a family emergency.

Marc says, "It happens. I'll be taking time off when Sasha has our baby."

Spidey says, "Families are no bueno. That's why I choose my own family members."

Tink says, "Is your dog as talented as you are?"

Bob Brows says, "Glad you're back. I have some ideas about your act to run through with you when you have a minute."

I say, "Thanks for coming to get me. Where's our next show?"

It's late evening when I board the bus, and we start heading east. Bob and Tink take turns driving so we can make it to Sedona, find our campsite at the festival grounds, and get a little rest. The next morning we set up to stay for the entire weekend.

I hadn't heard of the fest, but the lineup looks interesting. It's mostly musical acts, but there's also a speed painter demonstrating his amazing ability to paint entire scenes in under three minutes, a psychic who does readings for large groups of people, and us. We're probably the most alternative act at the festival, and that's how Tink plans it.

The Circus of Misfit Marvels relies on not only talent and shock factor but being in the right place at the right times. Tink manages our scheduling and venues while Bob and Marc handle the number crunching. We perform with as much enthusiasm and effort in front of fifty people as we do five thousand. However, the larger crowds yield more merchandise sales which means we make more money. The Sedona festival appears to be the largest crowd I've been to with the Misfits so far.

Bob borrows a festival van to go pick up a shipment of T-shirts and other merch from the post office. Marc says he expects this weekend to be our largest grossing weekend of the summer. I'm surprised at the number of boxes we unload from the van when Bob returns, but I'm even more surprised at the padded envelope he hands to me with my name on it from Denver—and by the size and feel, I think I know exactly what's inside. I tear open the top of the yellow envelope and pull out my journal. No note or message from Corban, but he couldn't be any closer to me. I make a mental note to call him later—on my *new* new phone—and thank him. Then I hold the book tight as I climb on the bus and stash it with my things.

Tink is in top form during our show later that night. All I can do is gawk and wonder at how his body is able to endure the masochism with little or no apparent pain and virtually no blood. He sticks pins, extra-long needles, and hooks in his skin and hangs ridiculous objects from them. Tonight, there are a series of pulleys and ropes attached to his body and various instruments on the stage. Twix runs on a makeshift treadmill which spins the pulleys and plays the instruments. As Tink moves his piercings, the instruments change notes, and somehow Beethoven's Moonlight Sonata is being played. The performance is twisted, hilarious, beautiful and bizarre. The full moon rises over the immense red rocks surrounding the festival grounds and we all watch in equal parts awe and disbelief. Tink finishes his symphony, disconnects from his strings and ropes, and takes a bow with Twix at his side. I'm sure Twix farted through the entire act, and I swallow a gag knowing how bad the stench will be. The audience doesn't have a clue about the smell, but at the end, they cheer for an encore.

After the show, I change clothes and go looking for a place to chill out in the desert. The moon is high and bright enough no flashlights are needed. Parties are happening all over the campground, but I don't want to party. I want to relax and settle down after such an amazing night on stage. The day had been so busy with rehearsals and set up I didn't get much time to myself, and now I can take a look around and visit some of the rock formations on the festival grounds.

As I stroll away from the bus, someone falls into step next to me.

"May I walk with you?"

"Sure." I wonder if Marc wants to talk business. Earlier, he cut back on some of the stage props for our set. He didn't explain why and I wondered if it's because of my last goof up, or disappearing for a few days, or because I'm helping Bob Brows when he's upside down, or none of these things.

Instead of enlightening me, Marc remains silent until we're out of earshot of any campers.

"Am I doing okay as your assistant?" I ask.

"You're splendid, Jasper. I appreciate your ability to work with both Bob and myself and still create your own act. It is remarkable what you're able to do and learn in such a short amount of time. Bob had a feeling about you, and I think he was correct."

I swallow. "Thank you. I'm trying my best to make this work. It's been difficult because of my personal stuff, but I'm trying."

"This is what I wanted to talk to you about. If you don't want to speak of it, please tell me."

"What's that?"

"The personal stuff. I've been considering your story, and I have something to share with you."

"This sounds awfully serious. Should I be worried?" I ask jokingly.

"No," he says. "Not at all. I have been through much in my life, like you. My family is far away in Turkey, and there is a reason I left them behind and will never go back."

"Oh." I'm genuinely surprised.

"I am going to share with you a thought, and I will ask you to keep an open mind. Only choose to accept it if it feels right for you."

He's using his stage voice and for a second, I wonder if he's using hypnotism on me. His way with people is rather spellbinding, but I don't think he would purposely influence me without my permission. He remains humble, and although he does nothing outwardly questionable, dread creeps up on me. My skin flushes with heat and sweat collects under my arms. My nervousness surprises me, an unwelcome response. We're having a conversation, and that's all, but a part of me knows he's about to say something hard to hear.

"Forgive them."

"Who?"

"Everyone," he says.

A bottomless well is in the sound of his simple word—everyone. Compassion, mercy, and understanding can be felt like a flood about to suck me under. I turn away from Marc's placid features and stare at the four-story high red stone. Forgive Keel for what he did to me. *The assbag loser.* Why should I? *And Geoff, and Mom?*

"You're thinking why the hell should you forgive someone who cheated on you, or stole from you, or hit you? I understand it sounds like lunacy."

"Yeah, it does. I didn't deserve being cheated on. I didn't deserve having a mother who's never there for me and will never stick up for me. And I didn't deserve being beaten by my stepfather. That's what I lived with. They suck. I can't forgive them for being horrible people. They should know better. They should be better human beings. I know better. I don't ignore and treat people like garbage."

"No. You don't. But you made a conscious decision to improve yourself from what they did to you. That deserves the highest level of respect. Imagine if you had not realized you shouldn't hit someone when you think they've done something wrong. Punishment comes in many forms, and many people feel they deserve to be punished if they do wrong. Many parents think hitting their child is a way to correct bad behavior."

"It's demeaning and soul-crushing."

"I happen to agree with you, Jasper. But, just because I agree doesn't mean we are right. Can you feel the difference in what I said? We agree, but that doesn't make someone else wrong."

"Hitting a child is wrong," I say with no doubt.

"Millions of people have done so."

"Well, they're all assholes then." I've been beaten. It's a soul-shattering experience that can't be repaired and made new again. Breaking a child's spirit is something I will never do.

He doesn't agree or disagree but goes on.

"In their minds, they think they're doing what is right to help a child learn. This is one example of how we all differ, but what is important is you try to see things from someone else's perspective. If you can put yourself in their shoes for one second, you will find it easier to forgive them."

"I don't know if I can do it."

"See a viewpoint other than your own, or forgive someone for their ignorance?"

"Maybe both. No, I take it back. I'm open minded enough to see things in a different way, but I don't think I can forgive someone for heinous crimes."

"Let me try explaining in another way."

"Okay, but I don't think you're going to change my mind."

"That's all right. Remember when I said, you can choose to entertain the idea without accepting it? We're only having a discussion."

He pauses, and we stop walking. Marc steeples his fingers and takes a breath.

Marc's tone of voice is monotone. His inflections are subtle but powerful. The way he performs illusions on stage messes with your head. I'm behind the scenes and should know how he's doing it, but I couldn't tell you his secrets even if I wanted to. He's that good. This is the most we've ever talked that wasn't work related and to be honest, I'm hoping he's not using his expertise on me.

"Did you ever do something you regret? Stolen anything? Lied? Cheated?"

I try to think, and my mind goes blank.

"Take your time, Jasper. Sometimes when our emotions are triggered, our mind empties, and it's hard to think. The mind and body have ways to protect themselves which are hard to consciously recognize. Something will come to you if you're ready."

I work my lips back and forth and take a deep breath. "I took this little stamp from a boy when I was like six or seven years old. It had a puppy on it. For whatever reason, I really wanted it. I asked him if I could have it, but he wouldn't give it to me. I waited for a couple of days and the next time we played together I stole it from him. I shouldn't have, I knew it was wrong."

"Okay, Jasper. Now tell me why you stole, even though you knew stealing was wrong."

"Like I said, I just really wanted it. It was stupid. Then I got caught by my mom when she found it by my bed. She asked where I got it, and I tried to lie, but she busted me right away."

"I hear you telling me you were caught, and you regret doing something bad. Now try to dig deeper and tell me the real reason you took it."

We start walking again because moving helps my mind function. We're headed back in the direction we'd just come from. I begin to remember the day, and it's surprisingly clear. Zachariah was the son of a couple of trapeze artists. He was already training with his parents to follow in their footsteps. He had a big family, and they always welcomed me over to play. The puppy stamp was cute and reminded me of a puppy stuffed animal I saw at the store with my mom. She wouldn't buy it for me, and I started crying. Mom was super angry at me for causing a scene inside the store. I just wanted her to buy it. She wouldn't get me a real dog, and I thought the stuffed animal would sort of make up for not having a dog since we lived in a small trailer, and we traveled eight or nine months of the year.

"I think I took it because my mom would never let me have a real dog."

"Do you understand now the reason you stole the stamp runs much deeper than, 'you just wanted it'?"

"Yeah. I guess. When I was six, I didn't understand I was trying to substitute my feelings of not being allowed to own a dog and being angry with my mom for a little blue stamp. Now I know there's a lot more to it."

"With a deeper understanding of the situation, can you forgive yourself for making the mistake?"

"I think so. I was only six, and I learned a lot from the situation."

We approach our bus and Marc says, "Let's go on the roof."

"Is Bob up there?"

"I don't believe so." Marc starts climbing up the ladder.

When we reach the top, I take in the view. The sweep of the Milky Way across the vast desert sky, the halo around the moon, and the scenic red terrain paints a portrait to remember.

"Imagine the day your six-year-old self picked up the stamp and put it in your pocket." Marc pauses to let me think about it. "Do you see yourself?"

"I do."

"What would you do differently if you could do it again?"

"I would tell little Jasper to leave it, and then go cry my eyes out because I wanted my own puppy."

"Picture the result you'd like to have instead of stealing."

"Okay." I do, then breathe through the vision of watching myself cry in my bed as a little girl. I sit by her side and rub her back until the tears subside.

"Would you like to tell her anything?"

"Yes. Do I need to say it out loud?"

"You can if you want, or you can tell young Jasper the words inside your head."

In my mind, I sit on the edge of the bed next to the curve of my little body beneath the covers, and I say, *Jasper? Guess what, sweetie?* My six-year-old self quiets down, and she's listening. *It's not the right time for a real dog. Because guess what, we get the best dog in the whole world in another few years. Just wait for her.* My kid self peeks out from under the sheet and smiles at me.

I open my eyes and look at Marc.

"Feel that?"

"What?"

"The shift in your heart."

I bite my lip. The feeling is a lightness of my entire being, like shedding a coat of armor I didn't I know I was wearing.

"That is what forgiveness feels like. If you can do that for something minor like a small mistake you made as a child, imagine what it would be like to forgive your ex-boyfriend, your stepfather, your mother, and eventually yourself."

"But it's harder when someone wronged you."

"The emotional charge intensifies the situation and can make it seem harder," he agrees. "But you recognize people are doing only what they are capable of in the moment. You knew you shouldn't take the stamp, but because of the other circumstances in your life at the time, and your past, you took it anyway. You were doing the best you could. You can understand it now, and you can forgive. Your father—"

"Stepfather," I correct.

"He raised his hand to you based on his experiences and other extenuating circumstances of his life. He was sadly and unfortunately doing the best he could. When I suggest you forgive him, I am in no way suggesting you give your approval of his bad behavior. He hurt you, and it was wrong, but can you forgive him despite that?"

"So you think I should say something like, 'Listen, you horrible prick. You screwed me up. You shouldn't have beat me with a spatula or a wooden spoon or caused my dog to have seizures. I'll never approve of what you did to Ollie and me, but I forgive you because you didn't know better. And even if you did, I still forgive because fuck you. You won't own me anymore, and I forgive you!'"

"Bravo, Jasper. You found forgiveness."

Chapter Twenty-four

"The most beautiful experience we can have is the mysterious. It is the fundamental emotion that stands at the cradle of true art and true science." — Albert Einstein

To my journal,

You were sorely missed.

To Evie,

Marc's right, you know. Forgiveness isn't about accepting the wrong, sick and warped versions of people and their actions. It's about allowing people to make mistakes because we all do. We're all trying to get along in this life the best we can. We do stupid, hurtful things to each other and to ourselves without realizing the damage we're causing—and it's not okay—but it's never going to stop. We're all learning in some cosmic, universal classroom. There are bullies and accidents and bad choices everywhere. Thanks to Marc, I understand it easier now. No one is perfect, including myself, and I need to stay away from those who mean to hurt me. They can revolve inside their own universe, and I'll keep my circle well away from theirs. I forgive you, Geoff, Keel, and Autumn, and even me, Jasper Alexia Pyrah. I'm doing everything I can to be better from this day forward.

I started a list.

The List.

Everything I learned and don't want to forget:

Mom – Numbness is the worst pain of all.

Geoff via Marc – Forgiveness is the ultimate freedom.

Keel and Caspar – It's okay to say no.

Vincent – Life lessons never stop. Question reality and keep picking yourself up even when you don't want to.

Aunt Summer – Live your life to the fullest every day, and always help someone up when they need you.

Spidey – Face your fears. And don't forget to laugh.

Bob Brows – All I need is inside myself. I am – and that's good enough.

Tink – Some things defy explanation.

Corban – Hmm… not sure if I'm ready to write this one down yet.

I shut the book and turn it over. As if propelled by an unseen force, I open the back cover and there it is. The unexpected. The surprise. The shock, and the worry at words written in unfamiliar handwriting inside my journal. Someone's been here, and they read my secrets, and they left their mark. Goosebumps rise over my bare arms. I take a shuddering breath in preparation to read the message.

Jasper,
I don't know if you'll ever get this journal back, but in case you do, I wanted to leave this inside for you.

"In the midst of winter, I found there was, within me, an invincible summer.

And that makes me happy. For it says that no matter how hard the world pushes against me, within me, there's something stronger – something better, pushing right back."
— Albert Camus

You probably know the whole quote, and I'm repetitive. Is this written somewhere inside in your own hand? Could be. I wouldn't know. I tried not to read any of it. I did glance inside briefly and noticed your affinity for quotes which is why I added one. I'll never be able to read Camus again without thinking of you—like words are bringing us together even though we're physically apart. First Albert's and now yours. I'm not a word guy. I'm using too many to write this.

But you need to know I didn't read your journal. I'm not an intrusive bastard. I like the mystery of you. I like how you are selective in sharing parts of yourself with me when the time is right. When I get anxious to know more about you, I think of time passing on Earth in comparison to the universe expanding, and I settle right the fuck down. I can wait a day, month, or year to find out if you would pick The Pixies over Social Distortion or if you would consider going out with me.

By the way, your journal was kept in a secret location so no one else can find out about you without your permission—before I do.

With the expectation of finding you again,

C.D.

A sigh, softer than a down feather but strong enough to tilt the world off its axis, escapes passed my lips as I lay my fingers over his initials on the creamy paper.

***

The next day arrives bringing with it another dose of Arizona sun and heat. Before work officially begins for the day, Ollie and I take a walk deep into the heart of a rock-walled canyon. Ollie can't seem to get enough of her new found freedom. She races over the sandy ground, exciting small birds, dashing after skittering lizards, and darting after anything even remotely resembling a rabbit. I find a seat on the sandstone beneath the shade of a scrawny looking tree and pull out my journal again. My entries yesterday and today are like a strange reunion. The journal was gone and has now returned. I'm okay with its departure. It's as if we had separate paths to take but those paths have brought us miraculously back together. I hope the words inside the journal found their freedom while they were on their own. My hope is they found a way to transform and become something larger than I meant them to be.

Here's what I need to put on paper today:

Olivia is pure joy. She's a shower of sweet scented happiness. My previous favorite scents were grape, watermelon, and peach. Ollie's like all that with a warm hug attached. In reality, she smells like a dog. Dirt, hair, slobber and fun. These are my new favorites.

Is it possible to love a dog more than a person?

I do, and I don't care if it's strange. Dogs don't ruin your life or make you feel anything you don't want to feel. Olivia is back in my life, and I am better for it.

So I want to write a huge thank you to Olivia. Thank you for not dying, and not running away, and not forgetting about me. Especially the last part.

And thank you, Corban, for managing to put my journal back in my hands. Without risking putting you on a pedestal, or something else lame like that, you're my knight in shining armor. Sir Vincent would be proud. And by the way, I would definitely consider going out with you again. And probably once more after that just because.... Because the rest of the answer isn't for writing down. It's felt too deeply beneath my skin.

"Life can be magnificent and overwhelming – that is the whole tragedy. Without beauty, love, or danger it would almost be easy to live." — Albert Camus

Since we're both fans of A. Camus, the above quote is for Corban even if he will never read it.

***

The tour rolls on.

We venture back into California and make our way north hitting all the major cities. We end up in Reno, Salt Lake, and eventually back to Colorado for a mountain festival near Frisco. The days blend into the nights and the nights turn into the days in a sort of squishy jelly roll of work and fun. About once every twenty-four hours I'm overwhelmed with how lucky I am to be part of The Circus of Misfit Marvels.

After leaving the mountains, we head east on I70 to Denver for two nights at The Gothic Theater. It's been on my mind since Sedona, and I can't tamp down my excitement and nervousness at seeing Corban again. A million thoughts buzz around inside my head like bees on speed. Not that I do speed, or meth, or would ever give drugs to bees, but you know, I'm über-excited.

We unpack the trailer and start setting up as soon as we reach the venue. I keep thinking I'll run into Corban any second now, but it doesn't happen... all afternoon. I don't text him, and he doesn't call. I refuse to be my old needy self and obsess and leave messages and pine over nothing, so I let it go. If he doesn't show up, it wasn't meant to be. The letters were enchanting moments and the phone calls, and texts were amusing while they lasted.

Without his distraction, I'm able to warm up, practice, and perform through the night. Misfit Marvels' fan base in Colorado is apparent, and the turnout is stellar. There's an after-party backstage, and everyone seems to know everyone. I'd forgotten Bob's family is related to Corban's in some manner, and I'm introduced to cousins of cousins and their significant others. A familiar face shows up during the shindig and offers me a beer.

It's Tully, Saul and Zeb's friend. I reach for the beer and take a sip.

"Tara. Wow, it's great to see you. You're working with the Misfit Marvels now? That's awesome."

"Crazy how things work out, isn't it?" I don't correct him on my name.

"Crazy cool," Tully says. "I saw you on stage. You expanded your act since you were here with Paradox. You were phenomenal."

He's grinning and looking at me with interested baby blue eyes. I've seen this look a hundred times, although Tully doesn't give off the pervy vibe, which is nice, and also the reason I don't make my excuses to step away. Spidey's sitting on the nearby couch and I can tell he's keeping his eye on me. Spidey sort of turned into my bodyguard over the last couple of weeks, like he's volunteered to become my older brother. I find it funny and sweet instead of annoying. He excels at giving off the creepy juju to most people and can usually discourage unwanted attention in a matter of seconds if I need him to. I don't think it will go to that level with Tully, but you never know. I didn't think Caspar would screw my boyfriend when I wouldn't screw her either, and look how that assumption turned out.

"Thanks. I'm able to do more of what I'm actually trained in, and I'm evolving, which is good."

"Sorry things didn't end so well the last time you were in town. Are you doing okay?" he asks. "No one could figure out what happened to you. Zeb and Saul wanted to call the police."

"It all worked out." I feel a twinge of pain remembering what happened. Tully doesn't need the details. I don't want anyone's sympathy. I take a drink of the dark malty beer to hide my face for the second I need to regroup.

"I still have the guest room if you need a place to crash," he says.

"We, umm, sleep in the bus most nights. It's pretty great."

"Yeah, I saw it outside. It's unreal. It's gotta be the greatest bus I've ever seen. You don't mind living in such cramped quarters?"

I shake my head, smile and take another sip.

"Jasper's the real deal, Tully. A Bohemian, Tzigane, gypsy, traveling artist. Whatever you want to call her, she's the 'it girl' to be sure."

The corners of Tully's mouth quirk at the description of my lifestyle and I turn to face Corban.

"No labels please," I say.

"But you earned them," he says.

"What's yours?" I ask.

"Asshole," he deadpans.

I can't even tell if he's joking or not, but I laugh at his answer because it's the last thing I would ever call him.

"Need a beer?" Tully asks Corban.

Corban nods. "Sure."

Tully wanders over to the keg to fill a cup.

"I thought you might have come down with the swine flu or something."

"Or something." He pauses and looks at my face. Not just my eyes but every part of me. His eyes land back on mine. "Swine were undeniably involved," he adds.

Now it's my turn to raise my brows. He doesn't clarify. Tully hands over the beer. As if the invisible bubble around Corban and me can be felt, Tully seems to bounce right off. He ricochets across the room and away from our space.

"Want to go outside to finish these?" Corban gestures with his plastic cup toward the exit.

"Okay."

We sip in silence for a few minutes, and I wonder if I fooled myself into thinking Corban is the friend I always needed in my life. Maybe we can only communicate through devices and not in person. Wouldn't that be a kick upside the head?

"I have something for you," I say.

Even in the mostly dark behind the theater I can tell he's giving me the side eye.

"Hold on. I'll be right back." I set down my almost empty cup on the patio table and skip over to the bus. When I return, I hand Corban the notebook I bought for him. It's nothing special, but neither is my journal, and he seems to have taken to it. There's still one more entry from Corban I haven't read. Ollie pulls on her leash until she's able to sniff at Corban's boots. It's good for her to get out of the bus and I want her to meet Corban.

"Paper?" he asks, as he strokes Ollie's head.

"Yep," I say. Her tail wags and she gives Corban's hand a lick. It's all the sign I need to know Ollie gives her approval.

"Thanks." He takes a closer look at it.

I sit down at the table, and I'm practically swallowed by the silence. *Okay, this is getting plain uncomfortable.*

"I can't decide if this is the real you, and I didn't meet him before, or if you're having a bad night." I scratch Ollie's ear. She lies down on the concrete directly between the two of us.

"Yeah. More like both."

I chew my lip for a second. "Want to talk about it?"

"No."

"Life stuff?"

"Yeah."

"It's bad?"

"It's not good."

"Want me to mug you at the bus stop and stick you with my crazy singing aunt for the day? Experiences like that can change your life."

He looks over at me with soulful eyes. I want to drown in those eyes for the rest of my life. *Shit. I'm not ready to fall for him yet.*

"Stay right there," I order Ollie, and tuck the handle of her leash under the chair leg. Walking over to the stage door, I tell Corban, "Be right back."

Returning a few seconds later, I hand Corban a cupcake from the catering table inside the theater. There's a Death Wish Bakery sugar wafer on top of the frosting.

He takes a deep breath before peeling the cupcake paper. I'm about to tell him I need to go walk Ollie when he finally starts acting more like himself, except in another unexpected way.

"Jasper, the way you dance. If I could bottle the feeling it creates inside me when I see you, you'd know how mysterious you are. It's sensory overload, Nirvana and Wonderland blended together."

"So you were working tonight." I lower my gaze.

"No. I had to take off to take care of something. I made it back in time for your act. It was unreal. You're like this perfect complement to Bob's Misfit Marvels."

"Stop. You're making me think weird things about you."

"You already have weird thoughts about me like I have about you. Now you're adding texture to those thoughts." He finishes the cupcake and folds the paper into a triangle.

"Still, I don't want to hear it. It makes me super self-conscious."

"Good. You can't be pulling maneuvers like that on me too often."

"I'm not pulling anything on you. I can't change the way I perform. It's how I am. If I'm not authentic when I'm on stage, I'll fail completely and fall on my face. It's all or nothing."

"The entire audience can tell. It was like seeing the universe created and destroyed in one person all in a moment. The possibilities of the world are exposed when you move. I can see it. You're making it impossible to live."

"Not true. Life will always go on whether I'm on stage or sleeping on a bench."

"Sure, life goes on, but not for me. When an event changes you, life stops. You start a new life where the old one left off. Something about you made me begin a new life, and you're in it with me. Somehow and in some way. Even if it's the memory of what happened tonight, you're going to be in this next life of mine."

"You're perfectly bonkers. Did you know that? Sort of like an ape at the zoo who puts poo on his fingers and sniffs it. There's sound reasoning behind those inquisitive eyes, but it still doesn't make sense to people on the outside."

"I like to consider it mental superiority."

"You or the ape?" I ask with a smirk.

"That's your call. And I would never examine my own poop. That's fucking mental."

"Ew." I wrinkle up my nose.

"Hey, you're the one who compared me to an ape. I think my observations run a little deeper than sitting around in a cage contemplating bodily functions."

"Sometimes I think we're not that different than animals. Our cage is bigger, but overall, we're just trying to survive."

"And procreate," he adds.

Right on cue, Ollie whimpers as if feeling my sudden shift of energy. "Nice. How did you twist my thoughts around so I can't think straight anymore?"

Ollie sits up and instead of coming over to me, she leans into Corban's leg. He begins petting her again.

"Maybe the same way you untwist my heart so I can't be mean and hateful anymore."

"You're not mean."

"I am. I'm vindictive and spiteful and angry, and you come prancing into the scene, and I forget what a punk I am and how I want to bury my ex in the wasteland of NGC 660 and overthrow the government. You're all wrong for me, Jasper. You're corrupting me. Next thing you know I'll be wearing a tie and loafers and heading off to teach Sunday school."

I snort and clear my throat which causes me to cough. I finish the last of the beer and give him a skeptical look.

"Too late—Jesus is moving through me already. He wants me to confess my sins even before I make them."

"You're watching televangelists on T.V. again, aren't you?"

"Nope. I moved on to immersing myself in cowboy rap with Sir Vincent."

I groan. "Forget what I'm doing to you. You're warping my innocent brain past recognition."

"What? You don't think I can be saved?" he asks, straight-faced. "I'll be the poster child for reformed delinquents."

"Wait. Hold up a sec. What is NGC 660 and why would you bury your ex-girlfriend there?"

A single dark eyebrow lifts and he gives me this look that says, *I can't believe you don't know what NGC 660 is.* "Seriously? How did I meet a girl who doesn't know her galaxies?"

Corban seems mildly disgusted with my ignorance. I think I know him well enough by now to be pretty sure he's only messing with me. But then again, he's not always the easiest to interpret.

"There are these rare galaxies in space where a lot of debris and galaxy stuff hovers around perpendicular to the disk plane. Astronomers think the pull of dark matter is causing the unusual shape of the galaxy. Gabrielle deserves to go there because she's as distant, unexplainable, and surrounded by dark matter with an unusual effect on her."

Ollie lets out a long whimper.

"Not you, girl." Corban gives her a reassuring pat and Ollie lies down at his feet.

"Ouch. I guess I shouldn't have asked," I say. "Talking about her is causing some hovering dark matter of your own."

"Yeah, well when someone says she's carrying your child and guilts you into staying with them so the baby won't be fatherless only to find out it's someone else's kid, you might attract a dark cloud of your own."

"That's what you were dealing with?" I ask, thinking of our previous conversation and his mention of taking care of things with his ex.

"Yeah. I would have taken care of the kid until the day I died. The real father petitioned for a paternity test, and now we all know the truth."

"I guess she does deserve to be cast into the universe," I say. "And without chocolate cupcakes, or air."

We share a moment of quiet contemplation. Corban's finally opening up about Gabrielle and the baby.

Corban interrupts my head space. "My daughter who turned out to not be my daughter is named Chastity Blair."

I let it sink in like sand absorbing sea water, and I burst out laughing. Bubbles of ridiculous giggles. "Ironic much?"

Corban's shoulders shake and he's laughing next to me.

"Couldn't she have just gone with, Don't-be-a-slut-like-your-mom?"

He scrubs his face with his palms and runs a hand through his thick hair.

"I thought we were going to buy this big house and start stocking up on diapers and baby formula. It was going to be my next life. The part that chooses you and says prison exists in all different shapes and sizes and timeframes. I escaped that kind of human oppression for the last twenty-two years. But over the last year, I convinced myself it was my time to suffer through duty and obligation. Suddenly, I'm not that guy, and I'm not responsible for a kid I never wanted in the first place."

I glance at him quickly. He's staring at nothing except the possibility of a future that would now never be.

"You make it sound like starting a family was going to be the worst thing that has ever happened to you."

"So far," he qualifies. "Life likes to take people out with wrecking balls. I'm keeping my eyes open for the next one, but the bastards go around in invisibility cloaks."

"Yeah, and goatees." I think about the dynamite Geoff brought into my family. He leveled us with one swift blow. "I don't do prison well. I escaped, and I'm never going back."

"Honestly, I wouldn't have minded if I had a choice in making that kind of commitment. I'm sure I would have walked into the long term relationship with Gabrielle easily, but she pulled out the emotional handcuffs without a split second's thought to how she was changing my life. I was preparing to go along with her reigning supreme because a baby needs parents. My misery was inconsequential."

"So, the real dad deserves a beer and handshake."

"More like a keg and a million bucks."

I peer up at the night sky and wonder how far away NGC 660 is. "When we're entwined in other peoples' lives, it's nearly impossible to break free. But we can do it."

"Let the unraveling begin."

I smile at the visual image his words create inside my mind. All the strings of attachment to those I don't want in my life anymore are flowing freely into the star filled night like multi-colored streamers. "You're not what I expected," I say.

"You either. Now go away. You're messing with my head again." He gives my shoulder a gentle shove.

I lean into the arm of the plastic patio chair and then right myself. "Wait. You can't do that. That was totally my line a few minutes ago."

He looks down, hiding his pale irises from me beneath those ridiculously perfect long black lashes. When he glances up, a challenge is on his face. "Then we're in agreement to walk away now before we make each other insane." He rises from his chair and reaches over to pick up the small notebook I gave him. He tucks it into his back pocket.

"Totally," I say. "Why would I ever want to take this any farther? You're crazier than my aunt with a box of blue glasses."

There's a tiny flinch of questioning wonder, but he lets it slide. "Goodbye, Jasper. You're a great dancer."

"Goodbye, Corban. You're not a great dancer." I follow his lead, grab Ollie's leash, and stand, taking a step toward the bus.

"You had to throw it in my face. Now I can't let you leave."

He snatches my hand before I can get away and starts pulling me toward him.

"Hey, we just agreed to part ways for our mutual benefit."

"You can't insult my dance moves and disappear into the oblivion of the masses, never to be seen again. You have to at least know I'm partially competent when the music is playing."

"You're not serious?" I ask.

His eyes are smoldering and intense like two peridot gems on fire. I swear I can feel his inner turmoil searing a path down his arm to our joined hands. But he's also wearing a minute smile which tells me how much he's enjoying this game.

"Put Ollie away and come inside so I can prove it to you." He releases my hand.

I do, and when I return, he's waiting for me by the door.

As we're about to step over the threshold and enter the dark club with its pulsing lights and haze of alcohol tainted air, I make him stop and place my hand on his upper arm.

Am I ready? Can I dance with the incredibly hot and mentally exciting guy and not fall in love with him? How can I tell if I'm making a huge mistake by letting him hold my hand? Won't my heart get broken again when he decides I'm his next prison sentence?

His muscles are hard beneath my fingers. The attraction I feel for him is life-altering. Everything about him feels right. His sexy eyes and body make my spine hum from top to bottom. And his damn mouth must have sexual attraction magnets built inside those lips. Even more attractive than the looks is his sense of self, quick intelligence, sarcasm, and thoughtfulness. The way he waits for me to answer and how he considers what I have to say before adding his own thoughts. How dare he walk into my life and tell me I changed his life forever?

He scares me in a way I've never known. I thought I knew what love felt like with Keel, but now I know being physically attracted to a guy isn't love, just lust. Relying on someone else to make you happy isn't love, only codependency. Unfortunately, knowing the truth doesn't stop my heart from making decisions.

"How long have you been thinking about dancing with me?" If he answers, since he saw me on stage earlier, or since we met, I'll go back to the bus and tuck myself around Ollie and forget about starting something with Corban. I can't be in a relationship based on lust again.

"About a minute. Since you made the assumption, you're the only one between us who can move like water."

He steps to the side so we're no longer blocking the door. He raises his free hand, and the tips of his fingers brush against the edge of my jaw. I slowly lift my gaze to his. He's watching me closely in the dim amber and black lights behind the club. He tips his head one way and then the other. The rawness between us is palpable.

We're both a mess, and we both know it. It's not condemning. Like he says, disaster is part of the beauty that makes life perfect. He's letting me go if I want to leave now.

I lead him into the club. The music is exactly right. He's not bad either. He's an exotic dream I don't want to wake up from.

Between songs, he leans down to my ear. "I take it back, Jasper. I think I've been thinking about dancing with you since forever. I just didn't realize it until now."

Chapter Twenty-five

"Fill your paper with the breathings of your heart."
— William Wordsworth

For the remainder of the show season, when I miss Corban, I reread his letters in the back of my journal. We're having this long distance, non-relationship thing. He drives to see me when I'm within a few hundred miles. So far, only once, but it was another amazing night. He's turned into my best friend—and God, he's a sexy friend. He's also a mind-blowing, amazing good kisser. But I could have told you that before we actually kissed. Lips like his couldn't be non-kiss worthy. He's going to come see me when we take a break from touring. I'll either be renting a yurt or cabin at the S & D Inc. base camp, or I'll be at Aunt Summer's in Chicago. Corban says I can stay with him in Denver, but I still need more time to figure out who I am and what I want for my life. Corban's recovering from his own unraveling with Gabrielle and Chastity Blair, so I'm certain I don't want to barge in on his soul-searching. He says living at base camp will be amazing, and I won't regret it. I'm leaning in that direction.

So once again, for like the twentieth time, I'm reading his last letter inside my journal.

Jasper,

I took over your journal again.

Sorry.

Not sorry.

These words play on repeat when you enter my mind:

"I am a forest, and a night of dark trees: but he who is not afraid of my darkness, will find banks full of roses under my cypresses." — Friedrich Nietzsche

I was floored after seeing you in Boulder. Literally, I was lying on the ground looking up at the Milky Way and the overwhelming need to write came over me. Since I'm a loser, I had nothing to write on. Using my phone to make a note to myself is a gross injustice to the bound pages of paper inside your book. My pen bleeds ink across the page and makes something real and tangible and physical right before my eyes. Creating is a gift of the universe. And the universe is what drove me to confiscate another page of your journal.

By the way, I still haven't read your personal entries. As you can see, I'm writing in the back and upside down. For today, I claim this as my side of the book. That is until I can give it back to you.

So earlier tonight, I lay in the yard behind my house, unable to move. The world is spinning, and I'm on this side of it looking out into the immeasurable universe. I'm overwhelmed and humbled. How can I be a part of everything and feel like nothing? Does my existence make one speck of difference in this world? How can I know? Do I move from one thought to the next with purpose like a planet revolving around the sun? Always on a projected course, destined to circle endlessly until darkness takes over and the big sleep turns the world to black? Am I wandering aimlessly like stardust with no destination in mind? Could I make it far enough to crash into something larger than myself and cling to its side hoping for osmosis or the very least shelter and a companion?

That's when I realized I am more like space dust than the revolving planet. I've been searching for something my whole life, even as I know I won't find it. The end of the quest remained elusive. Sure, there are occasional answers to provide a temporary spark in the darkness, but the fulfillment was always brief. Then I would revert to my old ways of rebellion and frustration over my life being as satisfying as eating air for eternity.

Then one day, I ran into this girl, and she looked as miserable as I was. Not on the outside. Her exterior was of the kind that leaves a man speechless. Her face was envied by angels. She had eyes the color of a Tiger's, all swirled with shades of amber and gold. And her body was almost too sacred to look at. I would lay down my sword for this girl without anyone asking. But a gorgeous body isn't what stood out to me. I knew she understood suffering and the internal struggle of existing in a place where answers are obscure and rarely ever found. She appeared to be surviving in this forgotten hell on Earth just as I was. This girl looked right at me and instead of telling me what a piece of shit I am, she invited me to stay by her side for a little while. The universe suddenly seemed much smaller and much larger all at once. Smaller because everything beyond our combined perimeter didn't seem to matter anymore. Larger because the exact opposite was also true. I was the stardust and I crashed into something spectacular.

Jasper, you're in my pocket, and you're on my mind, a new kind of hopelessness. The kind I anticipate. I see larger things infiltrating my immeasurable universe, and I want to know what these abstract things are, and I want to touch them and explore them in ways I never considered before. And, oddly I want them to stay around for a long time. You *give me ideas which create more ideas. I'm equally terrified and desperate to see you again so I can see what happens next.*

I need a drink after all this word vomit.

Cheers to messing with my mind, you awful tantalizing girl.

C.D.

***

After reading the letter from Corban, I flip the journal over and around and find a blank page to write on. This is the last page, so I try to make every word count.

Evie,

I'm sorry I can't be there with you. You know all the reasons why I won't be coming back. That doesn't mean I don't think about you all the time or that I don't wish things could be different because I do.

In my letters, I shared my humiliation, debauchery, shame, and blame. Please don't read this and think to yourself, *Wow, my sister was really messed up.* I admit, I am messed up—sometimes. Aren't we all? I'm trying to make fewer mistakes and be less screwed up in the future, but only time will tell if I succeed in this endeavor. If my letters can save you from one bad decision, or show you a path to a healthier life—not the day-to-day terror we experienced at home—then it's the greatest gift I can give you. Overall, I hope they leave a good impression on you. Without taking anything away from your own personal journey, I hope my advice helps you discover who you are and helps you learn without having to endure the pain I experienced. If you can find words of wisdom and use them for joy and happiness, then I did what I set out to do.

I discovered the future holds so much to look forward to. In the depth of the darkest parts of my life, I didn't want to go on. I didn't want to take even one more breath, but if I had given up, I wouldn't have discovered any of the amazing and wonderful people and experiences which happened to me this year. I can only imagine what else the universe has waiting for me—and for you. Sometimes we see or do things that are perfect and are meant to be, but these occurrences could have been absolutely wrong last week, or last year, or even yesterday. If you ever feel like giving up, remember, time is a mysterious creature. Be patient and be kind and she'll come around when she's ready, and she'll surprise you with something extraordinary.

So I hope you smiled when you read about Corban, Twix, Spidey, Bob Brows, and his bearded sister, Marjorie. True laughter and genuine smiles are equivalent to love. Find love where you can because love is all that matters. But, love is also a complicated endeavor. Love is painfully strange, happiness and devastation all wrapped up together and smothered with good intentions and dreams. Love is allowing and accepting without conditions. It's unconditional. And that's what Corban taught me. Maybe I'm a screwed up, judgmental and unforgiving person, but the more I can allow and accept these traits to exist in myself the less I am controlled by them. My messes don't own me. Freedom is a perspective. Love is understanding. Choose to love yourself first, Evie, because if you don't, there will be no love in your life at all.

By the way, I added "unconditional love" to The List next to Corban's name.

When you're thinking about me, or need to escape from your own life for a few minutes, open my letters and read another page. But don't forget to blur the lines. Nothing is exactly as it seems. When you think you know everything, that's when you couldn't be more wrong. My letters may give you a tiny bit of the truth, but remember that this little journal is just that—little. There's always more to the story.

If you enjoyed *When We're Entwined*, please help spread the word. The greatest compliment you could give is to leave a comment at your favorite online retailer, share with a book club, or recommend it to a friend.

Be on the lookout for *As We Unravel*, book 2 in the *When We're Entwined* series.

Acknowledgements

To John and Nancy. My books would not exist without the two of you. I want to thank my family and friends for their continued support even when I forget to cook dinner...or call you back. You're never forgotten even when my head is a million miles away in my next project. A very special thank you to my editor, Melissa A. Robitille, for every correction and suggestion. Your help is invaluable. Thank you to my beta readers and proofreaders—you know who you are. Lastly, I want to thank my readers. I appreciate every one of you.

About The Author

When Jody isn't navigating the terrain of her imagination and writing it down, she can be found exploring the wilderness of Colorado with her family, or in the kitchen baking cookies & brownies – and trying not to eat them all. She's passionate about continuing to learn and reads anything and everything that catches her interest.

Death Lies Between Us, book one in the *An Angel Falls* series, is the winner of RomCon's Readers' Crown Award for Best Paranormal Romance.

Jody A. Kessler invites you to stop by her website and see what's new at www.JodyAKessler.com.

You can also connect with her on Facebook at Jody A. Kessler, or on Twitter @JodyAKessler.

www.ingramcontent.com/pod-product-compliance
Lightning Source LLC
Chambersburg PA
CBHW020249200626
46816CB00001BA/210